Heroes & Ghosts

a yaoi novel by

S. A. Payne

Better With Boys Press, Pennsylvania

To read other novels by S. A. Payne, please visit
http://www.sapayne.com

The Better With Boys Press web site address is
http://www.betterwithboys.com

Make sure to check out Yaoi Magazine,
the magazine for the global fans' lifestyle, at
http://www.yaoimagazine.com

ISBN 978-0-9799397-0-4

PRINTED IN THE UNITED STATES OF AMERICA
10 9 8 7 6 5 4 3 2 1

This book is dedicated to all of the wonderful people who have subscribed to SAPayne.com over the years and have made my dreams a reality. With your support, I've been able to do amazing things.

Chapter One

"What?" Kenichi nearly screeched. Instead he drew a long breath and grabbed control of his voice. "What do you mean, you're turning your ship around?"

Captain Josiah Harvick shrugged and scratched his chin. "The order just came across, all ships are forbidden access to Avalon space. If already in Avalon space they must proceed to the nearest port for grounding. I'm not in Avalon space."

"Jos, come on, you're on our doorstep, you can be here in three hours! I can almost swim out to you, don't do this to me." Kenichi pleaded, clasping his hands in front of him to keep from balling them into fists.

"Nothing personal mate. You're my favorite bug doctor in the whole of the wide blackness here, but an order is an order and I fly a clean ship." The older man shrugged. "I'll come back when the ban is lifted. A week, two, maybe three until all this mess settles down, swear."

"Wait, you can't, surely we can work something out?"

"Sorry, mate, see you in a bit." The screen flicked off and went to its generic image of a sunny field of flowers.

Kenichi stood in the center of the main control room and tried not to swear. He really didn't believe in swearing, but a year's worth of planning had just been shut down. After a few more slow, steadying breaths, when he was fairly sure he could speak without sounding like a cat with it's tail stepped on, he went to the only person that might be able to get Jos' ship back.

The door opened to the small lab, larger than his own but he worked by himself. The lights were bright and the two doctors were perched on stools intently studying the scrolling results of some analysis.

"Don't even start with me, Ichi." The female of the pair spoke as the door opened, her blue eyes not even leaving the screen they were watching.

"Amanda..."

"Don't!" she warned as she pointed to a line in the information. "See, there, that's what I noticed."

"Huh." The man, William, nodded and leaned forward to peer more closely at the small print. "Hey, Ichi."

"Will." Ichi nodded, remembering his manners. "Amanda..."

"No. Look, you knew the risks when you signed up here. I'm sorry, this mess with the Flossin Guard is too dangerous, too messy to take any risks. I agree with home, we need to shut down our skies for a while." She sighed and turned to study one of their closest friends, which was saying something given that the station only had seventeen members and Ichi wasn't from Avalon.

"But, he's three hours away, another ten minutes and he'd be headed our way."

"And he'd be grounded here with no way of leaving. He's an independent contractor, he needs this job, he can't afford to break the rules, Ichi. Don't worry, you'll get your vacation."

"No, you don't understand, my work..." He sighed at her raised eyebrow. "I can't just up and go later. I was supposed to speak at the conference next week."

"So, give it over the vid, you'll get the credit."

"It's just, please Amanda."

"No. Flossin Guard nearly took out Jake's whole station, so we're in lock down until this can be resolved. No debate, no exceptions, we can't take any risks. You of all people should know the things we work on here. Avalon space has half a dozen stations like ours, it's just too risky."

He ran a hand through his dark hair and tried to find a logical debate that might get her to change her mind. "I've put almost a year into planning this. I've got a lot of money tied up in deposits. I was supposed to go from the conference to spend the rest of the month on the beach drinking fruity drinks and getting a tan."

"Avalon will reimburse you for any lost expenses, you know that."

"He means he has a three week stay at Xerolousia planned, and he's horny." Will chuckled and froze the code on the screen before glancing to the now blushing entomologist.

"It's not..." He tried to protest but the couple had a knowing look on their faces. "Alright, fine, happy? God, I'm only human. I haven't left this station in almost three years and, in case you failed to notice, I'm sort of isolated here."

Amanda grinned, knowing every one of the station's five single females would have happily tumbled the charmingly nerdish scientist into bed, and also equally knowing he had no interest in women. "Tell you what, I'll loan you Will for the night." She grinned at her husband.

"You will?" He sat up straighter. "Am I being pimped out?"

"The two of you should go do whatever it is you two do when you're up all night." As the de facto leader of the station, she wasn't supposed to know about the still that had been set up. She just pretended the home brew just magically appeared.

Ichi sighed and shook his head. "I guess I'm unpacking."

"I'll be over in about an hour," Will offered, trying to make it sound friendly and supportive but if it soothed Ichi's disappointment any he didn't see it.

The door shut behind their friend. "Well that made me feel like a heel, poor Ichi. You should blow him just for mercy's sake."

"Down woman!" Will laughed. "You know brunettes aren't my type." He slid over and wrapped his arms around his wife's waist. "I like redheads," he whispered, nuzzling his face to the nape of her neck where red springy curls the color of fall pumpkins had sprung loose.

⁓⁓⁓⁓⁓

"Tuk tuk tuk, tuk tuk tuk." Ichi clucked at the secure box full of bugs and they swarmed over to the nearest layer of clear, very thick polymer. They instantly started clucking back at him and jostling each other to be closest to the drop chute. "Oh, who's the piggy beetles? Who's my baby piggies?"

"You're a strange man, Ichi," Will tossed out, standing across the small lab from the boxes of secure, very deadly insects. Frankly he didn't like bugs much, but he wasn't squeamish about them. Yet seeing how they responded to Ichi made his skin crawl a little bit.

"They're smarter than people think. Hive minds, they're amazing." He was proud of the swarm, he was the only person, anywhere, to successfully keep a swarm alive and healthy in captivity. "Trillions are notoriously difficult to keep but we know so little about them." He tapped on his side of the window and chuckled as the carnivorous bugs swarmed for his finger.

"Yeah, because they keep eating their keepers." He swallowed bile as he knew what was coming. "I can't lie and say I'm sorry you're staying on board, I wasn't looking forward to feeding your children."

"You're too sentimental, Will." Ichi moved to the crate in the corner and pulled out three slender cylinders. He popped the latches on them and one by one they slid open. The storage gel evaporated at contact with the air and he pulled out the feeder rats from inside. "Those scientists were stupid and lazy, there's no way this swarm can get out, or me in." He clucked again as he dropped the rat into the feeding chute and started its cycling. The device of his own design would move the rat into and out of four chambers before dumping it into the main box.

"Ugh, even knowing, that grosses me out. Didn't you ever have a real pet as a child?" Ichi was just so clinical, so cold. It always amazed Will, he was from Avalon and nothing was ever too cold or clinical there.

"Hmmm?" Ichi hummed and watched the mindless rat be moved closer to the hungry swarm. "It's no different than the tissue samples you order in. The rat's heart beats, it breaths, but it feels nothing, it has no brain. The brainstems are fascinating, so underdeveloped to be nearly useless. That's why I only order from PETS, they take great care in their feeder stock." The system cycled and the rat dropped into the main container. The swarm was instantly on it and started its hour long meal. "And for your information, I had a cat as a child." He frowned as he turned back to where Will hovered at the far side of his lab. "The thing didn't like me much." He picked up the remaining two not-really-alive feeder rats and dropped them into other chutes to feed other deadly, hungry insects.

The sight of the swarm gathering on the brainless, lifeless rat churned Will's stomach and he scooped up the advertisement flyer from the PETS feeder rat box to scroll through it. 'P.E.T.S. Perfectly Ethical Transformation Solutions: Your source for all your needs', scrolled across the top as a happily illustrated woman guided him to select from the menu of options. It ranged from tissue samples, plant as well as animal and human, to the feeders. Simply for distraction he pulled up the files on the rats and studied the very empty, fluid filled brain cavity. That was a little too close to the current situation and while Ichi could watch the careful, slow consumption of the offered meal, Will tried not to.

"Companions?" He pulled up the final listing. "Huh, I didn't know they were the same PETS." The options for grown human companions specially made to accommodate any needs, and with the intelligence of a dim witted dog, as well as their line of artificial life sized dolls, scrolled across the flyer.

Ichi turned and pulled the flyer from his friend's hand. "Sadly, yes, don't even suggest it."

"I'd never suggest it. Why should we mail order you a pretty young man when you'd only feed him to your pets?" Will teased.

Only Ichi wasn't laughing, the idea that he'd maybe be able to order a human grown without a brain to feed to his swarm set his mind to whirling. "That's not a bad idea, a custom order, wonder how long it would take a swarm this size..."

"Ichi!"

"Kidding, kidding, of course, the cost of the human companions is just outrageous. I couldn't afford it and besides, they consider each one a work of art. They'd never make me one to feed to a swarm." But he glanced over his shoulder at the clicking, chirping beetles and sighed. "Mores the pity."

"Are you done now?"

Ichi nodded.

"Good, let's go get drunk." He tossed an arm around his friend's shoulders and guided him out of the lab.

"You know, I never drank until I came here. The stories are all true; everyone from Avalon is an alcoholic." It was a weak protest since he'd learned to drink almost as easily as his station mates.

"That's because everyone from Kakurega are monks and have sticks up their asses. You should thank us for showing you the grand zests of life and the joys of home brew." The ongoing debate was friendly; each mocked the other's home lightly and without malice. "You should come see Avalon with me, I'll show you around. We've plenty of handsome men inclined your way. Cute fellow like you? We'll get you laid in no time."

"I don't..." He sputtered. "I'm not looking to get laid."

"Blown, laid, whatever you want, we'll find it."

"Will!"

He was laughing now, gently, at the blush creeping across his friend's face. The man was far too prudish and it was one more wall Will was set to tear down. "Come, let's get you drunk. That's the only way I ever win at cards against you."

❦

It was hours later, and Will with less money to his name, when they staggered back to Ichi's set of rooms. He was leaning heavily on his friend, who was still far too sober for his liking, and clutching a bottle of the clear, flavorful alcohol.

"A royal flush, a royal flush! You're the luckiest bastard I've ever met. I had a straight flush, man, I thought for sure I had you."

Ichi got his room door open and let his friend stagger in. It was a nice set of rooms, nothing fancy by any means, but the small kitchen was a rarity on Avalon designed and built stations. They tended to assume everyone was like them and wanted to gather in a communal kitchen for meals.

Someone had thought ahead to the tiny size of the station and planned that occasionally privacy might be sought.

Ichi was grateful for it. As much as he'd grown to care for his station mates, there were times when the loud, cheerful, vibrant people really got on his nerves and all he wanted was a quiet meal, alone. That and his choice of foods rarely showed up on the communal kitchen's menu.

That meant that his living room was just an open space with a narrow table shoved along a wall and a small kitchen placed nearby. He had a sofa, soft and big enough for three that rarely got used, and a vid screen hung on the wall across from it. Except for letters or calls home, which weren't frequent, he rarely turned it on.

The first thing Will did once the bottle was safely secured on the small side table by the sofa was to turn the screen on and find a channel with softer music to shatter Ichi's preferred silence. The darker man sighed and moved to dig glasses from one of his cupboards, knowing if he didn't Will would drink right from the bottle.

"Seriously Ichi, Amanda's cousin, you'd like him. He's a farmer so he's all tan and strong."

"Let's not have this conversation."

"Ah, not drunk enough I see!" He poured out the clear liquid into the glasses and pressed one into Ichi's hand. "You're almost family you know, another year and we'll adopt you."

"I don't want to be adopted."

"Hush, of course you do! And family looks out for family." Will slurred drunkenly but there was something dark in his eyes.

Ichi knew that look, most everyone from Avalon had it when they spoke of family. The Concord's invasion, occupation and than near annihilation of their little colony had broken every family on the planet.

Will dropped himself onto the sofa and downed another swallow. "We'll find you some sweaty man loving soon, don't you worry about it."

"I'm not worried about it, it's just..." He was drunk to allow this conversation to continue, but part of him really wanted to whine to someone.

"Just what?" Will leaned over, squinted his eyes and than grinned. "You had a boyfriend meeting you!" he announced with certainty.

"Don't do that!" Ichi scolded and sat with more reserve on the other end of the sofa.

"Can't help it, I'm drunk and a level 22 psi, and you're horny as hell and disappointed about missing your meeting."

Ichi's grandfather had been a pioneer in the field of biophysics, he'd helped design and create the standard test that was now used to judge and rank a human's psychic skills. It was a field of science that was half mysticism and required either raw, inborn gifts or near mystical genius for mathematics. Ichi had neither and the field of biophysics simply confused him.

He was happy knowing the basics; that most of humanity, over 95 percent of them, tested as flat line, base zero, for psychic skills. Ichi's grandfather had given long-winded lectures to attempt to explain that a zero was just human standard. That it included a mother who knew her child was lost or hurt, and the person that knew to check in on a friend that they hadn't spoken to in a while only to find out the friend was in a rough patch in their life. His grandfather had debated that all humans had some base psychic attunement but that a rare few spiked higher.

Ichi was a solid, dead on flat line. He was happy with that. His life was complex enough without anything extra. He liked knowing the world was solid and real and definable. However, the vast majority of the people from Avalon were not flat lines. Seventy-four percent of the population showed a ranking of over five, adding in those five and under and the number jumped up to an astounding ninety-nine percent.

While it was almost unheard of in the general population for a human to have a psi rate of over twenty, it wasn't uncommon on Avalon. In fact, while a rating over twenty was extremely rare, statistically improbable, in the general population it happened often enough on Avalon to attract little notice. Ichi's grandfather had spent years trying to learn why.

Until the flaws in the Network drive system turned their study focus around. The Network drive was amazing; it let humanity cross vast distances faster than ever before. Ichi was like most people, his field of study wasn't advanced inter-dimensional physics, so his understanding of the Network drive was limited. It didn't bother him any, the same way when he turned the lights on in his room and the room lit up he didn't bother worrying about the complex wiring that allowed it.

He knew what everyone else did: it cut travel times down to manageable amounts, and the original Network drive was flawed. It had worked, yes, but it had also worn holes into the very fabric of dimensional space. As scary as that sounded it wasn't that big of a deal, those worn patches re-wove in short order. But sometimes, before they could, something got through. Something that tore entire crews apart and turned ships into floating morgues with only babbling nonsense about demons and monsters left on the ship's log.

Biophysics was the first feild to understand and find a solution. Ichi's grandfather's research had taken a turn from understanding the why's of human population to the why's of inter-dimensional beings.

Termed 'Demons' by the general population, it was his grandfather's research team that first learned these creatures fed on human emotional energy, and once fed they became strong enough to manifest a physical shape. It was his grandfather's team that first learned that some of the stronger psis were not only able to sense but manipulate the Demons' energy fields, and so effectively combat and remove them. It was shortly after that when his grandfather and his entire team had been found torn into parts too small to identify by the creatures he had been attempting to study.

Then the Network drive had been fixed and the engines no longer were scratching portals for the Demons to slip through, the entire science of biophysics became a quaint, almost old fashioned side venture. It was agreed that it was interesting to know just why some people were born with a higher skill ranking, but it no longer was important.

Until thirty years ago when an entire town on a colony in the middle of nowhere was found torn into shreds and their logs and files showed sobbing, terrified people speaking of demons and monsters. There had been no Network drives present to contain a flaw in and slowly it became clear that these monsters, once thought safely contained in their own space, missed the open buffet of their human feasts. Suddenly biophysics was all the rage and the scientific world started scrambling for solutions. They discovered that a tear between space worn open from the other side wasn't so easily closed from this side.

Now any place was a potential target as groups and gatherings of humans one by one were attacked. Survivor's only options became to run away, carrying the fears with them and acting like lightening rods for charging up new attacks. The scientific world went back to the original research and Ichi's grandfather's theory about high-level psis. Successes were slow but it became a proven fact that a high-level human psi was capable of shutting down, containing and sealing a rift.

Except when they were outmatched, in which case the psi was quickly overwhelmed and killed in horrible ways. This further limited the already shallow pool of people with the skills and the inclination to stop the Demons. And all the while, the place with the highest concentration of psis was embroiled in a shameful occupation and slowly was being pushed toward extinction.

Ichi didn't fully understand the politics. He was a Concord citizen after all, and the idea that any system wouldn't wish to join the Concord boggled his mind. But Avalon, like a handful of others, clung to their independence. Worse, they flaunted their scorn of the Concord, harbored smugglers and loosely defined inter-space laws. Ichi was starting to learn it wasn't done maliciously but it was almost a cultural need for the people of Avalon to cause trouble. If a garden had a sign reading 'do not walk on grass,' he was pretty sure they'd take picnics in the center; if a computer system had fourteen levels of security, he knew they'd find ways to hack in just to see why; it was just their nature.

It was deemed that Avalon needed to be reigned in. Why should the Concord go to the expense of terra-forming a new world to colonize when Avalon was eighty percent unsettled and filled to bursting with rich resources. Two birds with one stone and off the Fleet went with boatloads of colonists.

And Avalon, a world of mostly-pacifists that had no formal army and no Fleet except for a handful of merchant ships, was quickly overwhelmed and occupied. All property and land was seized and given to Concordant Citizen landlords, giving free rule to civilize the savage population. Tens of thousands were killed, on both sides, as the occupation pushed the normal peaceful nature of Avalon too far and they took up quiet arms with an informal militia. The resistance was met with greater laws, less freedom for Avalon citizens, more restrictions. And the harsher the laws, the more they fought.

Until the Fleet drew a line and dropped the Bare Earth Virus. It had never been used before but Avalon's isolated nature and the blockade that had been in place for a decade made it a likely test grounds. The Concord's own citizens were merely collateral damage, expendable and replaceable. The Bare Earth was insidious. It attached to everything--soil, air, plants, animals. It contaminated everything in an ecosystem so long as it was able to mutate and grow.

The first weeks, and even months, weren't so bad. A handful of the population fell ill, a handful died, most of Avalon had laughed and teased that the Fleet had underestimated their stronger constitutions. The Avalon scientists knew better, Bare Earth was only learning their system. The second wave killed thousands and each wave thereafter killed more as the virus changed to become deadly to another segment of the population. Some mutations caused madness, some killed quickly, and others killed painfully slowly. And now, cut off from any supportive order, chaos tore what little civilization that was left apart. The occupying clung to control as best they could, fighting the virus and the weakened Avalon citizens. The planet stood on the brink of extinction. Wiped clean of human life, it would only take five years once cleansed for the Bare Earth to degrade in the ecosystem and make the planet habitable again. Five years was a short time to wait when the Concord had been fighting for decades.

It was either chance or fate that dropped a street child with no family and no name into the hands of their doctors. Mercy Shillelagh had proven unusually resistant to the virus, but just how the Avalon researchers managed to find a vaccine was still a closely guarded secret. They saved their world, their culture and way of life with that vaccine and it gave them a weapon like none before. As they only people immune, the upper hand was instantly theirs.

And rather than seal themselves away, it was Mercy Shillelagh that stepped forward to combat the growing danger from the other-worldly demons that so plagued the Concord. As the human with the highest psi rating of ninety-four and an affinity for the Demons bioenergy like none before her, she became the founding member of the independent Psi Guard. Following her example, over half the

Guard's ranks were soon filled with Avalon citizens, all working as independent contractors and making the money required to rebuild their world.

Avalon had used that boost as a spring board. With their world ruined, their natural resources torn and tainted and decades of clean up and repair ahead of them, they encouraged the surviving citizens to exploit the one resource no one could take from them. Within a handful of years, Avalon was producing some of the finest researchers, scientists, computer programmers and academic elite anywhere. Their research facilities were of the highest caliber and their concerns for security meant that they were on a very short list of places that Ichi could bring his very deadly swarm to for a controlled study.

It didn't mean he was comfortable living around the unusual people, even without the added factor of psychic skills. Their informal ease with each other and their casual approach made him uneasy. So many from Avalon had lost so much that all of them now were bonded tighter than family, and it often left Ichi feeling even more like an outsider.

So he'd gone and befriended the most casual, most informal, and the one person on their little research station that had the highest psi rating. Will was everything that made Ichi uncomfortable but somehow, as the years had gone by, it was only around Will that Ichi ever found himself just being himself.

That didn't mean when he was drunk and knowing things he had no right to know Ichi didn't want to kick him. It was unnerving and well beyond intuition. Being drunk himself didn't ease the unhappy stab of pain or the bitterness of embarrassment at having his secret so casually uncovered.

"I'm not horny as hell," Ichi protested.

That only drew snickers from Will. "What's his name?"

"There's no name to tell," he muttered out around his growing blush.

"Bullshit there's not. Come on, come on, I'm not strong enough to pluck it from thin air, tell me?" He poured more drink into their glasses and nudged at his reserved friend.

"Andrew."

"Andrew." Will nodded, rolling the name across his tongue. "All this time and I had no idea you had a boyfriend."

"He's not my boyfriend," Ichi tossed back right away without thinking.

That just raised Will's eyebrows.

"It's just... I'm not..." He sighed and knew Will would never leave it alone until he explained. "We've just know each since University."

"Is he a bug doc too?"

"No, he's an ecologist." He'd given up trying to get them to not call him a bug doctor.

"Is he, you know?"

"I'm afraid I don't know."

"Sexy."

Ichi ran a hand over his face and prayed that Will would just pass out. "Will..."

"Show me a picture!" He hit on the idea and sat up. "Come on, I know you've got them, don't make me dig in your files!" Will lurched toward the panel access and had his hands smacked by the less drunk Ichi. "Ow!"

"Stop! Okay, fine, a picture." Part of him wanted the sympathy and part of him just wanted to poke at the wounds a little. He tapped a few commands and the vid screen lit up with a picture from the last time he'd crossed paths with Andrew.

Will whistled under his breath. The Ichi he knew, always serious, rarely smiling, looked different. He was relaxed, a shy, half-grin teased his mouth and actually touched the slightly almond shaped, light hazel blue-green eyes. The near black hair was crushed under a wide hat that shaded Ichi from the bright sunshine. He also wore a carefully buttoned up shirt with loose, long sleeves in an effort to protect his station-sheltered skin from the harshness of real sunlight.

Andrew hung across his shoulders, smiling brightly with startlingly white teeth. His shirt was white but cut to show the lean strength of his shoulders and arms. Will guessed that Andrew was shorter, so maybe five-six to Ichi's five-eight, but seemed larger just from sheer personality. His skin was darkly black, his eyes a lighter shade of brown, and he wore his hair into twisted dreadlocks that brushed the top of his shoulders. Even Will had to admit the man was handsome.

"I'm impressed, Ichi, didn't think you had it in you! You two are cute."

"Cute."

"I'm straight and I'd do him. Hell, Amanda would be all over him. Who knew you had such a cute boyfriend."

"He's not, it's not like that."

"Even kinkier, who knew you're into casual sex." Will chuckled and sprawled on the sofa, enjoying watching the normally unshakeable Ichi squirm.

"It's not, we're just friends. He stuck up for me at school. Entomologist are at the low end of the geek totem pole, I had tech nerds beating me up." He finished the contents of his cup in long swallows, trying to push down the awkward and uncomfortable memories of his years at school. Andrew had been several years older and the only bright spot about the time.

"Amanda's cousin, he'd be a perfect part-time boyfriend. He's dumb as a box of hammers, but that boy can bench press you."

"No, and I swear, Will, if you send him my name I'll do something awful to you with ants."

"You wouldn't." He refilled Ichi's empty glass.

"I would too!"

"You wouldn't because it would hurt the ants."

Ichi sighed. "Okay, so I wouldn't, but I can be clever if I have to be." He collapsed back on the sofa and rubbed at his eyes. "God, I'm so horny! It's been almost four years, Will, four years."

"I'm sorry, friend, I really am. As soon as this mess blows over I'll take some time off, we'll go home for a bit and I'll introduce you around. We'll get you laid."

"I don't want to just get laid, I…" He sighed and kept his eyes shut. His people simply did not discuss things like sex, and Avalon, well, on Avalon there wasn't much that wasn't discussed. "I'm not comfortable with people. I don't really like most people."

"No shit." Will teased, laughing again. "You talk baby talk to bugs that would happily eat you alive. I think we're all pretty clear on the 'Ichi isn't good with folks' concept."

"It's not easy for me to be… physical with someone. Andrew and I have a history, we're comfortable."

Will's laughter stopped. "I do understand." He reached over and took up the access panel for the vid screen. "Here."

Chapter Two

Ichi opened his eyes and saw the company logo across the screen. "No." He shook his head.

"Hush, just make a doll, give me some idea what type you like." He'd punched up PETS companion doll creation site. It would have been more fun to make a living companion, but that page was password protected for customers with bank accounts large enough to accept such a heavy cost.

"You first." Ichi mocked, knowing that Will wouldn't.

"Sure." He began to click on specifications adding hair and eye color to the generic female form, widening the hips, adding curl to the hair.

"Oh, that doesn't count, it looks just like Amanda." It didn't, not really, but the doll appearing on the screen was gaining an eerie resemblance to Will's wife.

He glanced up and grinned in a silly, besotted way. "It does, doesn't it? She's my dream woman, can't blame me for that. Only, I bet the doll version of her wouldn't hog all the covers at night."

"This is pointless."

"Your turn. Taller or shorter than you?" He switched the doll's basic form to male and waited.

"Same height."

"Hair color?"

Ichi sighed. "Brown."

"Eyes?"

"Brown."

"Build?"

"Average."

Will glanced up. "Ichi! I'm taking this seriously."

"You're drunk."

"So are you."

"Point taken." Ichi glanced to the bland, ordinary looking man taking form on the screen. "I'm ordinary, ordinary suits me."

"This is supposed to be fun, what's your ideal? And you aren't ordinary, you talk baby talk to swarms." He cleared the image. "Now, taller or shorter?"

Ichi dropped his head back onto the sofa and sipped at his drink. "Taller, just a little though, not too tall."

Will grinned with an evil bent. "Build?"

He shrugged. "I don't care."

"How about like this?"

The doll on the screen suddenly was built like a muscle man and Ichi raised his eyebrows in surprise. "Do I seem like the sort that would be attracted to that?"

"Naw, this seems more your sort." He punched a few more commands in and the body changed into a slender, lean waif.

Ichi forgot to be embarrassed. "No, not really, graceful, lean, but toned."

"Like Andrew?"

"Yes," he answered softly, watching the doll's body grow long, slender, lean muscles. He looked like a dancer now, strong but elegant.

"Skin? Andrew dark?"

"Sure."

"Be honest."

"Lighter." He admitted.

"How much lighter?"

Ichi glanced down to his own golden skin and shook his head. "If you laugh at me I swear..."

"I know, I know, the ants, now out with it."

"Lighter than me, I like seeing… it's just…"

Will nodded in total seriousness. "I understand, I'm the same way with Amanda, I like seeing my hand against her paler skin."

"Far too much information, but yes."

Will lightened the skin, made it several shades from pale but also several shades lighter than his friend. "Okay, eye color?"

Ichi shrugged, fascinated now. "I don't have a preference."

"Light or dark?"

"Light."

"Hair?"

"Again, I've never worried about it. Light, I guess."

Will nodded and clicked generic light for both, unspecific the computer would pick a random combination if the doll was ordered but for the display it just put on pale blonde with blue eyes. "Short hair? Long? Mid-length?"

"Shorter, but long enough to run hands through." A shaggy, layered, slightly longer than short but not quite mid-length cut appeared on the doll and Ichi found himself nodding.

"Endowment?"

"Tell me you just didn't ask that?"

"I'm your best friend, if you can't be honest with me?" He grinned and the doll's penis grew to a ridiculous length.

"Average!" Ichi finally admitted. "Just average, I don't think about these things."

"What kind of guy are you? I've spent hours thinking about Amanda's breasts, they're simply perfect you know. I couldn't improve them in any way."

"Again with the information I don't need." Ichi shook his head, but watched fascinated as the dolls penis returned to a normal size.

Will went all the way, showing dozens of eye, lip and nose shapes, face styles and cheekbone levels and bit by bit he plugged in Ichi's choices. He was surprised at the man being put together, he had expected Ichi to cling to his concept of ordinary. Instead, the doll that appeared body part by body part was becoming a rather handsome, unordinary example of humanity. It wasn't pretty and not the least bit feminine and, if Will was being objective, Ichi was closer to pretty than the doll had become but there was no denying the doll was quite attractive.

"My friend, you need to order this doll."

"I most certainly do not!"

"It comes with tight gripping ass action and a super suction mouth," Will read the specs off.

"You did not just say that." Ichi was too drunk to blush but he wasn't too drunk to flush with a tinge of interest.

"And get this, it has a tongue attachment! How neat is that? The central computer will regulate its skin temperature, it has real soft touch artificial skin, you can even set it to breath, blink, and have a heartbeat. It's designed for easy cleaning too."

"We aren't having this conversation."

"Aw, Ichi, no one would mind. I mean, you wouldn't be the first person to order one, I promise you. We all know how difficult it has to be for you. We've actually been toying with hiring you a professional."

"Okay, that's it, this conversation is over with." He was blushing bright red now, he could feel it. Apparently he wasn't too drunk to be embarrassed.

"Just for a couple of days, nothing long term. Mary wanted to send your name into one of those mail order spouse companies."

"Stop." He stood up and got Will up off his sofa by pulling on the man's collar. "Go home to your wife Will, just pretend tonight didn't happen. If there is any mercy in the universe you'll be too drunk to remember this conversation." He led the other man toward his door.

"Order the doll, Ichi, you'll be so much happier. It's just a sex toy for gods sake, it's not even immoral or kinky."

Which made Ichi wonder just what his friend would consider kinky. "Out! Go home!"

"Think about it, order it and you can always store it away if you don't like it. When have you done anything for yourself?" he asked as the door shut on his face. He stood, drunk and a little disappointed to be so rudely tossed into the hall, until he turned and made his way to his own set of rooms and his awaiting wife.

Ichi leaned on his door and locked it. He was the only person on the station that locked their doors out of habit. None of the folks from Avalon ever did, which seemed insane to him given all that they'd lived through, but Ichi had grown up locking doors and so he continued to do so. He was alone now, in his empty apartment, in his silence and facing the unhappy task of writing Andrew to explain.

Before he could figure out what to say, his screen beeped with an incoming call. There wasn't a long list of people willing to pay the cost of talking to him live so he answered it carefully but his face lit up with a smile when Andrew appeared.

"Hey." Ichi slurred out. "I was just about to write you."

"Ichi, I just saw the shut down order on the news, are you okay? That's not your station right? The one with the murders and bombings? And are you drunk?" Andrew frowned.

"Yeah, a little and no, it's not mine."

"Since when did you start drinking?"

He rubbed at his head. "It's a social experiment."

"Will you be able to make the conference?"

Ichi sat down. "It doesn't look promising."

"That's a shame, Steve was looking forward to meeting you."

"Steve?" The name was one he'd heard. "Your assistant, Steve?"

"The one, he's coming with me to the conference."

Ichi's alcohol muddled mind took a moment to process the look he saw on Andrew's face. "You're sleeping with him."

"What of it?"

"Andrew, he's nineteen and you're, you're old enough to be his father."

"You know I don't sleep with anyone over thirty."

Ichi had just turned thirty two. "But, I'm over thirty."

"And I thought we had an understanding about that, Ichi. It's never been more than friendly, right?" Andrew asked carefully.

He was too drunk to have his normal control, so some of the suddenly stunned, pained shock slipped onto his face but Ichi quickly rubbed his eyes and shook it off. "Of course, I'm sorry." He held up his glass before taking a long swallow. "I'm drunk and not thinking clearly." He suddenly felt like an idiot.

Andrew didn't look convinced but he nodded. "Okay, so, I just wanted to make sure you're okay."

"I'm fine, this is actually a good thing. I've so much work to do and the swarm is touchy about strangers taking care of them so it's better if I don't leave them alone for so long, this really is a good thing. I don't like traveling all that much anyway and I can't afford to get a sunburn again." He knew he was babbling but he was afraid if he stopped he'd just sit like a stunned animal unable to speak at all.

"And, we're okay, right? You and I?"

Ichi nodded. "Of course."

"Well, good, I was worried about you." He glanced off camera. "I need to run, I promised I'd pick Steve up for dinner."

"Of course," he heard himself repeating like an idiot.

"It was good to see you, Ich, you look good."

That made him flush again, but he wasn't sure if it was from pleasure or anger. "Thanks, you too."

"Write to me?"

"I will," he promised when he wanted to throw his glass at the screen and shout. Hating that manners and control prevented him from doing what he wanted. The screen went black for a second and than flicked back to the custom made doll that slowly spun in a circle to be inspected. "Oh, my." Ichi sighed and slumped forward over his knees, suddenly feeling lightheaded. "Oh."

This was why he didn't date, he always got dumped and that hurt too much. Will—outgoing, laughing, fun to be around Will—didn't understand that. When, if, he'd ever been dumped, he could see Will shaking it off. Ichi didn't shake anything off, rejection clung to him like sticky fingers.

He rolled the half empty glass in his hands and picked up the mostly empty bottle. If ever there was a night to get really drunk, this one was it. He finished the contents of the cup in quick swallows and proceeded to drink straight from the bottle.

The happy, helpful chiming of Ichi's alarm clock set his head to screaming. For a man that hadn't ever consumed more than a glass or two of wine or sake during the course of his lifetime, waking up with hangovers had been far from uncommon during the last few years. To his station mates credit, they rarely actually got drunk but the consumption of alcohol was a cultural sign of good times so even if it was watered or not even touched, every get together had something. He'd long since learned that most days, the jug of punch was often untouched and the kettles of tea were emptied. It was only on special occasions, celebrations and sorrows that they actually got drunk, and Ichi had been holding his own right beside them.

He groaned and sat up, wiping drool from the corner of his mouth, which felt stuffed with cotton. "Alarm, off." He ordered and tried to remember why he hadn't made it to his bed the night before. The empty bottle of home brew made it pretty clear that he'd simply drank where he sat and fallen asleep on his own sofa.

He staggered to his feet and stumbled to his kitchen. It was a sad day when he would find the hangover cure before the bathroom. Then again, it was even sadder that he'd sat alone drinking. All because of Andrew and his obsession with younger men, which Ichi had known about from day one and hadn't worried over. Thirty had seemed like a lifetime away when he'd been in university and he'd been too busy with work to really notice he'd slipped past that mark.

He shook out one of the dissolve tabs, the size of his thumbnail and mint fresh for the removal of the hangover vomit taste, and popped it on his tongue. It happily melted and instantly hit his bloodstream. Before he could turn on his morning tea, his headache started to dim and his stomach settled. With steadier hands he peeled off his shirt and moved to shower and change for the new day.

As he crossed his living room his feet froze and into his mind crept just what was glowing across his vid screen. "Oh, my, god."

The custom made PETS Companion Doll that Will had wrangled him into making still spun in a small circle, but now information was plastered over it. A shipment date was flashing in one corner and across the top repeated the words 'Thank you for your order, your request has been processed.'

Ichi's stomach turned over and he ran for his bathroom.

～～～

"I'm never drinking again." Ichi announced when he'd finally settled his nerves, cleaned up for the day and managed to find his way to Will's lab. Amanda, gratefully, wasn't in yet or had been in and was currently off seeing to station business.

Will just glanced over to his friend who outwardly appeared none the worse for the wear of the previous night. "You always say that and you always drink again. The threat is losing its strength."

"I'm serious this time." He dropped his screen notebook beside Will and dropped himself onto an empty stool. "I am never, ever drinking again."

Will paused his work and glanced to the screen that glowed beside him. It took a moment but when understanding dawned he started laughing. "You didn't."

"Apparently, I did."

"And you don't remember it?"

"Of course I don't!" He hissed back, trying not to blush and praying Amanda wouldn't walk in. "What am I going to do?"

"Cancel the order."

"I've already spent the entire morning trying, they don't accept cancellations."

"They must get a lot of hung over calls the morning after an order is placed."

"Will, what am I going to do?" Nothing in his experience prepared him for this.

"I would have thought a man of your age wouldn't need instruction." He teased dryly just to make Ichi blush.

"Will."

"What were you doing drinking after I left anyway? You know better." He scolded but picked up the notepad to read the fine print.

"Andrew, well, it's complicated."

"Un-complicate it for me."

"He doesn't get involved with men over thirty, I forgot and well, he's now seeing his nineteen year old assistant." He sighed and rubbed at his eyes, relishing the sharp pain.

"Ouch. You know, you picked him because you knew he'd eventually dump you." He kept scanning the fine print, hoping to find a 'my friend was drunk and wants to cancel his order' clause and not finding one.

"Don't, not right now Will."

"You avoid intimacy like the plague, and trust me, I've seen people avoid the plague. There's more to life than your creepy bugs. I'm actually impressed you placed the order, proves you're human after all," he grumbled.

"I like bugs, they're nicer than humans." His stomach felt sick again, he told it to shut up. "What am I going to do?"

"Well, it doesn't seem like you can get out of the order, so you're going to be the proud owner of your own sex doll. Who's going to know? I mean, I won't tell anyone, you won't tell anyone, and if anyone finds out tell them to walk to the nearest air lock and go swim in vacuum. No one here will care, so why worry about it? It'll show up in ahh..." He glanced down. "About three months. I'll help you move the crate to your room, no one will know."

"You promise?"

"I promise."

⸎

The ban on travel in Avalon space was lifted a few weeks later and the small research station paid it little mind. Ichi, with no further plans to go on holiday, tossed himself into his work without looking back. He didn't follow the news and the growing scandal of the Flossin Guard exposure. Neither did he take too much notice to the fact that a new push to expose the harsh treatment and condition of Avalon citizens during the occupation was started by a Captain Elliot Gore, a decorated Concord Fleet officer. It was a bit of news that had his Avalon station mates buzzing in concerned distraction, as Elliot Gore was the son of the commanding General that had torn their world apart.

It didn't matter to Ichi personally, he didn't belong to their world and he had his work to focus on. For weeks as Elliot Gore's efforts to bring about reparations for the harm his father had done was first met with suspicion and then grudging admiration, Ichi moved around the station as a virtual ghost. It was just what his uneasy, battered ego needed, the solitude of work and his pets to regain his sense of self that had been bruised with Andrews rejection, his canceled plans, and his own stupidity.

When three months came and no crate arrived in Jos Harvick's hold, Ichi sighed a breath of relief. Maybe they'd lost his order; he wouldn't protest it. Or maybe his order had been lost in shipment, it wasn't common but it wasn't unheard of either. It could have happened and it would have been a blessing. He didn't really care so long as that three-month window came and went and nothing with his name attached to it arrived.

So two months later he'd nearly forgotten the order placed one drunken night, even if his mind still shied away at the shocked pain of being dropped by his part-time lover. He had his hands full; his swarm had laid eggs, something that had never occurred in captivity before, no one had even observed them mating. Ichi had been near giddy with delight, as proud as any parent, and he'd been pouring over weeks of recordings trying to spot their mating. It had him distracted enough that he'd lost track of days and had forgotten that Jos Harvick was due back at their station. He wasn't just due, but overdue.

"Hey! Ichi!" Will poked his head into the small lab.

"Shhh, they're building a nest for the eggs." On a whim, he'd provided his swarm with different bedding material, of different styles, and the group had chattered happily before starting to weave a complex nest. He'd been watching them for hours, taking notes as he went; it was better to see it live anyway.

"You're taping it right?"

Ichi nodded and kept his eyes on the enclosure.

"Well, good because Harvick is docking and there's an extra couple of boxes with your name on them in his manifest."

"What do you mean?" He asked, quickly keying in a note about the males being skittish about getting knocked inside the growing nest.

"Your order." Will prompted.

"My order?" He frowned and thought and than remembered and blushed. "Oh, I'd hoped they'd lost it."

"I promised you I'd help you move it but it if sits in the cargo hold for too long people will notice. So, tape your morbid friends and get moving." He glanced over his shoulder to make sure no one was in the hallway.

"Right." Suddenly, watching the nest being built didn't seem the most important thing. "Do you think we can talk Mr. Harvick into just taking it back? Return to sender or something?"

"This is Avalon, there is no return to sender option on shipments, and besides he'll want to know why and what it is and I don't think you want to answer those questions."

"God, no." He didn't want anyone knowing. "You didn't tell Amanda did you?" He'd never thought to ask until now, but the idea that she might know made him uncomfortable.

"Of course not, I haven't said a word." He hurried them through empty hallways, which weren't unusual during the day but something had his nerves uneasy.

When they reached the cargo hold, he knew why. Ichi froze just inside the door, stunned and unsure if he could turn and run before he was noticed. There were seventeen people on the station; not counting himself and Will that meant there were fifteen others. A dozen of those fifteen waited in the hold, talking and laughing, two of the women poked at the boxes stacked to the side and marked with the PETS logo and Harvick stood in a small group talking and waving a notebook around with his wide, ranging hand motions.

"Will…" His blood froze and suddenly, the idea that his swarm might one day escape and consume him slowly over days was no longer the worst fate he could think of.

"I didn't say a word, I swear." Will hissed back but he eyed his wife near the boxes laughing.

Amanda glanced up when her husband's eyes fell on her and she smiled widely. "Ichi! Hurry up and open it, we're dying to see!"

Suddenly, thirteen pairs of eyes swung his way and a half dozen different conversations ended. He felt the blood drain from his face and his pulse pounded in his ears. It was just a matter of time before he turned on his heel and hurried back to his lab to die of embarrassment or until he flat out passed out from shame, he knew it. "How do they know?" He managed to whisper, not really asking Will.

Will pulled on his friends arm and got him moving. "They're Avalon, we're nosy bastards. Secrets tend to get out around us, I'm sorry."

"What's everyone doing here?" Ichi managed to ask when Will dragged him into the storage room. The large doors were open and the tube connected Harvick's ship's main hold to their storage hold cast a pinkish glow to that corner of the large room.

"Hush, we all known." Amanda smiled. "Open it up, Ichi, we want to see." A chorus of agreement followed.

"But, it's nothing…" he tried to lie and knew it sounded like a lie. Besides, they had an uncanny knack at knowing when people were lying.

"Aw, I told them Ichi." Harvick nodded, looking proud.

"You what?"

"Here, look." Harvick moved forward pushing buttons on his notebook as he went. He set it down and it projected a message upwards.

It was the same generic woman that illustrated PETS promotional brochures. She flickered a little and solidified into a slightly glowing and very fake looking spokeswoman. "Congratulations--" There was a pause, just a fraction too long, making it pretty clear that the message was generic and the specifics were simply plugged in. "Kenichi Vitorui of--" Another half-beat, too long pause. "Avalon Station S14592." Her fake smile broadened as she stared off to a point a good distance from where Ichi actually stood. "You've been randomly selected to receive a free upgrade. From time to time, here at PETS Companion division, one of our Living Companion models doesn't quite meet our expectations. When this occurs, if it's at all possible and compatible, we upgrade special clients like you--" A half beat too long pause. "Kenichi Vitorui, from a standard doll to a real Living Companion."

She smiled wider. "We're certain you'll have a grand time with your new Living Companion. You'll find included a full instruction manual on care and training of your new Pet as well as a complimentary six month supply of nutritionally complete kibble. The shipment crate converts easily into a housing crate for your newest Pet and makes a convenient bed. If you have any questions, our technical support line is open to inquiries at any time and we'd be happy to assist you. Again, congratulations and we hope you enjoy your free upgrade." She smiled for a second longer before the projected message clicked off and disappeared.

The room broke out in excited conversation again and Ichi just turned to go. Will caught his arm and kept him from going more than a few steps. "Want me to just kill you now?" Will teased.

"Don't tempt me." He drew a breath and turned back to the waiting group.

"Open it Ichi!" someone called out.

"No, no one is opening it! Captain, please, there's been a mistake."

He glanced to his files. "You didn't order a customized doll companion from PETS?"

"I, well, yes, I did, but that was a mistake too. I don't want this." He pointed to the boxes sitting, still sealed, nearby. "Send it back."

"Can't do that."

"Of course you can, I'll pay the transport, just take it away."

"Ichi…" Amanda spoke softly from where she knelt near one of the boxes.

"No," he snapped back to her. "It's going back."

"We have to open it."

"No, we don't." He met her eye and stopped. It wasn't idle curiosity there, or even cruel teasing, but real concern. "Why?"

"The date, this pet's been in storage for forty three days."

The conversations and whispering stopped and even Ichi paused. His rats had a longer shelf life, six months or more in gel storage, but they had no complex neural tissue and they were rats. For larger life forms, say, something as complex and large as a human, even an altered human, the longest they could safely stay in gel storage without a break was supposed to be twenty nine days.

"You didn't take it out?" Will snapped at Harvick. Somewhere along the lines of shipping the pet should have taken it out of storage at least for a few hours before putting it back in.

Harvick shook his head. "I just transport, that should have been done at one of the weigh stations."

All eyes turned to Ichi and he shook his head. "Open it."

Chapter Three

The box was a little more complicated than the cylinders his rats came in. Ichi knew to step aside and let Will and Amanda, both medical doctors, figure out the complex series of latches and locks. After a moment where they all stood tense, near to Ichi but not close to him, the box began to cycle open. The gel that had supported and stilled the life inside began to evaporate as it came in contact with the air outside of the sealed container, and the sheer volume of it created a very dramatic swirl of mist and filled the cargo hold with the smell of sharp chemicals covered with the added scent of fresh pine.

Putting his shoulder to the side of the door that had slid open, but not free, Will shoved against it to force it open. It unsealed all the way and swung off the crate, falling in a loud tumble to the floor. An extra billowing cloud of mist swirled out and someone behind Ichi sneezed.

"Is it alive?" Amanda asked from the side of the crate, but Will just stared into the rapidly drying interior. "Will?"

Movement inside caught every eye. A hand smacked out and caught the edge of the crate and a bare foot shuffled forward. The pet stumbled forward, squinting under the cargo hold's lights but alive and moving and as it stepped out of the shadows of the crate, nude and very obviously male.

Ichi stood, stunned, as a creature from his dirtiest, deepest, most hidden of fantasy realms stepped into the ordinary and very every day world of his stations cargo hold. Taller than he was but not overly tall, maybe five-ten at most, and entirely long, lean muscle from head to foot. Even dazed, in obvious shock, the pet moved with a jaw dropping grace. His skin was pale, milk pale, ivory pale, treasured fine china pale. The face was heart shaped, with cheekbones high enough to offset the strong chin and lips expressive without being soft. A straight, obvious nose was centered between sharp eyes. Eyes were the color of storm clouds, such a metal gray shade that they pulled all attention right to them. His hair was drying from the gel and clung in long tendrils to his body, it reached almost to his waist in the back but it was deep, black cherry red. Not the orange pumpkin red of Amanda or even a reddish auburn brown but a dark, blood, brick red.

The pet took one unsteady step forward, and than another. His eyes locked onto Ichi's and he froze. The look sent a thousand shivers across Ichi's body and made his face flush a red nearly as dark as the pet's hair. The pet shivered too, convulsed and fell dead forward like a fallen tree.

He hit the deck hard with nothing to break his impact and the crowd gasped. Ichi stood silent and startled as the pet so close to his feet started to have seizures. If the pet had six legs instead of two, he would have instantly had some idea what to do. Since he was human, he stayed out of the way and tried to pretend he was invisible.

"Mark! Help!" Amanda called out as both she and Will fell on the twitching creature on the ground.

One of the other researchers pushed past Ichi and joined the pair. "Over forty days, what's he doing alive?"

"Pets aren't people," Will reminded them. "Help me get him to the med lab."

The group of people easily lifted the pet and they gossiped and chatted and nudged each other along as the entire crowd followed behind Amanda, Will and Mark to the med lab. Ichi didn't move, found he couldn't move, and it took a long time for the silence to sink in and tell him he'd been left behind, alone and forgotten in the cargo hold.

His hands were shaking. "Oh my god," He whispered into the silence and sat down, hard, onto the cold deck floor.

⁂

Ichi wasn't sure how long he sat there but eventually curiosity got the better of him. He picked himself up and dusted his pants off before leaving the cargo hold. He took the turns of the hallways without thought and the door opened before him.

His hands stopped shaking. "Tuk tuk tuk, tuk tuk tuk." He clucked but his swarm was too busy weaving their nest to notice. Safe inside his lab again, back in the world he could make sense of, he felt his shoulder's unknotting. He eased himself back into his chair and just sat and watched his beetles.

Hours passed and the nest slowly grew. Soon his beetles were scuttling over their handiwork, inspecting it, tugging on loose fibers, giving it a very careful final inspection like he'd never witnessed before. Once they were satisfied with their work, they formed a fire brigade and passed one egg from beetle to beetle. The first one in line quickly scurried to the front and so the chain moved the egg toward its place in the nest. He smiled at seeing how each beetle turned the egg carefully, how their antennae caressed the smooth gray surface with almost-tenderness.

"That's it, careful now," he whispered to them, encouraging the awe-inspiring sight he was the first human to see. Well, the first human that had lived to report seeing anyway.

Beside him his notebook beeped at him and Will's face appeared. "Ichi?"

"Hmmm?"

"We need you to come down here to the med lab."

"Now?"

"Yes, now!"

"Alright." He sighed and pushed the off button on his notebook. Four of the six eggs had been safely transported, it wouldn't do any harm to wait and watch the last two get moved.

❧

The med lab was the size of his own research lab. It could supposedly handle nearly any medical emergency that got tossed their way, but Ichi hoped he'd never have to test that theory. There were only two beds and in a mass illness or injury most of the station members were to be housed in their own apartments. Normally both beds were empty and, other than a run of colds or the occasional flu, the station had little use for the medical facilities. A few bumped heads at parties, a turned ankle on occasion from a clumsy step, but never really anything of serious note. In fact, he hadn't set foot in the lab since last year's physicals and he counted himself lucky for that.

"Where have you been?" Will scolded and stopped pacing the room as soon as the door opened.

"You just called, I came as soon as I could." Amanda sat reading files, pointedly not looking at him or her husband. The lab's only other occupant was the pet, curled up loosely on his side on one of the med beds, apparently asleep.

"That was over a half hour ago, Ichi."

It hadn't felt that long. "I came as soon as I could."

Amanda held up a hand. "That doesn't matter. Ichi, sit, there's a lot you need to know." She caught her husband's wrist as he paced by. "And you as well, if you don't sit and settle down I will sedate you."

Will stopped his nervous pacing and drew a long slow breath. "I'm sorry, it's just, everyone is so ugh." He made a face and tried to shuck off the nervous, excited tension that their new arrival had brought with him. "I'm trying," he muttered and dropped himself into a chair.

Ichi's eyes had scanned the room and stopped on the sleeping pet. His face was slack now in sleep and there was still strength in it. Someone had twisted the thick tail of dark red hair back and tied it in place and it curled in a solid rope across pale skin. There was something magnetic about the pet, and it wasn't an entirely comfortable something.

"Ichi, sit." Amanda spoke and broke into the entomologist's thoughts.

He nodded and pulled a chair over to where his friends sat, waiting. "Yes? I'm sorry, it's just, my swarm, they've built a nest. There's no indication that they nest in the slightest and yet it's amazingly complex and when they'd finished--"

"I'm sure it's fascinating." She cut in with a small smile, knowing if allowed Ichi would ramble for hours about his bugs. "There's a lot you need to know before you take your pet home."

"Before I--what?" He tilted his head a little, certain he'd misheard what she said.

"Before you take him home."

He glanced to the sleeping form and back to Amanda's wide eyes. "I'm not taking that thing anywhere. I don't want it." It, it was so much better to think of the pet as an 'it' and not a 'he'.

"He's yours, you own him."

"I don't want it. You two keep wavering on having a child, so start out with a pet. I've heard every couple should raise a dog or something before they have a child." He waved in the general direction of the medical beds. "Feel free."

Amanda's face grew serious. "Ichi, he belongs to you. He's your responsibility."

"One I didn't ask for. I'm not good with pets, I'm sure Will's told you, I had a cat as a child that hated me."

"He's made to be the companion to another man, Ichi. He's never going to be happy being owned by a heterosexual man or a woman and, since you're the only gay man on this station, you can't pawn that poor creature off to someone else." She looked to Will for support but her husband was still twitchy and she knew the look on his face, he was slowly pulling himself together. That meant until he was more stable, she was on her own.

"What does that mean, it's ridiculous. A dog wouldn't care about the gender or preferences of its owner."

"PETS Living Companions aren't dogs and they aren't cats. Yes, the base of their genetic code is human, but they're not human. They're brains are built from the ground up differently. They aren't self aware, they aren't conscious, they don't have human emotions, and they're not capable of human speech. They're just barely smart enough to be trainable, like a dog, a rather stupid one at that. What's more, they make them for specific functions, they're built from their DNA up for this function." She punched buttons on her panel and brought up files.

"I'm not sure I like where this is going."

"You don't need to like it. This pet was built to be the sexual companion to another man, end of story, bottom line. Someone put a lot of time and effort, not to mention money, to customize this pet for that function. His nerve endings are double terminated."

Ichi frowned. "Meaning?"

"Meaning he's made to respond twice as strongly to touch. His libido? In theory is doubled or tripled from a base line human standard. He's been built to have a docile, pleasing personality. This pet wasn't created to be someone's doll or toy or as a platonic companion, he was created from the ground up to be someone's sexual companion." She half-pitied Ichi, the man was blushing and obviously flustered at the very idea.

"None of that means he was meant just for another man." But he thought about the curve of the pet's shoulder, the lean muscle, the way the deltoid tapered to a point on his arm, and he couldn't chase the thought away.

"Ichi, he's a rejected pet because the person that paid to commission certain specifications didn't get what he wanted. One of the modifications that wasn't successful was a self lubricating anus, now you tell me if I'm assuming the wrong thing."

He dropped his face into his hands and rubbed his eyes, hoping maybe this was some odd dream he was about to wake up from. "That's not a funny joke."

"I'm not laughing. It's all right here, a list of requested specific modifications and some are marked as failed and some unknown. Hair color, eye color, neither took exactly the right color, the self lube seems a touch odd but it's not a difficult concept, simple implantation of specialized goblet cells, but his body rejected them. The double terminated nerve endings are a difficult modification and that one took. Even his hair length was specified, and for most of it he passed fine, but when your client is willing to spend more than this station does in a year to buy a new toy, he expects perfection. One failure rejects the whole pet." It was beautiful in the sheer scientific perfection of the creation of these companions, and if she was slightly less ethical she'd admire them. As it was, it smelled too much like slavery to her, even if she knew that what was sat in the handsome pet's skull bore no resemblance to a human brain.

"So, how is this my fault? Why can't we pack it back up and send it back?"

"For one, he can't go back into the gel for a while. I know Pets are supposed to be hardier than a human but, frankly, I've no idea how he survived so long in storage. For another, if one of their free upgrade Pets get returned they don't shuffle them to another free upgrade winner. Apparently these upgrades are fairly rare, if the winner rejects the pet, the pet is assumed to be unforgivably flawed and is liquidated."

"Killed?" Ichi couldn't help it, he glanced to the sleeping form and the idea of something so handsome, so graceful and lean, being liquidated pained him. He really was a work of art and some gene designer had gone above and beyond the call of duty to make him.

"Killed. Self-aware or not, that's a living creature. You may not have asked for this but neither did he ask to be dissolved for spare genetic material."

Ichi slouched back into his chair. "Okay, okay, I'm not that inhuman. Just explain to me why it has to stay with me. Why can't we get it, I don't know, its own room or something."

"You never had a dog." She sighed. "What were you? Raised in a lab?"

"Well, yes," he answered.

Amanda glanced to Will and he shrugged, not sure himself if Ichi was kidding or being honest. The dark haired man had a very dry sense of humor and he'd never spoken of his childhood or home life before. "That's a joke right?"

Ichi just shook his head, a little surprised at the reaction. "No."

The look that passed between the married couple was softer this time and again Will just shrugged before Amanda took them back to the topic at hand. "It doesn't matter, just, he's a lot like a dog. He's a social creature. Even if we put him in a room and you gave him food and water and he was physically taken care of, he'd be miserable. We'd be better off sending him back to be liquidated."

"Fine but why does it have to be me?"

She sighed and looked to Will and he shook his head before answering. "Look, Ichi, he's a super-charged, horny sex machine in a human shape attuned to men. Every other man here is straight. You're cute and our friend and none of us have wanted to get it on with you, how awkward do you think it would be for one of us to have that pet trying to fulfill his function with us?"

Ichi blushed again, wondered idly if a person could die from blushing too much and couldn't meet either of his friend's eyes. "What makes you think it would be any less awkward for me?"

"Goddess sake, Ichi, this is a gift! Right here is a creature made specifically to be a sexual partner to those that can't afford the time of a relationship. He's attractive, I know you think he is, he's made to be your lover and you're having second thoughts?" Will shook his head. "You've been hanging out with bugs too long, my friend."

"But, I'd be taking advantage…"

"He's not human!" Will retorted but Amanda put her hand on her husband's arm and leaned toward their friend.

"No one is saying you have to do anything with him. Just feed him, be social toward him, make sure he's taken care of like any good owner should. He's trainable, if you don't want him coming on to you, I'm sure you can train him not to."

That made logical sense but he sat and tried to think of a logical debate against it. When none emerged he nodded. "Alright, you win, at least until I can think of a better solution."

Amanda let go of the breath she hadn't know she was holding. "Good. Now, I've sent his care instructions to your home system. He's housetrained, and he knows several commands. You're only supposed to feed him the provided kibble and it's considered bad for discipline to let him sleep in your bed. Mark and Henry were putting his crate together and they said they'd drop it by your rooms tonight."

"Wonderful."

"Ichi, this is serious."

"I'm the one with a pet that looks like a man, I think I understand how serious this is."

She sighed. "He's a little sick right now, and disoriented, so he's out of sorts and might be for a couple of days. I don't know how he survived being in storage for so long but it's going to take him time to recover. Also, you're going to need to think of a name for him."

"What?"

"He didn't come with one. You'll have to name him. Anna wanted to call him Fluffy, so pick one quickly before something stupid like that sticks. And, he came with a set of kilt-like skirts, apparently that's standard dress for Pets. We got him into one here so he's ready to go."

"Of course."

"Now, I've work to do, can you take your pet home so I can get to it?"

He opened his mouth to protest about his beetles and their nest but the look in her eyes was stubborn. She wasn't just his friend, she was technically in charge of the entire station. "Of course." He surrendered.

"Good." She smiled now and stood up. At the side of the medical bed she brushed back loose threads of dark red. "Hey there pretty boy, wake up now, thata boy, wake up."

The gray eyes fluttered and squinted open. A slender hand rose up to rub at his face and he half sat up. Those dazed, amazing, eyes slid from Amanda to Ichi and they widened in some quickly hidden emotion before a yawn split the handsome face.

"That's unnerving." Ichi found himself whispering. "Can it, he, understand us?"

Amanda shook her head. "No, his brain isn't built that way. Like a dog, he'll know only that the sound of his command word means to do a certain action, and like a dog he should respond to tone." She produced a slender silver silk rope from beside the bed and offered one end to the pet and his hand wrapped around it. "His leash." She offered the other end to Ichi and he took it carefully. "They recommend you use it until he figures out who his owner is."

"And what?"

"And walk, he'll follow."

"Just like that? He'll hold on to his end and follow?"

She nodded. "He's trained, remember? This isn't just a pet, someone spent a lot of money making him a very high end pet. Now, take him home, let Mark and Henry help you get his crate in place, feed him, name him and let him get some rest."

Experimentally, Ichi took a step or two back until the cord between himself and the handsome pet was tight. The pet slid from the medical table with graceful ease and landed softly on bare feet. His head automatically bowed, his eyes downcast but his grip on the rope was strong.

"This is wrong on so many levels."

"Read the files on him, once you study the science behind it, you'll see Pets only look like people." She tried to smile but her belief wasn't as firm as Will's.

"Okay." He took a small step toward the door and the pet mirrored it. Still shaking his head, he led his newest pet out into the hallway. He followed always at the same distance, always with his head down. It made Ichi uncomfortable beyond words but he led the creature back to his own apartment of rooms, one careful step at a time.

The pets' bare feet made only the smallest of slapping sounds on the deck floor, but the sound seemed impossibly loud to Ichi's ears. He knew he was blushing and he just couldn't help it. The sexual aspects of the pet's design function alone would have had him embarrassed, but adding in the overtones of bondage and how placidly leash trained the thing was, well, it was far kinkier than Ichi was comfortable with.

Chapter Four

Fortunately, the only people he ran into while leading his new pet home were Mark and Henry. They were pulling a supply cart loaded down with the walls of the pet's crate as well as boxes that Ichi didn't know about yet.

"Heya Ichi, how is he?" Mark nodded to the silent follower.

"Wow, that's amazing." Henry circled the unresponsive pet, poking at its arm occasionally. "He looks so human. There's no way Rosie is going to give me the time of day now with this pretty thing on board."

Mark elbowed Henry and shook his head. "Engineers, so uneducated."

"Hey!"

"Stupid, it's designed to be gay, it won't even know what to do with Rosie. Ichi's the lucky winner this time. Have you named him yet?"

Ichi stood as silent as the pet as both of the men turned from the pet to him. He forced himself to shake his head. "No, and Amanda says he's fine and just needs rest. And he's not staying. There has to be some group or something that takes these things in when they're unwanted. I just need to find them."

Henry tipped the pet's chin up and peered into his face. "I've a buddy with some shady contacts that could probably sell him for you. The secondary market for these critters has to be huge, given the costs involved. Be a shame for you to just give it away when you could get some money out of it."

"Thanks, I'll think about it." Avalon and its black market. When he'd first arrived, it had surprised him until he'd learned that even now the Concord still had a partial ban on the trade of goods to the smaller system. He unlocked his room and got the door open. "I'm grateful for your help."

Mark just laughed and pulled the cart in behind him. "No thanks needed, this is the most exciting thing that's happened since, well, since you arrived! We're easily amused."

Ichi got out of the way while the other men filled his living room and started unloading boxes. When they seemed to have picked their workspace, he moved forward, the pet following, and got the two of them inside his actual rooms. He dropped his end of the rope and moved to the small kitchen. "Would you two care for some tea?"

"Naw, thanks though Ichi, Anna's expecting me back and Henry, well, he's going to be going to the kitchen and drooling over Rosie. Like normal."

"I do not! It's just, she's so… so…" He sighed and held the side of the crate in place while Mark fastened it.

"He's so smitten." Mark teased and laughed but he glanced up to where the pet still stood where he was left. "Is he supposed to just stand there?"

Ichi followed Mark's nod to where the pet stood, swaying lightly in place, still clutching his end of the rope. "I don't know." He crossed around the growing clutter of crate parts and pet supplies to stand and study the creature. There were dark circles like smudged pain under the downcast eyes, the smooth skin looked a little ashen and if he was to assume the pet would show human-like reactions, he looked unwell.

Carefully, Ichi slipped the pet's end of the silver cord from its grasp. The pet shivered and instantly dropped to the floor. He literally folded up and sat right where he stood, bowing forward over his legs.

"Huh." Ichi glanced to the leash and down to the pet but when he went to take a step away the thing skittered backwards, startled, and pressed his back to the wall. "Jumpy fellow."

"He'll settle in, will just take a day or two."

Ichi nodded to Mark and moved to put the leash on his coffee table. "He must be trained to be tethered. If the leash is dropped he stays put."

"Useful, wish I could do that with Anna when we're back home and she wants to go shopping," Mark teased again, trying to get the tense entomologist a little more at ease and failing. "There we go, crates all together."

Ichi peered at the oblong box that looked too much like a coffin for him. Long and rectangle, even pressed against the wall it took up space. The upper half of the sides and back were a mesh screen as well as the top and one end was open. The whole thing stood no more than two feet tall, about three wide and less than six long. The floor inside had a thin, plastic coated mat but nothing else.

"The rest of these boxes, they're yours too. We only brought up one carton of kibble but the rest are in storage." Henry nodded as he worked the cart back into the hallway, tossing another glance to where the pet sat, knees pulled up to his chin, against the wall.

"Thank you, both of you."

"No troubles, just call if you need help."

"I will, I think I have a lot of reading to do tonight."

Henry nodded and smiled softly. "Have fun."

Ichi couldn't swear it, but he thought the tone of words and smile had a lewd undertone. He chalked it up to being over sensitive and nodded at the face value of the statement but, when the pair left, he locked his door. That left him alone with his new pet, which sat pressed to the wall watching him from behind his wide gray eyes.

"Absurdity," Ichi whispered and moved to open the boxes of supplies left.

One that stood knee high and was a foot by two feet wide was filled with walnut sized lumps of kibble. Ichi lifted one up out of curiosity and sniffed it. It didn't smell unpleasant but neither did it smell like food. He dropped the round back in the box and lugged the entire thing to set it along the wall by his kitchen.

He pried open the next box and found in it two metal bowls and guessed they were feed and water bowls, so they got stacked on top of the food bin. Below them, he found a small box of the thin fabric kilts, all in plain ivory, and the storage box they were in was obviously designed to clip onto the pet's sleeping create. Another small, clip-able box held grooming supplies. It looked to him like shampoos and soaps, a wash cloth and towel, but he didn't root in it too much, just snapped it on the crate next to the first one.

"Great, have to bathe it too." He sighed and wondered how he was going to drag the taller, obviously stronger pet into the shower or how he'd manage to remember it wasn't a thinking creature when something that pretty was wet and naked.

The rest of the box had what looked like a hairbrush and collar, different color leashes and other types of harnesses, but what caught his attention was a tiny box lost in the bottom. When he fished it out and opened it, two shiny gold bars tipped in faceted gold glittered inside.

Ichi picked one out and turned it over in the light. "What the?"

The hint of movement out of the corner of his eye made him glance over but when he glanced down he jumped, startled. The pet had crept silently over to him and now sat, watching him, almost at his feet. Gray eyes met brown before dropping submissively again. One slender hand extended outward, palm up, and simply waited.

"What?" Ichi glanced around, uncertain and confused. "I don't understand." But he saw he was still holding the gold bar. "This?" He carefully set the bar onto the pet's hand, prepared to snatch it back if he tried to eat it or something.

The pet didn't try to eat it, instead he popped one of the faceted ends off with deftly skilled fingers. Ichi watched with the same fascination that he did his insects as the pet glanced down, and then shoved the bar through one nipple. The bar went halfway and stuck, the hole that had obviously been in place had partially healed while the pet had been in storage. Instead of stopping, before Ichi could react, the pet forced the bar to pierce the newly healed tissue.

Ichi swore he heard a popping sound and he grimaced even if the pet's expression never changed. He did shiver, a slight rippling that twisted across the lithe body that Ichi couldn't swear was entirely from pain. The sight was disturbingly erotic and Ichi licked his lips without thought.

The slender hand extended again and Ichi glanced from it to the second waiting gold bar. There was a small trickle of blood, tracing its way down the pet's pale skin, and that made Ichi close the box. If he'd known what the bars were for, he'd never have let the pet have the first one. "No." he said in a firm voice and dropped the box with the bar back into the shipping bin.

The pet gave him a confused look that he ignored. Instead, he fetched a damp towel from his kitchen and knelt down to wipe the thin trail of blood away. The pet shivered again and arched backwards, exposing his chest to be petted or touched, his eyes going half shut in open pleasure. Ichi didn't notice right away but it did sink in and when it did, he blushed and grew very hard.

He stood up quickly and moved to the sink in his kitchen to rinse the towel free of the blood and try to settle his nerves down. "Bad, Ichi, bad of you, you've just been alone too long," he whispered to the running water before shutting it off. He turned around and startled backwards against the edge of his counter top.

The pet had followed him again. It knelt in front of him, eye level to Ichi's groin and those gray eyes weren't downcast. Having the beautiful creature kneeling there, openly studying his aroused state left Ichi clutching the counter top. In his mind he knew he should step away but he stood frozen, even as the eyes slid upward to meet his own. In his world, beautiful men simply didn't kneel and lick their lips at him.

Carefully the pet leaned forward and slid the side of his face against Ichi's groin in a slow, sensual nuzzle. It startled Ichi so badly that he jumped backwards far enough that he was almost sitting on his counter top. His hands snapped from their grip out and he caught the sides of the pet's face and pulled the head away from his body.

"No," he said firmly and was met with a confused look. "No, don't do that. No! Bad." Good, very good, too good, his mind whispered back. He shivered a little but stepped to the side and got himself out of being stuck between the pet and the counter. He hurried to the crate and patted it. "Here, now, here, this is yours."

The pet tilted its head and still looked confused. Ichi patted the top of the crate, which he saw was hinged and could be lifted up, and this time the pet carefully moved. Silently, gracefully, the creature crossed over and then almost darted into the tiny space. Ichi wasn't even sure how he did it, let alone so quickly. One moment he was a few feet away, the next he was turning and bending and quickly disappeared into the confines of the crates small space.

Having the pet safely tucked out of sight did a world of good for Ichi's fraying nerves. He sighed and moved to fill the food and water bowl before setting them down near the front of the crate. He peered inside and saw pale flesh and dark hair and that was about it, the pet was curled up near the back. That was fine by him, having the skittish creature out of the way was a good idea.

He sighed and moved to finish making his own tea, picking a soothing blend of mints to settle his uneasy thoughts and stomach before he dropped himself onto his sofa to start reading the care manual that came with the pet. Long moments passed as Ichi balanced his personal notepad on his fingertips as he read.

The sound of the pet moving in his crate drew his ears but a subtle glance out of the corner of his eyes showed him the creature was still hidden from sight. Another long pause came and went before the pet moved again and this time, Ichi saw a long slender arm extend from the crate to reach into the food bowl. The hand grasped and the kibble rattled before the arm quickly disappeared back inside. A moment later, Ichi heard crunching sounds and an odd smile twisted at his lips.

The manual was divided into two books, a plain overview and a more in-depth version. Ichi tackled the overview first, scanned it fairly quickly and found most of it to be simple sales pitch propaganda.

He learned from the overview that it was recommended that all pets eat only their kibble and not human food; that they sleep in their crate on the provided mat and not in a bed or with blankets. A collar was provided, which was highly suggested to be worn until those that might come in contact with the pet learned what it was. There was also supposed to be a discipline stick in the supply box, but it sounded awfully like a cattle prod to Ichi.

The pre-trained commands ranged from useful and fascinating to downright embarrassing. 'Change' would have the pet putting on a kilt, either removing the old or if naked dressing outright. 'Bathe' would have the pet stripping and washing; again, useful. There were normal commands like 'sit' and 'stay'; 'heel' to get the pet to come and stay near the owner. The order of 'crate' would have the pet returning to its crate instantly. All useful commands, and logical too.

But there were commands like 'present', which would have the pet assume a position for sexual intercourse. Ichi wondered just which position and then figured his imagination didn't really want to know. 'Mouth' would give the pet the command to please its owner orally. Both commands were adaptable with the use of secondary commands--harder, softer, faster, slower and a few others. That made his mouth fall open a little and even sitting alone he blushed.

He found a chapter on what to do when bringing a new pet home. Most of it was things Ichi had already covered, like the assembly of the crate and offering food and water, but he hadn't thought to show the pet where the bathroom was. That seemed pretty high on the list of important things so he finished his tea and got to his feet.

When he peered inside the crate again, the pet was watching back at him. "Heel." Ichi tried to say it in a firm voice and was surprised when the pet actually crawled from its crate to sit near his feet. The instructions had said something about praise so Ichi softened his voice. "Good boy." He tried to coo and just felt stupid.

A few experimental steps proved the pet was following and Ichi led them past his bedroom door to his bathroom. It wasn't large by any means, but space on the station was a commodity. The one upside to working on an Avalon station was the combination showers, both the fast vibe showers most smaller stations used, and real water ones as well. It was a testament to the organic nature of Avalon's culture, the same as the handmade blanket chest at the foot of every bed. It was just Avalon tradition. His combo-shower was small, but the water always ran hot so he was thrilled.

"Potty," he spoke, placing the location, hopefully, into the pet's mind. He turned to leave and see about getting the collar onto the pet, but the pale man stood in the bathroom.

"What?" Ichi glanced back and the steady face twisted up for a second and a small whine escaped from the back of the pet's throat. "Do you have to go? Well, go on then."

Another whine and a quick glance from the toilet to Ichi. It took a moment but Ichi finally understood the pet was trying to ask him to go. "Oh, sorry, I'll be out in the living room," he muttered, forgetting the pet wouldn't be able to understand him. It surprised him the pet would be shy about such primal, basic things like urination.

He was still digging in the shipping box when the pet quietly slipped back into the living room. Ichi stood up and smiled slightly. "Better now?" His hand swung forward and the slender stick he'd found came into view.

The pet instantly hit the floor. He just dropped and curled up, his arms wrapped around his head, his knees tucked up to his chin and he started whimpering. The reaction was so severe that Ichi stood confused for a moment until he remembered he'd just found the discipline stick. He dropped it back into the box as if it were a viper.

"No, no, shhh it's okay," he tried to comfort but when he moved closer to the pet it only made the whimpering worse. It made Ichi feel like a bully. He backed away, giving up the idea of putting the found collar on the pet and with careful movements sat back on the sofa.

Ichi sat down and tried to start reading again but his focus was on where the pet sat, obviously terrorized at the sight of the stick. It took a long time but the pet eventually stopped whimpering, his arms slowly lowered but he stayed across the room for far longer. Finally, when he did move, it was to scurry quickly back to his crate before diving safely inside.

That made reading easier and Ichi dove into the more complicated side of the manual. It detailed the process of how a pet's genetic code was spliced and re-made. It spoke in fairly scientific terms of how the brain was dwarfed, stunted, and unable to develop into human consciousness. It was fascinating and as he read he grew more comfortable with the pet's construction. Just like his rats--he had not a single doubt that they felt nothing when they were fed to his insects. His newest pet did feel, and obviously had some base line emotions, but there was no way a brain as underdeveloped as his could think, let alone process information. He was just an unusual dog, with a high libido.

He read until his eyes hurt and he was yawning. There was no point in staying awake and the day had been odd. He'd have a mountain of information to study and process tomorrow just going over the tapes of the nest's construction. Ichi needed sleep but he paused before he turned off the lights. In the end, he left a small light glowing. It was tiny and would be a small nightlight in the living room. That made him feel better and he kept his bedroom door cracked open in case the pet had to go to the bathroom during the night. Yawning widely, he laid down to sleep.

And found his mind too awake. He lay there, drifting into light sleep and starting awake, his mind buzzing about nothing in particular. The truth was, he wasn't comfortable sleeping with another living thing in his rooms. It made him nervous and a little worried.

After over an hour, he got up and figured he'd rest better if he checked on the pet and made sure he was okay. The nightlight seemed bright now that his eyes were used to the darkness of his bedroom and it gave him plenty of light to see by. Ichi crept with soft steps to the crate and peered inside.

The pet was curled up into a tight ball, asleep. Only, even in the dim light, Ichi could see goose bumps across the pale skin of the curved back. A body had to be exhausted to sleep when cold enough to shiver, but it wouldn't be restful sleep. He sighed and glanced from the pet to his notebook filled with the proper care instructions.

"Be damned," he finally whispered and disappeared into his bedroom. He turned on a dim light and opened the blanket chest at the foot of his bed. From inside he pulled out the largest, thickest of the quilts, the one he never used, and a spare pillow. They were a warm, heavy weight over his arm as he went back into the living room.

The hinges on the crate's top stuck and then rattled when he pried them open but the lid lifted easily. Only now the pet was awake, still curled up and watching him.

"Here now." Ichi tried to soothe and lowered the pillow into the box near the pet's head. "You looked cold, so, here." He spoke and draped the quilt over the chilled body.

The pet's eyes were wide and one hand petted the soft fabrics of pillow and quilt. There was something disturbing about seeing what looked like gratitude over such simple comforts. He shook his head, lowered the crate's lid and went back to bed.

This time, when he laid down, he fell soundly asleep.

⌘

He woke up several minutes before his alarm actually went off, which was normal for him when he wasn't drinking all night. He yawned and scratched and stumbled from his bed. The sheets were tangled around his legs and he kicked them aside as the lights in the apartment gradually rose.

As he always did, he found his way to his kitchen and fumbled to pull the tab on a carton of coffee. It started to heat in his hand as his eyes fell on the crate. It hadn't all been some overly vivid dream. He rubbed his eyes and sipped at the coffee, burning his lip in the process the way he did nearly every morning, as he shuffled over to the crate and peered in the mesh lid.

His pet was curled up in the quilt. The pillow was tucked under his head and partially along the slender body, the dark red hair spilling out everywhere. The blanket had been wrapped and twisted to engulf the long body, he'd even managed to get a corner pulled up over the side of his head. Only a hand and one bare foot stuck out from the quilt and the sight made Ichi smile again.

He shook his head and glanced down to find the food bowl half empty and the water bowl completely empty. The coffee was too hot to drink anyway, so he set it down and refilled both bowls. When he knelt down to put them on the floor, gray eyes peered out from the blanket at him.

"Morning," he heard himself saying, but the awkwardness made him retreat. Nothing was that different, he had work to get to and his morning patterns didn't have to be altered that much.

Another careful sip of the coffee proved it was too hot still and he yawned on his way to the shower. The carton of coffee took its normal place on the counter top and he got the water going, hot and steamy. He was half naked before he remembered the pet was in the living room and that made him glance out into the bedroom to make sure the pet wasn't lurking somewhere close at hand before he stripped off his pants.

Once he was under the hot water, all worry about the pet maybe seeing him naked fled. It was an irrational worry anyway, he wouldn't worry about a dog seeing him naked.

"It's the eyes," he heard himself saying. Those human eyes in such a haunting color, they made him feel ugly and plain and ordinary, a reaction he'd never feel around a very pretty cat or dog he was sure. The human shape made things so much more complicated.

But those eyes, Ichi sighed. If only he could find a guy with eyes like that and a mind to match. Unbidden, the idea of a lover with eyes like the pets came rushing into his thoughts. He imagined what it would be like to feel the slender lean body against his own, those cold, silent eyes watching.

It was there that his fantasy took a turn. Somewhere in his mind the idea went from the possibility of a lover with similar looks to remembering the way those eyes had glanced up at him while the pet had kneeled in front of him. That had his erection from the night before returning full force and demanding attention.

He stumbled back and leaned his against the cool shower wall, lightly thumping his head against it. "So not fair," he whined. It was some mocking joke, some comedy of absurdity. A single gay man on a tiny station surrounded by nothing but straight people and given a sexual Pet he was too uncomfortable and too proper to touch. It just wasn't right, Ichi reminded himself. He wouldn't have used the stupid sex doll he'd drunkenly ordered and he wasn't going to lower himself to fuck a Pet either.

That didn't mean he didn't have his own mind as comfort, and the steady touch of his own hand. What a man fantasized about wasn't wrong, he couldn't be blamed for that. The soap made everything slick and Ichi just dropped his head back and closed his eyes. He was too logical to deny himself the tiny pleasure of masturbating in the shower, even if it just made him feel more alone than ever when he came.

The coffee was cold when he finally got out of the shower and dried himself off. He wrapped the damp towel around his hips and slurped the cool coffee down as he moved to dress for the day and nearly choked to death on the swallow when he stepped into his bedroom.

His pet was naked, that was the first thought to sink in once the sight of all that creamy, exposed skin stopped shorting out Ichi's brain. He was naked, his hair was loose, and he was kneeling on the still unmade bed. Not just kneeling but almost posed, his knees parted and he was raised up enough to display anything that Ichi might want to glance at. The pet's hands were held at his middle, hovering in the center of his body and he was clutching a tube. It was one of the grooming items from the kit attached to the side of the pet's crate, the kit Ichi hadn't bothered to inspect too closely.

It sunk in slowly that the tube wasn't shampoo and, even in his limited experience, his mind recognized lubricant when he saw it. There would be only one reason the pet would be naked, on display in the center of Ichi's bed clutching a tube of lubricant and the total it added up to made Ichi grateful that his body was too spent to become aroused again. That didn't stop his heart from speeding up or his breath from catching in his throat; the sight was a stunning one, after all.

Chapter Five

Ichi stood frozen and the pet stayed in his awkward pose. Both men seemed unwilling to move, locked in some silent stalemate. Gray eyes raked across Ichi and the expression on the normally blank face grew to one of worry. As Ichi watched, trying to think logically, focusing on just how worried a pet could actually feel and how much of the expression was from the mobility of a human face, any thought of logical analysis melted when the pet turned.

When the first pose failed, the pet turned around and presented his back and ass to Ichi. It left little room for doubt as to just what was expected and Ichi felt his palms sweating. A small voice in the back of his mind teased him. It whispered about Amanda saying pets were social creatures, how they needed interaction to be happy. It whispered that this pet was built for sex and should then, logically, require sex to be happy. It whispered that it was almost cruel to deny the creature, not to mention cruel to deny himself.

He drew a long breath and nearly had himself convinced when the pet glanced over his shoulder and briefly met Ichi's eyes. It wasn't a look of lust or want or even one of unfulfilled need, it was a look of uncertain fear. It startled Ichi enough that he'd see such a human looking emotion that he thought he might be reading too much into the single glance, until he really looked at the pet, not just at how lovely the pet was.

The pale skin trembled and it wasn't from lust or a chill. The body was tense and it wasn't just in the muscles being used to hold him in the awkward pose. Even the pet's shoulders were rounded, hunched up slightly as if fearful of pain or injury, but it was the pet's hands that tossed cold water on Ichi's lust. They clutched at the tube, not just strongly gripped, but with white knuckles clutched it. Everything from the posture to the expression spoke not of a creature looking for comfort and pleasure, but one fulfilling a feared and unwanted duty.

The glance came again and the gray eyes widened at the frown Ichi wore. The lube was dropped quickly and the pet scrambled to drop his upper body down and support his weight on all fours. His head lowered, the round smooth expanse of his ass raised and his knees slid a little further apart.

As lovely as the sight was, as much as Ichi knew it would show up in his fantasies later, right now it churned his stomach over. "No." He spoke firmly and earned himself another fearful glance. "No, bad, no!" He scolded and tapped his hand to his thigh. "Heel."

Ichi felt a little like he might be trembling too now, from lust and disgust all mingled together but seeing the pet slink off the bed to come and kneel at his side in obvious fear upset him. He let himself pat the top of the worried head. "Good boy." He tried to sound pleased. "Stay," he ordered and left the creature kneeling in his bedroom.

He took the tube of lube back to the kit and dug out the more common items for grooming, the shampoo and soap, washcloth, towel and combs. There was no getting around it, he was going to be late getting to the lab but he couldn't just leave now. If he was going to attempt to retrain the pet into something that he could live with, even for the short term, he'd have to start replacing behaviors.

The combs he dropped on the bed but the rest he took directly into the bathroom. He got the water on and set the soaps and such around. "Come here." He shook his head. "Heel." He waited until the pet obediently, and still very nakedly, joined him in the small bathroom. "Bathe," he ordered and the pet nearly frowned in confusion but stood and slipped into the hot water.

Ichi hung around long enough to see the pet was actually washing off. Soaping up his hair and scrubbing his skin with almost human-like sighs of pleasure. It was almost disturbing how human the thing could occasionally be, he'd have to ask Will if dogs sometimes acted like people too.

Comforted that the pet was properly washing himself, Ichi took the time to dry off and dress himself. He brushed out damp hair and left it to air dry as he always did and heard the water in the bathroom shut off. He wandered in to see the pet trying to dry off with what was obviously too small of a towel. It seemed to be sucking the water off his skin well enough but at the same time did nothing for warmth, modesty or comfort.

Another choice had to be made and Ichi landed on the same side of the fence as he had last night. He opened the small closet and tugged out not one, but two of his own fluffy towels and shut the door.

"Here." He offered one to the pet who stopped in mid-rubdown to stare. "Go on." He shook the towel a little

Gray eyes scanned across the towel, glanced to where Ichi had hung up his own towel that matched it and then back to the offered towel. Eyes drifted up the arm and studied the face for signs of anger or hidden malice before very slowly the pet accepted the larger, softer towel. A small sigh slid from the tense and cautious body as the softer towel rubbed across drying skin.

Ichi smiled slightly as the gray eyes half closed in pleasure and remembered what Amanda had said about the pet having double terminated nerve endings. The towel that had come with the pet had been rough, scratchy even, and it made logical sense that the softer towel would be a very real physical pleasure.

"Better huh?" Ichi talked mostly to himself and moved forward with the second towel to start gathering up the impossibly thick and long hair. "I about purred the day I got them. Had to special order them all the way from the Pockelet Mills. Some small pleasures are worth the cost." He'd had the foresight to pick up a new, clean kilt and offered it to the pet. "Change," he ordered and the pet dropped the damp towel and fastened the simple kilt around his hips. "Come on, let's get this hair unknotted."

He led the pet back to the bed and got him sitting on the corner. The creature instantly tensed up again but when all Ichi did was towel out the worst of the damp and start tackling the knots, the shoulders in front of him slowly relaxed. He'd have to think about only letting the pet use the vibe shower, even if it meant denying him the pleasure of the hot water. It took some effort but he eventually got it untangled and quickly braided it back into a thick plait.

"There we go, now off the bed." He shooed and eventually the pet understood and moved to sit along the wall. Ichi made the bed with the pet watching, and found he was growing more accustomed to being watched. With his morning chores finished, Ichi moved to go to his lab and found the pet following.

He stopped and sighed. "Stay." He ordered but softened his voice. "I'll be back at lunch to check on you." It was to soothe his guilt and it didn't work. With the gray eyes fearful, Ichi let his apartment door shut with the pet inside.

❧

"Hey," Will called out as he came unannounced into Ichi's lab. "How're things?"

"Tell me again why the only way a lab door can be locked is in the case of an emergency?" Ichi muttered out, not looking up from his close up shots of the nest weaving.

"Ah, because that's rude?"

"So is being disturbed twenty times in six hours."

Will just laughed and sat next to his friend. "People are just curious to hear how last night went. I've heard stories all day, I'm dying to know which of them are true."

"It slept soundly, ate, bathed, nothing interesting."

It didn't take being a psi to know more had happened, Ichi's ears were tinged just a shade too pink. "For someone so good at bluffing at cards, you're a horrible liar."

He stabbed at the pause button and put his notes down. "Maybe it's because, unlike some people, I like my private life to be private."

"That good huh?"

"Will!"

"Hmmm, you didn't get laid, you're too crabby for that."

"Nothing happened, nothing is going to happen, but you were right, it did try to come on to me."

"He, not it."

"Whatever."

"Did you name him yet?"

"Not really."

"But you've an idea."

Ichi sighed and folded his arms over his chest. "You'll laugh."

"It can't be worse than Fluffy."

He mulled the advantages of staying silent or letting the name he'd been toying with all afternoon slip out. "Rimose."

"Reyemoos." Will extended the name as he let it roll around his mouth before grinning wickedly. "Have you been studying his cracks?"

"You promised!"

Will held his hands up in defeat. "So I did. Rimose: adjective, full of crevices, chinks or cracks and proof that my dear friend Ichi never had a childhood. You didn't name the poor thing, you classified him. Not sure why, but you did."

"He's skittish, like something fragile that was broken."

"Cracked."

Ichi nodded and waited for the snickering.

"It's better than Fluffy, if a touch technical and cold." Will nodded thoughtfully. "Rye it is than."

"Not Rye..." He tried to protest but then remembered he'd have to explain his reasons for 'Rimose' to everyone. Avalon folk took names seriously, and if Will circulated the shortened nickname it would save Ichi a lot of awkward muttering. "Guess I can't stop a nickname."

"Rye is way better than Fluffy."

A week and then two slipped by and life fell into an easy pattern. Ichi woke, showered, had his coffee while Rye showered and then untangled the long hair. The pet then retreated to his crate to crunch on kibble while Ichi downed his coffee and ate some oatmeal. He'd leave for work, ordering the pet to stay behind, and find Rye sitting near the door when he returned at lunch to check on him, and again when he came home from the lab. Ichi would eat to the sound of shy crunching from the crate and try to catch up on his scientific journals that he was hideously behind on, or watch the headlines from the newscasts. He'd eventually say goodnight to Rye and fall into his own bed to sleep soundly.

He only had to scold the pet about a dozen times in the first weeks for offering himself sexually, and each time he did it was longer between when he had to scold him again. Each time he refused, some of the uneasy skittish fear fled the eyes. And as the fear dissolved, it became more difficult to think about finding a new home for the pet. Ichi found he was actually getting used to having something else alive in his rooms and growing accustomed to the pet the way he would a new painting or end table.

Sixteen days after the pet's arrival, Ichi came home early for lunch with fabric tossed over his arm. He'd talked Mary into tossing together new kilts for Rye and she'd happily agreed when he'd explained. The pet seemed cold most of the time, running about half-naked, but Ichi liked his rooms at a temperature that was comfortable with clothes on. And he'd worried about the plain, almost rough woven fabric against Rye's obviously oversensitive skin. Mary had grinned like a fool, or a matchmaker, and happily agreed.

It had taken a few days but she'd quickly made a set of modified kilts. They'd found double woven flannel in the stations stores, in pale green, that felt luxuriously soft to Ichi's touch and she'd made the set from the original kilt he provided her. It would attach around Rye's hips the same but it would reach well below his knees and help keep him warm. He was so pleased with the results that he left the lab before his normal time to show the pet.

"Hey, Rye, I'm home," he called out, but the pet wasn't at the door. "Rye?" He glanced around the living room and still saw nothing. It was the first time ever he'd come home and not found the pet waiting.

Worry flashed through him. Maybe Rye had managed to hurt himself. He had the dexterity of a human but just because he was trained to touch only a few things didn't mean he couldn't have broken something or cut himself. Or, worse, he suddenly feared the pet had gotten out of the apartment and could be wandering lost on the station. Most of it was finished hallways, perfectly safe, but some areas were just catwalks or rough tunnels.

He moved to make a search of the apartment, suddenly fearing the worst, only to quickly find the pet in his bedroom. Between tending to Rye and watching his swarm, Ichi had fallen behind on his chores. His dirty clothes bin was filled and he hadn't had the time to toss the bin into the washing unit. For some reason, Rye had dumped his dirty clothes out onto the floor and sat in the center of it all. He'd even managed to wiggle into one of Ichi's loose cotton shirts that he tended to sleep in. The sight would have been comical if hunks of dark red hair hadn't lay strewn about.

"Rye, there you are…" He tried to keep his voice steady but the sight confused him.

Gray eyes went wide in fear and the pet scrambled to his feet. He ran full speed and pushed past Ichi. Before Ichi could turn around, Rye had dived into his crate still wearing the pilfered shirt. Ichi held his ground and frowned, confused. He crossed to the pile of laundry and found it was warm to the touch, so he knew Rye had been laying in it for a while.

It was the pulled hairs that shocked him. It wasn't just a strand or two but sections that were strewn about. Some of it looked chewed off, gnawed on or twisted until it broke, and other sections looked like they'd been pulled right from Rye's head. It was so obviously self-mutilation that it confused Ichi. Animals self mutilated from neuroses, but Rye seemed to be growing more comfortable, more at ease, not less.

He dropped the new kilts on the bed and moved to the living room. Rye was still hiding in the back of his crate, curled up into as small a ball as possible, but Ichi could see him through the mesh of the crate. "Come here." Rye didn't move. "Heel!" he demanded.

Slowly, Rye crawled out and came to sit in front of Ichi. He hung his head and trembled in fear.

"Stop that, I'm not going to hurt you." He sighed and wished they'd trained the pet for that command. He reached out and ran a hand over the dark head, comfortable now touching the pet as he would running his hand across the back of his sofa. There were definitely angry spots, one or two bloodied, where hair had been yanked out. When he slid his hand down to the thick length he found ragged ends still damp from having been chewed on.

"Why would you do that?" He folded his arms across his chest and tried to think. When he'd walked in, Rye had looked content, even--maybe--happy. There was no sense that the hair pulling was done from desperation or depression. So why would a pet chew off and pull out its own hair if not from a desire to self mutilate?

The idea he stumbled on seemed too human, too basic. Ichi knelt down and threaded some of the long length through his fingers. "Do you not like this?" He asked knowing that Rye didn't understand and couldn't answer. "Let's find out."

Ichi stood and had to rummage around to find the old pair of scissors--they weren't overly sharp but they'd get the job done. When he knelt again the gray eyes followed the blades with worried acceptance.

"Here, now, see?" Ichi picked up the tips on one section of hair and snipped it off. "See?" He knew he was testing the limits of the pet's intelligence, but not its dexterity. He pressed the scissors into Rye's hands and guided him to repeat the action. "If you want it shorter, you can cut it shorter." He helped the uncertain hand form another cut and than sat back a few feet away and watched.

Rye sat silent and serious, his eyes glancing from the scissors in his hand to where Ichi sat nearby and then down to the hair that had fallen away. Slowly, one hand rose up and gripped a thick length of hair. With eyes firmly on Ichi, Rye steadily cut the entire handful away. As the length fell to the floor an unsteady flicker of a relieved smile danced across Rye's face. It wasn't the look of glee at destruction, but the look of someone long denied the power of choice.

"It's okay." Ichi whispered softly. "You can do it."

Another handful, another cut, and more of the dark red length fell to the floor. Rye gained confidence now and quickly moved to snip the length away, cutting the thick hair to a ragged edge around his shoulders. It left feet of the hair severed and coiled around him and when the last cut was made Rye set the scissors down and shook his head with obvious delight.

For the first time, Ichi saw a real smile on the pet's face. Even though he'd been told it was just a natural reaction and didn't denote emotion the way it would with a human, it still thrilled him to see it. "Better?" He asked and gathered up scissors and hair. Insanely, he wanted to keep the length and he wasn't sure why.

When the bulk of the hair was gathered into a loose tail in his hand, Ichi glanced up to see Rye still tugging at the shoulder length hair. "Shorter still, huh?" He reached over and plucked at the shirt the pet wore. "Can't get a hair cut wearing a dirty shirt."

Gray eyes went wide again and Rye quickly twisted his way out of the shirt. He hunched down and offered the garment back to Ichi. When Ichi moved too quickly to retrieve it, Rye flinched even lower toward the floor.

"Hush now, I'm not mad, you looked cute in it." He smiled and petted the now shorter hair before he stood up. "Come on…" he patted his side and Rye had learned his mannerisms well enough that he followed. He picked up one of the new kilts and tossed the dirty shirt into the pile of spilled clothes in the corner. Rye moved to gather up the laundry, trying to quickly shove it back in its bin.

"Stop that, I'm not worried about the clothes. Here, change." He ordered and handed the new kilt to the pet.

Rye took the fabric and turned it around a bit until he found the same clasps. He stripped out of the thinner, shorter kilt and wrapped the new one around his hips. The soft fabric glided across his skin and his eyes lit up. His hands petted the fabric and another real smile darted across his face.

"Better, huh?" Ichi smiled too, even if how Rye was petting himself was oddly erotic to watch. To distract those thoughts he moved to his clean clothes and dug in it to find a shirt that was loose on him so he knew it would fit Rye. "Here, change," he said softer, offering the shirt.

Rye took the fabric and studied it for a moment before raising it to sniff. He made an unhappy face and stepped forward, closer to Ichi than he'd been in a week. The taller pet leaned forward and sniffed lightly at Ichi's hair and than stepped back to sniff at the shirt. He frowned, dropped the fabric and retrieved the dirty shirt from the pile.

Ichi was trying to focus on the memory of seeing his swarm feed in an effort to not become painfully hard. Rye was wearing his dirty clothes not for warmth but because they smelled like him. It was oddly the most romantic thing he'd ever seen, and he knew he was being absolutely stupid for thinking that.

"No, you can't wear a dirty shirt," he managed to tease and replaced the dirty one with the clean shirt.

Rye sniffed the clean shirt and again frowned.

"Of course it smells different, it's clean and not all stinky. Wear the clean one."

There was only a pause this time, no more sniffing, before Rye wiggled into the shirt. It amazed Ichi, pets weren't supposed to know how to manage anything more complicated then their kilts but Rye didn't seem to have the slightest trouble getting the shirt on. He'd have to think about leaving some of the bigger shirts out for the pet. It would certainly be easier on him not to have the fellow running around half naked.

He tapped at his side again. "We don't need the leash, right? Heel," he ordered and was confident enough in Rye's training that he didn't even glance behind him to see if the pet followed.

Half-way to the community kitchen Ichi glanced back to see not if the pet followed, but how he was reacting to being outside of the apartment for the first time since his arrival. Rye followed silently on his bare feet, head down, eyes locked to the back of Ichi's legs. He neither glanced up or around and he stayed at almost exactly the same distance behind Ichi even if the pace was altered. It kind of disappointed him, he'd been hoping for more of a reaction--but what could be expected of a pet, after all?

There were only six people in the main kitchen for lunch, Will and Amanda among them, but the conversation was loud enough for several times as many people. Ichi led Rye into the common room and the entire room went silent. All eyes turned to them and he considered that this might have been a bad idea. Only, a glance to the pet showed that Rye didn't seem to notice the situation and certainly was less embarrassed than Ichi was himself.

He cleared his throat. "I'm sorry, I could use some help. Rye--he wanted to cut his hair, but, it's rather ragged." He glanced up and then had to look down, remembering that he hated being the center of attention almost more than having to speak to a crowd. "Could someone help us?"

Five people hopped up and swarmed around them, all talking at once, and Ichi felt ready to run away to escape it all. Some of the women started talking about the new kilt and one of the men wanted to know how Ichi trained Rye to wear a shirt. It was too much and he was almost ready to walk them back to the apartment and risk styling Rye's hair himself.

"Enough!" Amanda teased and laughed over the small crowd. "We're scaring them both. Ichi, dear, leave it to us, can you get him to come in and sit down?"

He nodded, happy that she'd stepped up and wrangled the group into some order, then led Rye into the room. He patted a chair. "Sit, Rye."

The pet sat on command but kept his head bowed and eyes on the floor. Ichi let Amanda shoo him off and he found himself sitting at a table to the side, accepting a mug of tea from Will. "Bunch of harpies," Will laughed as scissors were fetched and a debate was started about styles.

"I'm grateful for the help."

"Poor fellow looks scared." The women had lifted Rye's chin to get a better idea of how to trim up his hair and the gray eyes had instantly sought out Ichi.

"I'd be scared too in the middle of all that."

"A wise man knows were not to tread." Will nodded toward the pet. "New kilts huh? And he's wearing a shirt."

"He put it on by himself. I came home and found him in a pile of my laundry, wearing a shirt."

"Aww, that's sweet, he must like you."

The idea he'd been rolling around in his head for a while solidified. "Will, I think someone owned him before me."

"Oh?" He didn't glance over, afraid if he saw the gentle look Ichi wore every time his friend's eyes met Rye's he'd be an ass and tease him about it. "What makes you think that?"

"Just, things, I don't know. He seemed conditioned to someone else's habits. It's pretty clear that he's frightened of being harmed. Whenever he thinks he's done something wrong he's so upset he trembles. The hair too, he wanted it shorter, it almost looked like he was casting more than hair off when he cut it."

"When you cut it."

"No, Rye cut it. I just gave him the scissors."

"Huh, risky letting him play with anything sharp."

Ichi didn't want to debate that. "Do you think it's possible he was owned before?"

"Possible, sure, they wouldn't advertise that fact. Who wants used goods, you know? Does it make a difference if he was?"

Ichi shook his head. "Not at all, it's just, I don't like the idea of anyone having hurt him. He's such a gentle sort."

Will glanced over to his friend and frowned. "You're falling in love with him."

"I am not!" Ichi sputtered back. "Don't be absurd!"

"I'm not, but you are." He shook his head. "It's okay you know, I loved my dog as a boy more than anything. It's just, Ichi, you need to remember he's a Pet, not a partner. He can make you feel better but there's no relationship there."

"You're being ridiculous." At least, he hoped Will was being ridiculous. He had grown more comfortable around Rye than he'd ever been around anyone.

Will waved it off. "Doesn't matter. Hey, do Amanda a favor and invite us over for dinner? She's dying for your futomaki and keeps making these really awful rolls and than making me eat them for dinner."

He shook his head. "Sure, next week though? I'm a little swamped with work and Rye. I'm worried about the swarms eggs, they haven't hatched yet. No one's really sure how long it takes for the eggs to actually develop or if they require certain conditions. I'd hate to lose this clutch."

"Next week. She'll be thrilled, so long as you don't put one of the swarm's eggs in the maki." He teased but laughed when Ichi looked horrified.

Chapter Six

It took almost an hour for the group to finish what should have been a ten minute hair cut. They debated about the length of Rye's bangs, about how layered to make the back and how short. They brushed and snipped and turned the whole thing into a social event. In the end, Ichi couldn't complain, except that Rye was now twice as attractive, if that was even possible. The dark, bloodred hair had been layered in the back to lighten the weight of such thick hair but it had been left long enough to curl around the back of his neck. Yet somehow they'd managed to cut the hair short enough that the slender curve of the pet's neck was exposed. The front was trimmed in layers too, only longer ones so the hair continued to fall in slender tendrils about Rye's face. It gave him something to still hide behind without being obscured by. It also gave him a tussled, coy, 'I've just stumbled out of bed', look that made Ichi itch to run his fingers through.

He wasn't sure who was more grateful to return to the apartment, Rye or himself. Ichi didn't stop there, he led Rye into the bathroom and the mirror he'd never actually seen the pet glance into.

"Here, look, do you like it?" He tapped on the reflective surface until gray eyes rose up.

Rye stood there, studying his own reflection for so long and with such a puzzled expression that Ichi wasn't sure the pet understood that it was him and not another pair of them on the other side. Gray eyes dropped and Rye's hands clenched into tight fists.

"Hey now, you okay?" Ichi asked and reached out to brush the newly formed tendrils of hair back. "I think it suits you."

Rye moved suddenly. His hands unclenched and reached up to capture the sides of Ichi's face. Slender fingers slid along his jaw line, back to tickle around his ears. Ichi started to jerk backwards and then lips pressed to his own. The kiss was quick, dry and over almost before Ichi's brain could register that he was being kissed.

Before he could either get aroused or scold Rye, the pet broke the kiss and dropped to his knees. Only this time he wrapped his arms around Ichi's legs and tucked his face against his knees. Ichi could feel Rye trembling where he knelt hugging his legs, and for a moment didn't know just what to do.

"I'll assume that means you like it." He reached down and ruffled the shorter hair, liking the way it feathered at his touch. "Stop that now, come on, I've got to get back to work." But Rye didn't let go right away, he clutched on as Ichi kept petting the soft hair and a few more moments ticked away.

As suddenly as Rye had kissed him, he released Ichi's legs and scurried from the bathroom. It left Ichi standing alone in his bathroom, a touch confused and having to remind himself that even dogs licked faces when happy. He shook his head and left to go back to the lab, surprised that Rye was now hiding in his crate but respectful of the space the pet wanted.

The next morning went as it had been going except that combing out Rye's hair took no time at all. Ichi went to leave and the pet followed him to the door and refused to stay. "I have to work, you should stay here."

Rye refused to step back and let the door close.

"You'll be bored." But then, what did the pet do all day anyway? Besides roll around in Ichi's dirty laundry... He didn't think the creature got bored easily. "Alright, but no fussing. If you bother me I'm taking you home."

And so it was, quietly, Rye started to go with Ichi to work. Word spread around the station almost before Rye arrived at the lab and the next day, when Ichi went into his lab, he found a cushion along one wall. A blanket was folded on it and someone had hung a sign over it that read "Rye's Space". Ichi never found out who had put the bed together, but seeing Rye instantly move to the softest spot in the lab and fold himself down on it where he sat, wrapped up in the blanket all day made him happy. After that, there was never the debate or question about whether or not Rye would go with him. Anywhere Ichi went, Rye followed.

A week later, Ichi came home a little earlier than normal to start the rice. There would be no shortcuts; when he set out to make maki, he did it from scratch. He'd dip into his stores of ingredients from home and everything would be cooked and prepared by hand. That was the trick, to take the time and make it, carefully and with the proper attention to detail.

Rye sat on the floor of the kitchen and watched, out of the way but absorbing everything with his alert eyes. Ichi didn't even notice it anymore, he was so used to the pet that it had become second nature. Only when he was rolling the first of the maki and Will and Amanda arrived did Rye scurry away to hide in his crate.

"Hello hello, gods it smells so good in here!" Amanda called out and came into the kitchen. She leaned over and pressed a quick kiss to the side of Ichi's face, startling him. "I brought sake!"

Will moved to pull the small table from the wall, as he did every time they talked Ichi into cooking, and plopped himself down into a chair. "Where's Rye?"

"Hiding." Ichi slid the sheet aside and carefully transported the first roll to the wide cutting board before starting the next. "He'll come out later, he's still skittish around people." He started on the next roll and let Amanda and Will pull out cups and plates and the nice set of chopsticks he kept on hand. While he finished rolling their dinner, his friends set the table and had everything ready to go by the time he had the maki sliced.

They ate dinner and drank the sake and Ichi found himself laughing at their comfortable ease and the stories they told. Amanda sat up and stared at the crate from where she'd been sitting, slouched down and rubbing her full stomach.

"He just reached out and grabbed a handful of food. Or have I had too much sake?"

Ichi shook his head. "He won't eat where he can be watched. I never see him use the bathroom either, or drink for that matter."

"Huh, that's odd. They aren't supposed to be shy like that."

"I think it has something to do with his original owner, I don't think the man was very nice."

Will sat up. "So you're convinced he had another owner?"

"I don't know, but it wouldn't surprise me." He toyed with his chopsticks, tearing the last bite on his plate apart into small sections. "Would you two think I was crazy if I asked if there was anyway he might be more human than intended?"

"You're just projecting human emotions onto him," Will dismissed.

"So there's no way."

"There's no way they could have made a mistake. They start out with base clones, if the clone isn't dead on to the specs it's not modified into a pet," Amanda reminded him. "You're just bonding with him, something I think you could use."

"Sometimes, he seems so, I don't know, expressive. And he learned to dress himself, I don't even have to order him to shower any more. He's far more adaptable than the specs made mention of. I don't know, sometimes, it's almost like he's thinking." He stared at the crate and wondered if they were going to laugh at him.

The couple exchanged a look before Amanda spoke up. "If you're worried about it, schedule an appointment for a medical exam. We'll go over him with a fine toothed comb and do all the in-depth scans and such."

He almost agreed, but it was silly. "No, I won't take up that much of your time. You're right, I'm just projecting."

Will stretched and managed to reach into the food bowl sitting outside the crate. He retrieved a single kibble chunk and eyed it suspiciously.

"What are you doing?" his wife asked.

"Well, his tastes should be human norm, right? I want to try one."

She started laughing. "Don't you dare!"

"Why? I've eaten plenty worse." He put the kibble in his mouth and crunched on it. It crumbled and his face twisted up as he forced himself to chew through the kibble. Eventually, after too much laughter from his wife and friend, he managed to swallow it.

"Well? What's the verdict, except that I'm never kissing you again?"

Will pushed the taste about his mouth for a moment. "Not the worst thing I've ever eaten, but it's pretty horrible. Augh, no wonder you're not supposed to feed him real food, there's no way he'd eat this shit once he's tasted something proper." They were still laughing at him when he tried to wash the taste out with swallows of tea.

It was a pleasant evening--certainly it always was when they got together for dinner and conversation. Only this time, something about seeing how easy and comfortable the pair was stabbed Ichi with loneliness. He was happy they were happy and suspected there was enough tragedy in their histories to long since have earned them the comfortable love they now shared, but he was also envious of it. By the time the sake was done, the leftover maki wrapped up to go home with Amanda and the couple was out the door, it was late into the evening and Ichi was warmly drunk and feeling very, very alone.

He lowered the lights since he was pretty sure Rye was asleep and, frankly, he wanted the dim intimacy of being alone to wallow in his loneliness. The dishes had been cleared and cleaned already and there was nothing left for him to do but drop onto the sofa and flip on the vid screen. He flipped around but nothing caught his eye, so he left it on one of the news channels simply because the man reading the headlines was handsome. Ichi slouched on the sofa and watched the way the man's mouth moved. The anchor's eyes were dark blue, not quite gray but fairly close.

He decided what he missed most wasn't even sex, but just physical contact. He'd been happy just kissing for hours, getting lost in the casual comfort of skin to skin contact. From somewhere in his sake induced haze, Ichi decided that the news anchor would be a good kisser, he could tell from how the man moved his mouth while reading the news. He just knew that he'd be the sort to press a lover to the sofa and neck for days.

Somewhere between trying not to be bitter about the idea that Will and Amanda were most likely happily tumbling each other into bed and the odd fantasy about how the anchorman's mouth looked, Ichi's palm had slid into his lap. It felt good to press the flat of his hand into his half aroused length. He was a grown man after all, in his own apartment, horny and lonely and allowed to touch himself if he felt like it.

Not that his justifications really mattered. He was lonely and masturbating was a very small pleasure. He dropped his head back against the sofa and deftly opened the front of his pants. In his mind the anchorman's steady voice was paired with slightly sad gray eyes and he slid his hand across his now exposed length. Maybe Will was right, maybe he should let his friend take him to Avalon and introduce him around. Goodness knew Avalon folk weren't what he'd call stuffy about sex. It would be okay, no strings or commitments, just two men enjoying each other's company, as friends, very friendly friends. He could allow himself that.

The hands that slid up his thighs were so perfectly entwined with his internal fantasies that it took a heartbeat for Ichi to register that they were real hands, really touching him. He startled and his eyes popped open to lock onto an unblinking pair of gray. He'd forgotten about Rye. Somewhere in the weeks he'd grown so used to the pet being in the room that he'd simply forgotten to not do this act anywhere that Rye might see.

He shivered to see the face between his legs, framed in wisps of dark red, eyes open and watching. It was a temptation, everything about the pet was a temptation, and it was physically painful when Ichi to tried to close his pants.

Weakly, his head shook against the back of the sofa. "No, Rye, no, shoo, go to your crate."

Rye didn't budge. He just stayed there, kneeling between Ichi's spread legs, his hands resting high on Ichi's thighs. Gray eyes locked with Ichi's hazel and there was no fear in them, not even a tiny amount of uncertainty. A pink tongue slipped out to wet slightly parted lips and the sight made Ichi groan.

"Come on, Rye, shoo," he forced himself to say and tried to stand up.

Strong hands gripped his hips and Ichi only managed to rise a few inches before being tugged back down, only now his ass was on the edge of the sofa far closer to that tempting mouth. One hand slid from Ichi's hips to wrap around his wrist and pull his hand away, exposing his naked groin for inspection.

"No, Rye, no, bad, go to your crate." He tried to scold but the sternness in his voice was weak because a hand not his own was lightly touching him. "Oh god."

Ichi's spine arched and he fell limply back against the sofa. He tried to remember all the reasons why this was wrong, tried to gather his will around himself to firmly refuse--but that hand, that slender, graceful hand was touching him. It had been so long since anyone else had touched him.

The hands grew more bold and pulled at Ichi's open pants, tugging them down with sure confidence and skill that a pet wasn't supposed to have when faced with clothing. "No," Ichi protested again and tried to push Rye's hands away. Only, the pet easily turned his efforts to stop aside, like an adult slapping away the fussing hands of a child.

Ichi lifted his head, trying to figure out if he could stand. His knees felt wobbly and his head felt light. Worse, he was splayed out on the sofa at an odd angle, his legs too widely spread to get a good brace to force himself to stand, and now with his pants open that made things more difficult. He glanced at his own body and shivered at the sight of Rye tucked so neatly between his legs.

Rye glanced up and Ichi's breath stopped. Not only was there no fear, or even worry, in the pet's eyes, but he had the softest of gentle smiles just teasing at the corner of his lips. Ichi's heart stopped and a small strangled sound caught in his throat.

"Bad, Rye, bad," he scolded without breath or conviction. "Stop, no..." He watched the head bow forward and his protests died into a twisted moan as a hot, wet tongue lapped against his overly sensitive flesh.

It didn't matter now if he fell on his face while trying to stand. Ichi needed to get away, right now, or he'd forget the reasons why this was wrong. He braced his arms and tried to push himself up, tried to push the slight draping weight of Rye from his legs. Again, strong hands caught his hips and forcefully pushed him back down, only this time there was no hesitation.

Before Ichi could even get his muddled brain to process the fact that Rye not only was directly disobeying a command but was also physically holding him to the sofa, a pleasure he'd forgotten poured into his body. Somehow, across the years of awkwardness and celibacy, Ichi had convinced himself that sex wasn't that great. Good, yes, fun and pleasurable, but not something necessary, not something as consuming as people made it out to be.

All illusions that sex hadn't been that worthwhile, that he wasn't missing that much, exploded when Rye simply took his tormented length into his mouth. Ichi's entire body trembled, his mind simply shut down and Rye's head bobbed, swallowing him whole. A forgotten fact drifted into his mind--on Rye's checklist of modifications the removal of the gag reflex had been marked as unconfirmed. There was no doubt that modification was a roaring success.

"Rye, no, no, oh god, bad Rye, this is so bad." He moaned and reached to try to pry the too delicious mouth from his erection. Except when he touched the top of that head, his fingers betrayed him and ruffled through the soft, thick hair. Rye moaned at the touch, deep and from the back of his throat, a sound of liquid pleasure. "Bad," Ichi sighed and petted his hand through the beautiful hair again. "So, bad."

There was no stopping, not without death, Ichi was certain now. He was hurtling out of control and the very fact that his own will had been overridden just made the entire experience more erotic. He collapsed onto the sofa, surrendering. His skin shivered at the feather soft brush of touch, Rye's hands ghosted across his skin. They teased the joint where leg met hip, fluttered up to lightly encircle Ichi's waist, just brushing his ribs before gliding down to torment the exposed tops of his thighs. And all the while, that eager, very talented mouth, devoured him.

Ichi heard gasping, shuddering moans and was startled to place them from his own throat. He'd never been overly vocal, ever. Andrew had teased him that it was a control issue but Ichi just didn't like to seem whorish. He wasn't the kind of man to moan and sob but here he was, doing just that, and the more the strangled moans escaped his control the more Rye worked to drag the sounds from him.

"No, Rye, I can't, I..." He gasped, shivering now on his sofa, trying to get the pet to stop before the last shreds of his control shattered. It was bad enough he'd allowed this but to come this way, it would be unforgivable. "Rye, stop, please, stop, I can't... I'm going to..." Hands gripped his hips again and held him in place, and just thinking about the word pushed Ichi beyond his last fragments of control.

"Oh, god, yes, Rye..." He moaned as his body broke apart into base elements and lost all connections to each other. For those few moments, Ichi became a thing of pleasure and he would have done nearly anything to hold onto that moment forever. It was beyond his scope, beyond his experience and he came with total abandon. "Oh, Rye..." he sighed as some small sense started to return.

He'd never come like that. Ichi's body still trembled, still twitched in lazy delights, and it felt like his body belonged to someone else. Someone sexy and sensual, someone not himself. Never had he so been overwhelmed, so lost in pleasure. He'd always felt awkward, reserved, even a touch fearful at such raw vulnerability, but in this moment there was total surrender. As Ichi's breathing slowed and his mind gradually restarted, he knew this was going to complicate things beyond measure. All the work he'd been doing to discourage Rye from thinking in terms of sex had just been unraveled.

As sense and logic returned Ichi found himself running his fingers across that silky hair. Rye had pillowed his head against one of his thighs, his bright gray eyes watched everything with what Ichi thought looked to be lust and sparkle of triumph. His pet was gloating about blowing him and the idea made Ichi blush slightly.

He tried to sit up, now with no forceful hands holding him in place, but Rye kept the side of his face tucked close to him. Ichi brushed the layered hair back from the handsome face. "That was bad, Rye." But there was only gentle affection in his voice.

Rye whined slightly and rubbed the side of his face against Ichi's leg.

"It's okay, I'm not going to punish you, though I probably should."

Rye whined again and this time his body arched slightly. Ichi felt the pet press himself against his leg, sliding, and then the unmistakable feel of neglected arousal. He sat up further and there was little doubt that Rye was painfully hard, the kilt, even the longer one, did nothing to hide his state.

"Shhh, it's okay, come here." Ichi wasn't sure what he was going to do but he wasn't leaving things like this. He reached for Rye's shoulder and the pet trembled and slid out of his reach. Ichi's thigh suddenly felt cold and empty without the comforting weight of the pet's head. He frowned. "What? You don't want to be touched?"

Rye's head bowed down and his hands hovered over his groin, nearly but not quite touching. He was shivering too, trembling, but the look he tossed to Ichi was lustful and almost desperate now.

It sunk in that Rye was trying to ask permission. "It's okay, go ahead." He tried to make his voice sound gentle and encouraging. but the idea that he was granting permission for Rye to masturbate made his voice break like a teenagers.

Rye's gray eyes flicked from the floor up to meet Ichi's and then darted to his crate. He whined-- low, desperate, needy.

The request startled Ichi but he nodded. "It's okay, go to your crate, it's okay Rye, crate."

The redhead didn't wait to be told twice, he moved with his normal fluid grace across the room and disappeared inside. It left Ichi sitting on his sofa, startled twice in a very short time. Pets were supposed to be utterly shameless about sex, as shameless as they were using the bathroom. There was no doubt what Rye was doing in the false privacy of his crate, low moans soon drifted out to tickle Ichi's ears.

He was masturbating, but he was doing it hidden in his crate, that denoted shame or at least a sense of self and a desire for privacy. None were supposed to be aspects a pet had; even a mistreated pet, one taught to be skittish and shy, shouldn't have that sense of self.

It left Ichi sitting on his sofa, wondering if he was simply reading too much into the situation. He'd been alone for so long, and than to have another living thing invade his privacy, topped off with an amazing blow job, he was getting too attached to Rye. It was only natural that he'd project human traits where there were none. Amanda had said it the clearest, PETS simply didn't make mistakes. He just wanted Rye to be more than he was, the way he overlapped the news anchor's voice with Rye's eyes in his fantasies.

He straightened his pants and closed them. Trying to think logically about Rye, to analyze his actions from a scientific point of view and trying very hard not to listen to the increasingly more desperate moans from the crate. Ichi was trained to observe things, so when the sounds drifting from the crate turned from random moans and stuttered grunts to syllables his ears sharpened and tuned to it.

It hadn't been so long since he'd at least seen pornography that Ichi mistook the sounds of release. The tone, the sound changed and Ichi felt his own pulse quickening at the desperate desire contained in it.

"Oh ahhh…." Rye moaned. "Oh…. Ichi… ahhh"

Ichi's ears tuned so sharply to the sounds that his entire head swiveled to the crate. There was no way, no earthly way that he'd heard what he'd just heard. He was imagining it, putting his own fantasy into the nonsense sounds Rye was making as he tumbled over the edge and came. PETS didn't make mistakes and he'd been alone far too long.

But, what if they had? The thought chilled his blood. It was something from a nightmare, just the thought of it. It left him sitting in dumb uncertainty, torn between his scientific need to know for certain, and his deep rooted fear of confessing what he believed and being thought an utter fool.

He was still sitting there, startled and uncertain, when Rye slinked from his crate. He was licking at his hand but his face, normally so neutral and steady, looked eased and relaxed, even mildly happy. Ichi sat silent as Rye padded on bare feet to the sofa where he happily dropped down to sit next to Ichi's legs. When he wasn't scolded, Rye scooted over slightly and very lightly leaned against Ichi, resting the side of his head against Ichi's knee.

Ichi reached over and petted a hand across the red hair. "It's okay Rye, we'll figure this out." His own worry of being the butt end of everyone's jokes seemed trivial. Ichi picked up his notebook and accessed the med lab's appointments, which were wide open. He scheduled an appointment for the morning, marked it as urgent and knew Will and Amanda would be waiting for him, first thing. He petted the hair again as he dropped the access panel. "We'll figure it all out."

Chapter Seven

Surprisingly, Ichi slept soundly. There was nothing to do until the morning anyway so he simply got them both ready for sleep and expected to lay awake lost in thoughts. His mind had a better idea; the surprisingly shattering orgasm had worn him out, drained him of stress and left him to sleep soundly.

In the morning he awoke before his alarm and found Rye awake and sitting near his bedroom door as he always was. Ichi moved for coffee with the silent pet following behind him and refilled the now empty water bowl and added new kibble. He showered, Rye showered and Ichi laid out a soft blue gray shirt for the pet. When he'd finished his coffee and quick breakfast, Rye was dry and dressed, his shorter hair simply shaken into place. Everything was very normal.

Things stopped being normal when Ichi made the turn that would take them to the med lab and not to his research lab. Rye stopped and glanced down the hallway that led to work and back to Ichi with confusion on his face.

"Not this morning, Rye, come on." He tapped his leg and kept moving, Rye followed, head bowed.

The med lab was well lit and Amanda sat at the one of the access screens while Will leaned against one of the beds. Both had cartons of coffee steaming nearby but their conversation stopped when Ichi joined them.

"Don't tell me, you've poisoned us?" Will teased as soon as Ichi passed the doors, Rye following.

"No, I didn't." He missed the joke and led Rye to one of the medical beds and patted it. "Sit." Rye obeyed docilely and Ichi brushed some of the stray hairs back from his face. He drew a breath and turned to his friends. "I need you to run full tests on Rye. I have to know how aware he is."

Amanda frowned. "What's happened?"

"I…" He prayed he wouldn't blush. "I think he said my name." But the memories were too vivid and he felt his face going red.

"Good god Ichi, we need to get you a boyfriend." Will sighed. "Stop projecting onto Rye, don't you get it? It's a thing. It's not capable of speech or thought, or even any complex emotion."

"I'm not…" He shook his head. "I'm not projecting. I would have thought people from Avalon of all folks would be a little more open minded, and a touch more sympathetic."

"I am sympathetic, you're my friend." Will went on. "You need a real relationship, some true human interaction. Rye's fine, don't get me wrong--but Ichi, he's livestock. Fuck him all you want, that's what he was made for. Use him, that's the point of livestock, but don't think for one moment that there can ever be anything more here."

"Will!" Amanda snapped. "Enough!" She understood his reaction, but Ichi didn't and she wasn't sure if the proud outsider would forgive her stupid husband if he went too far.

Only Will didn't need to be stopped, he'd stopped himself. His eyes were resting on Rye but they were unfocused. "Oh, gods, Amanda." He whispered. Will blinked quickly and stumbled backwards. "This can't be. I…" He shook his head but his wife was at his side, rubbing his shoulder and pushing him to sit.

"What is it?" She asked gently, knowing Will hated his ranking, just high enough to be a pain in the ass without really being useful.

"Humiliation and shame. Heavy, horrible shame." He looked to Ichi but found only confusion on his friend's face.

"From Ichi?"

Will shook his head. "Rye."

"But, that would mean he could understand you." She shivered at the thought and glanced to where the pet sat, as docile as ever, with downcast eyes on the medical bed.

"I'm sorry, Ichi, I can be an ass. I…" He shook his head. "You're right, we need to test him."

Amanda stroked her husband's head and smiled softly at his admission. "This is going to take a while. Did you want to leave him here or…?"

"I'll wait." Ichi agreed instantly, knowing there was nothing for him to do, but knowing he'd never be able to focus on work while Rye was here.

She nodded. "Then you'll stay out of our way and not bug us. We're not going to tell you a thing until we're done and have had a chance to look everything over."

"That's fine." He moved out of the way and took over a small workstation in the corner. He'd brought his notebook and there was work he could do from the med lab, but every time he glanced up Rye was watching him with wide, worried eyes. It made working difficult and he ended up sitting, drinking too much coffee and watching.

Amanda and Will had a half language of long term partners, sentences were unnecessary so it left Ichi in the dark for most of the morning. Some of the equipment they pulled out were things he knew, some weren't, and a few items were obscure enough that the couple had to hunt them down in storage. If nothing else, he was comforted that they were taking this seriously.

Around lunch Amanda stepped out of the lab to fetch something from their research lab and Will came over to sit by Ichi. Rye lay still and accepting on the medical bed, outwardly calm, but Ichi knew the pet well enough to see the tension in how he was holding his body.

"I had a puppy, as a kid," Will started as he sat down.

"And I didn't, for which I am deprived and pathetic. I know, you've told me."

"No, I..." Will glanced to Rye and than down to study the stations work surface. "The Concord landlords didn't leave us with much, if it was of value they took it. Even a family's garden, they'd just come in and take what they wanted. We were hungry all the time. My earliest memories are of a really bad winter and watching some of my neighbors slowly starve to death."

"Will, I'm sorry." But sorry really didn't mean a whole lot compared to that.

"Anyway, food didn't come in from outside, it went to the landlords and they made the choice to allow it to reach us or not, so we really had to scramble to find a way to make it. What livestock the village had we pooled together but the landlord took it. Some of the men were able to poach rabbits occasionally and once or twice a deer, but one of them got caught. The landlord had the man beaten to death in the village square, made us all watch. So in an effort to survive, the elders made the choice to start breeding dogs for food. It was something outside the landlord's imagination, they had large litters, and they matured quickly. Anyway, one spring when I was like seven, I got really attached to this one puppy. Named it, taught it to fetch. That stupid dog was my best friend until the following winter when my father slaughtered it so we could eat." He picked at a rough cuticle on one of his fingers in an effort to not have to look at Ichi.

"I'm so sorry."

Will shrugged. "It's just, sometimes I get a little twitchy about things. Times got really hard out in the rural villages; a lot of things were done. Amanda says I'm a walking emotional breakdown," he tried to joke but it fell flat. "I didn't mean to go off on you like that, earlier. It's just..." He sighed. "I haven't had a pet since, just can't do it. It's the biggest thing stopping us from having kids too. I just wanted to let you know I didn't mean to be cruel, that it was me, not you, okay?"

Ichi nodded but Will was looking down and didn't see it. "There's nothing to be sorry about. Thank you, for trusting me enough to tell me."

"Anyway, couple more tests and we'll figure out what's up with Rye. Okay?"

"Thank you."

"So did you… you know?"

He felt himself blushing again but he shook his head. "No."

"Aww, you just seemed, I don't know, less stuffy today." He nudged Ichi with an elbow. "Thought maybe you got some."

He had, he had gotten plenty. "And if I had, I certainly wouldn't share it with you." Ichi arched an eyebrow.

The med lab door opened and Amanda rejoined them with whatever item she'd wandered away to fetch. She tapped Will's head as she went by. "Back to work for you."

Will sighed dramatically and pushed himself to his feet. Ichi watched them, unable to work now with so much on his mind. He really did know far too little about them, as little as they knew about him. It was his choice to keep things that way, wrapped in his own privacy and awkwardness, he'd assumed the comfortable ease the Avalon folks showed was as deep as they ran. He was quickly learning the laughter, the joy in life was a learned cultural reaction to a suffering he'd only scratched the surface of. There was a great deal he'd been missing by being so nearsighted.

His thoughts distracted him so much that another hour slipped by and it wasn't until Amanda stood in front of him that he shook himself awake. "Well?"

"Well, you should take him home. We've a lot of data gathered but I want time to look it over. He's mildly sedated, let him sleep it off, okay?"

"But what do you think?"

"I think you need to take him home and let him rest and we'll let you know in a couple of hours."

"Amanda."

"Go, out of my lab!" She shooed.

He relented and gathered up a yawning Rye but he didn't lead them home. He'd just sit there and worry, so instead he went to his own lab. As soon as they were inside, Rye went to his cushion, pulled his blanket over his shoulders and curled up to sleep. Ichi tried to work, he really did, but it didn't work out that way. In the end he gave it up and simply sat and watched Rye sleeping, trying to make sense out of the mystery hidden in the pet's silences.

As dinnertime slowly rolled around, Rye stirred in his sleep and slowly woke up. He yawned and stretched but forced himself to wake and sit up. It was something Ichi had noticed; Rye had an amazing sense of time. Even in the mornings the pet would be awake before the alarm. He'd move toward the door close to lunch, he'd leave his crate to wait by the apartment door before it was time to leave to go back to the lab after lunch. Even asleep, it seemed Rye had a perfect sense of time.

"Ready to go home?" he asked and Rye climbed to his feet. He was too nervous to eat, torn between wanting to know and being frightened of the truth. Amanda and Will would be looking for him in his rooms, so he'd go there and wait.

An hour passed, then two, and Ichi was getting so nervous that Rye was picking up on it. The pet wasn't quite hiding in his crate but he was sitting close to it, watching Ichi randomly scan programs on the vid screen with wide, uncertain eyes. When the buzzer at his door rang, he sprang to his feet and Rye darted into his crate.

"It's okay Rye, it's just Amanda and Will." He hurried to let them in.

They looked serious and Ichi wasn't sure what that meant. "Sit down, Ichi," Will muttered.

"Where's Rye?" Amanda asked scanning the room, but spotted the pet in his crate. "There you are."

Ichi sat back on his sofa and let Amanda settle on one side and Will on the other. "Well? I'm knotted up in worry here, what did you find?"

Amanda reached over and took Ichi's hand. "He isn't a twisted pet, or a mistake," she started gently.

"Oh." He felt embarrassed, and grateful. He'd made a huge assumption and his friends were being kind about letting him down.

"Ichi, he's not a pet at all."

That made less sense. "What?"

Will leaned forward. "He's human."

"What?"

Amanda drew a slow breath. "The base of all pets is a human gene code, but because all of them start from the same base code they show up almost as twins of each other. The code is then tweaked, hair, skin, eye color, special modifications, the like, but the base code is the same altered human. Rye's gene code is as human as yours or mine."

Ichi felt the blood pound in his ears and he was suddenly very glad he'd sat down. "He's human."

"Yes, but stay with us. He's been adapted, not just once to be made into a pet but twice, maybe more than that but definitely twice. Another clue, the scans show massive amounts of healed injuries. Some of them are very old; he's had dozens of fractures, some along the bones growth lines while the bone was still growing." She spoke slowly.

"Meaning?"

Will shook his head. "Meaning some how he broke bones while still a child. Pet's don't have childhoods, they're grown to whatever age is requested and than adapted."

"You said he's been modified twice?" He glanced to the crate but Rye was still hiding inside.

"Well, we think the first was a series of modifications over the course of his childhood. His muscle density is way out there, totally off norm. His metabolism is faster, his lungs can process oxygen easier--" Will started but Amanda broke in.

"It's his immune system, Ichi, it's amazing. He has the t and b cells of a young child, his body is in overdrive. We found stem cells in his system, Ichi, stem cells. They're coded with proteins I've never seen before. Will and I are virologists, we've been studying immune system responses for years and neither of us has even read of something like this." The excitement tumbled out of her.

"What does it mean?"

"She's trying to say that you could break Rye's arm and so long as the bone was set in place it would heal cleanly in half the time. I'm betting his immune system would eat the Bare Earth Virus for lunch."

Ichi glanced to Will. "Let's not make that bet."

He waved it off. "Point being, someone spent a tremendous amount of money changing Rye as a child and yet during the same time frame he had a dozen or more broken bones? It doesn't make sense."

"So, what? They modified a human and than modified him into being a pet?"

Amanda punched up some of the displays on her notebook and handed it to Ichi. "Something like that, but his brain, here, this is the standard brain of a real pet. See the darker areas? They don't even light up on a pet, these are regions of thought, consciousness, awareness. They aren't even properly formed. Now, this is Rye's scan."

The image Ichi was looking at grew larger, brighter and the images peeled away in layers. "It looks normal."

"It's close, but it's not normal. The base line is a perfectly healthy human brain but what grants us consciousness?"

"A soul?"

"Mythical nonsense."

"We disagree, I think it's mythical nonsense in conjunction with biology," Will teased.

"When we're deeply asleep, before we reach REM, our brain shuts down. The different sections stop talking to each other and we lose all consciousness. Ichi, someone very skillfully severed a vast amount of Rye's pathways, they shut down or severely strangled his brain's ability to talk to itself." She enlarged regions and pointed out sections but it was all far from Ichi's study.

"So, they what? Damaged his brain and made him into a pet?"

"That would have been kind," Will whispered and leaned back.

"This is just theory," Amanda qualified, glancing to Will with a warning look to her eyes.

"Tell me," Ichi demanded and started to flip through brain scans, images of broken and long healed bones, body chemistry results and DNA tests too complicated for him to really understand.

"Someone was very careful, see here..." She took over the notebook again and pulled up the brain images. "And here? We're guessing, but we think they did this to cut off his memories; here, this section, it prevents him from being able to form words but look, this? Ichi this is where we comprehend language."

He studied it and frowned. "It looks normal."

"It is normal. They left it untouched."

"What she doesn't want to say is that someone very deliberately made it so Rye wouldn't remember who he was and so he wouldn't be able to speak but left him with enough intact that he's aware, conscious and able to understand. Our theory is that he's totally able to understand every word said around him but he's been disconnected from the experience of the words." Will sighed. "Like you can say to him ocean breeze and he'll know what the words mean but not what it feels like, really feels like to stand and feel an ocean breeze. And even if he lived years Oceanside, nothing will associate with the words. They'll be blank slates."

The truth settled on Ichi hard. "Oh, god, they left him locked inside his own head. Why? Why would anyone do this?"

"The only person who might know that is Rye, and he's not talking."

"But, he was someone, right? Surely someone is missing him?"

"Ichi we ran his DNA twice in all the databases and it came up blank. Nothing, not a whisper of an identity," Will spoke softly. They'd had over an hour to process the sheer horror of what they'd found.

"That's why, sometimes, he seems so human, so like he understands." He thought he might be ill.

"Ichi, that crazy immune system of his?" Amanda glanced to Will but he nodded. "It's undoing all of this." She waved to the brain scans. "The other things, like the double terminated nerve endings and the denser muscle tissue, his body has those written in as what's normal for him, but this surgical adaptation of his brain is contrary to it. It's slowly undoing it."

"Oh, god, how long?"

"How long until it's healed?" She shrugged. "We don't know. We don't have a base line to go from, we didn't do these scans when he arrived."

"Guess?" He asked, demanded, needed to know.

"A couple more months, maybe a year?" Will raised an eyebrow. "Some of our scans show healed tissue, the process of reversing this is almost halfway finished. The original surgical scars are at least a year old."

"You have to be able to do something for him, to help him?"

"What we could do would be like using an axe to chop berries. His body is doing such a fine, delicate job of repair that we'd only be making things worse. Yes, we can repair the damage, but the way his body is doing it he'll eventually return to how he was before the surgical procedures which may--if he's very, very lucky--may contain his memories."

"Oh god. This, this is barbaric."

"There's more." Will continued and pulled up another set of images. "Our scans of soft tissue found no real scars, nothing marring his skin or muscles, but that's a given once we saw his immune system, but look here." The tone of the images changed, the colors skewed and lines appeared. "We can see growth patterns. It lets us find old, healed wounds from the re-growth directions. They use it to look for signs of abuse, anyway, we found a lot."

Ichi frowned and tried to understand what the image was showing him. It took a moment, but he realized it was a back, Rye's back, and lines crossed it. It took another moment for the meaning to sink in. "These, these aren't whip marks, are they?"

"Whip marks or something similar." Amanda spoke gently. "Something tore up his back pretty badly. We found a lot of healed wounds."

"How recently? I mean..." He tried to process all they were telling him. "Can't they be from years? Maybe he was in some sort of accident, the broken bones the injuries?"

"This scan can only pick up re-growth patterns on the skin and underlying soft tissue for maybe a year in the past. With Rye's immune system, it'd be safer to say maybe six months ago?" Amanda was starting to worry about Ichi, the man was growing ashen and looked as shocked as she'd felt when they'd started to piece the information together.

"Oh god." He shook his head. "Is he, I mean, how intelligent is he?"

"Best guess would be that he's no less or more than any other human."

"And someone did this to him? Trapped him inside his own mind? Tortured him?" He was shaking his head. "Who would do that?"

"Better question might be why?" Will added softly.

"No." Ichi shook his head. "The better question is what can we do to help him?"

Will grinned. "Told you he wouldn't freak out," he tossed to his wife.

"You're very clever."

"You thought I would freak out?"

"Well," Amanda started carefully. "I was worried your first thought would be about contacting PETS, letting them know."

"Oh." The idea hadn't occurred to him. "Should we?"

"No." She shook her head. "This isn't a mistake, Ichi, this couldn't have just happened. Someone very high up there knew and let it happen. They sent him out here to the middle of nowhere because they figured you would never know. Don't tell them you know, no matter what. He's still a pet, legally he's property. If they think the secret's been blown they can claim he's faulty and replace him, take him back, give you another maybe or maybe not but in any case, Rye would be gone."

"I won't allow that to happen." Ichi knew it sounded melodramatic and silly but he meant it. "Now, what can we do to help him?"

"We've ruled out surgical options. Besides, we'd have to take him back to Avalon, it's too delicate of work for here. It doesn't matter, he's best left on his own anyway." Amanda rambled for a bit. "His brain is in the process of repairing and replacing a ton of neural pathways, we need to encourage them."

"Forgive my wife, sometimes she forgets that people actually listen to her when she's speaking."

"Hey!" She mock pouted at the scolding.

"What she's trying to say is that the brain is like our bodies, if we don't use it we lose it, and in this case we need to stimulate his healing brain to heal. If he doesn't try to speak, those pathways may re-form in an underdeveloped way. So, the word of the day is therapy."

Ichi nodded. "Okay, just tell me what has to be done."

"First, you, we all, need to stop treating him like a pet. Now, Rye is yours, good or bad, he's your responsibility. Amanda and I will keep our mouths shut about this but everyone here is Avalon, they can keep secrets. I wouldn't tell Harvick even, but the rest of the crew? No worries there, but the choice is yours." Will tried to see Ichi's eyes and couldn't, the man was clutching to Amanda's notebook and had his eyes locked onto their tests.

"I can't, I mean, I can't…"

Amanda soothed a hand across Ichi's back. "You worry about Rye, we'll tell the rest of the crowd. Okay?"

He nodded and felt punched in the gut. "Thanks."

"Now, Amanda and I differ here. She thinks no fuss should be made, that you should just start treating Rye like you would a normal person. I think that will confuse the hell out of him. I think you need to sit him down and tell him you know he's aware in there, that the jig is up and he needs to start trying to get better." Will glanced to the crate, unsure how much of this Rye was listening to.

"May I ask your reasons?" He needed that, the falling back on logic and reason when the world no longer felt as safe as it did.

Amanda drew a slow breath. "I think if you make a fuss, it'll upset him; but if you quietly just change things, he'll adapt. He obviously tries to please, that'll carry over here too."

"I think it's just the same, he's trying to please. Someone beat the shit out of him, that's a pretty good crash course on wanting to keep your owner happy. Fear of punishment, fear of pain, they can shut a mind down, crush personalities. He needs to be encouraged to express himself and know it's okay," Will countered.

Ichi shut the notebook off and handed it back to Amanda. The files on speech therapy and behavior therapy he knew would all be waiting in his home system and his stomach churned too much to read them now. "I don't know, I, this is, this is just so much."

"Ichi," Amanda started gently. "You can't fall apart here. If this is a lot for you to accept, imagine how it has been for Rye."

He sat up and ran a hand across his hair. "I need to think about this a little. I, it's just, this is so much more than I'd feared, I…"

"It's okay, now you know why we took the afternoon. We wanted to double check everything and stop feeling so ill over the results." Will grinned. "We'll go, get the others together and let them know and go from there. Okay?"

Ichi nodded. "Thank you, both of you, for trusting me."

Amanda leaned over and put a kiss to the Ichi's temple. "No dearest, thank you for trusting yourself. If this had gone unnoticed, that would have been so much worse." She tossed a head to the door. "Come on Will, buy a gal a drink would you?"

They left, with Will pausing in the doorway to turn and add, "Call any of us if you need anything." And then Ichi was alone.

Only he wasn't alone, for as the minutes ticked away and the silence continued to weigh on him, Rye slowly emerged from his crate. The pet, no, Ichi caught his own thoughts and corrected them, the man slinked out and came to sit on the floor in front of the sofa as he always did. Gray eyes glanced up to the worried look Ichi wore and the smallest of worry reflected on the normally empty face before Rye dropped his eyes and face to the floor. It wasn't an issue of coldly clinical facts with the handsome man sitting so docilely in front of him.

Chapter Eight

When Ichi's stomach had settled, he reached out a hand and stroked it across the soft red hair. As always, Rye arched into the touch and tried to get him to repeat it. Lately he had been, but not today.

"Rye?" He spoke softly and the head swung up to look at him again. "Come here, sit." He patted the coffee table and that earned him a frown. "It's okay." He patted the coffee table again and slowly Rye unfolded his legs and very carefully sat on the edge of the table.

The head instantly lowered, the eyes studied the floor. Ichi reached out and raised his chin. He studied those eyes, so fluid and expressive but he couldn't swear there was intelligence behind them. When he released the chin, Rye's head lowered again.

"I'm not sure how much of today you understood. Will and Amanda, they're good friends of mine and they're medical doctors. I had them run some tests on you. I know that you're not really a pet." He tried to speak gently.

Rye shifted unhappily on the table and his eyes darted up, worried, before dropping again.

"Will and Amanda know, and soon, everyone here will know. These are good people. No one else will. We aren't letting PETS know. No one is going to take you back, your home is here, and you belong here." He sighed. "God, I wish I knew how much you actually understood. They said you're healing, that what they did to your head is getting better. We're going to try to help you as much as we can. No one is going to hurt you again, Rye, no one."

A spot on the fabric of Rye's kilt grew wet, and than another. It took Ichi a moment to understand that tears were slipping from Rye's eyes to drop from his bowed head to dampen the fabric. He reached out and tried to raise the hidden face again, Rye was more resistant this time and the chin he held trembled.

"Aw, hey now, it's going to be okay." He tried to wipe at tears but Rye flinched a little and he stopped. "Guess this means you understand some of this, huh?" He tried to smile.

Rye just pulled his face away and tried to curl up over his own knees to hide. Ichi understood, he was private with his emotions too. He stood up. "I'm making some tea, would you like some?" He was three steps to the kitchen when Rye disappeared into his crate again. Knowledge alone wasn't going to be enough, they were going to need a lot of time too.

The tea helped settle his nerves but Rye stayed hidden in the crate, even though Ichi poured tea into a wide mug just for him. He sat and read the files Amanda and Will had sent him, but most of it seemed like common sense. The now comforting sound of kibble rattling shot across the silent apartment, and Ichi turned to see the hand carefully picking out two or three rounds.

"No time like the present." He nodded and moved to kneel at the crate. "Rye, come out here." It would have been simpler to command him but that was missing the point.

There was a pause but Rye crawled out to kneel in front of the crate, eyes downcast.

"Give them to me." Ichi held out his hand.

Rye didn't move.

"Come on, give me the kibble." He lifted the slender hand and stroked at the fingers until he got the hand to turn over and drop a couple of kibble chunks into his hand. Ichi moved to drop the kibble back in the bowl and caught a quick movement from the corner of his eye. When he glanced back to Rye, nothing seemed different except a slight difference to how the redhead was holding his mouth. "You sneak." Ichi laughed and held out his hand. "All of it now, spit it out."

Rye sat, his eyes downcast and looking stubborn but Ichi didn't relent. After a short stalemate, Rye gave up and spit the slightly soggy chunk of kibble out into Ichi's hand. The kibble was quickly shaken off into the bowl.

"No more of this." Ichi stood, taking the bowl with him as he went.

Rye stood and followed the bowl, watching with worried eyes as Ichi dropped it, kibble and bowl, into the storage tub. His stomach growled, angry and hungry.

"Don't worry, I'm not starving you. It's just that pets have unstable digestions, rich foods make them sick. You aren't a pet, there's no reason you should eat this." Which meant he'd be cooking for two and had to think of something that could be eaten with hands. He doubted Rye was up for handling a spoon or chopsticks.

"Pizza." He settled and went to grab a pair of the Neapolitan rounds from storage. Ichi tore the package off and dropped them in the cooker before moving to set two places at the table. "Trust me, this is way better than kibble."

There was only one wide mouthed mug in his store of dishes. He occasionally used it for soup, but right now it had the untouched mint tea in it. Ichi gathered it up and held the lip of the mug close to Rye's mouth. "Try it, see if you like it."

The gray eyes were uncertain, uneasy, but he parted his mouth enough to let Ichi tip some of the cool tea forward. The mint sprang across his tongue and Rye instantly pulled back.

"Not a fan of mint, huh? Well." Ichi dumped the mug and rinsed it out. He filled it with cool water instead. "Water it is, until we figure out what you do like." The cooker chimed and he moved to pull the plates out. The rounds of baked dough steamed, the tomato slices on it were properly crisped. Scattered over the pizzas were squares of bubbling cheese and wilted basil leaves. The smell was amazing and as Ichi slid the plates on the table, he caught Rye watching every move the food made. Ichi snapped the rounds in half along the pre-pressed crease and patted one of the chairs.

"Come here and eat, Rye. Before it gets cold."

Rye didn't move.

"Come on, I know you're hungry."

He held his ground but his eyes darted from Ichi to the food and off to the crate.

Ichi sat down and picked up half of his pizza. It crunched as he bit into it. The aroma of the herbs filled the apartment, and over it all Ichi could feel hungry eyes on him. He ignored it and kept eating.

"It's really good, sit and have some."

Rye held his ground.

Ichi finally set his half eaten slice down and turned to study the skittish pet--no, the skittish man he corrected himself. "I wish you could talk, I wish I could understand why you're so worried about eating in front of people. How about this, you can eat the first half wherever you want, but the second has to be eaten at the table."

With no indication if Rye understood or not, Ichi reached across the table and slid half the round pizza off the plate and offered it toward Rye. "Deal?"

Rye's stomach growled loudly. Gray eyes danced between the food and Ichi and settled on the floor for a moment, but before they could drop Ichi saw fear there.

"It's okay, go on. It's really good."

Very slowly, Rye crept closer and then with little warning he snatched the half away from Ichi's hand and darted hurriedly to disappear inside his crate. Ichi watched and his food grew cold while he thought. There would be no removing the crate quickly, it was pretty clear that it was the only place where Rye felt safe.

There came a small crunching sound and it was followed by a happy food murmur. Ichi grinned at that and another louder crunch was followed by more delighted food moans. He figured if he'd had nothing but the same food to eat for at least a year--even if it had been good food, which kibble wasn't-- he'd be making the same delighted sounds as well.

Before Ichi could get more than a bite or two finished, Rye was back, sitting just out of arms reach. He didn't even glance over. "If you want it, you'll have to sit at the table and eat it." He spoke softly, making a point to not make eye contact.

Rye didn't move.

Ichi finished his own pizza and still Rye sat there, his face a torn up mix of longing and fear. "Guess you don't want it, huh?" Ichi stood and started to clear the table but he knew better. As he took a few steps toward the kitchen with the waiting half round of pizza, Rye whined a little.

"What? I can't understand what you want if you don't let me know." He was being cruel, all he wanted to do was give the man the pizza and let him eat it wherever he wanted. "If you don't want it, let me know, tell me no." He said slowly, shaking his head no. "If you want it, tell me yes." He nodded his head yes and stood, waiting.

Whatever the internal battle was inside of Rye it must have been tremendous. Ichi could see him almost quaking with emotion but after a moment's struggle, Rye's head nodded. It was tiny and quick, but real, and the breath Ichi hadn't known he was holding rushed out.

"Well now, see, that's not so hard. Come here and eat it." He set the plate down and patted the chair again. This time he didn't sit and watch, instead he moved to make tea, a blend that was lightly toasted and mild, and very carefully watched from the corner of his eyes.

Rye moved slowly but he moved. He stood on shuffling feet and hovered over the chair, one of his hands brushed across the top of the back with the smallest of touches. With only a final glance to his crate, he gingerly sat down, on the very edge. He perched there, uncomfortable and uneasy but quickly scooped up the pizza and devoured it.

Ichi returned to the table and set his tea down as carefully as he could. "It would taste better if you actually chewed it," he teased and gathered up a napkin. "Hold still."

Rye obeyed but when the cloth swiped at the tomato in the corner of his mouth he pulled back just slightly.

"Water's in the cup, I know you can mange it." He nodded and sat down.

Gray eyes went to where the water bowl had sat for weeks and to the tiny cup sitting untouched on the table. Ichi had never seen the man drink either, in the mornings the bowl would be empty and occasionally if he went into the bedroom or bathroom he'd return to find it partially drained but, like the food, Rye never touched it where someone could see.

A hand, shaking and frightened, extended out and curled around the cup. When no harsh words arrived the other joined the first and the pair steadied the sloshing water. It was quickly raised to Rye's mouth and drained in long, thirsty gulps. Ichi was surprised at the skill Rye showed. Drinking from a cup was a fairly complicated effort and Rye, beyond his fears, had no difficulties.

"Here now, come see this." Ichi stood and cleared the empty plates away, plucking the empty mug from Rye's hands. "This mug, from now on, is yours. Okay? This is Rye's. Watch." When he moved further toward the kitchen, Rye happily followed, glad to be rid of the chair. He pressed the mug to the water dispenser and it slowly filled. "See?" The mug was pushed at Rye. "You do it."

Rye stood uncertain, but at an encouraging nod he extended the mug and let it fill up. With his eyes still locked onto Ichi, he quickly downed the second mug full.

"There now, your mug and you know how to fill it. I'm proud of you Rye!" He smiled and moved to ignore Rye and let him find his own level of comfort again, figuring they'd pushed the man enough for right now. Ichi set himself to tidying up the kitchen and getting the dirty dishes dropped into the washer.

He moved to step away from the counter and collect his cooling tea but a hand snaked around his waist. The touch startled Ichi, made him jump slightly but a second hand petted up through his hair, fingertips dragging across the nape of his neck in a teasing touch. The contact was like fire and Ichi shivered, feeling like a chill was melting in the face of such a blaze.

"Rye, don't," he sighed, but there was little conviction to his words.

The hand in his hair stroked more and tilted Ichi's head to the left, exposing the length of his neck. Soft, careful lips pressed behind his ear and Ichi's lungs forgot how to work. "Oh, don't, Rye, don't…" he sighed out but the lips didn't still. They moved forward, more boldly, carrying with them the spicy scent of basil, to gently feather across the tense cords of Ichi's neck.

At his waist, the hand that was holding him in place tugged his shirt free from its tidy tuck in his pants. Before Ichi's lust-muddled mind could make sense of any of it, the slender hand was under his shirt, resting on the narrow flat of his stomach, skin sliding on skin. Fingers curved gently around his waist and just held on.

It melted Ichi, he moaned and his head lolled back, his spine arched and a shoulder was there for his head to rest upon. That subtle difference in heights was perfection and his eyes squinted shut.

There were reasons for not doing this, he knew there were but with the hand curled around his waist, touching him skin to skin, and that tormenting mouth kissing and teasing the side of his neck, none of those reasons came readily to mind.

"Rye..." Ichi struggled to breath. "No..... This isn't right..." He needed stronger ammunition than that if he was going to remember what was right. "Your not well, not yet... oh god." He arched further back, his stomach hitching against the steady hand, begging to be touched, when Rye found a particularly sensitive spot on his neck. "You... you can't know.... Not yet.... This can't be what you want." He managed to whisper out.

If there was any doubt that inside Rye's head he was able to understand, it fled. He may not have been able to counter Ichi's protests with words but he could with actions. The strong hand around the slender waist tugged and pulled Ichi's body fully along Rye's own. Back pressed to chest, legs entwined, and a hard, hungry length crushed tightly to the roundness of Ichi's ass.

There were many things Ichi had missed during the long years of celibacy. The scent of another person was one of them. It wasn't something he could define, but the very scent and warmth of a lover's skin comforted him. Rye smelled like pine trees and open air. There was a hint of something under the green, living scent, something like lilacs and spring sunshine. It was too deliberate, too sensual, and Ichi wondered if that soft scent to his skin was a modification that hadn't failed. Under it all was something duskier, something heavier, the teasing scent of strong male. Ichi knew if he let himself, he'd grow drunk on the scent of Rye's skin.

There were things he had missed without knowing what he was missing. As Rye gently pressed his body along Ichi's, one of the empty hollows of his soul suddenly made sense. Rye was hard, achingly hard, eagerly hard, and Ichi had done that. It was heady and thrilling to know he was the cause of the handsome man's state. Simple, plain Ichi had done this to another person. Someone wanted him so badly that they were holding him, pressing themselves against his ass in silent pleas and it made Ichi ache as deeply. Knowing that someone needed him, was passionate for him was something he'd missed without being able to name.

None of the reasons of logic mattered with Rye kissing his neck and pressing into his ass. All Ichi wanted was to be allowed to melt forward over the counter, cling to it's smooth surface and let Rye take him. Nothing else mattered and inside Ichi's head he could feel it, the touch of bare skin to bare skin, the stinging burn of first being entered, then the trembling bliss of letting go. The desire was consuming.

But he needed to see those eyes, those gray eyes which had haunted his fantasies from the moment Rye had stumbled into his life. Ichi squirmed and for a moment the hand at his waist clung tighter before easing. It gave him just enough room to turn around but not enough to slip away, and he found himself pressed now between the counter and Rye's chest, face to face.

It was distressing how easily Rye breathed. Ichi was panting, gasping for breath, his heart pounding in excited emotion and physical need, but Rye's breath had barely increased. There was no missing the lust in the other man, his face was twisted with begging need and a flush colored his pale skin. Those gray eyes were dark, almost blue with desire, and the hungry look in them made Ichi shiver.

The hand at Ichi's waist had slid as he'd turned, still under his shirt, to now rest along the small of his back. It slid lower now, down to grip firmly the curve of his ass. The clutching touch made Ichi shiver, it made him want to strip naked and fall to his knees and devour Rye as Rye had for him. When the grip pulled, tugged at his body and Rye's hips slid forward, there was no room left for Ichi to think.

The pleasure of being so wickedly teased, of desire finding and meeting desire, shut his mind down. Rye moaned, low like a growl in the back of his throat and he held Ichi's head steady when the shorter man nearly melted backwards. Ichi was gasping, his mouth parted and his eyes shut. He never saw Rye lean forward, but he felt the strong lips cover his own and swallow his moans whole.

Ichi had nothing in him with which to fight the kiss. He knew he was about a step away from being fucked silly right there on his kitchen counter top and not even his logic was willing to speak up to offer a reason not to. Rye kissed him, not with the shy, joyfully grateful kiss after his hair cut, but a consuming kiss. There was nothing shy or uncertain here, his tongue explored and conquered as Rye's hips continued to slowly rub into Ichi's own.

Across the counter, Ichi's fingers scratched for a grip, something to ground himself on in a world of lust and want. They found nothing until they stumbled on Rye's arms. That was solid and real, if not grounding, and he let his hands travel up the arms to round over shoulders. The slender body he rarely saw undressed any longer was still hard to the touch and the memory of the long lean muscle that lay under the soft fabric sprang to mind. He felt Rye shiver under his hands and thought nothing of it, the kiss continued, the tormenting mash of hip into hip went on. Ichi found his target, his hands wandered down shoulders, across the strong back and the kiss stuttered. Down his hands roamed until they rounded over the kilt covered ass, gripping lightly and Rye froze.

The sudden chill, the cold emptiness around Ichi sunk in a moment before his mind understood that Rye no longer had him pinned to the counter. His hazed eyes opened and fell on Rye, standing a good three paces away. The gray eyes were storm clouds again, wide, and the breath that hadn't stirred for desire moved in uneasy fear.

That dumped ice water over Ichi and knocked a lot of the wind from his sails. He watched the blind, undirected fear that was bordering on panic fade to worry and then be quickly chased by a more direct, embarrassed personal fear dance across Rye's face before he dropped it. Ichi had to rewind the last few seconds to try to gather just what had spooked the taller man and it didn't take much to connect it with being touched.

"I'm sorry." He moved forward to brush hair back from Rye's eyes but the redhead ducked back before he could. Ichi stood, silent and trying to jump-start his thinking mind. He needed to process a complex situation and he could do that. Only, he was really bad at processing complex emotional situations.

Normally by the time Ichi figured out what to say or do the person he needed to take action with had grown frustrated and left. Rye just stood there, uncertain and uncomfortable, waiting for something, waiting for punishment.

"Rye," Ichi started carefully. "It'd be so easy for me to give in here, to just let you please me. God, people like you, as beautiful as you, don't ever look twice at geeks like me." He tried to joke but it came out sounding bitter. "I think I might understand; you're scared, things are changing. I know they've turned up your libido, but I can't do this. As attracted as I am to you," he found himself speaking slowly, picking each word carefully and still he felt clumsy. "As much as I like the fantasy of us together, I won't have it be as simple comfort or repayment, or from obligation or duty. I want to touch you and pleasure you, and I can't begin to imagine why that frightens you. All I need to know is that it does and that's okay, but Rye, this is why I say no."

Ichi rubbed his eyes and leaned against the counter again but this time it was because remorse was making him feel exhausted. "I'm a fool, I know it, I mean as soon as you've got your mind back you're not going to look twice at me, but I can't do this. I want you, Rye, god, when you touch me…" He shook his head and had hoped something he'd said would gain some reaction. Rye still stood, staring at the floor. "Until you can meet me as an equal, touch and be touched, until you're ready to face that, this is wrong. You may never get there and that's okay too. Or you may never get there with me and I can deal with that. For now, you focus on getting better and we'll deal with this--" he waved his hand between them. "We'll deal with this when you're ready to deal with it. Okay?" He felt like pounding his head against the wall, or crawling in bed and sobbing in frustrated anger.

Rye simply stood where he'd retreated to, unmoving and unresponsive.

It was too much, the swings of mood and emotion, worry and fear, lust and crashing stops, left Ichi exhausted. If Rye was an insect, he'd have no doubts how to handle the situation, but Rye wasn't even a pet, he was a human and Ichi knew he was horrible dealing with people. It just felt really important not to mess this up.

"I'm exhausted, let's go to bed." He pushed himself from the counter and moved to Rye's crate. The lid popped open far more easily now and he fished the blanket and pillow out. "No more sleeping in here, Rye, okay? Until I can think of something, the sofa is way more comfortable." He made up a quick bed on the sofa and patted it until Rye came over and stood near it, eyes still down. "Well, sleep when you're ready."

He shook his head and lowered the room lights down to the dim night light levels he'd been setting them at since Rye arrived. When he wandered to his bedroom, Rye was still standing next to the sofa, eyes downcast, looking as lost as Ichi felt. When Ichi woke the next morning, he found Rye curled up, asleep inside his crate. The blanket and pillows lay on the sofa untouched.

Chapter Nine

"Afternoon Ichi, Rye." Will tossed out in happy tones as he swung into the small lab. "What's new?"

Like always, Ichi was bent over his bugs doing whatever odd bug thing he did, and it made Will grin to see it. Rye sat in the corner, as he always did, perched on the blankets. It was still an odd sight to see the redheaded man wearing pants, but he was getting used to it.

"The swarm, they're on their fourth metamorphosis. I've never seen anything like this, the mouth is still malformed and the wings are barely functional."

Will rolled his eyes and knelt near Rye. The small smile at Will's quiet teasing grew into a wide grin when the chocolate was slipped from one hand to another and Rye quickly popped it into his mouth.

"What did you just give him?" Ichi asked without turning around.

"Nothing."

Ichi sighed and shut his system down. He turned and could tell by the way Rye was trying not to smile just what had transpired. "Chocolate. Really Will, it's not healthy." He scolded but his eyes danced. Rye had developed quite the love of the sweet candy and the darker the chocolate, the better.

"Hush, it was just a small piece."

"Well, what do you say, Rye?"

Rye grinned and nodded his head.

"Use your words." Ichi stood up and stretched his back. His spine popped as he worked the kinks out.

"Th... th... th... thank y...you." Rye managed to stutter out and blushed a little at the difficulties. The voice was shy and soft, with a quality of long disuse, but it was there.

Will marveled at that. Ichi had refused all outside help and took up working with Rye nearly every day. The redhead had made massive amounts of progress in a fairly short amount of time. Even the latest scans showed a shocking rate of healing and the only thing to attribute it to was Ichi's care.

"You're welcome, Rye. Amanda's waiting for you, want to go ahead?"

Rye glanced to Ichi before he forced out more newly found words. "Ma...ma... May I?"

"So long as you're not a pest." Ichi grinned to take the scold from the words. "We'll be right behind you, I just need to close up here."

Rye grinned again and the smile was almost heartbreakingly lovely to see. He nodded his head and hurried out of the lab.

Will shook his head. "That guy loves music."

"It's been good for him. The only nights he sleeps soundly anymore are after these weekly sessions." They'd stumbled on Rye's love of music by chance. Ichi had popped in one night to the common kitchen when the small group was playing, and Rye'd stood in awe. Music was as much a part of Avalon as their drinking and he figured of the two habits, this was the better one to pick up.

Ichi had never felt comfortable joining the group, he wasn't from Avalon. When he boiled down his excuses, he'd always been too awkward. He lacked a rhythmic bone in his body and couldn't sing to save his life, and everyone sang along to the old songs. When Rye responded with such delight, there was no way he could miss the weekly gathering, and while Rye stuttered when he spoke he could sing along to the songs without a hitch.

"He's still having nightmares?"

"They're getting worse, not better." Ichi ran his nightly checklists and finished his work. "He woke me up screaming last night."

"You're doing amazing things here, Ichi, you know that right?"

Ichi just shrugged one shoulder. "He's the one doing the work. He still won't say a word about before he got here. Will, do you think maybe, you and Amanda could take him for a while? He's really grown very fond of you two." He couldn't meet his friend's eyes without blushing so he kept them down while he fussed at the last of the nightly busy work.

"Why would you even ask that?" Will cocked his head to the side and frowned. "What's changed?"

"Nothing, it's…" Ichi gave in and sat down. "You're going to die laughing at me."

"Most likely, if I must go it will be while laughing at you."

"When he has a nightmare, the only thing to be done to get him back to sleep is to let him sleep in bed with me," he confessed.

"Whoa, Ichi, you dog!" He didn't laugh, not quite.

"That's the problem. I'm fairly sure he isn't thinking about me in those terms but I'm not getting any sleep. He stays on the far side of the bed, but he doesn't need to touch me. I, god, Will, he smells sexy to me, I can't say no to him but it's driving me insane." He ran a hand across his hair and tried to show Will how serious he was.

"Why would you think he isn't interested in you sexually?" Will knew better, Rye may still be hiding a lot of what he was thinking or feeling, but every time he stared at Ichi, Will nearly blushed.

"Why should he? He needs a big brother or a father right now, not a lover. And, frankly, we've no way of knowing if he was gay before they made these modifications. What if he's naturally heterosexual? What if they altered his preferences when they amped up his libido?"

"And what if they didn't?"

"That's worse. I'm not a fool, I know what I am. I'm not in his league, that's for certain, and the only reason he's even looked twice at me is because they've programmed him to be gay and I'm the only option. I may not have much pride but I won't be a lover of last resort. Celibacy isn't going to kill me, maybe, if I can get Rye out of my bed." The words tumbled out, chasing each other to be aired.

"You're an absolute idiot. Rye doesn't need a father or a big brother, he needs someone to love him, which you do."

"I don't."

"Bullshit. And you're very cute, in a geeky way. I'm straight and I might consider it, if we were the only two folks on the station and I was drunk."

In spite of himself, Ichi found himself laughing.

"My point is there isn't any reason why he shouldn't be fond of you, and there's every reason why he should be sexually attracted to you. I can talk to Amanda about it but really, Rye is doing amazing in your care and he doesn't seem to take to change well."

Which was the truth, it had taken over a month to wean him of his crate and even then, when really upset, Ichi found Rye sitting in the clothes closet or in the shower stall. "He still feels safest in small spaces."

"And he might never change that. Just because we're pretty sure he's going to make a solid recovery doesn't mean he'll ever be back to what he was before they did this. He may always have oddities that he won't be able to shake."

"I just want him to be happy."

"Compared to what he was when he got here? You've done that."

"And the nightmares?"

Will shrugged. "A lot of folks have nightmares." The tone he used was wistful, distant while holding a stab of personal experience. "Sometimes talking about it helps, just keep trying." He grinned again and tossed and arm around Ichi's shoulders to guide him from the safe world of his lab. "I can get you some medication to turn off your sex drive if you want?"

"I'm not even going to dignify that with a witty come back."

Ichi took his normal place in the back along the wall and tried to pretend to be invisible. It was enough that Rye had a good time, and watching the happy smiles dart across his face or the rapt attention he paid the musicians made the night bearable. He'd have sent Rye on alone, but the redhead simply refused to stay if Ichi wasn't there. Like most weeks, as the night progressed Rye found his way over to sit near him. Tonight Ichi let him sit on the floor without scolding him and toward the end of the night Rye was leaning against his leg, his head tucked tight to Ichi's knee.

Rosie came tumbling over, breathless from dancing with Henry for most of the night, and stumbled to a stop. "Hey Rye, darling, how are ya tonight?"

"G..g….go… go..good, thanks," he forced out.

"Good! It's good of you to get this curmudgeon out of his lab occasionally." She smiled and winked at the redhead and ignored Ichi's slight frown. "And speaking of curmudgeons, you've a vid call Ichi. It's marked urgent so it popped up here." She nodded to the screen along the side wall.

The frown deepened. It had been months since his last call, his mother had briefly contacted him to let him know his youngest sister was now wed and the call had lasted all of a minute. He wasn't expecting a call, let alone a call marked urgent. "Thank you Rosie."

"Welcome." She nodded and squealed as Henry dragged her back out to dance.

He set his drink down and slid a hand across the red hair out of habit before standing up. Rye followed silently behind him but paused outside of the vid screen's camera range. It was something no one had shown him, Ichi was pretty sure of that, but he knew it. Another odd fragment of knowledge from Rye's other life, and one that was just as puzzling.

Ichi clicked the accept command and it took a moment for the call to complete. When it did his father appeared, wider in his face, skin less golden and eyes less almond shaped than Ichi's. The elder's hair was going white and he'd made no efforts to alter the fact, but his dark eyes were still sharp even if they held a look of exhaustion Ichi had never seen before.

"Father," Ichi said and bowed slightly.

"Son." But the elder frowned and glanced behind Ichi. "Are you at a party?"

Ichi glanced behind him to where the music was still playing and the occasional dancer must have swirled into focus. "No, not really, it's just a thing they do here."

"I thought you were working at a serious research station."

"I am father, I…" He drew a breath and reminded himself that he wasn't a child any longer. "It's just their way. Forgive me, I will find a quieter screen." He bowed again but before he could push the pause button Will popped up behind him.

Will ruffled Ichi's hair and grinned before turning behind him and shouting. "Knock it off you animals! It's Ichi's dad!"

That stopped the music and a dozen folk tumbled over to hang on Ichi and ruffle his hair. They jostled each other with all the life and exuberance of Avalon to get closest to Ichi, to drape over his shoulders. They took turns waving and shouting greetings of "Hello, Ichi's dad!" Some stuck their tongues out and winked, others held fingers behind Ichi's bowed and embarrassed head to give him horns.

Through it all, Ichi held still and blushed. Knowing how it would look to his father and knowing if he protested it would only encourage his station mates to be sillier. He gritted his teeth and saw his father's tolerance level dropping.

"I'm sorry, father, it's just their way. They mean no offense. What is it you wished to speak to me about?"

"Yeah, Ichi-dad, what's the news?" Anna laughed and the group took up the chorus of pleading, ending with Rosie sighing. "It's an arranged marriage! Ichi's to be wed off to some buxom blonde!"

That made him blush a brighter shade of red but he ignored them.

"Kenichi, it's my duty to inform you that your mother has been killed."

The laughter stopped and the hands nudging him and poking at him turned to soothing brushes and comforting weights. It didn't help the words sink in.

"I'm sorry, father, what?"

"She was collecting samples and her equipment failed. It was a fall of several hundred feet and it took the rescue team several hours to reach her, by then it was a recovery operation." The man spoke calmly, as controlled as ever. "There's no need to return home, her services were today. I know she wouldn't wish her death to disturb your work." The word work was a touch strained.

Ichi bowed again. "She was kind that way." The words came out on their own but he felt his pulse beating in his head. "Thank you for informing me of her passing directly, father."

"Of course, son." The father bowed again and the line cut off without a further word.

"Oh, Ichi," Amanda whispered and tried to wrap her arms around him.

Ichi pulled back and stepped from the group.

"We're all very sorry about your mother, Ichi," Mark added.

Ichi backed away a little more. He knew they were and doubted a one of them had a living parent, but their way wasn't his. It was Avalon custom that the community was family. When the occupation and virus had taken so many, this tradition had become even more important and a birth, wedding or death was felt by the group. They gathered around each other as their strength was in their numbers. It wasn't something Ichi could do.

He bowed slightly. "Excuse me," Ichi muttered before turning to hurry from the room. He was halfway back to his apartment before he even noticed that Rye hurried along behind him.

Once home he moved on autopilot and found the items he kept in storage. The small, low table that didn't suit the Avalon provided furniture came out and he set it along one wall. On it went the ceramic bowl, made by his grandmother's hands and filled with sand from his home. It took a little searching to find the picture he wanted, the one of his mother smiling for a publicity image taken while he was still a child. She rarely smiled and the sight of it lit up her pretty face and made her look warm and approachable. He set the image on the table and gathered rice and water in two matching bowls to place beside the sand. Before the plain wood table he unrolled a red satin carpet made of thousands of tiny, intricate knots, work he'd made himself as a teenager, as all his people did to prove they were ready and mature enough to set up their own household. A tradition he'd found silly and old fashioned and now was grateful for.

Out of a wood box he removed three sticks of incense and the lit them on the built in lighter. The sweet smoke flared and curled and filled his quiet rooms and Ichi balanced the sticks between his pressed palms as he knelt on the red knotted rug. The prayers that tumbled out were whispers, a comforting safe ritual she had taught him as a child. He bowed and repeated them, the incense smoke filling the room.

Behind him he heard his door open but didn't glance to see who was there. It was a small station, he could guess. Only it wasn't a single pair of feet but many, and a half dozen men and women entered with subdued respect. On the small table, Amanda placed a glass of dark Avalon brewed porter ale before stepping back. Will moved to the other side and set a bottle of Avalon whiskey and again disappeared behind where Ichi prayed. The room was silent, and for once it was an uncomfortable silence. He finished his current set of prayers and tucked the incense into the sand.

The living room was filled with comfortable faces and Rye had tucked himself against a wall, watching with wide, uncertain eyes. "I'm sorry, I didn't mean to ruin the night," Ichi apologized.

"Hush, you." Will shook his head and stepped forward. Without asking permission he wrapped strong arms around Ichi and pulled the dark head to his shoulder.

Ichi tried to protest and pull away but Will held on and at the gentle, comforting hand across the nape of his neck, he gave in. It wasn't his way but his way felt cold and lonely. In his throat, his breath hitched and didn't quite sob, but he let himself wrap his arms around Will's back and he clung to his friend, feeling small and young.

"Shh, it's alright," Will soothed and the group around him moved. Some made tea, and others moved furniture around to form a comfortable grouping and occasionally some came by where Ichi clung to Will and stroked his back or hair and whispered words of comfort. It was okay to let them see grief and pain because they were a people that had seen more pain in their short lifetimes than most people saw in three. They understood and he didn't need to say a word.

Eventually Ichi was sat on his sofa and tea was pressed into his hands. Around him were his friends and they made dinner and saw to it he ate. Not one of them offered pity or false sympathy, they just sat with him and expected nothing. It was in that emptiness away from all expectations that Ichi understood why they gathered together in times of joy and pain. The biting sting of the sudden news would have been sharp if he'd been alone, but with so many around him to cushion the shock, it merely ached.

Eventually, they said good night. At his door he was hugged and kissed and patted in comforting acceptance. Offers of comfort and care were exchanged and he was left to his privacy. The apartment felt heavy with the fragrant scent of the incense still in the air and Rye sitting tucked in a corner looking uncertain.

It was easier to think about Rye than his mother. "You okay?" he asked.

Rye nodded carefully.

"Do you understand what it means, when someone dies?" He still wasn't sure how strong of a grasp Rye had on more abstract ideas.

"Yes," Rye answered without a stutter. More often than not, when alone with Ichi in the safety of the apartment, he barely stuttered at all. It was only around other people that he grew fearful and uncomfortable and the stutter shook him up.

Ichi stood in the middle of his apartment. "Do you remember your mother, Rye?"

Rye just shook his head no but he climbed to his feet and padded softly over to the small table. He knelt on the red carpet and stared at the picture. "She looks li... li...like you."

"Technically, she was here first so I look like her." But the observation made Ichi smile softly. "We weren't very close." He moved to kneel beside Rye. "She had six children but left it to the nannies and tutors to raise us. Her research was what she lived for. She did her best, loved us as much as she was able." They were words he couldn't say to Will and the rest of the folks from Avalon but ones that came easily when he spoke to Rye.

Ichi bowed again but didn't want to think about his mother. "Rye, you had another owner before me, didn't you?" He asked the question he hadn't directly asked yet. It had been an ongoing hope that as Rye learned not only how to speak again, but that it was okay to speak, that he'd share some clues to his past.

Rye hadn't ever willingly volunteered a single scrap of information. The question made him pause and he considered it for a long moment. "Y...y...yes."

"He wasn't kind to you."

It wasn't a question, but Rye shook his head. "No, he wa...wa...wasn't."

"You know, I don't own you. No one does, you own yourself. You know that right?"

Rye shook his head no and lowered his eyes to the floor.

"You're not a pet, Rye, and you're not stupid or a child. You don't need a caretaker. No one here is going to turn you out. There are other sets of rooms, you're welcome to one."

"No." Rye shivered.

"You're going to have to eventually. You can't keep sleeping on my bedroom floor. You deserve your own life."

"I ha... have a life."

"You don't need me, Rye. You can take care of yourself and you've been able to for a while now."

"No."

"Of course you can, you're even learning to cook." The things that Rye knew how to do were random, and some very basic things like cooking even prepackaged foods were totally unknown to him.

"No. I d…d…do need you."

"No you don't. We both know it. It's okay to be scared about being on your own."

Rye shook his head but his hands balled up in fists. He struggled but no words were willing to come out and he swallowed hard hoping to dislodge them.

"Shh, it's okay."

"No!" Rye forced out. "It's not!" He wrestled with his own hidden wounds that felt deeper than mere brain damage. "I do need you. I be…be…be…be..belong to you."

Ichi shook his head. "No, you don't Rye, you don't belong to anyone. You just think you do. Maybe it's in the modifications they did. I'll ask Will and Amanda, but no matter what it feels like you're your own man."

"No!" His balled up fists lashed out and he hit his own thighs with enough force to bruise. "Not t…to, I be…be..belong with you," he corrected. "Please, Ichi." The red head bowed forward, hiding the emotions that Rye couldn't control. "Please, don't se…send me away."

"No one's saying you have to go away, just that you need to move on with your life."

"I am!" he snapped back defiantly.

"Rye, you had a life before this happened to you. A family, a home, a real name. Will and Amanda think it's been over a year since this was done to you, you must have family that misses you, is worried about you." He folded his hands in his lap. "I can only help you so much and I know you're holding back from me. On your own, with your own space, you'll have the room to find what's been lost, maybe." In some small part of Ichi's mind he knew he was trying to push Rye out because he couldn't handle mourning when someone else was around. Especially if that someone else could so easily knock his emotions off balance.

Rye was bent so far over his own knees his forehead nearly scraped the red carpet. Only it wasn't a bow of respect but one of internal struggle. His hands slid across the thousands of knots, scraping lightly. Inside, he felt twisted into as many knots, tied up and restrained and everything felt so close to coming unraveled. He just didn't know which thread to pull on to start the process.

"It fe...fe...fe...feels like a dr..dream," he forced out around a clenched jaw.

The painfully forced words startled Ichi. Rye barely spoke, even when they were alone in the lab or apartment, the redhead was silent more often than not. When he did speak, it was when spoken to first, and little more than what was necessary.

"What is?" Ichi asked carefully.

"Before." Rye sighed. "Before here." He rolled slightly and curled up on his side on the red carpet of knots.

"You remember it though. Do you remember who did this to you? Or where you're from, what your life was before?"

"No." He closed his eyes. "Some. Being co...cold. Always cold and pain." He shivered a bit. "Ichi, I ju..ju....just remembered th...that m...much a couple of da...days ago. Before? He would be...be...beat me. He'd le...le..le..le...let oth..others use me."

"Rye..."

"No!" He stopped Ichi. "No. Let me sp..speak."

"Okay, I'm sorry."

Rye sat up and didn't look away. "When he p..put me to be dis..dis..disposed of, he said it wa...was because he'd broke me. Like an an...an...animal, and now I was bor..boring. He was right. He only wa..wanted me to br..break me and he did. But I woke up here, with you. Ichi, I ne...need you. You're the only thing that ma...makes me happy, makes me hu...hu...human."

"You are human."

Rye shook his head in protest. "Please, I'll li..li..live as your pet if you don't send me a...away."

"I don't want a pet," Ichi hissed back, startled by the painfully confessed words. "I never did! But you have to understand Rye, I was drunk, when I filled in the specs for the doll. I was honest. You're so close to those specs, I could have custom made you. It's like you've stepped from inside my head and it's not just how you look. God, every day, every time you let yourself be a little more alive, I like what I see more. That's not fair, to either of us, because look how far you've come in a handful of months, you'll be twice as far in another six. You're going to find yourself and be whole and you're not going to want me and I can't do this." The words tumbled out, falling on each other with his unspoken fear of rejection and isolation. It was better to stay tucked away and forgotten than to risk and be so badly hurt.

Rye reached out and strong slender hands cupped either side of Ichi's face and held his head still. The gray eyes held a horrible intensity, a seriousness to his level of focus that Ichi had never noticed before. "What makes you think you haven't stepped from inside my head?" The words came out, flawlessly and with more strength than Rye had ever managed. "That f..first day, all I saw was you. I th..th..thought, prayed, please, let h..him be my owner and I blacked out and wo..wo..woke up and it was so."

The grip on Ichi's head lightened and the fingers took on a stroking touch. The thumbs traced his temples, the fingertips slid across his hair. "Rye…"

"Say I ca..can stay?"

He still wasn't sure if Rye was even capable of making such a choice, and he certainly couldn't swear that he hadn't been modified to bond or feel loyalty to his 'owner', but Ichi wanted to agree.

"On two conditions." He drew a breath and waited until Rye nodded. "You share with me what's in your head. The things giving you nightmares, Will says it might help ease them if you talk about it. If it's something you can't share with me, you'll tell him or Amanda or someone."

Rye shook his head and glanced down. "Only you."

"Doesn't have to be me, just talk to someone. It might help."

"The oth…other condi…dition?"

"You let me touch you." The longing in his voice surprised Ichi and he hurried to correct himself. "Not like that, not… I mean…" He felt himself blushing at the implications. "Just… touch; casual, human. You can stop it at any point, but avoiding contact isn't healthy. Just as friends, not more."

The hands slid from Ichi's face down to cradle lightly to either side of his neck. "Maybe more," Rye whispered.

The whisper made Ichi shiver and he scolded himself for getting hopeful. "So it's agreed?"

Rye smiled lightly and his head tilted to the side. Words hadn't stripped the man of his easily expressed body language. "On one condi..dition."

Ichi raised an eyebrow, but he reached up and took the slender hands between his own. "Name it."

"You won't se…send me aw..away for anything I might te..tell you."

He raised the hands up and kissed them, softly, before rubbing the side of his face against them. "Never."

It wasn't good enough and Rye lifted Ichi's chin to stare into his eyes. "Promise."

Ichi nodded. "Promise."

Rye sat and let the promise sink in, the way he imagined sunshine would sink into his skin but he couldn't remember ever feeling sunshine. "Sleep?" He asked when it was obvious Ichi wasn't going to move and equally obvious that the dark haired man was exhausted.

"Sure."

It was easy for Rye to glide to his feet, but Ichi felt old and stiff and moved with none of the redhead's grace. His body felt leaden and he moved about the nightly rituals of preparing for sleep without thought. His mother was dead, the idea was a cold fact and had no connection to emotion. Somewhere, Ichi knew he should be feeling more, or at least feeling something other than surprised shock, but it just wasn't there. The startled uncertain confession of Rye's trust and truths sat closer to the front of his mind and those were feelings he'd rather think about.

In the bedroom, Rye lifted the stack of blankets from the bottom of the bed. Sleeping on the sofa wasn't restful, and with the crate gone all he'd wanted was to fall asleep hearing Ichi breath, and occasional snore. He'd taken to sneaking the blankets into the bedroom and sleeping on the floor and trying to wake early enough to sneak back out. After Ichi caught him the third time, they no longer pretended that Rye was sleeping on the sofa.

In a timid voice, Ichi had offered to share the bed or have a smaller cot brought in but Rye hadn't wanted that. He was just as comfortable on the floor and it seemed to make Ichi more comfortable to have him outside of the wide--but not nearly wide enough--bed. It was only on the occasions after really bad nightmares that Rye accepted the offer and crawled in under the heavy covers. They smelled like Ichi and, while he slept across the bed from the other man, he could feel his warmth. It was the only thing that soothed his mind after the dark images.

Tonight would be different. Tonight, Rye was pretty sure Ichi needed him to sleep in the bed for comfort. The confessed words had been almost physically painful to force out, but they'd won him security and a place in the quiet, thoughtful man's life. It wasn't something he was going to let slip by and he knew Ichi was too tangled inside his own head to ever ask.

He watched as Ichi yawned and slipped into the bathroom to change. His modesty made Rye smile softly while he stripped off his own clothes and slid on the soft flannel pants that were so blessedly comfortable to sleep in. His fingers slid across the shirt he normally wore to bed and rejected the item. Promises were made on both their parts and he was going to have to get used to being touched sooner or later. The smile at Ichi's modesty became softly self-mocking, he just wanted a chance for Ichi to brush against him in their sleep. The touch scared him silly but set his nerves on fire and made him feel whole at the same time. It was a conflict he wasn't sure how to resolve.

Chapter Ten

Ichi was yawning as he left the bathroom only to find Rye sitting on the far side of the bed, shirtless and not looking in any rush to put the shirt he was gently touching on his body. It was one of the things he'd noticed, the other man had a tendency to touch things, to simply trace textures and fabrics with his hands, absorbing the feel.

"Sleeping in the bed tonight, huh?" He tried to make the words sound light but his heart sunk. He was so tired and just wanted to be left alone.

Rye nodded and refolded the shirt.

Ichi could feel his shoulders tensing up in nerves, but he nodded and dimmed the lights down to near darkness before sliding into his side of the bed. "Good night, Rye." The covers were cool along his skin and it made him shiver a little. The bed moved beside him and fabric rustled against fabric. Warm fingers brushed across his shoulder in the dim light.

"Ichi?"

"Yes?" He kept his eyes closed, not wanting to see or feel or think anymore then he had to.

"I…" but the words caught and refused to move. Rye had learned to hate that shorted-out, disconnected feeling when he knew what he wanted say inside his head but couldn't make his body give it voice. He struggled for a moment and when he knew nothing was going to shake loose he gave up. It was easier to just pick up Ichi's arm and slide in under it.

"What?" Ichi questioned until Rye pillowed his head on his chest and let the lifted arm fall to drape across bare shoulders.

The touch of Ichi's hand along his shoulders made Rye shiver but the sound of the startled and too fast heartbeat below his ear helped chase away the fear. It felt good, right, to curl up so close to Ichi, to let their warmth intermingle, and Rye knew this was better than anything he'd ever had, ever. He closed his eyes and struggled to reclaim his words.

Rye settled in against his chest like he'd been doing it for a lifetime and Ichi shivered. The head pillowed on his chest was a comforting weight, but the skin his fingertips brushed was too silken over too perfect of a body. Ichi tried to tell his body he was too tired to think about sex, no matter how good Rye smelled or how nice it was to touch him.

"Ichi?"

Ichi had to clear his throat a little before he could answer. "Yes?"

"I'm ready."

He made the choice to be especially dense. "Well, I won't make a very good pillow. So if you're ready to sleep you should slide over."

"No," Rye whispered and found if he listened to the heartbeat below his ear and didn't think too much about it, the words almost slid out normally. "You said, when I was ready, we'd figure this out. I'm ready."

Ichi's mouth went dry. "Maybe I'm the one who's scared now?" He whispered into the darkness. He wasn't sure he could morally have wild, sweaty sex on the night he learned his mother had been killed. He'd never heard anyone say it was specifically disrespectful, it just felt like it should be.

"That would make us a pa...pair. I'm still scared too." It amazed him that Ichi's heart could be pounding so quickly but his voice could be so steady. Too often, Rye felt that every emotion he had slipped to his voice and face and he had no control. He wondered how Ichi was able to hold so tightly to his.

"What're you scared of, Rye? We don't ever have to do more than this," he forced out but found his hand gently stroking the bare shoulder, tracing the contours of arm, muscle and bone.

"I... I'm afraid wh...when you touch me."

Ichi frowned a little. There was a touch too much stress placed on the fact that the fear was when it was Ichi doing the touching. "But not when, say, Will or Amanda touches you?"

"No."

"Are you afraid I'll hurt you? I promise you Rye, I'll do everything I can to never hurt you. I'm not like the other man was, before."

Rye shook his head as much as he could while keeping it tightly pressed to Ichi's chest. "I know. I know you wou...wouldn't hurt me. I'm not afraid of be...being hurt. Even before, I wa...wa...was never afraid, just si..si...si...sickened."

Which was a statement that simply broke Ichi's heart. "Tell me what you're afraid of Rye, and I'll do anything I can to fix it."

"I'm af...af...af..afrai...afraid of you." The words came out and he squinted his eyes shut, frustrated and desperate to get things right.

"Of me? Why?" It was like being punched in the stomach and Ichi wasn't sure how to process the knowledge that Rye was fearful of him.

"No! No... I... damn it." Rye sighed and the hand on his shoulder moved higher to slide across his hair. It made him shiver a little but he felt his tension easing a little at the only touch that always made him feel better.

"It's okay."

"No, it's not! I'm af...afraid for you, n...not of, for."

"For me?" That made little sense but fear didn't have to be rational. "Why?

"I d..don't know. Just, I feel si..sick thinking if you tou..touch me, something bad will ha..happen to you."

"Nothing bad is going to happen to me," Ichi soothed and the steady slide of his hand across the thick, soft hair was comforting. "Did something bad happen to another lover of yours?" His heart skipped a little at almost counting himself as one of Rye's lovers.

"I do..don't kn..know." Rye leaned his head into the slow motions of the hand in his hair. "I ke...keep dreaming about blood. Seeing yo..you in a pool of blood."

"Is that what woke you up so badly last night?" Last night had been rough, Rye had been screaming and incoherent. Even once the lights had gone on he'd sat wide eyed and frightened, unable to shake off whatever dream images had so terrorized him.

Rye just shook his head. "Last night... was maggots."

"Maggots?"

"I ha...had a wound and it itched. So I we...went to see and the wo..wound opened and in..inside was a long wo...wo...worm. White, flat but n..not, tipped li..like a spear. I pulled it out and it wa..was soft. But another worked it's wa..way to the top of the wound from in..in..inside. I kept pulling them out and then there wa..was other wounds and more wo..worms and they we..were eating me from inside ou..out."

Ichi stilled and didn't think telling Rye that there was actually a maggot that did that would help him sleep any. "That was a doozy of a dream."

"It felt re..real."

"Well, it was just a dream and I promise you, nothing bad is going to happen to me if we touch. We're on a very small, very secure station. The only person who comes and goes normally is Jos Harvick with his ship, so it's not like anyone can even happen by here. They made us out of the way for a reason." He sighed and pushed his thoughts about Gorpahn worm life cycles from his mind. "We're on a very secure station."

Rye lay silent and still as he let Ichi's words settle into the stillness of the night. He understood, logically, that what he said was true, but it would take touching and being touched to prove his fears wrong. When he was certain he was up to the task, he slid his arms out and draped them against Ichi. "I'm sleeping like th..this," he sighed.

⌒⌒⌒⌒

Ichi had assumed he'd lay awake as he always did when Rye was in the bed beside him. It was different this time, this time there was none of the heavy weight of touch and not touching, this time Ichi was bone weary and the warmth of the body along his own was soul deep comforting. He was asleep before he had the time to worry about not sleeping.

He awoke nearly twenty minutes before his alarm was due to go off. Only he was rested, warm and safely tucked in someone's arms. In his bleary half-sleep he couldn't figure out who was holding him. Andrew was a cuddler but Andrew was gone, Ichi had grown too old for his tastes. When it all returned his breath caught. His mother was dead, Rye was letting him in, and the safe, warm feeling was because the legs wrapped around his own were a pair belonging to a certain redhead.

His slight start of surprise jostled Rye where he was wrapped around Ichi's back. He muttered in his sleep and nuzzled against Ichi's hair before the strong arms pulled Ichi tighter to him. It made Ichi feel rather like a full-sized stuffed animal, but it left him feeling warm and happy. Too happy to get out of a warm, snuggly bed twenty minutes before he had to. He sighed and took one of Rye's hands in his own and figured it wouldn't do any harm to just lay there and enjoy the moment.

The next he knew, he was hazily waking up. The angle he was sleeping in blocked the view of the clock but he could tell by how rested he was, how slowly he was waking up and just an internal sense that it was late. Ichi startled upright a little, or rather he tried to but hands caught his shoulders and pulled him back down.

Ichi blinked in sleepy, half-awake uncertainty and found his head again pillowed on Rye's shoulder. The scent of the redhead was everywhere but it was the feel of those arms around him, of the soft breath tickling the top of his head that made him blush. A hand stroked over his cloth covered shoulder and Ichi's eyes focused across Rye's chest and caught on the sparkle of the gold nipple ring.

"What time is it?" he asked around a yawn.

"Late," Rye whispered back and dared to stroke a hand across the sleepy body again.

"The alarm?"

"I tu…turned it off."

"What?" He tried to sit up and instead, somehow, Rye managed to get them turned. Ichi found himself on his side with Rye wrapped around him again. "Oh," he sighed and involuntarily wiggled a little to get tighter to the other body. "Why?"

"We bo…both slept too we..well to get up." Rye sighed and reminded his fluttery brain that the station was very secure and nothing bad was going to happen to Ichi.

"What time is it?"

"Late."

"But, what time?"

Rye shrugged. "Don't kn…know."

"The clocks right there, don't wanna get up to see. Just look for me?"

"Can't."

"Hmm?" He pushed himself out of the warm arms to glance at the clock; he'd overslept nearly three hours. "Really late, Mother would find this unforgivable. Lazing in bed instead of working, especially on the morning after her death." He flopped back down and let Rye gather him close again.

"She's de..dead, she doesn't get to dis…dis…disapprove."

"True." He nodded at the logic of words that should have felt insensitive but were oddly comforting instead. Ichi yawned again and something rattled in his sleepy mind. "What do you mean 'can't'?"

"Can't." Rye shrugged. "Can't remem…remember how."

Ichi squirmed and wiggled until he was turned to look up at Rye and saw no embarrassment at the confession. "I'm sorry."

"For?"

That was a good question. "For not knowing?"

Rye grinned and leaned forward. He pressed a kiss to the crinkled up forehead. "You're adorable," he whispered and felt himself pulling Ichi closer so the man couldn't see the raw vulnerability the confession exposed in him. He hated it, some things he couldn't force out of his head with all his will, and other things, like his most recent comment, just blurted out.

Ichi felt his face grow hot and he wanted to protest. Only, as he opened his mouth, what came out wasn't a protest. "We'll teach you." The arms tightened around him. "Isn't right, being around so many researchers and not relearning." It was inconceivable that Rye hadn't known how to read before he'd been taken and made into a pet.

Rye hadn't given it any thought. "If you wa…want to." But if Ichi felt it was important, he'd do his best to learn.

"I do, but first, got to get to work." He sighed and reluctantly pulled from Rye's arms. The room felt cold and the other side of the bed empty without that warmth near him. "Oatmeal today?" He asked as he slowly started his day.

Rye just nodded and sat up to watch Ichi scratch and yawn and shake off sleep. Getting a few extra hours of sound sleep had the brunette more awake than normal but it was still amusing to watch him stumble around. Rye was never like that; when he was awake, he was fully awake instantly.

"Ichi, Ichi, what are you doing?" he asked his reflection, which didn't provide any answers. "Moron." He just shook his head and got the water going in the shower. As he stripped off his clothes he caught a hint of Rye on them and it made him shiver. "Idiot."

The water did a lot to shake off the last of the night's cobwebs and he shook his head to clear it of improper thoughts and random water drops both. He slid his hand across the dispenser and caught the shampoo. For all the hassle, nothing could beat a real water shower. The lather was thick and dropped in foamy chunks down to his shoulders.

Which meant that when a blast of cooler air hit his back his eyes were squinted shut and Ichi couldn't see to shut the shower stall door. The latch had been loose lately and he'd kept forgetting to ask Mark to fix it. He shivered and groped behind him to get it shut by feel. His hand slid along warm flesh and the door shut on its own.

"What?" But his fingers slid across a strong side and Ichi knew. "Rye?"

Rye was silent, frightened just the smallest bit, but excited. The need to see Ichi undressed had been consuming, the desire to touch him even stronger. He'd been lucky so far and never been caught, but every morning Rye snuck into the bathroom and lurked there, listening. Ichi would sigh in contented pleasure when the water would hit him and then the tiny, hitching sobs of desire would drift out among the sounds of the water. Rye couldn't start his day without that, he'd sit near the floor and listen, touching himself in time as Ichi sought his own pleasure. He always finished first, touch was so much stronger now, harder to stop or back down, and Rye would find himself leaning against the bathroom wall trying not to moan or pant, focused on the stifled sounds from the shower.

It was a better way to wake up than coffee and, while empty, was at least better than nothing. Rye would sit and listen to Ichi finish and then linger longer to watch how the shorter man hurried to wash off afterwards. As if soap could remove the fact that for a few moments he'd been human with human wants and needs. Each morning Rye promised himself he would wait and when Ichi came out of the shower he'd be bold enough to repeat what he'd done to Ichi that night on the sofa. Each morning as Ichi grew closer to finishing his shower, Rye would quietly leave. He'd rather be lonely and horny than risk angering Ichi and being driven away.

Today was different. Today Rye couldn't stand to hear those quiet, muffled sounds or to find his own solitary release. He'd waited just long enough for Ichi to hit the water and had planned to surprise him in the act, but Ichi surprised him. Instead, today, Ichi went right to washing and Rye stepped naked into the tiny shower and found Ichi soapy.

Ichi wasn't as toned as Rye found his own body to be, but the smaller man had nice tone to his arms and chest and his legs were sleek and long. He'd known that Ichi met Will a couple of time a week to play Hold Ball and he'd watched the friends once. Only, the sight of Ichi sweaty, panting and being competitive, had left him in a dire state and he hadn't risked watching one of their matches again. He was really worried that if he did he'd drag Ichi back home just to toss him into bed.

It didn't matter that the muscles along Ichi's stomach weren't sharply defined, or most of his body for that matter. He was lean and lovely to look at and Rye drank in the sight of so much of the haunting golden skin. The hand groped out behind him and Rye let the probing fingers slide past his waist.

"Rye?" Ichi tried to remove his hand to wipe at the suds that had slipped down to his eyes but Rye caught his hand.

"I can't," Rye whispered barely louder than the water.

Ichi ducked his head under the spray. "Can't?" He was afraid to open his eyes, afraid to turn around and find his mind was being a touch too vivid this morning.

"I can't st...stand it," he whispered again, knowing he wasn't making any sense but so hard from just looking at Ichi naked that he was ready to beg for release. He stepped forward and stood just a hair's breath from touching Ichi. The tip of his cock just barely brushed across the side of Ichi's hip and he trembled.

It was ironic, the first time in a long time Ichi had found himself not hard in the morning and Rye managed to make him almost trembling with aching need with only a few whispered words. He felt more than heard Rye move closer but it was only for that single, sharp contact. Suddenly, Ichi found he couldn't stand it anymore either. He didn't care what Rye did, didn't care that he couldn't touch the other man yet, he needed something.

Ichi stepped those last inches back and pressed his back full along Rye's chest. He kept his eyes shut. "Please." He whispered.

It was enough. Rye reached out and pulled Ichi impossibly tighter against him. It was a repeat of how he'd pinned Ichi in the kitchen, and he attacked the shorter man's neck just as ruthlessly. He needed both arms to hold Ichi still, the instant his mouth fell to the slender neck Ichi was squirming. One of his mindless writhing motions twisted Ichi so his ass pressed fully against Rye's hips and it poured burning desire across both men.

"Oh!" Ichi cried out at the delicious feel of bareness against bareness and pressed back against Rye mindlessly. He stumbled a little and braced his hands against the shower walls. "Please, oh, please," he sighed.

Rye managed to reach a hand over and the shampoo was slick on his fingers. He wanted more, wanted everything that Ichi seemed to be offering, but it was too much, too soon. The soap made them slippery and Rye slid himself along Ichi's body, teasing them both. Each time the slow thrusts he allowed himself against the golden flesh slid across Ichi's entrance, or lower to tease between his legs, Ichi bucked and moaned.

It was too much. Rye closed his eyes and still he saw the way Ichi's hands clawed at the walls and the drip of steamy water from the dark tips of his wet hair. Silently, he lost control and pulled Ichi's hips tight to his own and spilled himself against the roundness of Ichi's ass.

"Oh, oh, Ichi," he sighed, trembling, into the ear he'd been nibbling on.

Something far more scalding than merely hot water spilled against Ichi's flesh and he shivered. Part of him was brokenly disappointed at not having been taken, but part of him was grateful. When--and it was when now, and not if--when they actually became lovers, Ichi didn't want it to be over the kitchen counter or in the shower. He wanted to be able to watch those eyes and spend hours, days falling apart into trembling pieces.

Rye's sighing breath of his name tickled his ear and made him arch backwards. He was lightheaded, which made sense since all of his blood seemed to have rushed to his groin and again Ichi found his flesh a foreign place to be. Whenever Rye touched him he felt sensual, felt sexy, he felt like need.

There was only a moment's pause between the scalding touch of Rye's shuddering release before one hand on Ichi's waist moved. He braced himself, expecting it to move lower and was surprised when those teasing fingers ghosted across his stomach. The touch was fluttering, and made Ichi writhe under it.

"Oh!" He gasped, surprised, when he arched back and found hardness instead of softness. "Oh, god."

Rye chuckled lightly. "Not done wi..with you yet." He whispered. "I ne..need you so much." He let his hands slide across the chest but Ichi nearly arched from his grasp when he slid the tips of his fingers across one nipple.

It was too much, the delicious length tormenting him with promises not yet fulfilled, the mouth on his neck that nipped and suckled, the hands across his body making his skin shiver--it was all too much. Ichi was as surprised by his reaction to the gentle touch to his nipples as Rye was, he'd never liked them touched before but something about Rye's careful contact was almost as thrilling as if he'd touched lower.

And when he thought he might have to beg for those teasing hands to touch him more, Rye took pity on him and lower his hands went. Ichi fell against the shower wall, clinging to it, his knees shaking too much to hold him upright on their own as Rye touched him. Only, when he fell forward even those few inches, it pried their bodies apart and he struggled for the words to ask for the tormenting contact he'd nearly been ready to curse at to be returned.

"So beautiful," Rye sighed and drank in the sight of Ichi lost to pleasure. He wanted him and Rye found himself sliding Ichi's legs further apart, pulling his hips back away from the shower wall. There was no doubt that Ichi would let him and it would be so easy, but that would just be sex and need and Rye craved more. That didn't mean he wouldn't unravel the man as much as he could.

"Oh, god!" Ichi nearly screamed and half stumbled to move toward or away from the single, slender finger that slid into his body. It was enough, the touch, the feel, the hand knowing just how to stroke him and that single, teasing finger. Ichi came with blinding force. His ears rang with the sound of his pulse and he missed his own desperate moans. His legs crumbled and it was only Rye's arm around his waist that held him upright. He was shuddering, lost in sex that was better than anything he'd ever felt, and they'd barely started. As his vision focused, he saw the last of his release wash away.

His breath was still burning in his throat and Ichi knew it was because he'd been trying too hard to hide just how turned on he was. The wall was cool under his hands but Rye's hand was still hot against his waist, only there was one hand now and from the gentle rocking motion transmitted along the soft contact, Ichi knew why. There was a sudden start of fear that if he moved or reacted the redhead would spook again, and Ichi had no desire to ruin pleasure for Rye. As he caught his breath, and his sense, Ichi squashed that fear.

"Rye," he whispered and turned in the light grasp he was held in. Ichi hadn't been sure just what he was going to do. He knew what he wanted to do but he wasn't sure Rye was ready yet to have the intimacy of a good, old fashioned blow job. It didn't matter, the sight of Rye hard, his eyes fluttering between open and shut in a losing effort to keep watching, his face flushed with desire, caused all logical thought to melt in Ichi's mind.

Rye gasped at being able to see Ichi's face and he fell into those eyes. There was something with Ichi's eyes that he simply adored, or maybe it was the shape of his mouth or maybe the way he tilted his head when thinking, or trying to anyway. It didn't matter, seeing the golden width of Ichi's back, the round curve of his ass had been delicious; seeing his face, his chest, pulled whimpering moans from his throat. He struggled to keep his eyes open, but they kept fluttering shut and he desperately clung to the need to make this moment last.

So his eyes were shut when Ichi's hands slid across his neck and up to his jawline but they sprang open when the shorter man's mouth found his own. He moaned into the kiss and let Ichi plunder his mouth, let the surprising dominance control him. It felt safer to be in control, to be the one pushing Ichi's limits, but having the normally reserved scientist nearly pounce on him was better.

He stumbled back, his hand faltering and release no longer the top most concern in his mind. The wall offered support and the shock of a cold touch to his shoulders, but he pulled Ichi along with him. The fear was starting to rise, a small screaming voice that was growing louder. It shouted at him to run, that if he had a single bit of affection for Ichi they'd stop before it happened again. Rye groped after what it was and found nothing but blankness. It wasn't something horrible to his person, but it would leave Ichi in a pool of blood.

"Shhh," Ichi whispered, breaking the kiss and seeing fear in the steady face. He let his hands slide across strong shoulders. "Nothing bad is going to happen, I promise, nothing at all." It was difficult to think in comforting terms when he wanted to bite the strong chest and bring back the gasping moans of a moment before to the redhead.

Rye shivered at the voice and bit his lip. He wanted to believe, but it wasn't simple, belief wasn't enough. His eyes popped open and he caught Ichi's and held his gaze. "I will die before I let anyone hurt you." The words came out easily, strong and with a voice that had a power he hadn't known before.

The intensity made Ichi shiver too, but he nodded at the solemn words that held the weight of a vow. "So let me…" He glanced down and trailed a hand across Rye's chest, swirling over the un-pierced nipple.

Pleasure exploded in Rye, his head cracked back against the wall and his voice disappeared. There was no room for thought or fear or anything but Ichi and the pleasure he was able to control. The voice that had spoken with such strength scoffed at him and mocked him for the whore they'd made him into, but he didn't care. It reminded him of how so very recently, people no where near as kind as Ichi had played his body's sensitivity against him and left him begging, moaning, needing pleasure and pain and wanting more. Rye didn't care.

On his neck, Ichi licked and nipped, tasting shoulder and collarbone, but it was when the uncertain hand found the piercing that Rye nearly collapsed. He hated it, hated the reminder of it, the pain it often caused, but he loved the way the smallest touch to the metal, the merest tug, created a pleasure beyond his words to express. The hand that had been carefully exploring where flesh and metal joined paused.

"I didn't mean to hurt you," Ichi apologized.

"Huh?" Rye gasped out and struggled to open his eyes. His breath was short and at every touch his cock twitched but he refused to touch it, liking the painful pleasure of need.

"This." Ichi touched the speared nipple gently again. "We can take it out."

Black spots exploded in Rye's vision and this time he heard the tormented moaning the small touch dragged from him. It did sound a lot like pain. "Oh.. N…no. Feels t…too good."

"Really?" Ichi questioned and tugged a little harder on the faceted gold.

Rye slid a half a foot down the wall before he caught himself. "God… ye..yes." He was able to come just from having that gold bar tormented and he was dancing along that edge now. "St..stop or I'll come," he warned and tried to get his legs to push him back upright.

Seeing Rye so lost in lust and need was almost enough to get Ichi hard again. His desire for days of lovemaking might not be such a fantasy and he smiled softly, wondering if Rye really could find release just from having his nipples tormented. One day Ichi was going to find out, but right now he wanted to watch Rye come. Right now, he wanted to be the one to make him come.

"So," Ichi sighed near one of Rye's ears, "Come already." He wrapped his hand around the ignored, begging, still soap-slicked cock and very gently stroked it. Ichi was learning what one aspect of double terminated nerve endings meant and guessed that too rough or demanding of a touch when Rye was already so excited would bring pain, not pleasure.

There was no shame in Rye and none of the lingering fear was strong enough to override the raw bliss of that hand touching him. Ichi knew and was gentle and it was perfect. It was better than any fantasy, any hidden thought or longing, any dream of what it would be like to have Ichi touch him and Rye moaned and struggled to open his eyes.

When he did, the sight was too much. Ichi wet, sated, with a happy, freshly-fucked look just from their mild playing, his hand wrapped around Rye's swollen length. It melted something in Rye's mind and for a long moment he forgot how to breathe. Legs moved to stand between his, golden around pale, thigh rubbed to thigh and Rye lost it.

His eyes were closed so he couldn't swear his vision went black, but he was light-headed enough that Rye felt he might have blacked out, if just for a moment. The only thing holding him up was the cool wall behind him and the thigh between his legs. Even his clenching grip on Ichi's arms was useless and Rye gave into shuddering, moaning release.

He was shivering, cold and spent under the hot water. Rye pried his eyes open and glanced down to the hand still lightly petting him, not even stroking him, just lightly touching his softening length. His release painted across Ichi's stomach and the dark haired man had a wicked, almost naughty look to his eyes.

Rye caught the hand still teasing him, knowing if he didn't stop the touch he'd be hard again and if he got hard again, all bets were off. He wasn't sure he could resist dragging Ichi from the shower, carrying him over a shoulder to the bed and dropping them on the covers while sopping wet. There, he'd fuck the shorter man silly, and that was a thought that he didn't need at the moment.

One of Rye's hands reached out and smeared the hot sticky release across Ichi's stomach. "You like this." It was a statement, but seeing his release, his mark on the other man made him want to lick it off. Rye dragged his thoughts back into line.

Ichi blushed, hoping that Rye wouldn't notice how he'd nearly pressed his body against the redheads in an effort to feel his climax. "Yes, I do." He'd always liked to feel his lover come in any way he could.

The embarrassed confession made Rye lick his lips and he let his eyes shut for a moment. "I kn..know I never did an…anything good enough to deserve some…some…someone like you."

"I doubt that." Ichi protested, but his mouth was stopped with a quickly stolen kiss.

"Sh..shut up." Rye shook water from his hair and forced his legs to work. He snagged Ichi's washcloth from its hanger and ran it over the soap dispenser. It lathered up easily and he quickly and thoroughly scrubbed his lover's body, which was amusing because the cloth drew startled, tiny gasps, even on normally less sensitive parts.

"I can wash myself," Ichi protested and blushed further.

Rye didn't even try to counter the protest, just continued the gentle washing. When he'd soaped Ichi from head to toe he hung the cloth back up and gently cupped water in his hands to help it slide off the suds. When his lover was clean and rinsed, Rye swooped in to put a quick kiss to the tip of Ichi's nose before wrangling him to the back of the small stall and moving to take over the hot water for himself.

Ichi stood a little baffled and overwhelmed and had to push his mind into working again. When it kicked in, he understood he was standing there, ogling a naked Rye. He blushed deeper shades.

"I'm going to…" 'Beg you to fuck me silly,' his mind filled in. "I'm going to go get dressed."

"O..okay." Rye nodded and glanced over his shoulder.

Ichi took the chance to escape and quickly stumbled from the shower. He snagged a towel as he went past and wrapped it around his waist before staggering into the bedroom. At first he sat on the edge of his bed but soon he collapsed down across it.

"Oh, god." He rubbed a hand over his eyes. "I just had the best sex of my life and he barely touched me. Ichi, Ichi, Ichi, what are you doing?"

Chapter Eleven

It felt a touch surreal to go from something that felt so far from his day to day life to fussing about grabbing a quiet bit of lunch before leaving the apartment. He couldn't rightly call it breakfast so late in the morning. Rye dressed and ate whatever was put before him, and while he no longer gave into the small, happy sounds of delight at real food, Ichi still would catch the other man's eyes sliding half closed as each bite brought pleasure. It made him more aware of his own daily life and the little things he just accepted, even if this morning the sight of the redhead made him want to blush.

The bottom line was Ichi had little real experience with what happened after a sexual encounter. What did normal people discuss over breakfast later? How were they supposed to react? His few encounters were limited, a fumbling lover in college, his tutor as a teenager and Andrew. The fellow in college had been a one-time thing at the only party he'd ever gone to, his tutor kept their sexual life and the educational life very separate and easily switched them from one to the other leaving Ichi free from having to worry about it. And Andrew? Well, he rarely spent the entire night with Andrew, and when he did the easier-tempered man would tease him. He'd laugh with no malice and tease Ichi about being as emotional as one of his insects when it came to pillow talk. Sad thing was, Ichi was more comfortable with Andrew thinking him cold rather than have him know just how socially clueless he really was.

Rye saved him by not making a big deal of it. Ichi took the cue and went about their morning as they always did and slowly some of the skittish uncertainty faded. It was in his patterns and routine that he found comfort and sense. Ichi clutched at the distance the order gave him, needed it to keep from melting into a puddle of nerves and lust. He would process everything, he just he needed time to do it in.

When they were done eating in their normal companionable silence, Rye dropped the plates and glasses into the washer while Ichi went to make the bed. It was normal, something so mind blowing had occurred and yet life went on as normal. Before he left he placed fresh water and rice on the small table by his mother's photo and bowed respectfully. Seeing her face made him blush a little, certain she wouldn't have approved of the extravagance of the morning.

Everything was just as it always was except, when Ichi left, Rye paused outside of the apartment. He turned, but the redhead looked thoughtful and more than a little distant.

"What's wrong?"

"I…" He glanced down the hallway they didn't normally take. "It's ju..just…" He drew a slow breath and tried to find words to put his desire into.

Ichi shook his head. He wasn't sure what it was that Rye was trying to ask but he suspected. "Go on, do what you have to do. You know where I'll be, it's about time you've gone off and had some time to yourself. Just be careful exploring around, a lot of the station is walkways, ladders and crawlspaces." He smiled gently. "Be back before dinner so I don't worry, okay?"

Rye nodded, grateful that he didn't have to try to explain his motives or thoughts. "O..okay." But before he left, he leaned forward and kissed Ichi lightly on the mouth and left him standing in the hallway startled and blushing.

It took him a long moment to stop standing in the hallway like an idiot, but with Rye off exploring or thinking or whatever it was he'd wanted to do it gave Ichi the freedom to go straight to Will and Amanda's lab. Only, when he got there, he found only Will inside.

"Morning," he broke into the softly playing music.

"Hey," Will sat up from where he was taking notes. "How are you?"

Ichi shrugged. "I'm fine. Where's Amanda?"

"Hen gathering," he answered, as if it explained everything.

"I'm sorry?"

"Oh, the women are getting together this morning. They do occasionally, every month or so, and spend the morning gossiping about us men folks. I'm sure you'll be top of the list, something about making sure someone comes by to make dinner or something. Thought you'd like the heads up." There was something different about Ichi this morning and it wasn't something bad. Will tilted his head a little and tried to sort it out, but it wasn't until he caught sight of the small bruises on the side of Ichi's neck that he understood. Grief did different things to different people, and if it had made Ichi horny enough to finally let Rye pounce, all the better.

"Thank you." He glanced around the lab. "I was wondering, you have some samples of Rye's blood on file, yes?"

"A couple, Amanda would like to study him more but I talked her into waiting until he's more comfortable. Where is he anyway?" It was unusual to see one of the pair without the other.

"He wanted to go off exploring a bit, needed time to think." He prayed he wouldn't blush and for once, he didn't. "If I send you an antibody protein, can you see if he has it in his bloodstream?"

"Sure, I take it this is to be kept quiet?"

Ichi nodded. "I don't want Rye to know, not yet, anyway. How long will it take?"

Will shrugged. "Not long, I'll page you when I'm done."

"Thanks." He nodded his head and disappeared out of the lab to make his way to his own.

For a change, Will behaved. He actually waited until the door was shut to start a chorus of 'somebody got laid' in a sing-song, childishly teasing voice.

❦

An hour later Will showed up in Ichi's lab and, in spite of the man's frown, he was a welcome distraction. The hour had been spent in thoughts that found no logical direction and Ichi was ready for any distraction. "Hello Will," he greeted before the man was even past his doors, disgustingly grateful for the interruption.

"What the hell is going on here, Ichi?" Will blurted out as soon as he'd glanced to the side and found the cushion and blanket Rye refused to surrender empty.

"Pardon me?"

"That protein, what's going on? And here, before any of the women see." He dropped a couple of small patches onto the desk beside Ichi.

Which made Ichi frown at the small films for bruises and felt like maybe he'd fallen asleep and this was a dream because nothing was making sense. "What?"

Will flicked a finger out to poke at the hickeys on Ichi's neck. "I'll assume they're from Rye and you weren't attacked by a vampire last night." He laughed as Ichi's eyes went wide and he hurried to find a mirror.

"Oh." Ichi blinked in startled surprise and frowned at the suck marks on his neck. He'd never had a hickey before, ever, let alone three at once. "Oh."

Will laughed harder and peeled the paper from the films. "Did you have fun?" he asked as he poked the sticky side to the small bruise.

Ichi was still fumbling, trying to recall when he might have gotten a hickey, and than he remembered how Rye had been suckling and nipping at his neck, how good it had felt. He'd always thought hickeys were supposed to hurt. "We didn't…"

That just made Will snort. "I'm your best friend, and those are impressive suck marks."

He flinched a little from the cool sticky film Will pressed over the last of the marks. "This will fix it?"

"In about a half hour with your skin tone. Now, out with it, did you have fun?"

"Will…"

"Look, I'll bug ya later. What's up with this protein?"

"You found it?"

"And how. How'd you know to look for it? I mean Gorpahn worm antibodies aren't common outside of Bentick Four. That's a pretty random thing to have me check for."

"Will…" Ichi sat back down and waited until his friend had settled in beside him. "Rye and I, we talked a lot last night. We came to an agreement, and part of it is that he has to start telling someone more of what's in his head."

"Wise, indeed, sage advice."

Ichi frowned. "I asked him about the nightmares, he told me about one and he described exactly the manifestation of a Gorpahn worm infection."

"Do I even want to know how you know so much about such creepy worms?"

"I did a paper on them when I was fourteen. It was juvenile and a touch sensational, but I put a lot of work into the research."

"Of course," he nodded and only half-teased.

"So you found the antibodies?"

"Yeah but here, look." He punched up the protein code. "See this here? This is the actual useful code, this is the antibody, but this down here? It's junk. Development companies fill this in like a fingerprint or copyright. You can tell who made the antibody and even under which patent. Okay?"

Ichi nodded.

"So, there are four patents for the Gorpahn antibody and only, like, three companies actually producing it, so it should be pretty simple to track the code print and get a good idea of when Rye was given it, maybe even where. Which is I assume your whole point to this? A clue to his past?"

"It was a thought."

"Well, we're shit out of luck, my friend. Look here." He switched files and the protein code changed. "This is what's in Rye's bloodstream. Look, the alignment is slightly different but that's not uncommon, but there's no copyright markers on it."

"Meaning?"

"Meaning, this is a naturally forming antibody."

"But, the survival rate of someone that reaches full manifestation is almost nil. With the synthetic antibodies, maybe they'd have a ten percent chance of beating it, if they were in a medical setting." Ichi stared at the protein.

"I take it the dream he shared with you didn't mention medical care?"

"He said he was pulling the worms out of his flesh and could feel them eating him."

Will made a face. "Ugh, which isn't a bad treatment. That's all a doctor will do, cut open the pockets and surgically remove the worms. Thing is, they sting when removed, you have to freeze them a bit. To just pull them out, gods, that must have hurt but it would improve your odds, if the venom didn't get you first."

"But I always saw it written that by the time a body made enough of its own antibodies the worms had consumed too much flesh to save the infected person." Ichi glanced up to his friend and hoped to find answers.

"So I've always been told, but Rye's immune system is a touch hyper. If anyone could do it he could, but to pull them out by hand?" He winced. "Another option is that the synth antibodies were introduced to his system and his body over took them."

"Is that possible?"

"Who knows? We haven't studied how his systems work yet so, sure, yeah, it's possible. Figuring you were looking for clues, I ran some searches. Looking for any reports of anyone who manifested and survived, came back with seven cases, none of which fit Rye."

"So he was infested and didn't get medical treatment and survived?"

"Maybe, but a lot of the hospitals in the smaller areas have been totally destroyed and their files are sketchy at best. The better question is, how did he get infected in the first place? Bentick Four has been in civil war for twenty years and for his antibody levels to still be this high I'd say he was infested no more than ten years ago, more likely about five. He isn't from Bentick Four, he doesn't even have the webbed finger gene in recessive. He wasn't there as a tourist."

Ichi shook his head. "So we can't trace him from that?"

"Doubtful, most of the folks running in and out of there aren't keeping passenger lists. You didn't tell him those worms were real, did you?"

"I'd like for him to be able to sleep again sometime. He'll remember or not on his own."

"Bentick Four is a shit hole, Ichi, even before the civil war. Why would he have gone there?"

Ichi shook his head. "Why wouldn't he have gotten medical care?"

"This is strange, very, very strange." And coming from Will, that meant a lot.

⧫

The topic of conversation in Will's lab once his wife rejoined him was about Rye and the rare and normally fatal exposure he'd obviously lived through. Amanda had done what she always did, she checked the results herself. If she'd been blindfolded and told it was night she'd only believe if the blindfold came off.

"I'm just saying, it needs to be studied more. If he really survived that, it needs to be documented," she argued back.

"And what? Tell the entire scientific community that he is a pet but isn't but is and oh someone messed with his genes when he was a child and guess what a neato side effect is?" He frowned. "What good would that do anyone?"

She opened her mouth to debate back but the lab door carefully opened. It was too timid to have been anyone from Avalon which ruled it down to one of two people. She smiled when a redhead stood in the half open doorway.

"Hey Rye."

"I'm so..sorry, I know you're wo..wo..working."

"Not a problem, how can we help you? Are you hurt?"

He shook his head but his words melted away. Amanda meant well, but it was Will he wanted to talk to which was ironic since he couldn't get a word out.

"Is Ichi okay?" she questioned and glanced to Will, but he had his listening thoughtful look on and wasn't speaking.

"I..." Rye sighed and shook his head. The struggle to find his words was overwhelming when they didn't want to play nice, and he was ready to turn around and try later.

"Naw." Will grinned. "Ichi's fine. I think I know what Rye's saying." He stood up and pressed a kiss to the side of Amanda's face. "I'll be back later, dearest." On the way out he tossed an arm around Rye's shoulders and guided the silent man out into the hallway.

They were at the kitchen before Rye was able to protest. "Will?"

"It's okay."

"Wh...where are we going?"

Will hurried in and snagged a couple of cartons of chai tea before again leading Rye away down hallways. "I'm going to show you a secret."

Rye's feet stopped moving. He felt a hand holding his face, fingers digging into his jaw and his head echoed with a threat from another lifetime.

"I'll tell you a secret boy, I own you. You don't get to say no to me!" The voice was strong, smooth, and set his spine to trembling.

Will missed the sight of startled fear that darted across Rye's face but not the shock of the suddenly spiked emotion. Only he noticed it a second to late to keep from pulling the redhead along beside him, his feet planted and frozen.

Rye stumbled and fell. The hard deck floor was something welcome and solid and he spread his hands across its slightly spongy surface. His stomach turned over and for a moment he thought he might be ill.

"Hey, hey there, it's okay," Will soothed and brushed stray hair back from the empty face. The gray eyes were blank, empty of emotion and it was a look Will had seen often. During the occupation, after Bare Earth had been released, almost everyone had eyes so dead. It was a look of shock, of surviving for far too long on empty. "Rye?"

A slender hand rose and rubbed across the still face. When it retreated the eyes weren't quite so empty. "I'm sorry. I tr..tr...tr..tripped."

It was a lie and Will knew it and he was pretty sure Rye knew. "Gotta be careful, Ichi will skin me if you get hurt."

Gratitude flooded Rye and it showed in his eyes. "Thank you." But the words weren't meant to the offer of help getting back to his feet.

"Now, as I was saying, this is my favorite place in all of the station." He smiled gently and started toward the access hatch on a mostly unused hallway. He pried it open and ducked inside and found the lantern he had stashed there.

By the time he had it clicked on, Rye not only was inside the access tunnel but he'd replaced the cover and managed to close it. The latches were complicated to keep someone without the knowledge of their working from wandering where they didn't belong. Rye sealed them without pause or thought and left Will standing, holding the cartons of tea and the light in awe.

It felt better not to say anything so he nodded. "Thanks."

"Wel... welcome." Rye answered and followed down the small corridor at a slight hunch to avoid cracking his head on the low ceiling.

Will led them down and around and up a ladder and finally to a spot where two corridors met and one branched off above at an angle. He set the lantern down and the small space was lit up warmly. "I love this spot."

Rye glanced around and saw no real difference.

"Here, there is wind." He grinned and pointed to two of the corridors. "When the climate control kicks on in the labs, it's filtered and circulated back here, so depending which labs' vents are running we can get a gust or a breeze." He turned and found Rye taking his words seriously but looking a little baffled. "Besides, I like the smaller spaces; feels, I don't know, isolated here, safe. Be proud, I haven't even brought Amanda here."

Rye sat when Will did and accepted the carton of chai, letting it heat up in his hand. Air gusted down the corridors and ruffled his hair and he shut his eyes in surprised delight.

Will laughed. "Told you. It's something you only appreciate if you've been planetside, a real nice wind."

Rye nodded companionably and sipped at the chai, surprised to find he really liked the spicy taste.

"Better than that tea Ichi drinks, huh? I swear it tastes like grass clippings mixed with dirt."

"It's not bad. Better than his mi...mint tea."

Will laughed again and let his head rest against the wall as a breeze picked up, gentle and soft. "Oh, Ichi and his mint teas! I keep telling him if he'd just relax a little he wouldn't get such upset stomachs." Will took a sip of the chai and the grin he was wearing faded. "He told me you liked smaller spaces too. I figured you'd like it here, and I don't mind sharing it with another lover of tight spots."

"I like kn...knowing where the walls are," Rye confessed.

"I used to hide, when I was a boy, in my grandmother's blanket chest. Every time the landlord's men would come around, I'd run off and hide there and it felt safe." He closed his eyes and let the air soothe his nerves. "So, did you shag him good?"

"No," Rye answered without embarrassment.

Will pried an eye open. "Well, why not? Ichi needs a good roll in the hay."

"It wasn't time yet."

"Yet!" Will shut his eyes again, knowing it was easier for Rye if he wasn't being watched. "Whatever is on your mind, you know you can tell me, right?"

Rye sipped at his carton. The closeness of the walls and the gentle light cast by the lantern made the space seem intimate and safe. "You ran those te...tests. Are you su..su..sure I'm really hu..human?"

It wasn't what Will had expected. "One hundred percent sure. Why?"

"I don't th..think I had a mother."

"Don't be silly, everyone has a mother."

He shook his head. "I've been thinking and th..there isn't even a feel of a conec...connection to the idea of a mo..mother."

"Rye," Will sat up and tried to meet the other man's eyes but Rye kept them lowered. "Someone took your brain and cut most of its ability to talk to itself off. That's no small surgery, you're lucky you remember what the word mother means. And so what? Maybe you didn't know your mother? Half the people here can't clearly recall their parents, it doesn't mean you aren't human. So don't you worry about that."

Rye nodded. "Ichi doesn't seem to remember his mo..mother well either."

"Oh, he remembers her. Look, Ichi's from a place where showing emotion is considered almost vulgar and his family was twice as bad. They raised him to be a logically thinking, icy cold scientist. I'm sure he's torn up about his mother but he won't show me and it'd be a great step if he showed you. He just doesn't express things easily."

"He's sm..smart." It was only a half question, Rye knew Ichi was smart.

"No, Ichi is brilliant."

"I'm dumb."

"Compared to Ichi? Amanda is dumb, and she's one of the smartest people I've ever met. His parents never understood why he went into entomology. That's like, if he became a musician or actor or something flaky. He used to get these letters from his mother about how he was wasting his talents playing with his hobbies."

"I really li..like him," Rye whispered around another sip. "I just... I don't kn..know how..." He sighed and tried again. "I have noth...nothing to offer him."

Will shook his head and kicked Rye's leg with his foot. "You're right, you are dumb. I've seen how he looks at you."

"That's ju...just what th..they did to me."

"No, it's not. Trust me, I can tell. Ichi doesn't need his intellectual equal any more than Amanda does. Graces know I'm nowhere near her smarts, so it's a good thing for me. Ichi's the same way, he doesn't need someone he can work beside, he needs someone he can live beside." He set his head back against the wall. "You've got everything he needs to offer him."

Rye didn't ask what that might be, but Will's words left him with plenty to think about. The breeze gusted up and he sighed happily at the feel of it against his face. Will was right, the wind was nice and the little convergence of corridors did make him feel safe. Together the pair sat in comfortable silence, sipping their chai and not speaking further.

Chapter Twelve

"That's it Rye, no more tonight," Amanda announced and closed the computer down.

"But--"

"No buts, that's enough." But there was nothing harsh in her words.

"Ichi wants me to le…learn to read."

She chuckled softly and shook her head. "Yes, but he doesn't except you to do it in a couple of weeks. Give yourself some time, you're making good progress."

It wasn't a lie to be kind, he was. The first week had been spent just trying to get his mind to comprehend that letters had meaning. Something in what had been done to his brain had cut that off as well and it was a strain to attempt to learn. Amanda had just patted his hand and assured him that if he kept trying, he'd overcome it, and he was. It was just slowly and with difficulty.

It made him grateful for Amanda's teaching, he knew he'd have been ashamed if Ichi had been the one. "I want to make him proud."

"Which is very noble, but he doesn't expect you to drive yourself crazy over it. You're getting there, really."

Rye just nodded. "Thank y..you."

"You are most welcome."

"Ichi wanted me to as..ask you if Harvick is still on his way?"

She nodded. "He's limping here, as per his last message. Two or three days, maybe a little sooner."

"He fed the swarm his la..last rat today. He's worried about the younglings if food is mi..missing."

"You can tell him not to worry, Harvick will be here before the next feeding. His children won't go hungry. And speaking of questions, Will asked me to ask you something."

"Yes?"

"Yet?" She shrugged. "That's all he said, 'Ask Rye 'yet'?' Said you'd understand."

Rye glanced down and tried to hide the grin. "No, not yet. Tell him 'soon'."

"I will, now, off with you. Go home and keep Ichi from worrying about his bugs."

The grin widened a little bit. "I will, thank you Aman...Amanda." Distracting Ichi was easy and it was just what he needed to get his head to stop aching. So far, he wasn't sure why Ichi felt it was so important that he learn to read, it seemed a great deal of bother and pain. But all he needed to know was that Ichi had asked him to try, so it was important he succeed.

⚜

"Ich! Hey, Ichi?" Will called out as he pushed Ichi's apartment door open. Will froze just inside the apartment. "Oh, man, sorry, the door was unlocked."

Ichi was pressed to the sofa, pinned with Rye laying on top of him. The reserved man's shirt was missing and in the back of Will's mind he noticed it had been tossed across the room. Ichi had twisted so he was able to look up and backwards at the door and, at seeing Will, he'd blushed almost the color of Rye's hair.

"It was unlocked because I logically assumed no one would be stupid enough to barge in!" He snapped caustically and struggled to free himself from the tangle of limbs.

For every move Ichi made, Rye countered in a subtle turns and twists, keeping Ichi pinned to the sofa. Will just laughed. "Hey, man, sorry, just thought you'd want to know Harvick is docking."

"I'll be right there." Ichi almost managed to sit up.

Before Ichi could slide away, Rye simply got a grip on his waist and tugged him back down to lay sprawled out and pissy below him again. "We'll be th..there shortly," Rye changed the answer.

"What?" Ichi almost choked but the look in the gray eyes was one he'd been learning well over the weeks.

"Take your time, want me to lock it on my way out?" He chucked a thumb toward the door.

"No." Ichi squirmed but found himself unable to get free of Rye's gentle grip.

"Please," Rye answered too.

Will nodded and, with a laugh, he locked the door on his way out.

"Rye, I have to go."

Seeing Ichi pull his mask of cool distance about his face again just made Rye feel wicked. One of the best things he'd come across was pushing Ichi beyond his own controls, snapping him loose to moan and gasp in shocking displays of emotion. Having him try to go back to his logical, day to day world after their small romp on the sofa was just a challenge to get him moaning again.

"Har..Harvik can dock without you and the others can unload without you. You are bu..busy right now."

"Rye!" But protesting was pointless, Rye attacked his neck again and the fight melted from him. "Oh, god."

And if Rye was disappointed that the night's play was cut short and what he'd thought might have been the right time turned out not to be, it disappeared as Ichi clung to him and shivered at his touch. Their fumbling on the sofa seemed safer than their explorations on the bed, but both left Rye feeling whole and content. The nagging worried fear had faded to a distant voice. He grinned as clothing was returned to place, knowing that as soon as Ichi had fed his swarm and returned home, the 'yet' to their relationship would merely be a memory.

It made the walk to the docking hold seem both too long and too short. Rye caught Ichi's arm before they made the last turn to reach the hallway to the hold. They hadn't told Harvick about him, so around the ship's captain Rye had to remain silent and pet-like. When Ichi turned to see why they'd stopped, Rye pushed him back against the hallway wall and stole a quick but passionate kiss.

Rather than blush or be angry, Ichi just grinned a little and brushed hair back from Rye's face. "Sooner I can feed the babies the sooner we can get home."

Nothing had actually been said between them, but Ichi's understanding set Rye's heart to fluttering. It meant that Ichi felt it too. They'd gone as far as they could without actually consummating their relationship. Rye had even let Ichi 'return the favor' as he kept putting it and found it to be a mind blowing--no puns intended--event.

The idea of finally moving further was a distracting one. In his mind he would play it out, knowing it would be a safe distraction with Harvick around and certain so long as he had his fantasies he wouldn't miss the found freedom of speech. It made little difference to Rye who was top and who was bottom. There was a distant sense that he'd, maybe, once preferred top and certainly reducing Ichi to the point of begging was an indescribable delight. However, if there was one thing his memories of his other owner had taught him, being taken, even in the course, rough manner that had befallen him, was equally delicious. It was a trade off, pain was worse but so was pleasure and Rye was finding many, many uses for that tradeoff.

The fantasy was distracting enough that he didn't notice the object of said fantasy had stopped inside the cargo hold. Rye stumbled to a stop behind him, his head bowed in typical pet fashion and he hadn't noticed Ichi had paused.

"That's him, that's the one," Harvick's voice broke the suddenly unnatural silence.

Rye glanced up. The Avalon folks were never silent and on days when Harvick arrived they grew even louder, more festive. What he saw set a spark of something off inside his stomach. It wasn't fear, or worry, but something closer to excitement. Harvick was down on his knees, his face a mottled bunch of bruises, with a newly red gash over his forehead. His hands were bound behind his back in locking cuffs and old blood had dried on his clothes.

Around him, the men of the station were kneeling as well, bound in similar manner, some with gashes or bruises. Henry lay unconscious and unmoving, bound as well, and Mark was leaning forward, his left lower arm bent at an obviously broken angle. They'd bound him also, cuffing his good wrist to one of his ankles.

They weren't what set the spark of excitement into the pit of Rye's stomach, it was the others. A handful of men, four in all, dressed in black and brown colors with splashes of red and wearing the fashion and styles from a hundred different colonies. Only one held a serious weapon, the small magnetic gun was old and held together with sealant tape and what looked like wire, the rest held knives and clubs made of weighted pipes or lengths of metal.

Rye knew the gun, knew the risk it offered. A mag slug wasn't a pleasant injury. At a lower setting it popped into flesh and cauterized the wound after it; higher settings could vaporize bone into small dust. From the repair work done on the gun, he could guess about a dozen things that might not function anymore, from actually firing to being able to control the force level of the slugs. From the look on the men's faces, it was only a matter of time until someone found out just how well the gun worked.

"Pirates," Ichi whispered, almost in shock at the sight of the thugs, his eyes going wide as the mag gun nudged Harvick's head.

Things had felt frozen. Stuck in surprise and shock, time had stopped. Until a hand reached out and gripped Rye's hair, pulling him in stumbling steps further into the cargo hold. He didn't offer resistance, something felt shut down or shut off. Much like his memories of those first days with his owner or the hazy awareness of before, there was a sense of being out of control, like the world was spinning around him.

Ichi, on the other hand, held no such disorientation. "Let him go!" he demanded and charged after where Rye was being dragged.

It was child's play for one of the men to kick the back of Ichi's knee and twist his arm behind him as he fell. The researcher went down with a cry that was more startled uncertainty than pain and found his eyes locking on Will's. His friend's nose was bloodied but his eyes were sharp, he shook his head in the smallest of shakes, silently begging Ichi to be silent.

The pirate dragging Rye across the hold held his grip firm in the red hair with one hand and just as firmly around a homemade knife with the other. Rye was pulled closer to Harvick and jerked to a stop. The one with the gun in ill repair nudged the side of Harvick's head once more.

"This the Pet?"

Harvick just nodded. For a second, his dark eyes met Rye's gray and they widened. He saw something there--something alert, vital, dangerous--that shouldn't be in the eyes of a pet. He frowned, surprised, and in the next heartbeat Harvick's head exploded. The whine of the mag gun was sharp in protest at being used, but it quickly recharged. Vapor from what had once been Harvick's head floated in a red misting cloud across Rye and he felt it landing, hot and soft against his skin.

"Get them on, the other's will be done fetching the rest soon. Secure the men and make sure the watch is on the women. No damaging the goods before sale!" the one with the gun ordered.

"But the Pet?" the man holding Rye whined as he jerked the red hair again.

"Sure the Captain won't reject some fun, just no touching the women. An Avalon witch isn't worth as much if the fight's been beat out of her."

Laughs were exchanged all around and the grip on Ichi's arm eased. It was pretty clear the pirates didn't deem him a threat and he couldn't rightly blame them. He'd never seen violence before, never seen anyone killed, and both sights had him cowed. Only the idea that these awful men, that any man, would dare to touch Rye shook him from his startled shock.

Ichi pulled hard on his arm and it slipped through his captors grip. "Leave him alone!" he heard himself shouting and found himself charging blindly toward the man holding Rye by the hair--which was stupid because he'd just seen what the mag gun was capable of and he had no illusions about how tender his flesh was.

They didn't waste a slug on him. The man that had knocked him down before recovered from his shock and swung his cudgel in a low arc. It caught the side of Ichi's head and dropped the smaller man to the floor. A booted foot kicked out and rolled Ichi over where he lay, sputtering for breath, stunned and unable to coordinate any movement.

"Kill him?" the man with the cudgel asked. "He ain't Avalon."

The one with the gun came over and ran quick eyes over Ichi before he shrugged. "Too pretty to kill, it'd be a waste. Pet can't keep all of you lot occupied and away from the women. Bring him; a mouth is a mouth, a hole is a hole." He grinned in a mocking way. "Someone will buy something so pretty even after you lot's finished with him."

The taste of blood was in Rye's mouth and it felt more familiar then nearly anything he'd crossed with since arriving on the station. The smell of blood was sweet in the air. Only one thing mattered; it wasn't what the pirates wanted on the station or what they planned to do with the small research crew. Harvick's murder hadn't even surprised him and didn't offer fear or shock, nor did the threats to his own person. He'd already learned what he'd been made into, he may never have willing accepted a single member of the attackers as a lover, but there was no love in what they wanted. Rye knew he'd been remade for sex, they could and would use him and he'd beg for more, it held no fear for him.

Until they'd hurt Ichi. That set off a cascade of fear and rage inside of him like nothing he'd felt. Even the heights of ecstasy he'd found with Ichi paled compared to the horrible anger that consumed him at seeing the gentle man harmed. When their words sunk in past the pounding, boiling anger that made his head throb and he knew they planned to rape Ichi, his Ichi, the rage froze. It became ice and the anger and fear froze and shattered. Suddenly, without actual thought or words, Rye knew what he'd originally been made for.

His elbow sung back, with no thought, no wasted time for concern, and with all his force it buried into the neck of the man holding his hair. The man released his hold on Rye's hair and his own blade, gurgling in surprised pain as his windpipe was crushed. Rye didn't think, he dropped and rolled, snatching the blade from the air as it fell. He came up on his feet behind the startled pirate just as the one with the mag gun swung toward him and fired randomly.

It was as if the entire moment had already been played out a thousand times inside of Rye's head. He knew the speed of the slug, the angle it would be traveling in, knew the actions and reactions of everyone around him before they even thought it. It was simple to kick out, knocking the gasping pirate to the side to stumble. It put him directly into the path of the slug, the shot Rye hadn't even known had really been fired until the man beside him suddenly had a hole the size of his fist appear in his chest.

The air floated with the dazzling mist of blood again and the mag gun slowly whined back to full charge. The blade was no longer in Rye's hand, he'd thrown it as he kicked the now dead pirate. His mind had judged the balance of the surprisingly well made knife with the distance to the one in charge with the gun. Without conscious thought, he'd judged that a moment would appear and he had to take it.

The blade appeared again, sticking from the chest of the attacker in charge. The hilt and a bit of the blade sticking from flesh wobbled slightly. A look of shocked surprise crossed the man's face as the mag gun dropped to the floor, breaking into parts as it hit. The pirate stumbled back, his hands touching the spot where metal met flesh.

"Bloody hell," he gasped before tripping and landing as brokenly on the floor as the gun.

Rye slid to the side as a cudgel raced past him. The man was slow with it, bringing it in lazy arcs and counting on the weight of the club to do the work. It made it easy to learn his timing and Rye slipped inside the arc of an attack. His hand flew up and the heel of his hand caught the stronger man's nose, breaking it and spouting blood and curses into the hold.

Again, instinct said to move to the side and as he did a blade from the fourth attacker danced dangerously close to both Rye and the man with the broken nose. Rye watched with detached interest as his own hand punched out, landing on the knife attacker's wrist. He felt and heard the bones snap under the force of the punch, the knife dropped from twitching fingers.

The blade didn't stay on the ground for long. Rye snatched it up and spun, knocking the cudgel to the ground with a smooth kick. The knife, not as well made as the first but sharp, lashed out and slit its original owner's stomach open. Rye didn't wait to see if the blow was lethal, he turned the knife and dragged it up to the center of the man's ribs.

Which delayed him long enough that the man with the cudgel got in another swing. Rye ducked and pulled the dying man with him. The cudgel landed on the trembling pirate, smashing collarbone and knocking him off the deeply buried blade. Rye kicked out from where he was crouched and was pretty sure he'd broken or dislocated the cudgel swinger's knee. As the man was following, Rye stood and the blade cut out again, slicing the man's throat open as he tumbled to bleed to death on the cargo hold's floor.

Rye ducked again and froze, waiting for the next attacker and finding the hold empty of any. The hilt was reversed in his grip, the blade running parallel to his forearm ready for defense or offensive moves. Blood dripped on his hands and made the grip slick. He did a final check of the four men, ignoring the moans of the ones still capable of sound and found them all fatally wounded. The idea that he'd just coldly murdered four people didn't even show up as a blip on his conscious. They'd tried to hurt Ichi.

Which reminded him of what had set him off and he hurried to where Ichi was struggling to sit. Blood ran down the side of his love's head, thick, and it matted up the dark hair. Ichi's eyes were wide and frightened but Rye wasn't sure if it was the situation in general or his actions.

He knelt down and ran his hands across Ichi's head. "Are you okay?" He asked with that odd voice of someone else again. The one that had vowed to die before allowing harm to touch Ichi.

Ichi nodded, unable to speak.

Rye was satisfied.

"Rye!" Will called out. "Get these cuffs off! They have the women on the ship! Hurry!" he hissed while pulling on his arms.

Rye glanced to the desperate men, men long used to waiting for the right time to act, before he glanced off to the tube that connected the hold to Harvick's ship. He shook his head. "Ichi? Can you get them loose?"

"I think so." He whispered, shivering as Rye smeared blood across the sides of his face again.

"Good." Rye nodded and turned back to Will. "How many? Any more guns?"

"Don't be stupid, get us loose we'll do it together."

"How many?" Rye demanded.

There was something cold and frightening in the gray eyes, something that made Will do something he'd never done before. He backed down. "Three more we saw on the ship, the Captain has a better mag gun. Five others on the station, knives and clubs. They're looking for some of our projects."

Rye nodded and left Ichi kneeling, surrounded by a wreath of corpses. "Keep him safe," he ordered, pointing a bloodied blade at Ichi before he bent and pulled the second knife from the corpse. It would take too long to piece together the broken mag gun and frankly he wasn't sure why it hadn't simply exploded in its user's hands before. "Ichi, move it, get them loose!" he ordered with a cold, hard voice.

It was one that Ichi responded to. He nodded again and forced his dizzy head to move him toward Will. "Rye?" he called out and the redhead stopped on the way to the connecting tunnel, but Ichi didn't know what to say. 'Don't die' seemed silly, 'don't get hurt' even more absurd.

Rye merely inclined his head in a small bow, accepting all that wasn't said, before he turned and slipped down the connecting pathway.

Ichi had trouble getting himself moving. Head trauma, he figured, blood was making his shoulder sticky in an unpleasant way, but he got himself moving toward where Will waited. Once he reached the other man's side he felt down his arm and got a grip on the cuffs. They were cheap and simple, a tri button release, but Ichi struggled to gain the focus to push all three buttons at once.

When the cuffs jumped free, Ichi sat down uncertain of what he was supposed to do next. Will didn't wait, he slid a hand across Ichi's shoulder and moved to start releasing the others. As soon as a couple more were free, Will hurried across the room and pried the emergency med kit from the wall, and before he could even worry about things he was slapping out pain killer patches to those that needed it.

"Ready?" he asked as he checked and made sure Henry was still breathing and his pulse was steady. Will glanced to the handful of men still able to fight and saw the abandoned cudgel weighted in one's grip. "Mark?" Will questioned where the other man sat, trying to piece together the broken gun with one arm.

Mark raised his eyes and caught Will's sideways glance to Ichi. "Got it covered."

"Good, let's go!" Will shouted and waved the small group to the docking tube.

Before they could move, protesting shouts echoed down the tunnel and one of the remaining pirates burst back onto the station. He was bleeding from a slash along his chest and moved in stumbling, wide-eyed panic.

"Help me!" he screamed to his former captives. "Oh god, help me! He's going to kill me!" A knife appeared deep in the back of his thigh and the man fell hard to the ground, moaning in fear.

Rye didn't stop his run when the blade stopped the last of the pirates from the ship. He hurried over, swinging the cudgel he had in one hand in a quick arc. It connected to the begging man's head, once, twice and again and the man fell silent. Rye wasn't in the mood to take chances, his other hand swung out and the mag gun in better shape fired, cutting a hole into the man's chest. For good measure, Rye smacked the man with the cudgel just to make sure he was going to stay down.

The men of the station stood in horrified silence. Rye glanced over his shoulder to where the first of the women were bunched in the tubes entranceway and saw the startled surprise in Amanda's eyes. His eyes sought out and found Ichi, but the man sat empty and blank, in obvious shock. All the violence was so quickly resolved and Rye hadn't even started to breath hard.

"Where were they headed?" he asked Will, who seemed to be the only one still functioning.

He shook his head. "Don't know for sure, there are a lot of sensitive items here. Mark's lab most likely, ours too. They'll be after Bare Earth, the vaccine and any information on how we made it." He moved and took the mostly repaired gun from Mark.

"You know how to use that?" Rye questioned.

Will charged it, checked the prime and shrugged. "Yeah, I can manage."

Rye just nodded in response, spared one last look to Ichi and hurried from the cargo hold.

Mary pushed past Amanda and she was holding a long blade. She fell in beside Will with the ease of a former fighter, one that had long since put aside war but not forgotten it. One or two other's fell in beside him and Will nodded. "Amanda, see to them?"

She nodded and moved forward and watched as Will went off to a difficult fight for the second time. Her only hope was that, like that first battle when the odds were so high against him, he'd find a way through again. She prayed so anyway.

That was all there was time for, the open med kit was scattered about and there was some work she could do other than merely passing out pain patches. She moved among the group, checking obviously serious wounds and simple ones alike and trying not to worry about Will and the others.

"Better?" she asked Mark as she worked the sling across his broken arm.

He nodded.

"Don't worry, we'll get it fixed up. I need to get the lot of you to the med lab."

"Henry?"

"Still breathing, lucky for him his skull is all bone," she tried to joke. "More worried about Ichi at the moment. He's never seen this before, he's going into shock." Between the emotional trauma of seeing violence for the first time and having violence done to him for the first time, added in with the head wound and bleeding gash to the side of his head, Ichi was by far the most worrisome case. Amanda knew the folks from Avalon were tough, but Ichi? Ichi was raw and new to this and she seen people die of shock that didn't have a single wound on their body.

"Where'd you leave him?"

"Who?"

"Ichi." Mark had glanced around but Ichi was nowhere to be seen.

"Over there…" she glanced to the side. "Oh, shit."

But, in the confusion, Ichi was gone.

Chapter Thirteen

Ichi wasn't thinking. He started moving in an effort to return to his apartment. The cargo hold was filled with blood and horrible things and he wanted to get away from that. The apartment seemed like a good safe place, but his head was pounding pretty badly and he was dizzy.

He reached the turn where one direction would take him to his apartment and the safe locks he could hide behind and the other way would lead to his lab. Something about the labs was important and he stood there, swaying, trying to think.

A scream, a man's, but fear made it sharp and high pitched, echoed up from another hallway and Ichi remembered. There were pirates, actual pirates, on their station. He'd read about them, sure as anyone in the Concord had. Men and women manning crews of unregistered ships that floated on the outskirts of civilized space. They ran raids inward, stealing what they could and dragging other crews off to be sold in slave markets on the most distant of worlds. One story of a man taken and held in a small mining colony for over a decade before he managed to escape had given him nightmares as a child.

That was all they were supposed to have been--stories, nightmares of children and childhood. The Fleet was the finest military force ever and they declared piracy extinct. Only, there were pirates on his station. They'd herded the women into their ship, were preparing to take the men too. They'd killed Harvick and worse, they'd planned on taking and using Rye. He remembered they'd planned on using him too and he shivered and wrapped his arms around his body. Never, even in his most dark childhood fear, had he ever worried about rape. It wasn't a threat or even a suggestion of a threat, and these pirates had made it clear his safe idea of the universe around him didn't exist.

Now, they were running loose on the station, looking to steal their work. Which was logical, a pure sample of Bare Earth was worth a lifetime's fortune on the black market. The vaccine was worth more, but the real score was the information on how Avalon had made the vaccine to the supposedly impossible-to-protect-against virus. That would be worth a thousand lifetime's money on the open market and no one would ask where it came from.

"The babies," he whispered. His swarm was valuable too. Nearly impossible to collect in the wild, never successfully held in captivity, Ichi's swarm was a rare prize. If they knew anything about what was on the station, the swarm would be on their list too. He considered himself a reasonable person and even he'd had idle fantasies about how evil owning such pets could be. The mere threat alone would be enough to make most people do what you wanted.

Ichi brushed blood out of his eye and turned to go to the lab.

Rye had started at the most obvious labs first, killing two in Will and Amanda's, one in Mark's, and that was the extent of his knowledge of what might be valuable on the station. He simply didn't know just what everyone else was studying, only that it was high risk and needed high containment. So he ran a lab by lab, hallway by hallway search and all he found was Will and his group.

"Check below," he snapped as he sprinted by, sending the group to check the other storage holds and the kitchen, the communal areas and if needs be their apartments room by room.

"Right." Will had just nodded and they'd moved to get out of the blood covered redhead's way.

That was the last he'd seen another person, but on he hurried and on he checked. He froze when he darted around one last corner and found Ichi standing in the hallway. The shorter man stood, stiff and wide eyed, just on the hallway side of his lab. He was staring into the workspace with an expression of confusion.

Rye didn't pause, didn't blink or breathe. He ran faster and slid to a stop in front of the doorway. Inside, one of the pirates was gingerly setting the swarm's central habitat on the counter and how he'd worked it free of its layers of default protection Rye wasn't sure. Until he saw the second man and the mag gun he was holding, a nice one, and knew from the fragmented clear polymer sections that sprinkled across the room that the fellow had actually risked shooting the layers away.

Which meant the man wasn't that smart and was willing to take chances. He couldn't tell if the first man was armed but he knew Ichi was about to be shot. As his feet slid on the floor, scrambling to stop himself and do something, Rye judged everything and figured out what was most important.

He fired his gun. It whined at full charge and the swarm's last containment shattered. Lights in the lab went red, an alarm sounded and the lab doors instantly closed. As they shut, a small dent appeared. It was at Ichi's head level and if the doors had stayed open a breath longer there would have been nothing between Ichi's head and the fired mag slug.

It was the first screams from inside the lab that broke Ichi away from the startled shut down his mind was in. "No," he muttered and ran toward the door. "No!" He scrambled for the lock and tried to remember if he'd ever designed the system to have an override for a full breach.

Rye caught his lover by the waist and pulled him away from the door. "Stop it!"

"No!" Ichi squirmed and fought but his motions were sluggish and random. "It'll kill them, the system, it'll kill them!"

"Ichi." Rye struggled to hold the other man without hurting him. "Stop."

He felt something hot on his face and it wasn't blood. "The system, for a full breach, it'll kill them!"

"It's too late!"

"No!" He stumbled and fell, taking Rye with him and landing wrapped in the other man's arms. "If the code isn't input in the first two minutes, the room, the system will gas the room! I have to get in there and put the code in!" He'd made it so the code had to be entered inside the lab. To prevent heroics, he'd thought, in case things went really wrong. The gas default was to prevent a death that would linger for days, but it would also kill his swarm and prevent them from getting loose. Ichi's own stubbornness had demanded a two minute window to have the attempt at re-containment. "There's still time."

Rye wrapped his arms tighter around Ichi and pulled him close. "Nothing is going to allow me to let you go in there." The screams inside the room grew worse, more tormented, more horrible. "Nothing."

But Ichi continued to struggle until the seconds ticked away and the screams mercifully ended. Rye released him then and Ichi crawled to the door and hit it. "No!" he sobbed. "No." Tears rolled from his eyes, sobs wracked his body. It was too much and he cried as he'd never cried as a child. Something inside of him broke; it was too much to carry in silence. The grief for his mother, the mourning of not only her death but the lack any mothering from her had been a horrible weight to carry. The isolation he'd wrapped himself in and the loneliness that went with it sparked by the promise and fear of more with Rye was too great to tuck inside and pretend not to feel. The horror and shock of being attacked, by pirates of all things, was more than he'd expected to ever see--but the death of his swarm and most likely of every other collection of insects inside his lab? That broke him. That was too much.

He crumbled there sobbing, each gasping breath making his head pound worse. Part of him wished that Rye hadn't acted, that the mag slug the door had stopped would have shattered his head like Harvick's. In that moment, everything felt empty and futile. His chest felt tight and hollow, he felt like a shell, empty and alone. The tears fell and he had nothing left within to fight them with, found nothing worth facing another day for.

Until warm arms wrapped around him and gently lifted him from where he'd collapsed in front of the door. There was strength there and comfort and Ichi let it wrap around him, clutching at Rye's shirt, simply unable to stop sobbing.

"I'm sorry, I'm sorry," Rye whispered. "I couldn't let them hurt you. I'm sorry." He pulled Ichi tighter to him and wondered if the other man would hate him now. To save his life he'd destroyed the only thing he loved. "Can you stand? We should get you to the med lab." There might have been more pirates on the station, but Will and his group would find them if there were. They didn't matter now, Ichi was all that ever mattered.

♋

Rye was half carrying Ichi by the time they reached the med lab, but he got them there and reluctantly passed the still sobbing Ichi over to Rosie's care. The med lab was packed, which wasn't difficult given how small it was. He pressed himself against a wall and tried to be invisible because there was no way he was going to let them shoo him out. Ichi wasn't going to leave his sight.

There was no room to put Ichi on a bed but Rosie pressed him to sit in a chair. He could still sit, unlike some of the others. Rye stood silent and apart, watching the controlled chaos move around him directed by Amanda's strong sure voice. He watched as Ichi was spoken to softly, watched as his wound was carefully treated. He was so focused on Ichi that he didn't notice Amanda approach him until she ran a wet cloth across his face. It came away bloody.

"You hurt?"

Rye just shook his head no.

"You sure?"

"How is he?" He pulled his face back from another cleansing swipe.

She lowered the cloth. "We've worked on the concussion. The gash was sealed up but it'll take a while to fully heal. I've given him a sedative, a little one, but it'll help calm him down."

"He's okay?"

"He's upset but he'll live. You should take him home, put him to bed."

"But what about…" In his mind he saw again the men he'd killed, it replayed in clear and brilliant detail but brought with it no remorse or guilt. "I should help them clean up."

"Don't worry about it, we got it. Will and the others can handle it, but you're the only one I think can handle Ichi right now. So go, get him home. Put him to bed and let him sleep some of this off, things always look better after a good nights sleep." She patted Rye's arm. "Okay?"

Rye nodded. "Okay."

Ichi came along willingly when Rye tugged gently on his arm but he didn't glance up and he didn't look around. He let Rye lead him out of the med lab and down hallways and didn't even glance up until they were back in the apartment. His only reaction then was to turn and lock the door.

"You're covered in blood." Rye said gently.

Ichi looked to the red head. "So are you."

"Yeah, but it's not mine. Let's get you cleaned up and tucked into bed."

Ichi dropped his head and sighed but didn't protest or complain when Rye led him to the bedroom and further into the bathroom. Steady hands stripped him and soon Ichi was being pressed into the shower. The hot water felt perfect and he shut his eyes and let it pelt across his skin.

Rye moved as carefully as he could. Ichi seemed frightfully silent and he suspected it wasn't from the drugs. With gentle hands he scrubbed them both clean, washing blood tenderly from the matted dark hair and roughly washing away the blood from his own skin. He wanted to wrap Ichi in his arms, hold him as the water soothed them, but he wasn't sure it would be welcomed.

When they were clean, Rye lead Ichi out of the shower. The fluffy towels were a nice way to keep the shivering man warm as Rye patted his skin dry and lightly towel dried the short dark hair. He quickly wiped the water from his own body before leading Ichi into the bedroom. The clothes Ichi slept in were right where the other man always kept them, neat and orderly. Rye helped him dress, Ichi moving like a doll with no free will of his own.

"Here now." He pressed Ichi to sit on the bed and hurried to pull on his own clothes. "Amanda said you're supposed to rest." Rye pulled down the covers and Ichi slid under them without protest.

"You're not coming to bed?"

Rye shook his head and brushed wet hair back from Ichi's face. "Not yet, but I'll be here. You just rest."

Ichi shut his eyes, giving into the exhaustion, giving in to the gentle touch of Rye's hand soothing across his head. Some of it was the drugs, he knew that, but a large part was just emotional exhaustion. He couldn't go another step, he was just too tired, so he happily surrendered to sleep.

Only to wake feeling heavy and groggy but finding something wrong. His head was sore but didn't hurt, thanks to Amanda's care, but the bed felt cold. The emptiness was what had woken him up.

There was no Rye, sleeping curled up in unpleasant dreams or tangled around him. It made getting back to sleep impossible and suddenly made him horribly lonely.

When he sat up he felt a little drunk, his head was light and things felt unattached. Whatever Amanda had given him, he was grateful for because he'd happily trade the numb emptiness to the twisted pain of everything that had been lost. He wanted a cup of tea and he wanted Rye and neither was to be found in the bedroom.

He padded on bare feet--Rye hadn't bothered with socks when he'd been pulling clothes for him--into the living room. The lights were dim, a touch brighter near the small kitchen space and near the vid screen since it was on and glowing. Rye sat on the sofa, near the edge. His lips were moving as he was trying to read the information on the vid screen, a small line of a frown between his eyes as he struggled to concentrate.

"There's an audio for it," Ichi spoke softly.

Rye nodded, not the least bit startled at the voice behind him. "I know, I wanted to practice. You're supposed to be resting."

Ichi shrugged even though he knew Rye couldn't see him. "Woke up." He moved to the kitchen to make tea and found a pot brewed and waiting. Rye didn't seem to be drinking any, it made him feel a touch better as he poured himself a cup.

"What are you reading?" Ichi asked just above a whisper. Something in the night, the mood or how broken and drugged he felt made it feel necessary to whisper, as if a real word, spoken in a real voice, would shatter something.

Rye shook his head. "Nothing of importance." He tried to click off the files but Ichi stopped him.

Across the screen were images with brief titles of the twenty most common weapons used in the Concord. Each one could be highlighted and more information called up. Ichi remembered seeing Rye moving as fluid as a dancer, as destructive and deadly as any of the weapons on the screen.

"You're not stuttering."

"No." He couldn't look at Ichi, couldn't bring himself to see the disgust that had to be there.

"Do you remember?"

Rye shook his head. "No. I..." He drew a slow breath. "I know things." One hand waved to the weapons on the screen. "I know them. I know distance, use, levels, materials. I can tell you how to assemble each of them. I know how to smuggle them and modify them. I know how to pilot Harvick's ship, most ships I think."

Ichi sat silent, eyes on the screen and the things so far from his world. "You know how to fight."

"I know how to fight."

"But not how you know?"

"No, nothing, it's just, blank."

The tea was a comforting warmth in his stomach, settling some of the unease. "Well, maybe you were Fleet? Fleet ground, special situations officer, maybe?"

Rye knew it wasn't right, knew he wasn't anything nearly so nice, he could feel it, he just couldn't admit such to Ichi. "Maybe." He reached out and clicked the vid screen off. "You should go rest."

Ichi didn't move, his mug cupped in his hands, hot, and yet still he felt chilled. "What am I going to do, Rye? Everything I had was in there. It took me a year to get enough to make even a small swarm, not to mention the others. It's gone, it's all gone."

He wanted to comfort his lover, wanted to take it all back, but he couldn't. "Go, rest, worry about it tomorrow."

"It is tomorrow."

Rye shook his head at the logic. "Worry about it when you're rested."

Ichi was too exhausted to protest much, he stood but didn't go a step further. "Come to bed with me?"

"I'm not tired." Which was only a half truth, he was and he'd give his soul to wrap himself around Ichi and pretend the day hadn't happened. Things weren't so simple.

"The bed feels empty without you." The tight, unhappy whisper he couldn't help using almost made it okay to speak so boldly.

It was too cruel. Rye clenched his hands into a ball. "I thought I'd just lay down out here when I was tired." It was the drugs, that was it, and the shock. As soon as Ichi was rested, he'd remember who was responsible for the death of his work.

Rye's whispered words became a blow that was only lightly padded in the cushion of the drugs he'd been given. It was a sharp reminder of the lessons of his childhood, and of why he lived a solitary life. He didn't take rejection lightly.

"Oh." Was all he could say at first and he swallowed hard to clear the lump from his throat. "Well, I understand. I'm glad you're remembering more about yourself, that's good." He couldn't make himself look happy for Rye, the drugs didn't extend that far.

"What?" Rye glanced up, startled by unexpected words, and found Ichi's face a cold, barren mask.

One of his hands soothed out to brush through Rye's hair purely on instinct and partly because he was afraid he'd never be allowed to again. "I understand."

"Well, I don't!" Rye stood up and willed his body to behave and not think lewd things at the soft, shy touch.

"It was only time until you healed enough to remember your true preferences. It's okay." Somewhere in the back of his mind Ichi had always known that Rye would eventually remember enough about himself to remember that what they'd been building wasn't his natural choice.

Rye pulled Ichi close, their legs entwining as always and his hands came up to cradle either side of the closed face. He lifted Ichi's chin so his eyes should have been meeting his own, only those mocking orbs were lowered and not taunting him. "You are my true preference."

Between the strong hands Ichi shivered, feeling the stirrings of desire in Rye where their bodies were pressed together. "It's okay, they made it so you'd need touch more. I understand, it's like letting pressure out so it doesn't build up."

It was a harsh truth. Rye had long since learned that anyone could touch him and soon have him begging for more--and he meant that, anyone. They were harsh truths that he'd spent a lot of time thinking about. "There's a difference between response and desire."

Ichi nodded and missed what Rye was trying to say. "Exactly, I understand."

"No, you don't." It was odd, having words come so easily and yet still struggling to put his thoughts and emotions into a logical form for words to explain. He closed his eyes to make it easier. "Send me away, that's the only way I'll leave you. You should, for all I've done."

"Send you away?" Ichi squeezed his eyes shut and dropped the weight of his head into the strong hands. "Can't you see? It's killing me to try to do what's right. To respect what you want."

"What I want is to stay by your side but I did… things today. I killed your swarm, I don't expect you to overlook that, just, let me stay near you." He wanted to kiss Ichi, toss him on the sofa and remind him how useful it was to have him around. It wouldn't have been fair and Rye held the desire in check. "Please."

"You saved my life, kept them from…" Ichi shook his head. "You saved most of this station too."

"But I killed the only thing you loved."

The reminder of the loss of the swarm twisted pain in his stomach but something worse twisted him more. "Do you think me so cold?" Like ice, Andrew had teased him, but the words had hurt because he was icy cold. "You think what we've been doing has just been physical?"

Rye found his hands sliding over the almost angry face, trying to soothe some of the torment he could see but didn't understand. "I hadn't wanted to hope."

That forced Ichi to look up and the emotions in the gray eyes were beyond his skills to translate. "Losing the swarm hurts. I don't even know where to go from here, but I'll go on." It was a lesson hard learned while sitting and watching his parents. His mother had always warned him that he grew too attached to things, and maybe she'd been right. "If I'd lost you…" He shook his head. "When they tried to take you…" His voice broke.

Soft fingers slid over the sealed wound on the side of Ichi's head. "You tried to save me; they would have killed you."

He flinched a little at the touch; the wound was sore and would be painful once the drugs wore off. "I couldn't lose you."

It didn't matter that Rye was pretty sure he wasn't a good person before someone he couldn't remember turned him into a toy. It didn't matter that he'd slaughtered people as easily as he made tea. In that moment, it didn't even matter if he never remembered another detail of his life before he'd been altered. The only thing that mattered was that Ichi didn't want him to leave and, more, actually felt something for him.

"Ichi, this is desire, not response. It doesn't matter what I might or might not have been before, this is what I am now." He glanced down. "If you don't hate me for what I've done, please, don't send me away."

He stepped forward and wrapped his arms around Rye's waist. It felt good to let the lean strength hold him, to bury his face into the slender neck. "I promised, no matter what you remembered, until you wanted to leave."

Rye slid his hands over the shoulders that he could get drunk touching and pulled Ichi just far enough away to kiss him. The lips were stiff, uncertain before they yielded and some of the tension faded from the rigid body. He kissed Ichi silly, kissed him until his breath was short gasps and only then did he break the kiss long enough to whisper. "Never, I'll never want that."

Ichi held back a snuffle and wiped quickly at his eyes. "No one's ever said that to me, wanted to be with me."

Rye kissed the worried forehead. "We're quite the pair," he teased. "You thinking I want to leave, me being scared silly you'll ask me to leave."

"Rye," Ichi sighed and pressed his head, the non-injured side, tight to Rye's chest. "What are we going to do? I don't know what to do."

"Shhh. For now, you're going to go back to bed and get some rest."

Ichi found himself nodding in agreement, feeling lost and tired. "You'll join me?"

"When I'm tired. For now you go, get some sleep."

It seemed a sensible idea and Ichi slipped back to the bedroom. He found himself sitting on the edge of the bed and not sleepy enough to lie down. There was something distracting, something he was missing or needed. There was something misplaced or overlooked and he sat trying to resolve what it might be. When he understood, he knew it was because he did want to do something and he knew just what it was. In one moment, a very clear, painfully honest moment, he knew exactly what it was he wanted to do.

"Couldn't sleep?" Rye asked gently as soon as he heard the footsteps lightly stepping behind him. There was no reply and when he glanced up Ichi was standing to the side of the sofa.

Rye wondered if maybe he'd been the one to take the blow to the head. What he was seeing had to be a hallucination. A very nice hallucination for certain, but what his eyes were seeing couldn't be real. Ichi stood by the edge of the sofa, face turned slightly down and eyes on the floor a foot or two in front of where Rye sat. All of that would have been perfectly normal, if Ichi hadn't been completely nude.

The sight stole his breath and made him forget to worry about all the long list of things to worry about. Ichi was body shy and covered up whenever he could, and while Rye had seen and over the weeks mapped out, the entirety of the luscious golden skin, to have it offered for his sight was intensely erotic. There was no doubt that Ichi was nude for him. Rye often begged, whined and pleaded to get more of Ichi undressed in visible light and Ichi always blushed and avoided the request when he could.

He was blushing now. The flush to the down-turned face, the way he was standing torn between trying to be comfortable and being intensely aware of his state of undress, it all screamed that it hadn't been a slight or easy choice to strip to his skin and stand to be studied. Rye drank in the offered vision and begged his heart not to fail.

"Ichi," he managed to breathe out in a whispery sigh. "God, you're so beautiful." That wasn't what he'd meant to say and he shook his head at his ongoing tendency to say what he was thinking. "You should be resting," he forced out, trying to be logical and reminding himself that masturbating another half dozen times tonight wouldn't kill him.

Ichi shook his head but couldn't quite raise his eyes. "I don't want to rest."

There was a velvet touch of desire in the softly spoken words that made Rye nearly swallow his own tongue. It was the same tone Ichi moaned in when he'd lost control and gave in. It was the same tone that played over and over again inside of Rye's fantasies. His body jumped to respond, begged to take the nude, shining, perfect man into his arms, but his mind reminded him of all the real solid facts. "You're hurt."

Ichi shook his head. "Not badly."

"Trauma, shock, a head wound, you're hurt, you're drugged and you don't know what you're saying." He could behave, he could wait.

"I know what I want." Ichi said in the same velvety voice and glanced up.

Rye stumbled and fell into those eyes and thought for certain he was drowning. So much so that he didn't notice as Ichi took the last few steps over to him. It was as if he was entranced and suddenly Ichi went from one side of the sofa to gently lowering himself down to sit, straddling his lap. The warm weight of the careful contact made him moan and his hands dug into the sofa to keep from gripping the offered flesh in front of him.

It was easier for Ichi to act on what he wanted if he didn't think about it. He slid down onto Rye's lap, holding his weight on his folded knees and barely balancing on the slender legs below him. They hadn't even touched yet and Rye's breath was moving in short gasps, something that normally didn't happen until much further into their explorations. Ichi leaned forward and kissed Rye, tilting the willing head back to rest against the sofa, liking the way the softer fabrics Rye wore felt against his bare skin.

As the kiss deepened, the grip Rye had on the sofa loosened. It was impossible to not touch all of that offered skin. Rye was sure that Ichi knew that sitting on his lap and kissing him would remove any further protests he might have. Once he was started, Rye found his desires too great, his body's responses too strong for his will to shut down. His fingertips slid across the silken flesh, up across hips and higher to tickle the bottom of shoulder blades. He didn't touch with thought or direction, just with the aching need to feel.

Ichi broke the kiss, breathing faster himself and no longer embarrassed at being naked. He leaned back, blinking a little at the still unexpected delight and shivers of desire that flooded him every time he saw Rye even the slightest bit turned on. From his hand he uncurled his fingers and let the ampoules drop to the sofa, keeping one small sealed tube. He broke the seal and let the slick lube coat his fingers.

"Ichi…" Rye swallowed hard but the look in the eyes that met his was steady, not clouded by drugs or confusion.

Chapter Fourteen

The whisper of his name, so hungry and uncertain, made Ichi smile a small, tiny grin. He kept his eyes locked onto Rye's, wanting him to see, wanting to be seen, and very deliberately slid the slicked up hand around to slide a finger into his entrance.

"Oh, god," Rye moaned and the hands that had been exploring Ichi's skin fell aside, stunned and useless. He watched as Ichi whimpered slightly and arched, his slick fingers sliding in and slowly out of his body. It felt almost pornographic to sit and watch, down right dirty to have Ichi sitting facing him, across his lap while the normally shy man finger fucked himself, but Rye couldn't refuse or protest.

It was beautiful and shockingly delicious. Rye found his hands on Ichi's calves, just gently touching the man's legs. His eyes hurt from the beauty of what he was being allowed to see. Ichi rocked slightly, forcing his fingers into his body, his face going from uncertainly embarrassed to erotically lost as the pleasure swept him away. His free hand slid across his own chest, circling a nipple, gliding over a shoulder, lightly palming his cock, all for Rye to watch.

It was the sight, he knew it was, but the slightest of amounts of friction of fabric across his aching length tormented Rye also. He wanted to rub himself, or better he wanted to rub himself against Ichi, or best of all, he wanted to replace those teasing fingers. His breath was short, he couldn't stand to watch but neither could he look away, and in the end he gave in. Rye's hands clenched onto Ichi's legs and his soft moans spiked a bit in desperate need. For a few heartbeats, release and pleasure stole the sight of the most beautiful man he'd ever seen pleasuring himself as he couldn't keep his eyes open and his body shuddered.

Ichi paused and watched, uncertain Rye had just come until the front of his pants dampened in proof. "You just…" But he wasn't sure how to ask and blushed a little.

Rye tried to get his breathing to level out a little, but he thought it was a losing fight. He'd come and the first sight of Ichi naked had him painfully hard again. He pulled the naked man down, forcing him to lean forward instead of sliding further down his legs, and kissed him. "Yes, I did," he whispered, inhaling the scent that was Ichi, a mix of shampoo and sterile lab cleaner.

"But, we haven't… I haven't done…"

Rye kissed the tip of his nose. "You're beautiful enough without touching me, but thank PETS, once is never enough for me where you're involved."

Ichi's mouth opened but he was too turned on to speak. Actions were working better for him, and since he'd made up his mind to do what he wanted to do, he may as well do anything he wanted to do. Emboldened, he slid from where he was balanced and with a smooth touch slid Rye's knees apart so there was room for him to sit between them. He glanced up, pinned lightly between the strong, long legs, and caught the near desperateness to Rye's expression.

"Ichi, I…" But it was too late to protest. Ichi stretched and his face nuzzled Rye's lap ever so softly. "I… oh god, please!" He moaned, loudly, as Ichi's mouth found the shape of his hidden desire. He shivered, he whimpered, he begged, but all Ichi would do was continue the slow mapping of his fabric covered groin.

Ichi tugged on the waistband of Rye's pants. "Take these off," he whispered just before he ran his tongue along the hardness hiding under the soft fabric.

Rye nodded and obeyed, unable to think enough to form words and unwilling to protest anything Ichi wanted. Right now, if Ichi had said he thought staking Rye over an anthill and pouring honey on him would be sexy, Rye would nod and agree. He slithered out of the fabric, and kicked it aside.

The scent of Rye was suddenly everywhere, a mix of desire and sex, and that haunting scent of his skin. Ichi licked out, dragging his tongue across Rye's thigh, knowing the effect it would earn him.

Rye moaned, his hands struggling not to grip into Ichi's hair. All his struggles to regain his words went out the window at the feel of Ichi's tongue, hot and wicked, tracing lines along his length. The sight of it shut everything down to a narrow window, nothing in the universe existed but the amazing man that actually wanted him.

There was a point where mercy had to be offered. Rye was gasping for breath, struggling to remain still, and it was because of everything he was doing. It was intoxicating, Ichi had learned that the modifications done to Rye amplified his reactions but also that a lot of it was strictly because of him. Which he found, he really, really liked.

Mercy was needed and Ichi was willing to offer it. He sucked in just the very tip of Rye's cock, teasing it gently with lips and tongue in velvet touches. His experience didn't lend to amazing skill or talent, but what Ichi lacked in that department he made up for in sheer delight and desire. Fortunately with Rye there wasn't a need to do much that was fancy. So long as he was gentle, so long as he remember that everything would feel more strongly to the other man, that was what mattered, and Ichi knew how to walk that knife's edge between just enough and painfully too much for Rye.

Rye bucked a little bit as he struggled to watch Ichi slowly swallowing him. He wanted to offer warning but there was no hope of being able to speak. Ichi's hands were petting his legs, stroking his hips, touching him in tormenting contact. He heard his whines grow more desperate and his head fell to the back of the sofa. He came with startling depth, shuddering, moaning, his skin breaking out in a light sweat and his eyes struggled to stay open to watch Ichi the entire time.

He hadn't planned to stop until Rye tumbled over the edge for the second time but he hadn't expected Rye to react so strongly either. It made him even harder, even more turned on, and he moaned as Rye finally let go and came. Ichi sighed and moaned and slid a finger or two back inside of his body while he closed his eyes and swallowed Rye whole.

He'd taken it for granted that Rye would stay hard, or at the least, be able to get hard again almost right away. Ichi liked it better when Rye would be spent enough to go soft and flaccid only to quickly be driven to moaning hardness once more. That and with his higher libido and stronger sensations, Rye almost needed to come several times, something Ichi was happy to help with.

It took careful planning, to tease him long enough so that Rye would enjoy a full torment during his release but not too long after so he'd grow hard again. Ichi wanted him to go soft, and hard once more, wanted to give him the excuse of biology to stop if he wanted to. Ichi slid back a little and stopped stroking his hands across lean and, now he knew, deadly muscles and waited until Rye recovered enough that some sense returned to his eyes.

"Want to stop?" he asked softly.

Rye shook his head. "Never."

There was no smile, just intensity, and Ichi sat up a little. "Take your shirt off."

There was no need to think about the order, the demand alone made him shiver and off his shirt was peeled. Ichi being aggressive was something from his deepest fantasies and he would happily obey. Even if seeing him slide back up to straddle his legs, Ichi's knees tucked up near his hips, being able to feel the bare skin of his legs and ass on his own legs, nearly made him hard again. He wanted to be hard again, wanted it so the moment Ichi had made would never end.

"Not finished with you yet," Ichi teased with Rye's own words before leaning in to steal kisses. His hands ran across the red hair that was just long enough to toy with. He wanted to slide forward and press his hips hard against Rye's body, grind against him until he found his own release, but that wasn't his goal and, if Ichi was able to do anything, he was able to achieve a goal.

Ichi arched forward and kissed Rye's neck, nipped at his shoulder, tormented down until before him was one lovely nipple glittering with gold. He glanced upward and met startled gray eyes, grinned at how Rye's mouth hung open from the last of their kisses.

"You wouldn't." Which was silly because obviously Ichi would as he carefully drew his tongue across the already hyper sensitive nub. "Oh, Ichi…" His entire body arched a little, in directionless need. When Ichi closed his lips over him, flesh and gold and all, Rye lost his words again. They fell, scattered about him like broken glass. His cock stirred, swelling, returning to life as Ichi slid forward.

There was nothing more than the press of flesh to flesh, but Ichi needed to feel Rye growing hard again. Wanted to feel the trapped length against his legs, his hip, feel it twitch as he flicked a tongue over the hypersensitive flesh. And just as he was sure Rye was as hard as he could get, Ichi very gently dragged his teeth across the tormented nipple, caught the gold bar, and slowly tugged.

"Oh!" Rye arched off the sofa, nearly causing Ichi to bite too hard on the captured flesh. "Oh my fucking god!" He fell limp and trembling back to the soft sofa and wondered if the walls were sound proofed, but he was saved from finding out by Ichi releasing his nipple and giving him a moment to catch his sense and breath.

When he opened his eyes he saw Ichi cracking open another of the tiny tubes of lube. The slick drops coated his fingers again and very carefully, very lightly, Ichi reached down and stroked the lube, slick and warm, across Rye's cock. "We need to go slow," Ichi said softly, blushing again, glancing down. "It's been a long time."

Rye was so startled he almost didn't feel the hand touching him. "Ichi…" He sighed out, shivering at the thought alone. "God, you're beautiful." He wanted to soothe his mind and confirm that Ichi really wanted to go further but he couldn't. Rye wanted the other man so deeply, so totally, he wasn't sure he could live another moment without knowing what it was like to, for just a few moments, be so totally joined.

Ichi leaned forward, Rye's hands naturally lifting to support his arms and help hold his weight. He locked his eyes onto the glazed, stunning gray and held the slick, hard cock steady below him. The head pressed to his entrance, slick but still tight, and both men moaned at the slight contact. Very carefully, Ichi lowered himself down, just a bit, and the pressure was horrible. He trembled and found Rye's hands petting him, helping to hold his weight and approving of the slow joining.

Then, the pressure eased, just enough, as Ichi's body adjusted to the demanding length pressing into him. The head slipped easily into his body, making Ichi want to drop all the way down and not care of he got hurt. His world was flesh and pleasure and the sight of those clouded, desperate gray eyes.

Rye saw the look flit across Ichi's face and he tightened his grip on his lover. He shook his head. "No, slowly," he forced out in a harsh whisper. Ichi wouldn't be hurt by this, he wouldn't, or he'd never let Ichi bottom again. It didn't matter if Rye was hurt while being taken, he healed so much faster, but no harm would ever touch Ichi if he could stop it.

The grip that stopped him from forcing the delicious length deep into his body made Ichi whimper. His eyes went shut and he dropped his head, trying to will his body to relax, lost in the tight, burning delight of first being taken and the thrill of the promise of pleasure. Fraction by slow fraction, he lowered down closer to Rye's legs and more and more of the redhead slid into him. Until he was there, his ass spread and taken fully, his body trembling and his voice breaking from the gasping whimpers he heard himself making and couldn't stop.

"Shhh," Rye soothed and leaned forward, wrapping his arms around Ichi's waist. He was moving by feel, blinded by the shivering delight, the sheer painful pleasure of how tight Ichi was. He soothed himself as much as the shy, shuddering body he was buried in. "Shhhh." He petted Ichi's spine, stroked the curve of his ass and felt sick with the need to move.

Rye wasn't the only one ill from the need to move. Ichi lifted himself up slightly, just a little, and slid back down. The experiment produced no pain and only blinding pleasure. Ichi's head fell back and he moaned, moving again, sliding Rye further from his body and deeper back in. "More," he begged and found Rye's mouth kissing, nipping the long exposed length of his neck. "God, Rye, oh more!"

"Ichi..." Rye gasped into the ear he'd been biting. "It's too much... it's... god... I can't..."

Ichi shook his head and brought his head forward. "I want to feel you... oh oh Rye, I need to feel you."

He took that as moaned permission and Rye took a hold of the teasing hips. He moved Ichi a touch faster, a little bit deeper in long sliding strokes. The need to come was a pain, a horrible chewing ache in his stomach that slid like molten fire to the spot of delight and torture. Rye's mouth fell open but only a strangled gasping hiss escaped as the fire spilled from his body. He forced himself in as deep as he could, frightened he would actually hurt Ichi with his need to be so tightly buried in his body but unable to be gentle.

Rye fell into Ichi's arms as the feel of his trembling release triggered new shivering in the shorter man. He held the redhead close, touching more boldly, more forcefully, across the sweat dampened shoulders and neck. They'd stilled with his release and Ichi waited to see if his gamble would pay off. Neither of them really knew how Rye's body would respond to their lovemaking. Rye's memories of his owner before were ones he didn't like to share and ones he fully admitted offered no clear guideline to what joining with Ichi would be like. Ichi knelt there, shivering a little, his cock weeping in neglect, waiting to see if Rye would soften inside of his body after such a desperate release.

Rye found he could still breathe and, while pleasure had swept him away, he was still aching and unsatisfied. He moaned softly, more of a hushed whimper, and kissed the bare shoulder he was tucked against.

"Better?" Ichi asked softly, feeling the cock still so deeply in his body twitching, the thighs on either side of his own trembling.

"Somewhat," Rye whispered but he lifted Ichi up and before the startled man could protest, laid him tenderly on his back. "My turn." He grinned into the darker eyes. Only, the sofa was cramped and there was little room to get the deep, serious angle he was looking for. Rye leaned down and kissed Ichi, sliding gently from his body.

The sudden, shocking, hungry emptiness made Ichi nearly sob in protest but Rye brushed hair back from his eyes and smiled gently. "It's okay, just trust me." He tugged and guided and got Ichi onto his feet and with kisses and touches led the other man to the bedroom. There he pressed the shorter man down, tumbled after him onto the bed's width and soft comfort. It gave him plenty of space to hook Ichi's legs over his arms and slide back into him, deep, full and solidly.

Ichi shivered and cried out, the fullness, the need to be taken hard and deep spiking in him. He tugged at Rye, clutched at his shoulders and back and begged him with words and sound to take him harder. He wanted to stroke himself off, frightened of the demanding need for release that was building in him but longing for it to continue. He wanted to spend the rest of his life splayed across his bed, stark naked, with Rye pounding hard into his body.

Then there was a shift in angles, subtle and small, but it lit up breathtaking delight in Ichi. Not every stroke in hit that spot, but a fair number of them did and he found himself torn between the sheer overwhelming pleasure of the outstroke and the stunning glare of the lucky in strokes. He was moaning, sobbing, not caring how he sounded, struggling to keep his eyes open and locked onto Rye's steady gray. Rye looked pained, tortured, as needy as he felt and it only made Ichi hotter.

"God, Ichi…" Rye groaned. "God, I love you."

The words, forced out and almost as painful as the clinging need for release, were words Ichi had never heard spoken to him before. Not in any context, from anyone, and it was the last thing he needed to break his hold on the fragments of his control. He shuddered, moaned a warning as best he could, and came. He lost all sense of himself, all control, all shame and pride, it all dissolved and poured from his body. He clung to Rye as the only thing tangible in a world that had exploded and as the only thing he wanted to be tangible.

It was the gasping, hot, short pants that grounded him, helped ease Ichi back to the real world. It was just in time, Rye was driving harder, shorter, deeper into his body as he came and was swept away by the sudden, shocking increase in tightness. It was too much, seeing Ichi come, feeling his entire body explode below him, on him, around him, it was what he needed. He surrendered, knowing that this time coming would be enough, and his release stripped him bare. He came from his depths, his soul, from whatever hidden, buried part of him remained from what he had once been. He came with all the hope and fears of never again facing a day without Ichi.

The clock that ticked off time inside of Rye's head woke him before the alarm was set to go off. Only, he wasn't sure they'd remembered to actually set the alarm, but it didn't matter. The one in his mind was a better keeper of time anyway and it was easy enough to wake up, make sure the alarm was off and curl back into bed.

Two things became instantly apparent. The first was that the alarm wasn't set, which made sense given the day before. The second was that there was no point to snuggling back into the bed because Rye had woken up alone. Normally he was a light sleeper, and if Ichi so much as sneezed during the night he was awake to some level and aware. Yet this morning Ichi not only had woken up, but had gotten up without waking him.

Rye groaned, rubbed his eyes and blamed his deep sleep on the incredible sex. Memories returned like scattered pictures, moments burned into the black empty spots in his mind where other memories should be and it was vivid, perfect, enough to make him shiver. Just the memories, with no Ichi in sight, were enough to take him halfway to aroused. He grinned happily, feeling really warm, really safe and really, deeply content.

He stretched and shook out his hair. There was nothing for it, he had to find Ichi. Even if the other man wasn't interested in a repeat of last night, Rye just needed to see him. He glanced around the bedroom and didn't see the pants he'd had on the night before, which made sense because they were kicked somewhere out in the living room. Rye pulled himself from the warm bed, scratching his hip as he went and found another pair. He didn't mind being nude but it made Ichi blush so he tied the cord lightly and let the soft fabric hang from his hips.

One moment, frozen like a bug in amber, floated up to Rye's hazy mind. Ichi was pinned below him, his face a twisted mix of pleasure and need, Rye had been in him, taking him, trembling with emotion and sensation. Somewhere in that perfect moment, Rye's brain had burped again and shorted out and he spoke without being able to censor his words.

Rye stopped and stared at the sex rumpled bed. "I told him I loved him," he whispered to the empty room, and suddenly Rye knew why Ichi wasn't there when he woke up. "Stupid, stupid!" He cursed and literally smacked the heel of his hand into his forehead. "Stupid!" he hissed once more and sat on the edge of the bed.

It wasn't stupid because it was a lie or because Rye wasn't ready to say the truth. He'd struggled for a short while, trying to pin down just what he felt around Ichi. It wasn't easy. It wasn't like pointing to the color blue and asking someone if that was blue or green. He'd needed time to think about it, figure it out and watch how other couples interacted to know the word to pin on his feelings. There was no doubt, after studying how Amanda and Will and the other Avalon couples interacted that he was madly, crazily, obsessively in love with Ichi.

What was stupid was that his idiotic, half screwed up brain had twitched and when he'd opened his mouth words he never meant to say came spilling out. It was becoming a habit, saying his thoughts without being able to stop them sometimes, and it wasn't one he liked having. He'd heard that small whisper of hope last night, that small hint that the relationship he had with Ichi wasn't just physical and his stupid mind, lost in pleasure, had spurted out the one truth he'd tried to bury too deeply to ever escape. He may not have been able to remember life before his change into a pet, but, like the weapons, some things he just knew. He knew Ichi, made a study of him and he knew Ichi didn't really know what to do with emotions.

"And what do I do? Dumb ass!"

He stood. There was nothing to be done for it now. He simply had to find Ichi and explain. There was no point in denying the words as truth, that would be too complicated and painful and Rye was learning he wasn't the sort of man to be subtle or hidden with things. No, Ichi knew, there was no back peddling about it now. The task offered him was more difficult, now he had to convince Ichi that it was okay. That Rye asked for nothing more than what they had, that the words that had slipped out didn't change anything. More importantly, Rye needed Ichi to understand that the reserved man wasn't required to do a thing more, feel a fraction more, be anything more. That was a task he didn't feel he was eloquent enough to achieve.

"Ichi?" Rye asked as he found the darker haired man in the living room. Ichi was not only awake, he was showered, dressed and ready for the day.

"Ah, good, you're awake." He glanced up from where he'd been looking across lab supply wholesalers and wild crafting companies that should be able to replace most of his collection. "Amanda has asked to do a follow up exam this morning, I'm on my way over, and I've got to clean up the lab."

Rye stood, uncertain for a moment. Ichi was so cold, so closed off and distant that he wondered if maybe the creature of sensual moans and shy abandon the night before had just been a very solid dream. There was nothing in the entomologist's voice or face to betray that less than twelve hours ago he'd nearly been kidnapped and raped, that he'd been beaten and nearly killed, or that his entire life's work had been lost. There was certainly no hint to Ichi's outward appearance to even suggest that he'd then seduced Rye.

"I..." Rye glanced from where Ichi was fussing with the last of the information on the vid screen to where he could still see the rumpled bed. "We?" Admittedly, Rye knew his brain was more than a touch off but he doubted it could have produced such a real hallucination. Then he remembered hearing Ichi's voice be so steady, so controlled, while hearing his heart pounding in uncertain fear inside his chest. He remembered how silently, how coldly Ichi had mourned his mother when Will said he was actually broken up over it.

It made Rye frown as he finally put the pieces together. "They can wait," he demanded and moved closer to where Ichi was fussing, moving toward the door.

"I have things that have to be done."

"No, you don't, not more important than this."

"Rye--"

"No, don't you run from this."

"I'm not running from anything," Ichi protested a touch too sharply. Inside he was begging to get away before Rye could carefully explain the many mistakes from the night before.

"You're running away."

"I am not!" he snapped back quickly and it sounded childish and harsh even to his own ears. "Amanda and Will are busy, it would be rude to put them off."

"We need to talk about this."

"There's nothing to talk about." He was halfway to the door. A few more steps and he'd be in the hallway and away from the conversation he wasn't sure he could survive.

"Just tell me, are you running away because we had sex or because I said I loved you?" The words tumbled out in anger and fear and without any way for Rye to stop them. He'd really have to see if Will or Amanda could tell him if this lack of censorship when he was emotionally distracted would continue.

Ichi simply froze, more frightened in that moment caught between Rye's words and the escape of the hallway than he'd been the night before facing a pirate. He couldn't look at Rye, standing with his hair mussed up and without his shirt. "I don't know what you're talking about."

"Ichi, you need to understand…"

"I can't…" He turned toward the door, set now to escape before more could be said.

"Don't run!"

"It's rude to make them wait," he muttered but his voice was dead, empty and he wanted to drop and never get back up.

"Ichi!" He moved closer, uncertain if he wanted to physically stop the other man from leaving or not. "Just let me explain."

The breath hitched in his throat. "There's nothing to explain." He hurried out the door, unable to hear Rye take back the words he knew he'd always treasure. Even if they hadn't been meant, he needed to hold on to them a little longer.

"Ichi," Rye sighed as the door shut. "You're running away, you fool." He could make the choice to follow. He could force Ichi to face what he had to say but something told Rye that backing off was a better choice. Ichi was obviously upset and needed space and it was only fair to offer it. It was simple, it was a small station and Ichi couldn't avoid him forever.

Chapter Fifteen

Ichi was halfway to the med lab before his hands stopped shaking. When he walked in Ichi was pretty sure he outwardly looked as normal as ever. Mary passed him on her way and smiled gently but he dropped his eyes and couldn't return it.

"There's our next victim," Amanda teased and guided Ichi into the lab.

Ichi just nodded and meekly sat on the edge of one of the beds.

Amanda tossed a look to where Will sat, his head tilted a little and where he was trying to hide a frown. "Sleep well?"

Ichi shrugged. "Well enough."

"Any pain?"

"I took something this morning." He'd woken up with a pounding headache and sore muscles from both the attack and the unusual occurrence of really great sex.

"Any blurred vision? Dizziness?"

"No." He held still while she did her job, wanting to get away as soon as possible.

"Nausea?"

"No."

She tossed another worried look to Will but finished what had to be done. "Before you run off, I need to speak as station leader for a moment."

"Okay."

"Your lab unsealed about an hour ago. I've told the other's to leave it untouched. I did some research this morning. No one's had access to the early stages of a swarm's attack on humans. It's either they've gotten out in a lab and the kill switch was automatic or they've gotten people in the wild and the bodies are found much later. You're the only one crazy enough to give yourself two minutes. Chance like this might not come about again. The bodies are still there, did you want to autopsy them before they're disposed of?"

He hadn't thought about it. "The toxin that was released will make it difficult for me to distinguish between the swarms toxins and the gas' effects. My background isn't in humans. I'd like to collect samples if I may?"

"I'll help you with the autopsy if you wish? I can help you sort out what is from the gas and what from the swarm." She smiled gently but Ichi's eyes were still down. "Will's no use, the bugs creep him out."

"It's a generous offer."

"One that you'll accept, right?"

It was generous and it would be just the help he needed. Not only technical help, but personal. Ichi needed the time to focus on logical work and not his emotional unease. "Thank you."

"Good! Give me a moment to grab some things and we'll head over. Okay?" She stepped back and waited for Ichi to nod before leaving. They'd discussed it and figured it wasn't a good idea to let Ichi back into his destroyed lab alone.

"You should tell me what's wrong now before she gets back. You know you'll be elbow deep in lower intestines later today and you'll tell her and she'll go all girly on you." Will spoke with only the slightest teasing.

"There's nothing wrong."

Will stood and came to sit next to his friend on the med lab bed. "I've known you for four years Ichi, don't lie to me. I can see behind that stupid mask you wear, something's chewing on you."

Will was his friend, maybe his first real friend ever. He blushed a little. "You've... been... with other women right? Not just Amanda?"

That made Will smirk a bit. If Ichi knew the half of his history he'd blush for a year. "Yeah, you could say that."

"Did you ever, I mean..."

"It's okay. I'm not ashamed of my past. I'm from Avalon, remember? We think sex is fun." He did grin now, knowing most Concord citizens thought of them as a colony of sluts.

"Yes. Well, did you ever say anything to one of them that you didn't mean?"

Will sighed. "I think everyone has lied to a lover at one point or another. But, you're not asking me if I ever lied when asked 'does this dress make me look fat,' are you?"

Ichi shook his head.

"What did Rye say?"

"It's nothing."

"Bullshit it's not."

Ichi sat silent, trying to figure out how to speak about something so personal, so painfully private without speaking about it. "Your mother loved you, yes?"

The sudden change of subject caught Will off guard, but he was used to how Ichi would often attack a personal issue from another angle. "Of course."

"How did you know?"

Will shrugged. "She'd tell me and I just knew."

"She actually said 'I love you son'?"

"No, she'd say 'Willy, you're a goofball but I love you to pieces.' Just like that, like a dozen times a day until the day she died."

"That's normal?"

"On Avalon? Yeah, we're a little obvious with our feelings. Difficult to hide things when half the population is a high enough psi to at least be mildly empathic. But yeah, I hear it's normal."

"My mother never said anything like that," Ichi whispered, unable to say something so personal in a normal voice.

This wasn't about his mother. Will knew that, but it was about her at the same time. The pieces and clues fell into place and he blinked, surprised. "Rye told you he loves you?" Will hissed out in a whisper too.

"I didn't say that."

"You don't need to!"

Ichi started to protest again but sighed. "I hate when you do that."

Will grinned and nudged the sullen man with an elbow. "No you don't, you like not having to pry the words out."

"Stop it."

"Okay, but seriously, I'm right, aren't I?"

Ichi just nodded.

"About time one of you got your act together and started talking." But all the pieces had clicked in and Will hide a grin. "You and he, he told you during, didn't he?" He was trying, really trying, to be delicate.

Ichi nodded again.

"Wow, great sex and a confession of undying love all in the same moment."

"This isn't a joke, Will." He meant to snap and be angry but he couldn't bring himself to feel it.

"I'm not kidding! Okay, maybe I am teasing you a little, but you're such an easy target." He nudged Ichi again. "I'm happy for you."

"It's just, no one's ever said that to me before and he couldn't have meant it and Will, I can't, I just can't hear him take it back. I can't. I know this won't surprise you but I don't know what to do in these situations."

"Yes, I'm shocked beyond words to learn you have no clue how normal humans interact." He teased dryly.

"I'm serious."

"I'm sorry." He tilted his head again. "You really mean it don't you?"

"What?"

"That no one's ever told you that they loved you? Not your parents, not your siblings, not a lover or friend?"

Ichi shook his head.

"Ichi, I'm sorry. Might not mean anything, but you're a brother to me, I love you as much as I ever loved them. I know Amanda feels the same way. You're family to us, and to a lot of the people here. We're stupid for never actually telling you."

The confession floored Ichi. "I..."

"And your family is messed up. The only thing a child needs is to know their loved, really, deeply loved. That's how you raise a kid, not to be a little scientific machine. What they did was unforgivable, Ichi, I'm sorry." It broke his heart and was close to one of the cruelest things he'd ever heard. "But help me see the problem here. Your family is a bunch of cold blooded pricks and I have to get you formally adopted into mine, and Rye not only loves you, he's told you and you got steamy, hot man sex. Why are you giving yourself an ulcer?"

"Because he doesn't mean it."

"What ever gave you that stupid idea?"

Ichi blushed. "Because of when he said it. It's not like he was thinking clearly, he couldn't have meant it. It just was so nice to hear," he finally confessed and hated that he felt like a child.

"Goofball." Will grinned and nudged Ichi harder with an elbow. "Look, you two have been doing just about everything but actual sweaty man sex for weeks, right?"

Ichi nodded.

"And not once, ever, did he say that he loved you, right?"

Again he nodded.

"Okay, so if it was like a reflexive thing like 'oh god, oh god, oh god,' something mindless that he says and doesn't mean, you'd have heard it before now. Right?"

"I don't know."

"Isn't it far more likely that the moment was so overwhelming, after such a difficult night before, that he let the truth slip out by accident?"

Ichi sat silent, unsure. "I don't know," he finally admitted.

"Well, you've heard my advice, think about it logically and then talk to the poor man about it." He knew that both men had fallen for each other and that neither one was speaking about it. That had to change or Will was going to get headaches from all the suppressed emotions floating around them. "You'll think about it, right? And talk to him?"

"I'll think about it," Ichi agreed.

"And, no, I've never told any woman I was with that I loved them when I didn't," he confessed softly as Amanda returned. As Ichi followed Amanda out of the lab, Will could almost see the cogs in the dark head turning, thinking, trying to figure out what to do next.

Will took a guess and found Rye at the third location he checked. The space was ready for expansion and was technically labeled as cargo storage overflow. It was, in reality, a mostly empty, fairly dimly lit large open space with gray walls and no personality. It had been left as a place for growth, but it was out of the way and mostly forgotten.

Rye was in the center, moving with fluid ease. Will stood in the door he'd opened and watched the lithe redhead glide easily from one posture to another, stretching, moving, and not even having to think. It made it pretty clear that the fighting skills the former pet had displayed weren't a mere fluke as Will caught postures from at least three separate and very different fighting styles. It wasn't just grace, but strength and speed, and it made Will shiver a little bit, grateful that Rye was a friend and not a foe.

"Thought I might find you here," Will spoke carefully into the room, interrupting the seemingly endless stream of moves.

Rye froze and stopped. He found himself almost falling back into the same submissive stance of a pet, head bowed, eyes down, braced for punishment. Will had caught him, found him and seen what he'd been doing and it oddly made him uncomfortable. "I'm sorry."

"For what?" Will lightly tossed Rye one of the bottles of water he'd snagged to take with him on his search.

Rye snatched it out of the air without looking up. "Thanks."

"What're you sorry for?"

He glanced up and half shrugged. "Not sure."

"So, you're a fighter, huh?"

"You too," Rye tossed back.

"Retired and only semi-trained, what was that? Three different styles?"

"Five I think, might be six, I'm still trying to straighten it out." He cracked the seal on the water and happily downed several long swallows. "How'd you find me?"

Will shrugged and dropped to sit on a forgotten crate, letting Rye move closer to him not the other way around. "I thought, if I was Rye and I just recalled that I could kick serious ass, what would I want to do? I'd want to see just what I knew but not where I'd be too easily found. That limits where you could have gone." He slid over and made room for Rye to sit on the crate next to him. "So, you remember huh?"

He shook his head. "No, just know things, not how I know them."

He shrugged. "It's a start." He took a sip of water. "Ichi was a little upset this morning."

"He told you why?"

"I guessed. Amanda says it's not my place and to stay out of it, but she's helping Ichi cut up those dead pirates his swarm ate so she can't stop me. You don't fool me, Rye, I know you really do love him. Just don't give up on him, okay? He's an absolute dork but he means well."

"I'll never give up on him." He closed the bottle of water. "You sought me out to tell me that?"

Will shook his head. "Not really. Rye, how much do you know about Avalon?"

He shrugged. "Only what I've learned from you and the others."

"Great gods help you then!" Will laughed. "Seriously, Avalon is sovereign and we do things a little differently here. We don't have a king or a president or a prime minister or lead council or any of that nonsense. There are virtually no laws on Avalon. When we have an issue, crime or dispute, the community settles it. Even in a city or large village, a community is the neighborhood, it normally looks like chaos to outsiders but it works for us. When something happens that is larger than the community, or complicated, we ask advice of our elders."

"You're a theocracy?"

"Not really. See, the elders are priests but no one is required to listen to them. Oh, we do cause they're actually really good at their jobs, a lot of them are very high psi's too, but no one person or community has to. They offer advice and guidance only."

Rye drew a slow breath. "I suppose these elders have suggested I be removed from the station?"

"No, not yet anyway." Will was a little startled by how perceptive Rye was. "This station is a community, yes, we answer to Avalon, but we're our own village. This raid affects all of Avalon, we need to consult with the elders. We need to get their input on what to do with Harvick and his ship and the pirates and, yes, with you and Ichi as well."

"Ichi will rebuild his collection."

"Don't worry, we know that, but he isn't from Avalon. And you? What you did yesterday was rather impressive."

"And too dangerous to be allowed to stay."

"I didn't say that and don't you say that. This community, the people of this station, will have final say but the elder's advice will be weighed in heavily. There is a meeting tonight, to discuss things with them. There'll be questions for you, you should attend and answer as honestly as you can." Will watched the steady face for signs of worry or anger and saw only set resolve.

"What kind of questions? I might not remember the answers."

"They're not looking to nail you to the wall and make you into a villain, but, Rye, you just killed a dozen people without breaking a sweat. I'm not wrong in saying you want to stay near Ichi, I think he needs to stay near you, so for his sake, you need to answer their questions honestly."

"What's in my head is personal, Will."

"And that will be respected. It'll be myself and Amanda, as two we hope you feel comfortable around, and a third member from the community that you may pick--Mark, Henry, Rose or Mary, Annie I know you've at least spoken to. It'll be your choice too if you want Ichi there or not, I'd understand either way."

"Mark's fine." He liked the logical engineer. "What kind of questions?"

Will turned the water bottle around in his hands. "The elders will most likely want to know everything you can remember, in detail."

"I don't like this."

"I'm sorry. They're going to want to know if you're a threat. They're going to want to know if you're what we say you are and not just a smart pet. I'm not going to lie and say it'll be comfortable or easy for you, I know how unwilling you've been to talk about your life before you came here. But Rye, unless you want to make Ichi pick between going with you and staying here without you, you'll be honest and forthright."

Rye bent forward, his forearms resting comfortably on his knees. "Will... the things he did, I, it hurts to remember them." He rubbed at his neck, trying to force some of the happy unease from his body. "I don't ever want to speak of them."

It would have been easy to toss out a cliché or empty comforting words but Will sat silent. There was no point to mentioning Ichi again, he had no doubts that Rye was very aware of the other man. Instead, when Will did speak, it was very carefully.

"When the Concord came and took over Avalon, we had no military, no way of stopping them. We had no means of negotiating with them. They made us into serfs or slaves literally overnight. It became unofficial policy for the Fleet and the landlords to use rape to break our spirit. Just on this station, there are only three people who haven't been assaulted or directly affected by being personally attacked or forced to watch a love one be hurt. Ichi's one of those three. I'm not," he said very carefully. "Rye, no one is doing this to open old wounds or for sick curiosity. The elders aren't fools, they might see something in your words that will help us figure out why this was done to you, or maybe be able to offer advice on how to go from here." Will sat back. "Even if you were Avalon, no one would force you to speak to them. Think about it, okay?"

Rye nodded but he still sat, silent and uncertain as Will stood and carefully left.

⚜

Ichi was told of the meeting as they were finishing up the second autopsy. Working with Amanda was amazing, they fell into an easy pattern and almost instinctually understood each other's skills and experiences. It made it easier to forget that each of the dead beetles they removed from the body had been his baby and Ichi gratefully took the distraction.

"I'll get these samples to the lab. Leave the bodies, we'll take care of them, but we both need showers, we stink," she teased.

"Amanda…" He tried to find a way to say what he was thinking without sounding condescending.

"Hmm?" She turned as she pulled off the thin gloves she'd worn.

"Thank you, it was an honor to work with you. I… I'm not used to people understanding." He glanced down to the container of dead beetles, their menace stilled in death.

It took a moment but she understood what he was saying, it wasn't always easy or comfortable being the smartest kid in the class, she knew that. "For me as well, next time you need help, just holler at me."

"Will do." He nodded and smiled a little. She was right, time was running out and they did stink. He carried samples to his lab and finished up the little details before he went home to clean up. At the door, he was braced for avoiding Rye, using the coming meeting as an excuse, but Rye wasn't home.

It made the rooms feel empty and lonely. The emptiness surprised Ichi, he thought he'd feel relieved. He shook his head at his own confusion and hurried to clean up and change clothes. Too much time had already been spent thinking about Will's words and Rye's words and he was tired of it. The meeting with the elders was actually welcome, even if the circumstances weren't.

He wasn't worried about it. Ichi had already been interviewed several times by several elders. Avalon was twitchy about letting a Concord citizen onto one of their most secure stations and they'd asked him all manner of questions before agreeing to admit him. The mess with the other station and the Flossin guard, sabotage and murder, only proved Avalon's point. Sometimes being paranoid was a good thing, and Ichi respected that.

His only worry, the only thing that nagged at his thoughts when Ichi sat down in the communal kitchen near the large vid screen, was where Rye might be. The entire station was there, but not Rye, and while Ichi sat and answered questions about reacquiring his swarm, the efficiency of his kill switches, his work in general on the station, his thoughts were focused on Rye.

"Thank you, Mr. Vitorui." One of the two elders said when Ichi finished. "Your understanding and cooperation have always been above criticism." The woman smiled gently. "Now, what was his choice?" She asked of Amanda.

"For Mark to stay, and Ichi as well."

"Very well." The elder nodded and the room slowly broke down, people shuffled out. Whispers talked back and forth and Ichi glanced to where Will was sitting near him and didn't show any signs of leaving.

"What's going on?" he hissed out in a whisper.

"It's Rye's turn."

"What? No one told me that."

Will glanced over and smiled gently. "You didn't ask."

Which was a truth that shut him up. It wouldn't have mattered, Rye came into the room as the bulk of the station left. He was dressed in somber colors and moved with obvious nerves. Gray eyes glanced up and brushed across Mark, Will and Amanda but settled on Ichi.

Rye wasn't scared as much as extremely uneasy. He had been invited to join them during the other conversations, but sitting there knowing what they were going to ask him would have been too much. It seemed easier to be in a mostly empty room when his time came, instead of kicking out everyone while he sat there waiting for them to leave.

His choice to have Ichi stay was one that he'd made at the last moment. He wasn't sure if he'd ever be able or want to be able to say some of the things they might ask of him again. Ichi deserved to hear it, he deserved to know just what he was taking as a lover. If it ruined what they were building, so be it, it was what was fair. That didn't make seeing Ichi sitting there looking startled any easier.

Chapter Sixteen

"Hello Rye." The male elder on the screen said with a smile and a bob of his head. "It's nice to finally meet you."

"Elder." Rye nodded back but kept his eyes lowered on the table. Somehow, he'd expected the elders to be really old and wizened, and while they were older than anyone on the station they still looked vital, healthy and not ancient.

"Would you like something to drink, water or tea, before we start?" The female elder asked.

Rye glanced up across the table to where the other's sat and his eyes fell onto Ichi's before he dropped them to a point on the table again. "No, ma'am, thank you."

"Very well. Now, Rye, our meaning in this isn't to cause you harm, just to understand. Do you believe that?"

"Yes, ma'am."

"We've heard about you, about what was done to you, and we're very grateful you found kind hands by chance and a safe haven here in Avalon space, but it is our belief that this attack on your station wasn't random and we must learn if your presence might have contributed to it."

Rye shook his head. "It wasn't random."

"How so?" Will spoke up. They'd figured he should be the one from the station to speak, to keep as many voices and questions silent as possible.

"Well," Rye drew a slow breath. "The pirates had no secondary ship waiting for them, which means they must have smuggled themselves onboard at some point. That was a lot of people to hide with no chance of escape. They knew Harvick's routine as well. And once onboard they went directly to three labs, no where else. They cloned Will and Amanda's entire computer, took all the samples from their storage. In Ichi's they shot away the outer containments, which is either very bold or stupid or a sign they had no idea how dangerous the insects inside really were, which suggests someone gave them a list of what to take but not information on just what it was. They were more concerned with the profit of selling the crew instead of the more profitable items they were stealing." He shook his head. "It just felt like they'd been hired for the job, it wasn't an attack of random chance."

Looks were exchanged but it was the elder who spoke again. "Very perceptive. We've seen the tapes of your counter attack. Did you know you were able to fight before that moment?"

"No ma'am, not until they hurt Ichi."

"And you've no recollection of how you learned to fight with such skill?"

"No, ma'am."

"What's the earliest thing you can recall?"

Rye sat silent, his eyes never moving from the point he'd picked on the table. "Being cold," he finally said, and it was easier than he feared so long as he didn't look up. "And pain, there was a woman with brown hair. A lot of pain after she was around, none of it makes much sense."

"And then?"

"A room with white walls, a couple other pets and a trainer. I think he knew I wasn't like the others, they were so empty looking. I tried to fight but the discipline sticks hurt too much."

"Elder? We've run some tests on the stick that was sent here with Rye. The paperwork says it will deliver a mild annoyance to gain attention, but that isn't quite true. It's quite painful, we've tested it on ourselves. And with Rye's nerve endings being doubled?" Will shook his head. "It would be intense."

"The others were trained until they obeyed instantly, I was only trained until I'd completed each command once. When the trainer tried to get me to present, I refused, fought, they brought in others and other sticks. I blacked out, when I came to, I didn't fight the second time or again in training." Rye spoke with a hollow, empty voice.

"How clear are the memories of your time in training?" the elder asked gently.

"They're not, ma'am. They're hazy, like a dream. It all feels like that until after I arrived here."

"And after training?"

"I was put in a box, awake, not storage, and moved. I've no idea where but it took less than a half hour. I was left in the box for hours." He shook his head. "I can't, I'm sorry, ma'am, I can't."

"Anything, Rye, anything you can tell us? It might be useful."

He drew a long breath and steadied himself. "I... I think he knew me before. Some of the things seemed personal."

"What did he look like, your first owner?" Will prodded.

"Older, white haired, heavy set, five-eleven, brown eyes." The description poured out like he was reading it without thought. "Which is odd, because I can't remember what he looks like."

"His treatment toward you...?" the elder prompted, not wishing to put words into Rye's mouth.

"Was unkind," he finished.

"How?" She glanced to where Amanda was giving her a nervous look and hushed the woman.

"He enjoyed hurting me, having me hurt. He let others use me." The words were empty, there was nothing connected to them. Rye felt lightheaded and a touch dizzy.

"What makes you think he knew you before?"

The words echoed inside of Rye's head, sluggish and distant. "What makes me think...?" He muttered back. He fumbled after a memory that felt slippery and when he caught it he screamed.

The memories were there, right there, vivid and real and more solid then the current moment around him. Rye stumbled from his chair but tripped on its legs and landed hard on the ground. He gasped for breath and couldn't fill his lungs and the voices around him vanished to be replaced by the voices of memory.

⚜

"So, this really is him, huh?" One of his owners' guests questioned and nudged his bare side with a booted foot. "Brave man, keeping such a dangerous toy."

Rye heard his owner laughing. "My toy to keep, as always, he's just a little more mannerly now. Go on, try him out."

"What?"

"I know you've thought about it, he's made for it now. Take him to the other room and the lot of you give him a good riding. Nothing like it, I promise, knowing so much death is moaning for your cock."

It hadn't taken much more then that before the trio of guests were leading Rye into the small sitting room to the side of his owner's office. They'd been timid at first, but as soon as they saw he really was different they'd laughed and used him roughly.

He remembered when he was first taken from the transport box, thirsty and tired. His owner had stood there, watching silent as Rye had crept to the waiting water bowl. He'd picked it up to slake his thirst when he received no direction and before the water could touch his lips a stick landed on his shoulders.

"No! You're an animal, you'll eat and drink like one!" His owner had shouted at him and brought the flexible piece of wood down across Rye's back again and again.

In the end, when he lay there beaten, Rye watched the tips of the man's finely made shoes hover near his head. "I told them I wanted you aware in there, but to do that they said you've forgotten everything. Pity, this would be better if you remembered who I was. Just know I remember and that I kept my promise." The shoes had stepped back and Rye felt the man spit on him.

He remembered stumbling back into his owner's apartment, his private rooms not his office, naked. Trembling, feeling broken, covered in cuts, bruises, coated in his own blood, his hair knotted and left with no illusions of what had just happened even if his fragmented mind couldn't remember where he'd been. His body was shivering as the come and spit was drying on his body, sliding across his skin. He could taste it in his mouth, mixed with his own blood, and he knew something very bad had just happened.

He was dazed and felt shattered and knew he didn't want to remember where he'd been. His feet crossed the thick carpet to where his owner sat, watching something on the vid screen. Rye drew closer when he was called over--he'd learned not to delay or stall--and stopped at the edge of the man's chair.

"Look how pretty you are," the man mocked. "You never believed I owned you, but I do and always will." He tossed his head to the screen. "Next time, it'll be twice as many."

Rye glanced uneasily to the screen and the moaning that came from the video. Horror filled him as he saw himself being used and beaten by a room full of men. He couldn't see how many, they kept laughing and moving, suggesting more and more horrible things as he watched one of them crush a lit cigarette on Rye's arm. He watched as the pain mixed with the forced pleasure made him come and the group laughed and shouted out a number.

He felt along his arm and found the fresh burn that he was too numb to feel. It was real, even if he couldn't remember it, it was real. Rye turned and his knees gave out. His stomach turned inside out he vomited across the thick, expensive carpet. When his ears stopped ringing he heard his owner laughing.

"Puked, huh? Never thought I'd see the day you'd get a weak stomach. Clean it up later, boy, right now you've work still to do."

Rye glanced over and saw the man opening his pants. He lost it and vomited again to more harsh laughter, his hair, the hated long hair, dragged in the vomit as a thick hand pulled him closer, dragged already torn up knees across the carpet. The hand tangled into that hair and held his head in place and Rye froze for a moment before doing what was required of him.

"That's it, good whore. I made you, I own you, for as long as it pleases me. Nothing's changed, you'll do whatever I tell you to, for as long as I tell you," his owner growled out. All Rye really could hear was his own recorded moaning, sobbing, and the drunken encouragements of the men at the party he'd so obviously been the entertainment for.

⁂

"Rye!" A worried voice broke the memories. "Oh god, Rye?"

Hands petted his face and supported his body. His mouth tasted like vomit again but this time it was just vomit. The voice calling to him wasn't from his last owner, but his current--and not just his owner, his lover, his love, his life.

He forced eyes open. "Ichi?"

"Yes, I'm here."

Rye didn't cry, there were no tears, no emotion that could express what had been done to him. He clung to Ichi, trembling in memory and hate, knowing that it was truly what he'd been remade to do and it wouldn't have mattered if they'd taken his mind as well. "He knew me, he knew me. Oh god, Ichi, he made me, he was my father."

The room stood silent in shock and it was Amanda that recovered first. "Mark, go to the med lab, quickly, and grab my kit." Will had crumbled with Rye and, while he hadn't vomited as well, it was pretty clear that the strength of the redhead's flashback was hitting him hard too.

"Will do." He nodded and headed out of the room at a dead run.

"You okay?" Amanda asked carefully when she knelt beside Will.

"Peachy," he forced out between clenched teeth, shivering. "Sedate me, please, Mandi, sedate me."

She brushed hair from his forehead. "Soon, love, soon, hang in there." He nodded, so she took that as a chance to move and kneel beside where Rye had fallen, where he still clung to Ichi like a broken doll.

"He's shivering so hard," Ichi noted worriedly before she could settle in.

"Shock, it looks like." She reached out to try to see into Rye's eyes but he jerked away from her touch. "Mark will be back soon with medicine. Rye?" She bent, trying to see into his face. "Rye?"

"Yeah?" he forced out.

"You're having flashbacks, it's normal. Okay?"

"Okay." But he buried his face tighter against Ichi.

"And you're most likely having a panic attack too. Just hang in there."

Mark made it back in record time, winded, but he passed the case off to Amanda and sat down. She popped it open and dug out the dissolve films she'd been looking for.

"Here." She handed one to Will and knew he was smart enough to take it without protest. "And here Rye, put this on your tongue and let it melt."

He didn't question, he took the offer and popped it into his mouth. There was a hint of mint but the thing dissolved almost before he could taste it. Right away he felt the tight fear that had him twisted up easing down. Ichi sensed it as well, he stopped holding onto Rye so tightly and slowly started petting across the sweat dampened hair.

"Is everyone okay?" the male elder asked. They'd turned the sound off on the screen and had been talking privately until the scene of the small drama appeared under control.

Amanda stood. Rye was still ashen looking but visibly easing and Will didn't look ready to pull his own hair out. "Yes, sir, we're okay."

"Good. Please, when you're ready, allow the others back in. We're ready to offer our advice."

"So soon?" She was surprised; normally the elders took some time to discuss things.

"When you're ready." He smiled gently.

Amanda nodded but she gave both men a chance to get a bit more pulled together. Mark helped her clean up the spot where Rye had gotten sick and they made tea to settle rattled nerves. When she was sure they'd stalled as long as they needed to, Will sat with the bridge of his nose pinched between one thumb and a finger, obviously trying to settle down, and Ichi had gotten Rye off the floor to sit, perched uneasily on the very edge of his seat at the table. He was staring off at nothing, hands loosely cupped around his tea and not moving.

"I think we're as ready as we're likely to get," she announced and, with Mark's help, got the room opened back up. The rest of the station slid in, all whispering, which was about as sedate and quiet as any gathering from Avalon got. It was a good thing because she wasn't sure either man's frayed nerves could handle a loud crowd of people.

"Thank you for honoring us in allowing our input into your community," the male elder said and the words felt like ritual.

"We're blessed to have your input," Amanda answered.

"First, all property and possessions of Avalon should be fully restored, replaced or reimbursed. We could find no fault in your community's response to this threat and, to the contrary, your systems have now been tested and proven successful. We agree, all efforts to identify the dead should be made. But if family is unable to be located there is no dishonor in offering them a proper burial, if that is the wish of the community. Harvick will be replaced. A ship will meet with your station in two weeks and it will contain a small crew. They will assume command of Harvick's vessel and his flight run. It was foolish to allow him to make such a dangerous run alone, but it was kind given his grief over the loss of his wife and child. A small crew will make it far more difficult to smuggle aboard anything and offer more safety while running supplies." He paused and drew a breath, glancing to the female elder before continuing.

"Kenichi Vitorui, it is our thoughts and our advice that you do not belong to the Concord. From what we have seen and heard, you have become as much a part of Avalon's community around you as any true children of the green hills. We see no harm in extending the invitation to stay to you as you rebuild your lost collection, for one does not need to hesitate to offer an invitation to family. It is our recommendation that you be formally adopted as a citizen of Avalon. However, we're not so blind to see that it would make regaining your collection more difficult because as a Concord citizen you retain access to so much more. Our hope is that some of your neighbors will remember that not all Avalon souls were born in the right place and perhaps one of them will adopt you, off the record, into their family line. Such an adoption would be recognized by Avalon folks but not the formal government.

"Now, Rye." The man sighed and glanced to the woman beside him and she nodded gently. "What was done to you is unforgivable. We can't express our sympathy for what you've endured in words that would carry enough meaning, nor can we express how it comforts our souls to know you've found a way here, and we hope that with Kenichi and your Avalon neighbors you might find healing. However, we would be blind fools not to notice or see that before you were so altered into being a Pet, you were something more, even how you spoke to us carried the feel of a solider offering a report. We've seen the videos of your fighting abilities; there is no room for doubt, you are a very dangerous man. We can not see what you were before but both of us see a great deal of death and blood on your hands." The man paused and drew a breath while the men and women standing around the silent Rye held their own. "Time and circumstances have made many of Avalon's people into dangerous men and women. A great deal of death and blood is staining Avalon hands and we are no longer so innocent as we once were. It will have to be up to your community whether or not they wish to embrace someone so dangerous among them, but we speak for Avalon as a whole. It is our recommendation that the Pet be killed and be reborn as citizen of Avalon. Perhaps we will be able to find one of our people willing to claim you as a cousin and offer you a name."

"I will." Will spoke up instantly, interrupting the elder in an unheard of fashion.

The elder only smiled softly. "It is our hope that among Avalon you find solace, Rye, and maybe some measure of peace, perhaps even lay your past to rest." He paused again and glanced around the silent room. "Was there anything more we may be of service to?"

Amanda stood. "No, thank you for your time, elder."

He bowed softly. "So may it be." The screen clicked off.

"Well," she turned to the group. "I doubt there are any objections to one of us adopting Ichi into our family line or about his staying on here, but for formalities sake any protest needs to be spoken now."

The room was silent.

"Very well. You all heard what the elders had to say about Rye, any thoughts?"

The room shifted feet and glanced around. It was Mary that stepped forward. "What's to be said? He killed them as easily as I sneeze, but he's one of us."

Rye collapsed forward and almost had his head resting on the table in front of him. Ichi ran a hand across his back very lightly.

"He's family," another added and there were noises of agreement.

Mark waved his hand for silence. "This shouldn't be brushed aside lightly. Rye is a killer, everything we've been learning of his past shows he was some highly trained killer. Everything is pointing to the fact that the people that once had him kill made him into a Pet, which means they know where he is. This is a risk we'd be taking, a large one."

Rosie shrugged into the silence. "Life is a risk, we all know that."

"Also," Mark went on before the group could fully land on a decision. "If we fully take Rye in as one of us, there's no going back. No matter what he did before or does again, he stays one of us."

"None of us can claim innocence," Will whispered.

"One more thing, we'd be committing ourselves to actively helping Rye however we can. The same as we would any Avalon that has lost their past. This isn't to be accepted lightly."

"Are you done yet, you old windbag?" Annie teased.

Mark shook his head. "Yeah, I think I am."

"Are you actually protesting or just being a cynic?" She grinned.

"Just being a cynic, of course."

"Then there's nothing left to be said, except who will take him in?"

"I will," Again Will spoke up. "I'll formally take them both. I'm the last of my line, there's no one to protest the additions or contradict it."

Rye sat up and his eyes were cold and empty. "I can't accept."

"Don't be stupid, of course you can." Will answered.

He just shook his head. "The pet can't be killed, they'd know I was still alive and what new name I was using. It would change nothing. Besides, as a pet I'll retain access to the Concord and my answers may be there."

"A pet doesn't travel alone," Amanda reminded them.

"He's right though, it might be foolish to kill off the pet." Mark spoke softly. "But why not set up an Avalon name and citizenship in the meanwhile, and what's stopping us from getting him a new Concord citizenship under another name? That'll give him three identities to move between."

Ichi frowned. "Can you do that?"

"This is Avalon, we can do anything." Mark grinned.

Will stood up. "Knife?"

A sharp blade was quickly fetched from the kitchen and handed to Will. The group gathered around, silent.

Will took the blade. "Tell me right now if you don't wish this Ichi."

"What would I be refusing?" He glanced around as the others of the station gathered nearer to him.

There was no joking, no light-hearted teasing to Will now. "You'd be refusing to be my brother, and that's okay."

Ichi ran his hand over Rye's back once more--the redhead hadn't lifted his head from the table once yet--before he stood up. "What do I have to do?"

Will nodded and turned his left hand up, the point of the knife cut deeply into the fleshy part under his thumb. One line, two parallel to each other and then a third diagonally cutting joining them. He didn't even flinch as blood welled up and began to drip from his palm. When all three lines were cut he turned the blade around, hilt first and offered it to Ichi.

Ichi took the blade but stared at it blindly. "I don't know how…" He glanced down and Rye was at least looking up now.

It was Amanda that stepped forward. She nodded a little and took the knife from Ichi. He offered his hand, the left as well, and she cradled it in her own. The cuts were quick and deep, the knife sharp. Ichi hissed a little in startled pain and watched in fascination as his own blood welled up to slid in small rivers across his skin.

Will reached across the table, blood dropping in startled specks to the clean surface below. Amanda guided Ichi's own bleeding hand out and he understood and extended it. Left hand met left at an angle, Ichi's bottom line met and mingled with Will's top line and vice versa. Blood from both hands mixed and joined, combined as one and flowed across both wounds.

"All things are born in blood," Will said softly. He glanced up to meet Ichi's startled hazel eyes. "My brother."

The solemn seriousness of the small ritual made Ichi shiver. Will held their hands tightly together for a moment more as blood combined and dripped down arms and to the table. A heat spread from the contact that went beyond the physical and Ichi couldn't explain logically. Will released the contact slowly, smearing blood made one across palms.

"As it was witnessed, so let it be recorded," Amanda announced to the group before she moved to bandage both wounds. "So it is that Kenichi Vitorui Sullivan is born." Normally such an adoption would set off a celebration, but the past day didn't warrant much joy. "I'm taking Will home. Ichi, I suggest you do the same for Rye, they're both shaken up."

He nodded, shaken up himself, but before he could help get Rye to his feet and moving Amanda touched his arm and stopped him. "Bring me everything that came with Rye, everything."

"Why?"

"I'm going to test it all for DNA. Maybe I can get a hit on his last owner, if they simply passed any of his equipment along, traces might remain."

Ichi nodded now. "If you can figure that out, we might be able to figure out who Rye was."

"It's a step."

"I'll have it to you right away." He slid a hand across Rye's shoulder and at the gentle touch the taller man stood up. "Come on, Rye, let's go home."

But Rye didn't answer, he didn't even look up, he just wanted to be invisible.

Chapter Seventeen

Rye followed as silently and submissively as a good pet should all the way back to the apartment. It was something Ichi was unwilling to address, if Rye needed to retreat into his own thoughts, who was he to prod him back out? It was a mannerism Rye might never fully lose, when upset or frightened he might always fall back on the training of being a pet.

As soon as the doors shut behind them, Ichi locked them and moved to the kitchen. "Are you hungry? I haven't eaten, thought I'd throw something together?"

There was no answer and when he turned around Rye wasn't in the living room. Ichi put his plans for food on hold and instead set tea to brewing, the rich black version Rye liked better. He moved to the bedroom looking for the other man and heard the shower running. He stood, torn between checking on Rye and giving him his space, and in the end he landed on retreating to the kitchen to wait for the tea.

The tea finished and he fixed one with a touch of honey and the other with sugar and soy milk the way Rye liked it and waited. The tea cooled and still no Rye appeared. Finally, nervous now, Ichi picked up the lukewarm mugs, reheated them and carried both to the bathroom.

The shower was still running. This time he pushed the bathroom door open and was met by a billowing wall of steam. The water must be running very hot to fog up the bathroom so, and the damp humid air carried the scent of soap with it. Ichi pulled the door shut and set the mugs on the counter.

"Rye?"

There was no answer.

Ichi popped the door open a little and peered into the stall. Rye sat on the floor, knees pulled up under his chin in a painful display of flexibility. His head was bowed and the water, nearly scalding, beat down across him. A washcloth lay forgotten on the floor nearby and, either from the scrubbing or the too hot water, Rye's pale skin was flushed red.

"Rye? You okay?" Which was an absurd question because it was pretty obvious the man wasn't.

"I can't get clean," he muttered out under the water. "I can't get the feel of them off my skin."

Ichi reached in and shut the water off. "I don't think you can scald it away or scrub it away. Here now, let's get you dried off." It made him feel like someone had kicked him in the chest, but Ichi knew enough to at least get Rye out and dried off.

Rye moved as he was directed, but with little will of his own. When Ichi wrapped a towel around his hips he simply held it in place, not able to summon the energy to care that he was dripping water everywhere. He let himself be towel dried easily, shivering a little in emotion and not cold. When Ichi pressed the mug of tea into his hands he accepted without protest.

He left Rye leaning against the countertop and pulled clothes for him to wear. Ichi dug out the loosest, warmest clothes they'd gotten for Rye. It was all soft fabrics that were cut in generous sizes, what Ichi called comfy clothes that Rye had seemed baffled by. He also dug out the thickest, warmest socks, knowing the other man was still getting used to being allowed to wear socks or shoes and, like chairs, still not fully comfortable in them.

"Here." He offered the stack of clothes over to the still and silent man. "Before you catch chill."

Rye took the clothing and petted across its soft fabrics. The smallest of smiles tugged at his mouth. "Comfort clothes." He dressed quickly, even pulling on the fuzzy socks without protest.

The clothes made Rye look smaller, younger and more vulnerable as he literally was swimming in the fabric. It made Ichi wonder a little bit about how old Rye might actually be. Pets had no real age, grown to the desired age and then modified, they had neither birthdays nor childhoods. Rye had both, even if he couldn't remember either. Ichi only knew that Rye was an adult, Amanda guessed maybe in his mid twenties. But suddenly, standing there, Ichi felt he was much younger.

Rye petted the loose clothes that hung from his body. "They're nice, thank you."

Ichi held the mug of tea out to him and Rye accepted. He led them out of the bathroom back to the living room and got Rye pressed down onto the sofa. The tea was set aside, untasted, and Rye pulled his knees up under his chin again.

"Want to talk about it?" Ichi asked softly, feeling completely out of his depth.

Rye just shook his head no.

Ichi tucked his own legs up under him on the sofa and just sat. There was plenty to think about, plenty had changed in both his personal and professional life, but he found his mind empty. He sipped his tea, but only to have something to do, and just sat while Rye struggled with whatever thoughts were buzzing around inside his head.

"Tomorrow I'll talk to Amanda about getting a different room," Rye finally said, his voice empty of emotion.

"What?" That snapped Ichi's thoughts from the empty wanderings they'd been in.

"I have no right to stay here." If he did he'd not be able to resist Ichi, he wanted the other man so badly, so deeply, and he knew he shouldn't touch the reserved man, that he had no right.

"Is leaving what you want?" He managed to make his voice steady but his heart started racing.

Rye slowly shook his head, unable to glance over to where Ichi was curled up at the other end of the sofa. "What I want and what I should do isn't the same thing."

"Stay."

"I can't."

"I thought you said you wouldn't leave unless I sent you away?" Ichi's voice broke, his control was crumbling and he wasn't sure if he was hurt, angry or scared.

"Ichi, I can't, I, you don't know." But Rye did, he knew it all now, he remembered it now. It was no longer hazy or the wrapped-in-cotton-feeling, he really knew what had happened with his first owner. There was no backing away from that knowledge.

"Tell me or not, I don't care."

"You should!" Rye stood up and started pacing. "I'm a whore."

"Don't say that."

"I am! I have no right to love you!" He almost shouted but the words drained the anger away into embarrassed horror. "Damn it! Worse, I'm a brain damaged whore! I can't even think something without blurting it out!" His legs refused to hold him and Rye dropped to sit on the floor.

Ichi stood and moved carefully to sit near the openly tormented man. "You are not a whore, they made you do it. That's rape, you didn't want it."

Rye groaned a little and folded forward over his bent legs, curling up again. "But I did want it; they made it so I would want it. God, Ichi, he even took that from me. Made it so I wouldn't even be able to stop that."

He sat silent and tried to process what he'd been told. When he thought he had absorbed it, then and only then did he speak. "I don't care. I don't care if you've been sexually involved with every Concord citizen and their dogs. I don't care if you enjoyed it or hated it, begged for it or refused. It doesn't matter to me, so long as you don't leave."

Rye sat up, sniffed hard and rubbed at the unshed tears in his eyes. "You can't mean that." But the spat of anger and pain was draining away into exhaustion, thanks in large part to the drugs Amanda had given him.

"Of course I can, I'm not a child," Ichi nearly snapped back. "Naive, yes, I will grant that, but I'm not ignorant. It hurts me that anyone hurt you; now, in the past, or tomorrow, the very idea makes me ache. But Rye, how can you think I would hold that against you? How can you think I would be jealous or upset or sullied by your past? You don't know, I could have slept my way through college, or across the universe and you wouldn't know!"

The idea of Ichi sleeping around made Rye half-chuckle. "Did you?" he asked in a weakened, tired voice.

"Well, no, but I could have. I'm not unattractive, you know."

"I've noticed." Rye reached out and brushed stray hair back out of the hazel eyes. "I have nothing to offer you."

"What?"

Rye shook his head. "I can't even offer you this body, there's nothing I haven't done, no innocence left to share, not one aspect that isn't dirtied or broken." He'd been thinking about the conversation he'd had with Will a lot and hadn't liked the raw and truthful answers he'd found. "I have no money, no job, no future, not even a name. The only things I seem capable of doing is killing people or fucking them. I have nothing to give you." He swallowed hard and couldn't meet those steady eyes. "There's no reason for you to keep me here, no role I can fill except being your whore, and while I would totally enjoy that, you deserve better."

It baffled Ichi. "But, last night, you said… I mean, and now, didn't you mean that?"

It took Rye's clouded mind a second to translate what Ichi was trying to say. "That I love you?"

Ichi nodded.

"I do."

"I, Rye, I…"

"It's okay, I don't expect you to feel anything toward me. I know what I am."

"I just learned today that it's unusual for someone to have never heard those words before. I don't know what to do with that, Rye. I, god it makes me feel so good and scares me silly." Ichi confessed quickly before he got frightened. "So I don't really know, but isn't just...being together, enough? Isn't that offering enough?"

Rye suddenly understood why Ichi had been so freaked out that morning. "Oh, Ichi..."

"Just, offer me yourself, okay? That's all I want, just a chance to know you, be with you, trust you and have you trust me." The raw honesty of his words surprised him and made him blush. Ichi glanced down to the bandage cut on his hand. "Seems Will's crazy Avalon blood is screwing with me. My father would have a fit if he heard me spouting about love like some mad poet."

"So, I should stay?" Rye asked carefully, unwilling to believe, finding it too painful to hope.

Ichi nodded. "I don't know what I'd do if you didn't. It's just, Rye, you have your past, I have mine. If I can't catalog it, explain it, document it, I can't understand it. And relationships, emotion? I've no idea how to process that. Give me space to figure out things and I'll give you space to figure out yours. Okay?"

"Sounds like a plan." Rye agreed. It didn't make him feel any less dirty, any more worthy, but he no longer felt cut off from the only thing he'd found that really mattered.

"Now, how about some food?" Ichi asked as he pushed himself up off the floor to move toward the kitchen, needing to retreat to the practical world of day to day care to settle his uneasy nerves.

"Ichi?"

"Hmm?"

He wanted to tell him how much he loved him, how much he needed him, how right and whole and normal he felt when they were alone together, but the words melted when Ichi glanced back to where Rye still sat. He'd be blind not to see how much the other man needed to back away from such raw, vulnerable emotions.

"How about pasta?"

There had been a long enough pause between whatever it was Rye wanted to say and what he actually did say that Ichi knew he'd changed it. He smiled softly, gratefully, and nodded. "Anything you want."

Cleaning out his lab was one of the most difficult things Ichi had ever been forced to do. He refused help from his station mates and Rye alike. Only Rye didn't listen to his protests and helped him anyway. Over the course of the days it took to tear apart and dispose of all the containers, Ichi found himself stopping on several occasions to just sit, overwhelmed by all that had been lost. Some of his collection he'd maintained the same line of since university, raising and caring for generations of insects--and it was all gone.

"You know..." Ichi said late in the afternoon, the lab nearly stripped to the walls around him. "This might be a blessing."

Rye dropped another sheet of containment plastic onto the cart and wiped at his forehead. Working, the hard physical work of tearing apart, felt good. "How so?" His only regret, other than the pain that often flickered in Ichi's eyes, was that his cushion and blanket and the sign hung over them would most likely be too contaminated to save.

"If we lay out the room better, the containments can be laid out better. Compartmentalize the areas, gas only the sections with breaches, save anything not being threatened? Might even be safer for us too, if we can rig up a way that seals the room into parts, might only get caught with one or two of the swarm. Two won't kill you." He was trying to picture the new system in his head. "And if we do this right, I can have a larger habitat for them, maybe divide it into sections. Seal them in one section to make modifications or testing in another? It'll give me a lot more flexibility."

Rye leaned against the side of the cart and downed some swallows of water. "You just figure out what you need and I'll build it." He was finding he had a good knack for that too. He seemed to have an innate knowledge of how things fit together, how to build or take apart and the sheer physical strength to wrestle even stubborn panels in place.

"Will do, I..." but his notebook beeped at him and broke his thoughts off. "Hang on." Ichi had to stretch to reach where it had been set on one of the few work surfaces they hadn't torn out. "Yes?"

"Ichi?" Amanda popped on to the screen. "When you two get a moment, swing by here okay?" She glanced off camera. "We have something to show you."

"Sure thing." He clicked the notebook off and glanced up. Rye was covered in a light sheen of sweat, his shirt sleeves pushed up to show off strong arms, and he was so stunningly handsome that Ichi forgot how to speak for a second. "Want to take a break and go see what's on their mind?"

Rye licked the last clinging drops of water from his lips and felt his skin grow hot from the way Ichi was watching him. If he'd known working for the quiet man would get him so turned on, Rye would have been lifting heavy things for weeks. He set his water bottle down and nodded.

"Sure, just one thing first." He crossed the space between them and rested a knee on the crate Ichi was sitting on before he lowered down to kiss him.

Ichi moaned into the kiss, letting his head tilt back into Rye's hand, loving how the redhead towered over him. "Rye?" he gasped when his mouth was released.

"Not fair looking at me like that and expecting me to walk away," Rye whispered into an ear before nipping it. His hands sliding across Ichi's clothing covered body to draw out more startled gasps.

When those teasing hands started to open his pants, Ichi tried to pull away. "Rye, no," he hissed out, breathless and embarrassingly hard from such little contact.

"Yes," Rye chuckled softly and deftly finished parting the fabric.

Ichi tried to protest again, but Rye was quicker and the words he was trying to form melted into a needy moan as Rye swallowed him whole. "Oh, god." He managed to gasp out, unwilling and unable to stop Rye. "The door…. Oh oh please, yes…." He shook his head and half fell across the crate. "Rye, the door doesn't… oh… doesn't lock," he managed to get out in what he hoped was a clear manner. He could feel how red his face was at just the idea that someone could walk in on them.

Rye paused long enough to glance up, catching hazel eyes nearly green with desire. "Let them watch, let them see how beautiful you are like this," he whispered and was rewarded with a long shuddering moan before Ichi fell across the crate and melted.

As he lay there, overwhelmed and happily so, Rye swallowing him like some rare candy and roughly stroking himself off with his free hand, Ichi found he didn't care if anyone walked in. In fact, he was starting to wonder if he might need to add exhibitionism to his growing list of newfound kinks. Wouldn't be a bad one to add to the list, a small voice teased him, given that Rye seemed willing to pounce on him anywhere. Even as he writhed, moaning while his hands ran through red silken hair, Ichi knew he'd never really want Rye to stop pouncing.

"Graces mercy you two, you're worse than newlyweds," Will teased as soon as Rye and Ichi crossed into their lab.

"I wouldn't know what you're talking about," Ichi denied but his blush confirmed.

Rye remained silent and Amanda just rolled her eyes. "Leave them alone," she warned her own mate and thumped his arm.

"Where's the sport in it if I'm not allowed to tease them a little bit?" Will grinned, but it turned into a happy smile. He rubbed at the healing cut on his hand and the smile grew more contented.

"You wanted to see us?" Ichi ignored Will and addressed Amanda.

"Yes, please." She motioned for them to come all the way into the lab. "Rye, dear, you might want to sit down."

"Why?" he asked, suspicious, but he took the offered seat. Will was in the seat nearest him but Ichi hovering to his side.

"Rye, we asked Ichi to send over all the equipment and supplies sent along with you. We've been going over it all forensically, looking for gene code samples in the hopes that something might have been carried from one owner to the next," Amanda explained and leaned against the counter nearest the vid screen she'd pulled the files up on.

"Hoping to learn who owned me and who I am?"

"Yes, exactly. I didn't want to tell you, didn't want to get your hopes up in case we weren't able to pull anything."

"But you have."

She nodded at him. "We have."

His stomach turned over but he nodded. "Okay."

"Most of what we found is incidental. We ruled out any hits we got from Ichi or yourself and we found one hit on a man that comes back as an employee of PETS. He works in the shipping department and most likely just roughed off some skin cells while packing the supplies up. We blacked out his code and kept looking." She folded her arms and wondered if this was the best thing to do.

"What did you find?" Rye asked carefully.

"Most everything was either new or clean enough to not matter. However, the collar you were sent with is ornate. Scroll metalwork over leather, perfect collector of DNA. It's been cleaned but not sterilized and we found plenty of trace evidence of your blood on it in the scrollwork of the metal."

"And?"

"And one trace semen sample with a gene code that wasn't blacked out."

"Who?"

"Ready for this?" She asked and waited until Rye nodded before calling up the picture. "His name is Howard Conti." A standard identification image appeared of a man with thick white hair, a face that was carrying a touch too much weight and neutral scowl. "Five-eleven, brown eyes, aged 68."

Rye had to close his eyes to keep from getting sick. A warm hand slid onto his shoulder and Ichi's touch gave him a current point of reference to focus on. "That's him."

"Who is he?" Ichi asked for them both.

"He's CEO and grand poombah of Lerman Securities Limited. Real big-wig and connected enough and wealthy enough to keep most of his profile secured." She checked with Will but at his nod continued. "What he isn't, Rye, is your father. At least, not in a biological sense. Even when we deconstruct all the mucking that was done to you, there's virtually no chance that he is related to you by blood."

"We called him Father...Papa Conti." Rye whispered but he forced himself to open his eyes and look at the man.

"We?" Will asked carefully.

"I don't know. Just... we." Rye sighed. "His name has been right there, on the tip of my tongue and I haven't been able to get it out. I'm not his son?" The truth was comforting, in at least a small way.

"Not by blood," Amanda confirmed.

"Don't some religious orders call their priests father?" Ichi asked, glancing from one of his friends to the other.

Will snorted. "Some, yes, but there's nothing priestly about this bastard. Lerman Security Limited is one of about four high-level freelance security firms. So skilled, so exclusive, they don't deal with people, they deal with governments."

"Will's being dramatic. They've worked with high-end celebrities and the like, but for the most part they deal with classified, never-to-be-spoken-of, behind-the-scenes work for large companies or governments," Amanda corrected.

"Anyway," Will went on. "Lerman is one of the oldest. Talking top of the line, need someone to train your private army or kill your rival? They're who you call. Hell, they've run armies, controlled cities, arranged accidents, you name it. Total mercenaries, from body guarding and little work like that to guiding coups."

"Illegal things, like the Flossin Guard?" Ichi asked, trying to understand.

"Not illegal." Will glanced to Amanda but she was keeping her mouth shut. "Flossin Guard were a secret offshoot of the Fleet military, which is supposed to be illegal to do. Companies like Lerman? Totally legal, they pay taxes for god's sake. There are loopholes in the law, one of their workers could help slaughter two dozen people and if caught they just have to say oops sorry, thought it was a staged fake, didn't know it was real people, not my fault. Or if they train a small army, oops, thought it was for personal security didn't know they were planning on overthrowing the whole colony. Loopholes make it very vague on the responsibility of companies like this. So long as the agent caught can justify their actions, no matter how thinly, they're legal and safe. There's never even been any arrests."

"And you think what? That I worked for this company?" Rye asked, glancing from one to the other and neither one willing to meet his eye.

"It's a high probability of it, yes," Amanda finally admitted. "Trouble is, their files are all sealed, locked up. We can't touch them. It gets more interesting though. Lerman is a growth company, they've bought shares in a good three dozen different companies and firms. One of which they own a majority share in is PETS Living Companion Division. Not a single share in the other division's of PETS, just the Living Companion one."

"So he did do this to me." He wasn't sure if he should feel better or worse and right now just felt queasy and numb.

"Looks that way, but Rye, if he had access to their labs, it would have been easy to work the original modifications on you."

"And there's nothing else you can find out about him? Nothing about me?" He glanced away from those cold eyes and the memory of what warmed them up.

"Little more. He lives in the same building that Lerman owns and operates from, which, incidentally, is in the same secure complex that Living Companions operates from. He doesn't travel and he's the third generation Conti to run Lerman, his grandfather established it. Other than that? Nothing else is in the public domain," Will added.

"Not married, no family?"

Will shrugged. "Not that we can tell. Trust me, Rye, there's no chance this man fathered you, he's not your family by blood."

"Howard Conti," Rye tried the name out on his tongue. "Thank you, both of you, it's a start."

His vid screen was beeping, not the one in the main room only, but all of them. Will snuggled tighter against a warm body and curls tickled his nose, Amanda was wrapped in his arms, one of his legs tossed over hers, and he was too asleep to move.

"Answer it," she muttered and thumped his side, sleepily yawning.

"No." He pulled her closer.

She whined and elbowed him. "No one would risk calling me at this ungodly hour. It's for you."

"Meanie," he muttered but untangled himself and sat up to flick the answer button and let the screen in the bedroom light up. "Yeah?" he nearly barked out and rubbed at his eyes.

"Will?"

The voice was so small, so shaken that Will didn't instantly know it and he had to drop his hands from his eyes to peer at the vid screen. "Rye?"

"Oh god, Will," he sobbed out, his eyes red. The normally empty, passive face was twisted up in tormented pain, tears streaked unnoticed down his cheeks and even in the dim light of Rye's apartment the wild, broken look to his eyes was clear.

"Rye? What's wrong?" He reached back to smack at Amanda's leg but she was already getting up.

"I killed him," Rye sobbed out. "It was me, I killed him, there's so much blood! Oh god, what have I done?" He sobbed.

"Rye? Rye?" Will's blood was chilled, but the redhead had wandered away from the camera's pickups and left the line connected. "Oh god." The healing cut on his hand ached. "I knew he took today too well, I knew it. I should have known it was just shock, oh, god, you don't think...?" He turned to Amanda and a med kit flew at his head. Will caught it on instinct and the heavy weight knocked some of his panic down.

"I don't think losing your head will help. Keep it together and get moving," She snapped, kicking his shoes at him as she shoved her feet into her own.

He nodded and pushed his feet into the shoes. "It's just, Ichi, I..." He couldn't say it, but he couldn't bear to lose another brother.

Will didn't need to put his fears into words. "I know, but we don't know anything, and if Ichi's hurt sitting here won't help him." She knew, she knew all about the fears and loss that still woke Will up late at night.

Chapter Eighteen

There was no way either of them could walk to Ichi's apartment. Will took off at a dead run with Amanda close on his heels and both prepared themselves for the worst. The apartment door was unlocked, which wouldn't have been odd for anyone but Ichi who locked his doors out of habit. Inside the apartment lights were dimmed low but it was enough light to see by and the pair hurried for the bedroom.

"Ichi!" Will called out as he hurtled past the bedroom door. "Ichi!" He braced for blood or cold flesh.

"Go away," Ichi muttered from the mound of covers in the center of the bed.

Will smacked the light switch and raised the lights all the way up.

The lump on the bed protested again and pulled covers tighter.

"Ichi? Are you okay?" Will pulled the covers from his grip and yanked them away. It exposed the body underneath, shirtless and in only a thin pair of sleeping pants and very much unharmed.

And very much pissed. "Will? What do you think you're doing?" He snapped awake, cold and now frightened.

Seeing wasn't good enough. Will tumbled onto the bed, dropping the med kit and running his hands across Ichi. "Are you hurt anywhere? Are you okay?" He ran his hands up over Ichi's scalp and felt no wounds and even went so far as to run hands across arms and legs looking for injuries.

Ichi blushed bright red and pulled away, or tried to, but Will didn't stop groping him until he'd checked all limbs. "I'm fine, confused, but fine. Stop that!"

Will nearly sobbed in relief and pulled the slighter man against him into a tight hug. "Oh gods, if you'd been hurt."

The hug startled him but Ichi sat blindly and allowed it. He locked eyes with Amanda who stood to the side and didn't pounce on him. "Care to explain to me why your husband has lost his mind?"

She sat on the side of the rumpled bed. "Where's Rye, Ichi?"

"How should I know, I was asleep!" Will started to pet his hair in a comforting gesture the way a parent would a child and it made Ichi's skin crawl. He hit at Will until he could push the other man away. "Stop that and so help me if you start cooing baby talk I will hurt you."

"You're okay."

Ichi shook his head. "I am but it doesn't seem like you are. What's going on here?"

"Rye called us." Amanda answered since Will was obviously still scattered. "He was crying, upset, kept saying he'd killed you, that there was blood everywhere. Then he just walked away and left the line open. We feared the worst and came right over."

Ichi slid out of bed and found his shirt. "Rye would never hurt me."

"Wait, he didn't say he'd killed Ichi, he just said 'I killed him.' Just him, no names." Will corrected as sense returned in the fading wake of cold fear.

"He has a reoccurring nightmare about seeing me in a pool of blood." Ichi pulled his shirt on. "He's phobic that if he lets me care about him that something bad will happen to me."

"He must have had a dream, seeing Conti today must have upset him." Amanda glanced to Will and was pleased to see he was looking almost normal.

"He seemed okay about it," Ichi admitted and glanced around the room. Rye had come to bed shirtless and his shoes were still lined up against the wall.

"Doesn't mean it didn't freak him out. He's picking up your bad habits, Ich," Will muttered.

"We need to find him."

Will climbed off the bed and pushed Ichi back down. "No, stay here in case he comes back. I think I know where he might be. Let me go get him."

"But…" Ichi protested from where he sat.

"Trust me, I know a thing or two about nightmares." He winked at the pair before slipping out, not wanting to have to explain more.

He stopped in the kitchen long enough to gather up some supplies and to make sure Amanda or Ichi hadn't tried to follow him. When he was sure it was all clear he hurried along to the access hatch, popping the complicated latches by feel in the night dimmed hallway. The lantern was inside, which didn't surprise him because he was pretty sure Rye didn't need the light to move around any more than he did.

Will turned it on anyway the moment he got the latch back in place. He knew it was a very bad idea to startle anyone trained to kill, knew it first hand. It had been the primary reason he'd kept his distance from Amanda for almost a year after the surrender, until he was sure his nerves had settled down. Even then, it had taken years more for him to be able to sleep without a weapon at hand, something that Amanda hadn't understood but just accepted.

The twists and turns passed quickly and Will wasn't sure he'd find his quarry when he heard a sobbed breath be held and shakily released around a darkened corner. "Rye?" he called out, unwilling to do anything to spook the other man. "It's just me, mind if I join you?"

He crouched there but no answer came either way. "Well, I'm going to come over there." Will moved carefully, letting the light go ahead of him and he found Rye, huddled against the wall.

The redhead was barefoot and shirtless. He was sitting crosslegged, and while his eyes were red he wasn't crying any more. Balanced in one hand was a slender, very sharp kitchen knife, but he just sat there, holding it. He didn't even look up as Will settled in across from him.

"Thought you might like some," Will said softly and pushed the small packet of tissues across the way with his foot.

"It was a dream, wasn't it?" Rye finally spoke, his voice low and broken. "I didn't hurt him, did I?"

"He was still sleeping like a baby. Scared me about half to death, but Ichi's fine."

"I'm sorry."

Will shrugged. "Happens." He forced his shoulders to relax. "So, what's the knife for?"

Rye shook his head. "If I'd hurt him…"

"You didn't."

Rye just turned the blade around in his hands, the metal glinting in the dim light.

"You don't really want to. Well, that's bullshit, I'm sure right now the idea feels pretty nice. Finish it all before you can actually hurt him? Hurt him a little with your death and know he'll get over it instead of waiting and maybe really hurting him later? A little bit of pain to end a bigger one you don't want to deal with, an end that's easy and mostly quick?" Will spoke gently and earned a quick glance up from

Rye. "No matter how much you might want to right now, you won't in an hour. Trust me, I've held that knife a couple times myself."

"If I'd hurt him..."

"You didn't. It was just a dream."

"Didn't feel like a dream!" Rye forced out between clenched teeth.

Will nodded and pulled the tab on one of the cartons of chai he'd picked up. It heated quickly in his hand. "Here." He held the carton out to Rye and made the man either refuse the offer or put the knife down and accept it.

The choice wasn't an easy one. Rye set the knife down carefully, the metal making tiny clinking sounds that the unnatural wind carried away. The blade lay between the two men, within reach of either, but Rye took the chai and wrapped both hands around it.

Will nodded and pulled the tab on the second one. "Tell me about it?"

"The dream?" Rye asked but his eyes were on his chai.

"Yeah, Ichi said you keep having a nightmare about him being hurt. Was it like that?"

The dream had felt so real. "I don't really remember calling you, that feels like a dream and the dream feels real."

Will shrugged. "Mixed up in nightmares and waking, I'm not surprised. You dreamed you hurt Ichi?"

"I didn't want to, I had to."

"Why?"

"I don't know, I had to. He was lying there, dead in his own blood, his eyes were open, watching while..."

"While?"

Rye shook his head.

"You won't shock me, or upset me. While what?"

Rye just shook his head again. "Just a nightmare."

"Was Conti in it?"

"Yes."

"It's not uncommon for memories to mix with current fears in nightmares."

"Will, I think maybe, it was from before I was like this, it felt different."

"That's good isn't it? If some of those memories are starting to slip into dreams, that means they're still there. Looks promising on you remembering more."

Rye shook his head. "What if I don't want to remember?"

"Don't you?"

"I like my life now." He studied the carton of chai but it offered no answers. "I don't think I liked it much before."

Will sat silent and let the breeze ruffle around them while he tried to pick apart what Rye was saying with what he wasn't saying. "I used to run with a gang," he finally said into the lingering silence.

Rye just glanced up, unsure where the confession was coming from.

"After my family died. Bare Earth took every one of them in less than two years. That was unusual, but happened with some families. Everyone but one or two was taken in the first waves of the virus, I was just the lucky one. I was fifteen, my village was mostly gone to disease and fighting and I joined a gang of Avalon kids." It seemed foolish now, but there was safety in numbers, and someone to bury you when you died.

"That's where you learned to fight?"

"Yeah, rough and tumble Avalon style." He sipped at the cooling chai to wash the bitterness from his mouth. "I didn't like myself much, figured I was living on borrowed time like everyone else. I did a lot of things I'm not proud of. Eventually the group I was running with ran across someone bigger and badder and those of us that survived scattered. I ended up in the city, mixed in with the docs that were scrambling for a cure because of my high level of resistance. That's how I met Amanda, her mother was one of the top doctors, brilliant woman.

"See, though, I was barely literate, rough, rude, violent, anti-social, drunk half the time, but they took me in. Wanted to keep their test subjects close at hand and well, I was used to fighting for someone else. They fed me, I helped out, kept the building secure, that sort of thing. I showed an aptitude for medical work, research, and Amanda, this stunning glowing angel made sure I could read better, taught me enough to be useful as an assistant. They were pretty short-handed, what with people dropping over dead every wave. I was seventeen and horny and she was stunning. I would have swallowed ground glass if she'd asked me to." Will laughed and glanced to where Rye sat silent, listening.

"Bare Earth took Amanda's mother in that last wave, just as the vaccine was being mass produced. The militia smart boys had an idea to get the Fleet out of our skies, but it was a suicide run. I got picked, had no family, no reason to live, no worry about dying."

"You agreed?"

"Of course." He nodded. "Nine of us smuggled up there and only four lived to touch Avalon soil again, five made it to the escape launch but one bled to death on the way down. Anyway, twenty minutes before I was to leave Amanda comes running up, sobbing her eyes out, telling me I had to come back, that I couldn't leave her, that she loved me. Me, the sociopath, Mr. Fuck-the-world-before-it-fucks-you, she loved me. I mean I was hot for her but love? Not even in my dictionary. She saw me at my worst, my absolute worst, saw and knew all the horrible things I'd done and still loved me, even though I didn't love myself. Pretty powerful stuff, love. It's something people like Amanda and Ichi don't hand out randomly and people like you and I have to struggle to accept."

Rye downed the last swallows of the spicy tea. "You think my dreams are a metaphor? My fears that if Ichi knows me too well it'll kill what we have?"

"I don't know." Will shrugged. "I work with immunology all day, not psychology, but it is a fear you've been holding in. Even if the dreams aren't stemming from it, that fear is getting mixed with it."

"I'm sorry I woke you." He was calmer now. When he'd fully woken up, tucked in the darkened tunnel, he'd felt like he'd been vibrating like a poorly made bell.

"Don't worry about it. We should have known seeing Conti would trigger something, it's okay. We'll leave some sedatives with you, if you're feeling unsteady take one before bed. It might not stop the nightmares totally, but it'll knock them down. Trust me, I still keep a supply on hand for personal use." He nudged Rye's bare foot with his own shoe covered one. "Feel like heading back? I'm sure Ichi's worried about you."

Rye followed, silent and a step or two behind Will for the walk back to Ichi's apartment. The knife discarded in the access tunnels was tucked lightly along Will's body, half out of sight from Rye but the redhead knew it was there. He also knew seven ways to take the knife back and myriad uses for it once in his possession. He shook his head and followed, trying to push those unwanted thoughts away, hating how easily such things came to mind now.

There was an easier thought to distract himself with. Ichi would rightfully be pissed. Not only had one of Rye's nightmares woken him, again, but he'd called and frightened Will and Amanda pretty badly too. It would almost be easier if Ichi did beat him; that was something he could understand, and once the flurry of blows was over Rye knew his guilt would be washed away with it. It was something he understood, even if he didn't like that understanding.

The apartment door opened and Will lead him inside. Amanda and Ichi sat at the table, tea cooled and forgotten in front of them. Rye glanced up and saw the tense, unhappy way Ichi sat, his spine perfectly straight, his hands clasped in his lap, eyes directed ahead but unfocused, and it hurt him to see it. Even when Amanda glanced over at the door opening, Ichi remained unmoved.

"Found him!" Will called out, grinning a little as he moved slightly to hide the sight of the knife from the pair at the table.

It wouldn't have mattered, as soon as Ichi blinked and glanced Rye's way, his eyes wandered no where else. He stood up quickly and hurried across the small room, stubborn focus set on his face. Will hurriedly side stepped to get out of the way, uncertain what Ichi was up to, actually frightened by the intensity in his normally shy brother. Will flinched a little as he stepped aside, ready to stop Ichi if the man actually did unleash violence.

Rye flinched too, hunkering his shoulders a little, ready to take whatever Ichi was silently moving to deliver. He dropped his eyes as Ichi's hands swung out and startled so strongly when those same hands grasped the sides of his face with pressing force. Before he could glance up or protest, Ichi was tight to his body, his lips covered his own. The normally reserved man met him in a blistering kiss, mouth parted and demanding and Rye surrendered to the kiss as fully as he was prepared to surrender to a beating.

Will shook his head and slipped into the kitchen to return the blade back to Ichi's collection. Amanda noticed, since she was trying not to watch in slack-jawed awe at the burning passion across the room. She raised an eyebrow at seeing the blade, but at Will's gentle shake of the head she held her tongue.

"Who knew Ichi had it in him?" Will teased as he came and put an arm around his wife. "Enough you two, geesh, get a room already!" He was laughing now, as much at the sight of the unusual display of lust as from the emotions rolling around the pair. Ichi had been near broken with worry and now floated on relief and love. Rye had been dripping shame on the way back and now stood in startled lust and acceptance.

Ichi broke the kiss but whispered something to Rye and waited for the nodded answer before he pulled the redhead into a tight hug. Slowly, Rye's arms rose to enfold Ichi as well. There was another whisper, another nod before Ichi ran a hand across Rye's hair and released him.

Will pulled Amanda toward the door. "We're going back to bed. You two try to get some sleep or something." He hurried them out the door without giving either man the chance to say anything, but he stopped on the other side and quickly kissed his wife.

"What was that for?" she asked with a soft smile.

He just shrugged. "Just reminded how much I love you."

She slid an arm around his waist and hid the larger smile. "Silly romantic."

Chapter Nineteen

"Rye, you've pestered the poor crew enough, come back to the passenger cabin." Ichi tried to sound stern, but the look on Rye's face made it difficult.

Will and Amanda had been personally requested to perform the annual physicals on Station 843. It had been nearly a year, and still they'd been unwilling to accept another full-time medical officer. Jake Ellia had delayed the paperwork as long as he could, but in the end he'd given in and called in two doctors he knew he could trust.

Which worked out well. Ichi had been toying with asking Dr. Ellia and his group of programmers to review his kill switch program and make any modifications they felt were helpful. He really did plan to make his new lab better, safer and more efficient before the first of his restock arrived. By the time he could replace his swarm his lab would be an ideal setting, incorporating all that he'd learned about them over the years and all he had already known.

But hiring Dr. Ellia could be done by vid screen, and when stripped away it was just a cover. Will had been confident that Jake could slip in a new identity for Rye right into the Concord mainframes and more than that, when Jake learned of the situation, he'd do it gleefully. But Rye would have to be there in person, the scanners taking retinal images had to be key-coded Concord issued scanners, or skillfully made clones. Will didn't know which it was that Jake had, clone or original, he just knew the man had the highly illegal-to-own equipment.

So when the intra-system shuttle arrived with the replacement crew for Harvick's waiting ship, Will, Amanda, Ichi and Rye casually got on and hunkered down for the nine hour trip. The shuttle was crewed by nine people that lived and worked on one floor of the small, sleek craft. In theory, crew sections were off limits to passengers, but Rye had shown such open delight at their vessel the Captain, a handsome blonde woman with wide hips and small breasts, had made an exception. Rye had spent four hours touring the ship, being shown everything from crew space to cargo holds, and apparently ended up in the flight cabin talking the current shift's ears off.

The second in command shrugged at Ichi's arrival and protest. "No bother, sir, we've just been going on about Zurlish Points."

Rye shook his head again. "Too unstable for the benefits they offer. Horrible addition."

The man shook his head. "They were too unstable, but with a little tweaking the new models are acceptable. Fish tail a bit when grabbing air but nothing that a good pilot can't handle."

Ichi didn't know what a Zurlish Point was and didn't want to seem ignorant and ask. "Still, it's late, Will is tossing some food together." Passengers were given a deck to themselves, lined with two dozen seats paired together and able to recline for sleep, a small bathroom with an even smaller vibe shower cabinet, a tiny kitchen with simple pre-packaged foods. They were expected to board there and stay there until the shuttle docked. Most passengers never even saw the flight crew, but the high security clearance to even approach 843 was still in place and the Captain saw Rye's delight in the ship she was proud of. The rest had just happened.

Rye nodded. "He's right, thank you and your friends for the time you've given me."

The man shrugged. "Anytime, always good to shoot the shit with another flyboy nethead."

More terms Ichi didn't know, but Rye shook his head. "I'm not..." he sighed. "Not really. Not anymore."

"Well, if you ever want to be again, figure you're Will Sullivan's relation, right? Sort of makes you Avalon I guess, our fleet needs all the skilled hands it can get."

They'd been vague as to just who Rye was but not that he was partnered with Ichi in more than a professional way. Rye smiled warmly at the praise but part of his mind scoffed. He had a hint that before all that had happened, the idea of pushing an intra-system shuttle around Avalon space would have been a demotion. "Thanks."

It wasn't until they reached the narrow stairwell that Ichi asked. "Flyboy nethead?"

"Flyboy, pilot."

"I gathered." He led the way down to the passenger deck.

"Nethead, someone that takes apart ships or Network drives for fun."

"But, aren't they unstable? Can't a Network drive explode if you tinker with it?"

Rye shrugged. "Only if you're unlucky or stupid."

Oddly, the causal way Rye spoke of a quick and fiery death made Ichi smile a little more. "Hn, I'm in love with a madman," he muttered, not thinking and trying to chase the fantasy of Rye picking a ship apart just to see how it worked, all sweaty and intent, out of his thoughts.

The words almost made Rye lose his footing on the short steps, but he caught the handrail with one quick grab and Ichi's shoulder with the other. The touch stopped the dark haired man and Rye quickly turned him around. "Say it again," Rye demanded, his breath short in his chest.

The intensity in Rye's eyes startled Ichi into forgetting just what he'd mumbled that had gotten him such a glare. "What?"

"Say it, while I can see your eyes, please." It wasn't a request and Rye's tone held no begging inflection.

Ichi dropped his eyes and fumbled his thoughts for what he'd muttered but when he stumbled across the words he blushed. He'd been distracted by the travel and seeing Rye so excited at being able to talk about ships, by thinking of him as the person he was becoming and leaving behind the broken thing he'd been, the words had slipped out. Everything in Ichi wanted to shout the words again but the only course of action his stiff pride and stricter upbringing left him was avoidance.

"Only a madman or a fool would play with something that could blow up on them if they sneezed." His face was burning but his expression was steady.

"No, the first part."

"Rye..."

The intense need dissolved and Rye dropped his hand from Ichi's shoulder. "It's okay."

The hands at Ichi's sides balled up in frustrated fists. Rye started down the steps, brushing past where he stood, frozen in spot, and now it was Ichi's turn to stop him. He deliberately raised his eyes and locked them with the resolute gray pair now a step below him. "I do, you know. I'm just, it's not something I can say while I'm thinking about it, but I do."

Rye didn't tell him it was okay or that he understood. He studied the emotion in the hazel eyes that Ichi couldn't seem to force out in anything but mocking jest and it made him smile a little in a darkly bitter way. Without another word, he continued down the steps to join the other couple and the simple food they'd tossed together.

"Damn it, Ichi! What's wrong with you?" Ichi cursed himself as he stood locked in his own inhibitions on the narrow steps. He wasn't blind to the sharp spike of hurt that he'd seen in Rye's eyes, but that wasn't the worst. The worst was seeing that Rye felt he deserved that hurt. Ichi steadied his expression and clenched his jaw before following in Rye's wake.

"Just you wait to meet him," Will began when Ichi joined the small group, grinning a little as he handed out the quickly made food. "Jake Ellia is a force unto himself. Not a computer system alive he or his group can't sneak into, tough sort that you can count on too."

"And able to bend steel with his bare hands," Amanda added with a smirk. "Will's still a little awestruck by the man. Jake was the only commanding officer able to keep his unruly stubbornness in line. The only one Will didn't pick a fight with!"

"Oh, I picked it, Jake just ended it. Cracked me upside the head a good one, too. I learned right quick to shut up and mind my manners around him." The confession only seemed to make Will happier. "Jake was always good folk, dignified and pulled together, not street rat filth like me. You'll like him Ich." He forced the smile a little brighter but Will wasn't blind to the underline of tension between Ichi and Rye.

"I can't wait to meet this Olesckian," Amanda added around a mouth of food. "Do you have any idea how rare it is to be able to examine an Olesckian? They're so phobic about technology, no idea how one ended up as a computer programmer."

"You just behave around him, no turning him into a lab rat, woman." Will warned. "Jake says he's still fragile and he should know. Fool crazy man going bonding to him and all that. Gods, it'll be good to see him again."

Will and Amanda kept up a running conversation with only a few small words added from Ichi or Rye. By the time the food was finished and cleaned up, Amanda was yawning. It was both real and a touch forced, something had happened between the other pair and she knew enough to get Will out of the way. Both men were private enough to not want too much interference, and both were smart enough to figure their complex relationship out without too much outside help.

"Come on, you." She tugged at Will's arm. "Help me go over the last of the med charts before I crash and take a nap."

"But…" he started to question, glancing to the tightlipped and silent men before nodding. "Yeah, yeah, all work and no play and that rot."

Being left alone did little to improve Ichi's skills at communication. Rye seemed to have forgiven him which only made Ichi angrier at himself. They ended up in a pair of seats several rows behind the set Will and Amanda had claimed as theirs, and sat silently. Ichi turned on his notepad, intending to read something or get some work done, and Rye stared mindlessly ahead, obviously lost in thought.

He needed a way to reach across the gulf of silence to Rye, and when Ichi found the idea he figured he had nothing to lose. He nudged Rye with an elbow to get his attention and when the gray eyes slid his way Ichi turned his notebook so they both could see it.

"This is my home, Kakurega." The pictures were from a tourism site he'd called up and showed the mountainous region quite nicely. Tall, craggy mountains sprouted up, small trees grew in twisted shapes and looked lonely and windswept. "It's in the mountains of Heidkio but see? There are seven peaks taller than the others. We call them the Seven Ancestors. The seven inhabited valleys nestled around them are the Seven Descendents. Each one has a name, a personality. On each of the mountains is a temple."

Rye found himself fascinated by the lush green shades of grass and trees and the dark smoky grays of stones. The tourist description under the images he scrolled through spoke of the community of priests and scientists, a secluded place of learning and austere beauty. This made Rye smile a little because it reminded him of Ichi, his own personal austere beauty.

The images highlighted carved wood shrines and temples and the sleek modern city that sprawled around the natural valleys. There was high praise for the efficient public transportation system and incorporation of natural landscape. He read carefully, picking up that most of the residents were of mixed Asian decent which explained the dark hair, golden skin and dark almond-shaped eyes of most, and the strong Asian influence in the structure and architecture of the city.

Rye slowed the text down, trying to read it and not move his lips at the same time. Learning, or relearning, how to read was a slow process but he was stubborn about it. "Tourists are granted some leeway in behavior and the natural beauty of the stark mountains, lush landscapes and breathtaking waterfalls attract some tourism. Most visitors to Kakurega, however, are business travelers, scholars or those seeking spiritual retreat and are expected to understand and follow local custom. Many a business deal has fallen apart due to basic misunderstandings; to the casual observer, the residents of Kakurega are a solemn, serious group. Emotion is held as a private affair not to be expressed in public, if to be expressed at all. Those free with their emotions are looked upon with suspicion; a visitor that smiles too easily will be thought of as empty-headed and frivolous. This emotional restraint has led to the continued practice of arranged marriages and near-shunning of those few unable or unwilling to enforce such tight personal control. To be respected academically, socially or professionally in Kakurega control is the most important issue and given that it is the seat of scientific research and religious contemplation, as well as being the home to some of the sectors top universities, it is a lesson best followed."

It made Rye wonder what the tourist site said about Avalon. As the words scrolled by he didn't need to wonder what Ichi was trying to tell him. He glanced up. "It looks very pretty."

Ichi nodded. "It is. Clean, safe, well laid out..." He glanced at the photos and shrugged a shoulder. "Even in the heart of the city, you can smell the rain in the mountains, or the trees when they're in bloom. I went to local universities for the first couple of my degrees but I was offered a chance to be the assistant to a professor of entomology off-world. She was a casual friend of my father and she rarely asked anyone to fill the spot. He felt it was too high of an honor to refuse, even if he didn't like the field of study. I guess he figured if I wanted to toy with it that was fine, I could pick up another graduate degree later. He accepted on my behalf and she became my advisor."

"Without consulting you? He agreed without speaking to you?"

"Why should he?" Ichi asked. "He knew my wishes, and as my father the final choice was his. Acceptance had to be made the year before I was to go, and I wasn't yet of legal age to make the choice."

Which hit Rye like a fist. It was just another reminder of how smart Ichi was and how Rye still had to move his lips to read. The man had already earned several degrees from top schools before he was of age. It made Rye feel dull and dim-witted.

"I'd read all of her papers, but it was my first time off world. My parents tried to warn me that outsiders were different." The memories made him smile softly, the very small up turning of his mouth would have made his mother frown at him in warning. "Dr. Foorsberg is an outrageous woman, full of mirth and life. It was difficult to align the serious, solid research in her papers with what appeared to be such an empty-headed, frivolous woman. I learned a lot about the outside world at university. My father would be appalled if he could see how much I've changed. Yet, by Avalon standards?" Ichi shook his head.

Across from him, Rye was studying the photos a little too intently and Ichi reached over and brushed hair back from the man's face. When those gray eyes glanced up Ichi drew a careful breath and held that gaze. "I do, I am, it's just not easy for me to say. I'm no good at this sort of thing." He felt his face grow hot, embarrassed by honesty and his own emotions. "I'm sorry, I… excuse me." Ichi hurriedly stood up and scrambled to escape but the only place to go was the small bathroom. He ducked inside, shut and locked the door behind him.

Rye sat stunned, staring off in the direction Ichi had scurried away to. It wasn't until Will sighed, kneeling on the seat one row in front of theirs turned to face him, that Rye pulled his sluggish and uncertain thoughts in line.

"He just told you he loved you, you dolt. Go after him."

"But…"

"The actual words don't matter. Trust me, I seem to have a built in Ichi-to-human translator. That's about as close as you're going to get for a while. Now, don't let him run away. Press the advantage, be bold!" Will grinned and tossed his hands up in mock outrage. "Geesh, kids these days, they know nothing of love." He was still muttering when he wandered back up the aisle to sit next to his wife, sparing a final toss of his head toward where Ichi was still hiding in the bathroom.

It took a few heartbeats for Will's words to sink in. Ichi had just looked him right in the eye and told him that he loved him. The truth of his words, the uneasy vulnerability he'd shown, made Rye's heart thud painfully in his chest. Something so simple, so human, made him feel like he could do anything, take on anything. He shook his head and stood up to hover outside of the locked bathroom, waiting for Ichi to emerge.

There was no running water in the small bathroom, most vessels didn't have such luxuries and vibe cleaning his hands just didn't have the same impact as being able to splash cold water on his face. The bathroom was small and the lighting had several intensity levels, but most of all it was private. Privacy and dim lighting worked almost as well as cold water and Ichi struggled to get a hold on his uneasy emotions.

When he was fairly sure he could hold onto his control, and the blush on his face had backed down a bit, he slid off the lock and opened the door. One step outside the small room and he'd nearly stepped on Rye's feet. "Rye?"

Rye shook his head and caught Ichi's arm, pushing the man bodily back inside the small bathroom. He reached behind him and shut and locked the door, trapping them both in the tiny room. It was just enough space for two to turn around in but little more and, oddly, Rye found it comforting.

"What're you doing?" Ichi frowned, but Rye was between him and the door and unless he was willing to knock the other man down and crawl over him he was effectively trapped.

"I'm not from Kakurega," Rye announced.

Which left Ichi wondering if Rye was saying Ichi's sad, tiny attempts at intimacy weren't enough. "I know you're not."

"I've heard your say, now hush and listen to mine."

The intense focused look on Rye's face gentled Ichi's own worry. He nodded. "Very well."

"All I remember of my life is about a year long, and what little bit I'm getting now about the time before this was done to me, well, I don't think I was a very nice person." Rye began to explain, but saw how Ichi dropped his eyes. The dark haired man was even uncomfortable with other people's expressions of emotions, and Rye let him hide just a little bit. "I'm not sure I can explain what it was like, to not know, to wonder if maybe this is all I ever was. Conti broke me, Ichi, because this is all I had to fight him with. It hurt too much to fight him when there was no ending to it."

"Rye, it's okay…"

"No, it's not," he broke in. "Just, hear me out."

Ichi nodded and held his tongue.

"He made sure I knew he was throwing me away and why. He could have given me to one of his friends but he didn't, there wasn't enough of me left for that, I was nothing when he finished with me. He tossed me out like trash or… or the broken toy I was and I knew that wherever I went it would be just as bad, or worse, forever. I actually hoped that being put into storage would kill me." His hands had balled up at his side but it was in anger at his own past weakness, even if he could understand why, he was still resentful that he'd allowed anyone to take him so far down.

"You were the next thing I saw and god, Ichi, you stopped my heart. When you took me home that first night, I figured it wouldn't be so bad being owned by someone like you. Someone so reserved, so handsome, so…" words didn't seem to fit how deeply Rye had been attracted to Ichi. He shook his head and didn't try. "That night, when you gave me a blanket and pillow?" Rye shook his head and blinked quickly to clear his eyes of unshed tears.

"It was nothing. You were cold."

"It wasn't nothing to me! That was the first time in my memory that anyone had done anything kind for me. And you asked for nothing in return, even the next morning? Conti would have beaten me for not being naked and waiting for him the moment he woke up. I overslept and you didn't hurt me for it. When I offered myself to you, you wanted me. I could feel it, and yet you didn't touch me. You have no idea what kind of man you really are, how amazing you are."

Ichi shook his head. "You've said yourself you don't remember very much. It's only natural that you'd bond to someone that treated you kindly."

"I may not have active memories but I suspect that I know more of human nature and people than you do." Rye grinned and knew he was right. "I don't love you because you're kind to me, or because you gave me back myself. I love you because you're a stunning, handsome, smart, stubborn, frustrating, annoying, hardheaded, closed-off, wonderful, talented, amazing man. I will do anything, anything, to protect you and that includes being careful with your emotions. I know you love me, you don't need to say it. Just as I know there is no reason for you to feel anything for me. I know you do. I would spend a thousand years with Conti to have known one moment of what it's like to be loved by you."

The words, spoken so boldly with an almost painfully obvious honesty, made Ichi blush again. Such things were never said about him, such emotion wasn't supposed to be inspired by him. He was ordinary, focused on his work and the goals of research, not the center of such romantic ideals. It made him want to escape the small intimate room and the too-raw emotions he didn't know how to process.

"I should…" He drew a slow breath. "I should go, see if Will and Amanda need help with anything."

When Ichi tried to slip around beside him, Rye caught his shoulders. "No."

"No?"

"No, I'm not letting you run away this time."

"I'm not running away." But he was and he knew it.

"Bullshit," Rye cursed and caught Ichi again as he tried to press by him, only this time he found himself pressing Ichi back against the wall, pinning him in place.

"Let me go!" The words snapped out, angry now and near panicked at not being allowed to flee. It was a sick feeling in the bottom of his stomach, but he was embarrassed to admit, even to himself, that having Rye force him to confront the feelings between them was highly erotic.

Rye shook his head. "No."

Erotic or not, Ichi wasn't going to stand for it. He pushed back against the hands holding him and felt for the first time how much stronger Rye really was. He may as well have been a child pushing at a grown man, and the sheer power in his lover's strength made his cock twitch and his knees wobble. He pushed again and was easily pinned to the wall and found both of their breaths were a little ragged.

Rye slid a leg between Ichi's, pressing his body closer to the one he'd trapped against the wall. He hadn't meant for things to turn sexual, but the small power struggle had mixed with the raw vulnerability of such emotional confessions and changed things. There was a heated, fiery look in Ichi's eyes, they sparked, but it wasn't really in anger. It was that look that nearly turned Rye into a moaning puddle of lust. The hand that was holding so tightly to Ichi's arm slid upwards and fingers ghosted across the silky dark hair.

The gentle touch turned rougher as he fisted the hand into the hair and Ichi's breath turned shuddering and needy. Rye watched as the lips so close to his own parted and the tip of a pink tongue slid out to moisten flesh that wasn't dry. Those eyes, hazel and so often closed off, shuttered halfway as Ichi tilted his head back in partial surrender. It was that needy look between anger, fear and lust that made Rye take that final step forward.

Ichi's body didn't instantly yield when Rye pressed close to him. The man really did want to run away from all the soft confessions and emotion that he'd rather avoid then accept. From head to foot he was tense, angry muscle, and not even the press of hidden arousal to hidden arousal weakened his resolve. Rye leaned forward and brushed his lips to the parted pair, teasing, not fully kissing, and quickly pulled away. The contact simply made Ichi's body tense further against his own, but his breathing hitched and grew more frantic.

Even the hand fisted in his hair didn't stop Ichi from throwing his head forward, his lips chasing the teasing pair that had barely tickled across his own. His mouth nearly smashed into Rye's and there was no teasing now. The kiss was ravaging, bruising, consuming, and Ichi gave as fully as he received. The hands at his side uncurled from angry fists and slid up Rye's body, both trying to pull him closer and push him away at the same time. The hand Rye had gripping his arm slid down his back to settle on the curve of Ichi's ass. With a grasp that was close to painful, that hand tightened and pulled their hips even tighter together.

"Stop," Ichi hissed out when his mouth was again free. His hands came up and he pushed at Rye. "Let me go."

That was cold water tossed over Rye. How many times had he begged inside his head for other people to stop or release him? The hungry, lustful violence was appealing, but only if it was mutual, and the idea that he'd pushed when Ichi hadn't wanted him to made him feel a little ill. He dropped his hands from the lithe body and stepped back, horrified at his own loss of control.

Chapter Twenty

There was no matching shock or pain on Ichi's face. He pushed away from the wall and caught the hem of his shirt. In a smooth motion, careful of elbows in the small space, he tugged it up over his head and discarded it. The quick, short breaths made his chest rise and fall and his nipples stand out, begging to be touched.

"What are you doing?" Rye asked, trembling with the need to slam the other man back against the wall and lick the exposed skin.

Ichi toed off his shoes and started working at the front of his pants. "I want you to take me, hard," he stated, eyes downcast. While he was flushed, it wasn't from embarrassment or shame but from lust and desire.

The sight of Ichi stripping and those dark, clinging words nearly swept Rye away and he was so hard he thought he might die. "What?" he gasped out, convinced he had to have been hearing things.

Ichi paused, his pants open and half slid down his hips. It exposed his stomach and hip bones but hid everything else, and he saw Rye's eyes trail down to the cut of the open fabric. "Make me tell you, don't let me come until I have." Then the fabric was pushed down and Ichi stepped out of it to stand naked and aroused, still tense and intense, displayed in the harsh bathroom light for Rye to see.

"Ichi…" Rye worried he may faint, so much of his blood had pooled in his groin.

"Make me tell you," Ichi repeated, eyes locked to Rye's gray in challenge.

It was one Rye knew he could meet. He patted a hand over his pockets but he knew the answer already. "No lube." Lately, he'd been very careful by always having one or two of the small ampoules on his person, knowing that it didn't take much to talk Ichi into a little physical one-on-one time, but he hadn't thought about needing any on the shuttle trip. He glanced around but the waterless bathroom offered no solutions.

One, two, and then three fingers slid into Ichi's mouth, his eyes never leaving Rye's. They emerged slick and moist and Ichi backed away and faced the small countertop that had the tiny vibe hand sink built in. He glanced up, watching Rye in the mirror above the counter, and those slick fingers were quickly forced into his body.

The mirror allowed Rye to watch the pained, hungry look that crunched Ichi's eyes shut as the poor substitute for real lube did little to help such a rough invasion. Nothing had hinted that Ichi had even the slightest bit of a masochist streak, but neither was the man weak or unwilling to achieve what he wanted. And no matter how erotic it was to watch Ichi prepare himself, to watch the saliva slick fingers forcefully disappear into that tight body with a moan to accompany each thrust, Rye's deep fear of Ichi being hurt overrode any lust.

He caught Ichi's wrist and pulled those plundering fingers away. "Stop."

Ichi writhed, his hips arched out. He gasped for breath and moaned. "Please, make me, please," he begged.

"I can do that," Rye heard himself whispering, running his free hand over the round, exposed ass, loving the contrast between his paler skin and Ichi's golden. "But I won't watch you hurt yourself."

The words and the gentle touch made Ichi moan. He needed to be taken hard, needed it rough and didn't know how to ask a second time. The teasing hand slid from his ass and Ichi dropped his head, letting it hang loose over the counter.

"Shhhh, it's okay, turn and watch." Rye whispered as he released Ichi's wrist and quickly opened his own pants. He held Ichi's hips in place, ass still toward him but encouraged Ichi to twist at the waist to see behind him. The hazel eyes widened slightly as Rye began to stroke himself and when Rye slid those long, bare legs further apart Ichi moaned.

"Watch!" Rye gasped out again, burning under the feel of those eyes. He'd learned of Ichi's little kink easily, the man liked to feel his partner come. On him, in him, against him, clothed or bare skin to skin, it was dirty and kinky and got Ichi horribly turned on. Given how fastidious he normally was in his day to day life, it was amusing how much he got off at the feel of come on his skin. "That's it, watch me," Rye whispered as Ichi moaned and let his legs slide even further apart.

It didn't take much for Rye to come, with the stunning body displayed out before him and those eyes eating him alive. His release splashed out, white pearls on Ichi's skin of gold, and the sight kept him hard and aching. Ichi moaned and his ass arched out toward Rye. He shivered and his eyes fluttered shut, close to coming himself from something too erotic for even his deepest mind to imagine.

"Shhh," Rye soothed, his hands sliding along the trembling body in front of him, comforting. "I got you, it's okay," he whispered and stepped forward.

Ichi's entire body arched, twitching, as Rye stepped closer. The feel of that hard length gliding against his ass, sliding sticky sweet come across Ichi's skin, teasing with what he really wanted, made Ichi lose his mind. It was those whispered words, the voice he'd grown to love so dearly lowered to dusky bedroom tones, telling him he was safe, telling him it was okay to let go, that kept Ichi together. He writhed under the teasing hands and managed to glide the hungry length hard along the cleft of his ass. That made both of them moan.

"Hard," Ichi sighed, his voice a begging sob. Even he knew what he sounded like, the tones dripping with honey-thick passion and whorish need. It was emotion that a man from Kakurega never voiced, but Ichi was unmanned, dissolved, deconstructed and he needed to be torn apart by the talons of desire even more.

Rye's breath stopped in his throat. He was still fully clothed, his pants merely opened, and the contrast between his cloth covered body and Ichi, naked, sweaty and writhing, made his fingers dig into the golden skin before him. Stripping was a passing notion, one that skittered across the surface of his thoughts only to fall away. It didn't seem important now, what felt important was to bury himself in the flesh of his lover. When Ichi moved, like an erotic wave, and the sensitive tip of Rye's cock slid between strong, beautiful legs to just tease at the begging entrance, he forgot how to undress.

The word hard danced across Rye's mind and he couldn't stop himself. He pushed and Ichi's body was horribly tight but it parted in welcoming heat. It made Rye's head feel light and dizzy, and he paused trying to adapt. Ichi moaned under him, his face twisted up in a needing ache that Rye was only barely able to absorb. He wanted to soothe the primordial creature of desire he was making love to, but before Rye could form the words Ichi growled. His hips snapped back and in one quick, nearly violent push he impaled himself back onto Rye's throbbing cock.

It was too much. Rye's brain melted. He leaned over the trembling, moaning body that he was buried in, his hands gliding up to ghost over ribs and nipples. If he didn't come again--now--he wouldn't survive, and his body acted on instinct and self-preservation. His hips snapped a few times, hard, deep and quick, and he was gasping. Hot breath tickled the side of Ichi's neck as Rye moaned and came, Ichi nearly sobbing at the feel.

Rye paused, buried deep in his lover's body. His pulse pounded in a half dozen spots in his body, adding a counter rhythm to his shuddering breath. He had a moment when release ebbed desire back to a controllable level, before his cock began to ache in painful need of Ichi's pleasure, to have what they'd just done really sink in. Their times together had always been careful, gentle. Passionate, yes without a doubt, but thoughtful. This wasn't, this was nearly violent in its need and Rye paused, buried in the shivering flesh of Ichi's perfection and wondered if he'd gone too far.

Ichi's hips pulled away the short inches allowed them, caught between counter top and Rye's strong body, then instantly thrust backwards, demanding more. His sweat dampened head raised and clouded hazel eyes gone nearly green with desire half-opened to meet Rye's overwhelmed gray in the mirror's surface. He licked his lips and impaled himself again on the trembling length still deep in his body. "Harder," he demanded as he arched backwards.

Suddenly, Rye found himself with armloads of Ichi. His hands slid across the taut stomach, tickling hip bones and teasing the soft skin so near the weeping, ignored length. The palms of his hands glided roughly over already hypersensitive nipples dragging broken moans and clinging gasps from the slender arched throat. Below his mouth, Rye kissed and licked, nipping on any skin or flesh that floated within his reach. Without his thoughts to stop him, his hips were moving. Deep, hard, long strokes and on each thrust both men shivered.

Rye kicked the bare feet further apart and the tiniest touch of a request had Ichi sliding his legs even further than asked for. Back Rye stepped, pulling Ichi's hips with him until his back was nearly to the locked door and Ichi's elbows were barely supported on the counter top. The only thing in his mind was that Ichi had asked for harder and Rye couldn't stop himself. He gripped the slender hips and let himself go.

Each deep, hard stroke in rocked Ichi almost onto his toes and dragged a keening sob from his soul. Hands dug into his skin, tilted his hips and suddenly those long, consuming thrusts were making his vision go white in fiery pleasure. He choked near to death on a scream and in his shattered mind was vaguely aware that the sound carried Rye over the edge again. The thrusts grew shallower, barely leaving his body, pounding deep and hard, hitting that hidden spot in rapid fire--and then came the wash of molten release.

Still Rye was hard. Ichi could feel the trembling in the hands and knew wound up like this the little orgasms did nothing to ease the other man's torment. Instead they merely built up to a larger release, a pleasure that often left Rye insensible and unaware, gasping for breath and thoughts for long moments after. It was an intensity that might have made Ichi jealous if he didn't see first hand how close the pleasure blurred with pain.

Instead, Ichi got to feel his love and lover come, not once or twice but often four or more times. He'd be able to taste him, feel him, touch him and still know that Rye could take him as far as he needed to go. He would have blushed if his face wasn't already flushed in overwhelmed lust at the dirty, lusty, wonderful feel of Rye moving in his begging body again. His release was slick against and in Ichi, the feel of it sliding from him, down to tickle across his ignored balls, slick on the top of his thighs, made Ichi feel safe and sultry and desired.

Long moments passed as Rye took Ichi as hard as he'd asked for. His body was a place of lust and torment, begging to be fully released, for the blinding pleasure he'd found when his reserved love let himself go. It was a tone to Ichi's sighing, begging, sobbing moans that he was waiting for. The tone that didn't demand release but sung for it, and when Rye finally heard the subtle shift in the trembling keen that escaped with each hard thrust, he stepped forward.

The move forward forced Ichi to half-stand again, arching back to be cradled in Rye's arms. The strokes were deeper, barely leaving his body before pounding hard back in. Their bodies nearly joined from shoulder to feet, the feel of Rye's clothing, soft as it was, turned into a scratchy tease. Fingers teased his chest, rolling aching nipples in tight circles and ghosting over the ticklish divot of his navel. The hungry mouth returned to nip and kiss at his neck and ear, down to his shoulders.

"Open your eyes," Rye demanded, coarse and rough directly into the shell of one perfect ear. "Look."

Ichi's eyes fluttered, struggled to open under the onslaught of so much delight. When he managed to get them to obey, what he saw nearly made him come. Rye hovered behind him, his eyes dark like cold steel from hungry need, his face intense and almost frightening deadly. He could see a hand stroking across his own chest, teasing collarbones and dancing over where his heart thudded madly below. He could see the near bite marks left behind as Rye nipped his shoulder, eyes still locked onto his own.

"Say it!" Rye demanded.

Ichi's eyes fluttered shut but one of the hands stroking his flesh turned to a mildly painful claw and nails scrapped across his stomach. That allowed him to open his eyes again and this time he saw himself. He looked sexy, primal, wild. His dark hair was stuck to his head and spiked out, his mouth was parted in panting breaths. It struck him like a bolt that this was how Rye saw him, not as the bookish, cold, repressed little scientist but the real human under all of that.

"Let go, tell me," Rye sighed against the heated flesh, shuddering now, needing to hear the words he was trying to drag from Ichi's stubborn mind. There would be release but little satisfaction if he didn't hear those words.

Rye had promised to protect him, to be gentle with the emotions he was so fragile over. Rye saw him, which was how he was so able to strip away a lifetime's training in control and dissolve him into a creature of maddening need. Rye loved him, not the kindness he'd offered or the shelter he'd provided. Rye loved him.

"Oh god!" Ichi sobbed, feeling his own release swelling, pooling, gathering in his belly, melting his will.

One of Rye's hands slid lower and the barest tickle of contact fluttered across the weeping, trembling tip of Ichi's ignored length.

Ichi's eyes flew open and locked on Rye's, those knowing, darkly deadly gray eyes that haunted his dreams, waking or sleeping. "Oh god, I love you!" he sobbed out, broken, shattered. The teasing hand closed around his cock. It didn't stroke, it didn't need to. Just the touch of the heated skin against him, the gentle loving touch, pushed him beyond control. "Oh, Rye, I love you so much, love you, love you!" He sobbed, his eyes rolling back under his fluttering eyelids as his release poured out with his confession. His legs dissolved and Ichi collapsed into Rye's arms. He recovered enough sense to feel the last pounding thrusts into his body, the scalding, claiming fire of Rye's consuming release mixed with mumbled words of love.

"Love you so..." Rye gasped, his thoughts and words fading in and out of being spoken. "... protect you... for you.... Anything... oh Ichi..." Rye managed to get them lowered to the floor before his body gave out, but his now limp sex slid unwillingly from Ichi making them both moan in regret.

Ichi turned in the cramped space and laid down against Rye's slouched chest, leaning up to kiss him. Both their bodies were trembling, exhausted, broken and remade whole. He twisted one hand into Rye's shirt and the other into his hair before he buried his face along the pale neck.

"Love you, so much, I'd be lost without you," he muttered, trying to get everything out while he still could. "Thank you, oh Rye, thank you." He half sobbed as the strong arms came around him.

Rye kissed the top of the head hidden against him. "Adore you, love you, need you," he whispered and just held Ichi closer.

It started out as a tickle in the back of Will's skull, the same way one of his migraines began. He rubbed at his eyes and adjusted the contrast on the notebook files they were studying. Amanda gave him a questioning glance, but he waved it off and went back to looking over the files with her. When the threat of a migraine spread into a general sense of unease, Will half stood up to glance around the cabin. No one else was in sight but he knew that, locked in the bathroom, Rye was following his advice and pressing the advantage.

"What's wrong?" Amanda asked, careful to not look up from the notebook. Will was often uncomfortable with his skills, not liking how unbalanced it often made him.

He just shook his head and sat down. "Ichi and Rye are just figuring things out. Better do it quick, because it's giving me a headache."

Only as the minutes passed it wasn't a headache that formed. Will fidgeted in his seat and tried to push the tickle away. He rubbed at the bridge of his nose and sighed. The medical reports that so fascinated Amanda made him feel restless and he found himself watching his wife instead. The small cleft in her chin, the curve of one pink shell-like ear that peeked from the barely controlled tumbles of red curls, all grew endlessly fascinating. He found himself grinning gently at the spatter of freckles across her nose.

"What?" she asked without glancing up, feeling his eyes on her.

"You're beautiful."

That made her smile but she snorted in protest. "Will…"

He knew that tone, that was the all-work-no-play tone. It made him sigh. "I know, Mandi, but they aren't fighting back there and it's making me just as itchy and gods you're amazing."

She flipped across another file. "Besotted fool," she muttered, grinning.

"Completely." He sighed and shut his own notebook down and tried to settle back in his seat. Only the seat no longer felt so plush and comfortable. He squirmed and shifted and nothing helped. "How am I supposed to meditate and try to block that when I can't get comfortable!" he finally snapped.

Amanda snickered. "You shouldn't be eavesdropping on them anyway."

"I'm not!" he protested, but his spine arched a little as a tingle of pleasure shot across his nerves. "Oh, lady's blessing, I'd like to see you block this out."

Beside him, Amanda noticed his growing state of unease and pretended not to. "He's your brother."

"I'm not being a voyeur!" he protested, shifting to slouch lower in his seat. His lips parted and his eyes drifted shut. It felt like he'd been dipped in honey, and he was close to asking Amanda to lick him clean. "Remember when we used to go at it like rabbits in shuttle bathrooms?" He asked in a voice that was floating, dreamy, remembering vividly himself.

She chuckled softly. "Public shuttles too, with half the passengers getting all hot and disturbed from our tumble. Damned psis." She tried to sound stern. "Not so funny when the shoes on the other foot, now is it?"

Will moaned softly and firmly told his hands to stay on the arm rests. He wasn't going to touch himself, he wasn't, not even to run a hand across an arm or chest. "I don't know, it was pretty damned funny when we were the ones in the bathroom."

"Well," she shut her notebook. "We're not and don't you dare ruin this for Ichi by making him all embarrassed. He doesn't know you could pick up on them." She leaned over and kissed the side of Will's head, but the chaste press of lips to his flesh made her husband moan. "Pull it together, you."

His eyes drifted open and saw no equally languid look in his wife's eyes. She was in work mode and there was never any way to sway her from that. Will sighed. "Trying." It wouldn't kill him to wait until the bathroom was empty. He'd be able to slip inside and indulge the memories of when he'd not been alone in the small space. Until then, he just had to try to not think about it.

Which wasn't easy to do as he watched Amanda stand up, the smooth fabric of the long skirt she'd worn floating about her. He liked the way the fabric clung to her hips, the way it tucked a little to the curve of her ass. It made him want to pet his hands across the curves, down to the hem to find the bare legs underneath. He licked his lips again and swallowed hard. "Damn it, no fair when Ichi gets more action than me!" He shut his eyes and pressed himself back into his seat.

Will was starting to wonder if maybe the pair had taken some sort of love potion as the tingle along his nerves was quickly turning into a fire. It might have been a good thing that Amanda had gotten up to go back to the kitchen area because he knew if she was still sitting there he'd be pawing at her. That would only piss her off. If she wasn't in the mood to play there was no moving the woman when her mind was set on something, it was one of the things he normally loved, but right now it didn't seem like such a good trait.

Something fell into his lap and Will started a little at the unexpected touch. When his eyes opened he saw, resting over his growing erection, pink and purple lace. It made him frown but he picked it up, the lace was attached to silk which was cut high on the side and tapered to a lean thong line. His breath caught in his throat at the warmth still held in the silk as he turned Amanda's panties around in his hands.

"Oh, gods." He groaned and glanced up to see Amanda standing a little behind him, grinning evilly. "You were wearing these?"

She nodded, leaning on the back of his seat.

"Mrs. Sullivan, were you planning on seducing me?"

She just shrugged. They were his favorite pair of panties and she'd worn them with seduction in mind.

"Are you being mean to me? Cause you know, it's horrible to kick a man when he's down." Not that he'd complain about taking her still-warm panties into the small bathroom later. He never claimed not to be a kinky bastard and anything that touched her skin became an erotic artifact to him.

She moved around the seat and came to their row. She'd let her hair loose and kicked off her shoes with the panties. "Now, Mr. Sullivan, are you saying I'm mean?"

Will's breath stopped as she leaned over him. "Only if you want me to," he whispered, watching her hand reach toward him. Then he watched it reach past him to the seat's controls. The slender fingers pressed the right button and both seats reclined back.

She shrugged and started to gather up the hem of her skirt. "I think I'm being very nice." The feel of her husband's eyes on her legs made her smile brightly. When the skirt was hiked up high enough she slid forward to straddle Will's lap.

He crushed the panties in his hand and groaned as she settled, totally bare under the skirt, across his groin. "Oh, mercy, very, very nice. Nicest woman in the whole universe... oh." This was her game and he'd happily let her play it. "What about them?" he managed to ask, not caring if Ichi and Rye emerged from the bathroom and found them, but unsure if Ichi would survive.

She shook out her curls and let them shower down over Will. "They're going to be busy for a while but, Will, so are you."

"Oh, thank you, Lady, thank you." He prayed until his lips were busy kissing his wife.

⸙

Vibe showers weren't Ichi's first choice any more. Sure, they got a body cleaned off and dry and they were efficient and fast, but it lacked the raw pleasure of a hot water shower. For him it was just a preference, but for Rye the vibe showers actually bordered on painful. The tickling, crawling bug feeling the vibes left Ichi with were far more intense for the redhead and he emerged shivering and trying to brush the feel from his skin. The upside was with clothing, as any traveler could witness too. Vibe showers didn't freshen clothes the way a real cleaning would, but they made them almost as fresh and ready to go. That was a good thing since Rye hadn't undressed and their luggage was in storage.

Ichi had lost all sense of how long they'd been in the small room, but out in the main compartment the lights were dimmed. Rye moved to get some water, downing long swallows before passing the bottle to Ichi. Ichi drank from the same container without thought, something that would have horrified his mother if she'd seen.

When he handed the bottle back, Rye caught his wrist and pulled him close. Lips pressed quickly to his before Rye pulled away to yawn which made Ichi have to yawn.

"Sleep?" Rye asked, hopeful.

Ichi nodded and the pair found their way back to their seat. It took a little arranging but they got the seats reclined and the small pillows and blankets out. There was some shifting of elbows and legs before they managed to snuggle down together, under the same blanket. Rye pillowed his head against Ichi's chest the way he did every night and yawned again as a hand stroked over his hair.

"Love you," Rye sighed, dropping quickly down into sleep.

Ichi opened his mouth to answer and couldn't, the words stuck. Instead he pressed a kiss to Rye's head and it made the warm bundle he was holding sigh happily. The meaning delivered in actions, if not in words, and just as easily understood. It made Ichi sigh himself and he closed his eyes to sleep in the dim light.

"Huh," Will spoke softly, a couple of rows ahead of the other pair and on the opposite side. He was curled up with Amanda under a blanket but neither one was really asleep.

"What?" She asked, nuzzled against him.

He shifted them until Amanda could follow his line of sight and see between seats and aisles to where Rye was curled up like a kitten against Ichi. "Just figured Rye was top."

She yawned. "He is."

"But…"

"Will Sullivan, do you think I snuggle against you and let you hold me because you penetrate me?" she asked as she turned in Will's arms to look in his eyes.

"Well…" It felt like one of those questions that couldn't be safely answered without getting thumped across the head either way.

"Silly." She shook her head. "I snuggle against you because you make me feel warm and safe, not because of who is doing what to who." She whispered so as not to disturb the other couple. They were going to wait until she was sure they were asleep to use the bathroom themselves. Will had come a long way in learning about intimacy, but sometimes they still stumbled across something that just made her shake her head and feel sad.

"Huh," he grunted softly, holding tightly to the warm feeling that Amanda's words put in his chest. She felt safe with him, it made him feel strong and loved. "So, Rye feels safe with Ichi. You'd think it would be the other way around what with how Rye is like a killing machine."

That did get Will thumped, lightly, against his chest not his head. "Emotional moron, has nothing to do with butt kicking skills." She yawned and slid out of his arms. "Going to shower so I can sleep, you should too."

He nodded. "Is that an invitation?"

Amanda rolled her eyes but didn't tell him not to follow.

Chapter Twenty One

The shuttle docked slowly and very carefully, wary of spooking the station that was still skittish. The crew would see to unloading the luggage with the other supplies they'd carried with them but left the passengers to find their own way off.

"There you go folks. Tubes connected and pressurized. See you for the return trip," the captain announced via vid phone, not coming down to see them off.

"Thanks." Will nodded and slid a hand across Amanda's back, leading her to the exit.

"Anytime." The captain smiled and the screen went dark.

Will seemed in good spirits, but his friends could see the nerves under the upbeat manner. The final lock opened and standing in the well lit entranceway were two people. One human man, with the sketchy age of past-thirty-but-not-yet-aged-looking, maybe five-six if he was lucky and strong across the shoulders. He had the look of a man capable of anything and his green eyes took in everything. They crinkled up in lines when he smiled and it made him look younger, not older. Standing beside him and slightly behind was a man that towered over him, well over six feet and pale to the point of nearly being corpse-like with subtle blue tints to his skin. It took a second glance to notice the differences made him something not human.

His forehead was a bit shorter than a human's, his cheekbones a touch too angular, his chin a fraction too sharp. The ears were a touch too large and sat a bit too high on the sides of his head to be human. The pale light blonde hair was feather soft and fine but his eyebrows were so pale as to be virtually invisible. The lashes around his slightly too large eyes were twice as thick as a humans but so pale as to nearly be clear. They fluttered over eyes with pupils in an oval slit like a cats and the color of pale cornflowers. Over all the man looked bleached of any living shade of color. It was the split upper lip and long, extra jointed hands as much as his coloring that gave him away as an Olesckian.

The effect was of someone so close to being human but so oddly distorted that it set most people aback.

"Permission to come aboard, sir?" Will asked crisply, not quite coming to attention but not slouching as much either.

The human laughed. "Of course!" And the pair fell against each other laughing, hugging and slapping backs. "Gods, you look good! Married life agrees with you!"

Will nodded and grinned like a fool. "Completely, still waiting for the invite to your hand fasting."

"You'll keep waiting, too."

"Jake, you remember Amanda." Will waved toward his wife.

She stepped forward and accepted her own hug, placing a gentle kiss on the side of the man's face. "Good to see you again, Jake. You look well, considering all the stories we've been hearing."

"I am well. And you're lovely as always." Jake grinned wider and motioned to the Olesckian standing so silently behind him. "Will, Amanda, this is Cardel'soli Narin, my bondmate."

"Yeah, about that Jake…" Will started to scold.

Jake waved it off. "A story to share over a good drink."

Narin had moved forward and inclined his head to the pair. "It's my pleasure to finally meet you both."

"And you Narin, it's a real treat to meet an Olesckian." Amanda nodded back.

Will wasn't so sure, still oddly protective of Jake and the inherent dangers of bonding to an alien psychic. To cover the disapproving emotions he didn't want to show, he reached behind him and tossed an arm around Ichi's shoulders.

"And these are my brothers, Kenichi Vitorui Sullivan and his partner Rye Sullivan."

Ichi nodded in greeting and half pushed Will's arm off his shoulders. "Nice to meet you. We have some favors to ask of you and your programmers. Will said we should tag along."

Rye remained silent and Jake locked eyes with him. For one moment, the wide smile on Jake's face faltered just a little bit. It was for only a second before it bounced back. "Any family of Will's is my family. Now enough of this, let's get you settled in before dinner."

One station looked much like any other, but while on their home they could go from one point to another without crossing another person's path, here people moved everywhere. They were still a smaller station but far larger than what Ichi was used to and he hadn't understood how comfortable he'd grown with the quiet station he lived on.

Jake and Will talked steadily about unimportant things like how odd it was to know Will was actually a doctor and how unsurprised Will was that Jake was the one in charge of the whole station. Amanda and Narin followed the pair in the slightly too-narrow-to-walk-more-than-two-wide corridors, leaving Ichi and Rye to bring up the rear. As they met with people, introductions were made and greetings exchanged in the same warm welcoming way of Avalon, which made getting to their assigned rooms twice as long of a trip.

"I like the paintings." Ichi commented quietly, speaking to Rye or Narin or no one.

Narin heard and turned, a small smile teased his lips and made the split upper lip more apparent. "Thank you. It was Jess' idea once all the chaos settled down, to brighten everyone's spirits. One corridor was painted, and then another and, well, I doubt it will be finished until every wall is so adorned."

Ichi nodded, the walls around them alternating from scenes of highly realistic landscapes to abstract blends of color. It gave the corridors personality and vibrancy and broke up the monotony of seeing the same thing over and over again. "It's a wonderful idea."

"Even if the paint fumes nearly killed us…" Narin agreed, trailing one long fingered hand across the current section, designed to make them appear underwater.

"Here we are," Jake announced and opened a door. It led into a small living room with room doors off to either side. "One of the family suites, didn't think you'd mind sharing space. Luggage should be here soon. If you don't mind, we'll be back to pick you up for dinner. Thought we could picnic in the garden, since it's been how long since any of you have seen real grass?"

Amanda snorted. "Too long, and we'd be honored."

"Until later." Jake smiled and there were more hugs and soon they were alone in the set of rooms.

"He looks really good," Will admitted.

"Maybe that's Narin's doing?" his wife suggested carefully, knowing how protective her husband was of the other man.

It made Will frown a little. "Well, if it is, I can't blame the man too much. This place is huge, almost makes me agoraphobic."

"Station rat." Amanda laughed and they moved to explore their new rooms.

Their luggage arrived a little while later and the pairs broke off to unpack. The rooms were plenty large enough and the common living room was comfortable, but there was no kitchen in the suite. The station was just a touch too large to allow everyone to cook in their own rooms, which was one advantage of either the very largest of stations or the very smallest.

They took real showers and changed their clothes and the very fact they were no longer traveling was refreshing. Rye was silent, struck by being someplace different and surrounded by so many faces he didn't know, which made Ichi silent as well and only Will's excitement as dinner drew closer countered that.

"Will!" Amanda finally snapped. "Calm down!"

That stopped his babbling and giddy excitement. "Sorry," he grinned sheepishly. "Babbling wasn't I?"

"A little bit."

"It's just a lot of people here and Jake and well…"

"It's okay."

And it was because even though Will continued to pace about the living room, he stopped talking so rapidly. When the door chime sounded even his pacing stopped but he hurried over to open.

"Hey!"

"Will." Jake nodded. "Ready? Narin and the others went and set everything up, so all we have to do is show up and eat."

Jake led them around hallways, some painted and some not, to a large set of doors. "The doors are new, the bomb blew them clean off. Had a fifteen inch piece of one stuck in my spine." Jake grinned at the talk of such horrible, nearly fatal wounds. "We've reinforced them and a lot of the damage to the gardens has been repaired. It's almost back to what it was, anyway, hope you like it, we're really proud."

The doors opened with a hiss of balancing air and the four visitors stood near open mouthed in awe. "Wow." Will said for them all. "We'd heard it was nice but this, this is amazing."

Jake beamed. "We've put a good chunk of money into it and, well, it's a lot of space to just grow things in. The dome's reinforced now too." He moved them inside. The garden was in a late afternoon cycle and the artificial light over head reflected it. "It's mostly a naturally occurring cavern in this rock, but we domed it in thinking it would be an observatory. Well, before we could afford the equipment someone started a vegetable patch and it sort of grew from there."

Gravel of the pathway crunched under their feet and the air was moist with green growing things. "This is amazing." Amanda breathed in the fresh air and tilted her face up toward the fake sunlight.

"Nearly ten acres. The dome does a good job of faking sunlight but at night it clears to give a view of the stars." He got them herded inside and the doors shut behind him. "Pathways are finished, the lighted ones go to completed areas. There's at least three acres of bare rock around here but we're working on it." He pointed across the wide open grassy lawn near the entrance to scattered boulders. "They were pulled up when the dome blew, we're going to leave them as reminders. Vegetable garden is over there, the pasture is open for whatever but some areas are marked off. The biology department often tests new grass strains and such, so if it's marked don't tromp it."

"The trees." Will breathed but a breeze kicked up and ruffled hair and clothing. "Oh, wind!"

Jake laughed. "We added that after the dome repairs. Programmed the air filters to randomize gusts, directions, duration, it's worked nicely. Going to add in rainfall too, I think, still working on it. We've dwarf fruit trees and berry bushes too."

"But those trees, they're so large." Amanda sighed as Jake moved them closer to the small forest across the open pasture.

"Anything anyone's missed from home. Willows, oaks, maple, elders, we'll try anything. Some took better than others. We've insects too, butterflies and bees."

That perked Ichi up. "In a controlled environment?"

"Yup."

"And they're surviving? What about overpopulation?"

"We're managing them, but it's worth it. We've streams all about, one large pond for swimming with some trout in it, frogs now too and a smaller koi pond back this way. Thought we'd eat by the meditation grotto."

The pathway was winding and made them feel like they were going miles from the sterile life of living on a station. Small lights were set along the pathway for night visitors and moss grew on stones. Ichi had to pause because Rye was no longer following. He let the rest of the group move on and backtracked to where Rye stood, hands pressed to the trunk of a tree.

"You okay?" He asked gently.

Rye shook his head. "Trees." He let a grin chase across his lips. "They feel nice to touch, I didn't know."

For as tactile as Rye was and how limited his memories, Ichi wasn't surprised. "Promise you, we'll come back and spend hours exploring here, okay?" What would Rye think of being planetside?

"I'd like that, the air even smells nice." He pulled his hands from the tree's bark but slipped a hand into Ichi's. "I mean I knew, but I didn't know."

Ichi nodded. "I understand, I'd forgotten too." He wondered if it would be possible to get Rye to Avalon for a couple of weeks' vacation. Their lakes and oceans, tall mountains and snow would fascinate the redhead.

They caught back up pretty quickly and turned a corner to enter what could only be called a forest glen. It looked like it had sat in place for centuries. A waterfall fell a dozen feet, the water splashing across chimes that filled, dumped their water and tapped into each other in musical randomness. Flowers bloomed around the trees and a fallen log crossed the stream to let the pathway continue away.

On their side of the stream was a wide clearing and spread in the center of it was a bright red and white checked blanket. Cushions and overstuffed pillows were tossed around to lean against, and a large basket sat to the side being emptied by a buxom woman with dark curly hair. She smiled when Ichi and Rye finally joined them.

"There they are!" she called out and patted the spot near her. "Thought you'd gotten lost. I'm Jess, that fellow over there is Ryan, you already know Jake and Narin."

Ichi nodded to them but, as was his people's way, he found himself the silent guest.

"We're Jake's other programmers, the ones he doesn't brag about."

Jake laughed. "Not true! I only hire the best. This crew, they could program circles around anyone else, I promise that. You won't find better in the universe."

Ryan shook his head. "We lost two of our own last year, it's been difficult to imagine letting anyone else come in to replace them."

"That and hiring folks to come to the middle of nowhere to maybe get blown up isn't all that great of a recruitment pitch." Jake laughed, passing food around.

"Fresh vegetables." Amanda sighed and filled her plate. "Oh, my."

"Hydroponics lab, thought you might like it." Jess smiled.

"So, is it socially unacceptable to ask about this whole bondmate thing over dinner?" Will's voice was light but his face was serious. "I mean, wouldn't want to be lout and have to sleep on the sofa tonight."

Jake grinned. "Being a lout was always one of your best qualities Will."

"Very true," Amanda agreed.

"Hey, I'm being serious."

"Not one of his better qualities, seriousness." Amanda poked again.

"Seriously?" Jake continued the tease. "There isn't much to tell."

"Jake is being modest. His courage saved my life," Narin added softly.

"That sounds like story to me." Will frowned.

There was enough uncertain and undirected tension in Will's voice that the two human programmers shifted uneasily. Jake held a hand to them, just slightly. "Narin's people are social, they can't survive without a bond on a psychic level."

"So, you what? Woke up and made you mind up to risk scrambling your brain to see if you could maybe form a bond with an alien?"

"It wasn't quite like that, but sure, that's what I did." Jake met Will's eye and didn't back down. "It needed to be done. You of all people should know I don't leave a man behind if I can help it."

Ryan glanced between the two men, sensing the underlying tension there and the protectiveness in Will. Jake had spoken little about his visiting friend, only that they'd fought together and nothing more. Like so much of Jake's time during the occupation, he refused to speak on it. "We were all pretty worried too, but it's worked out fine. Jess and I have both even shared communions, sort of a lesser version of bonding. It's nice."

"You're welcome to join us," Narin offered.

"Hm." Will shrugged. "Maybe." Amanda nudged him. "Thank you for the offer."

"So," Jake asked, tearing a hunk of bread apart and trying to delay dealing with Will's protectiveness until later. "What's this favor you wanted to ask of us?"

Amanda and Ichi shared a look before Ichi sat straighter. "I've been redesigning my lab, making it more efficient, safer. I wanted to know if you or your people have the time to look over the kill switch procedures."

A look was passed between the programmers but it was Jake that answered. "Of course, but you could have asked that over the vid. What's this really about?"

Ichi looked toward Rye who had his eyes down. One of his hands ruffled the slender blades of grass at the edge of the spread blanket. That didn't help offer him any answers. "Amanda?"

She nodded. "They're all Avalon, well, except Narin and he's as good as Avalon as you are."

"Rye, was…"

"Is," Rye corrected.

"Was, a Pet."

That started the ball rolling and Ichi and Amanda, with occasional help from Will, conveyed the entire story. Rye sat silent, head down, preferring to be talked about instead of to. As the horror of the situation grew on the faces of the programmers they seemed to grow easier with that set up as well.

"Oh, Rye, we're so sorry!" Jess finally forced out around the lump in her throat. "What an awful thing!"

Rye didn't even look up.

"We're lucky for it though. Rye took out those pirates without even blinking an eye," Amanda bragged for the silent redhead.

That made Jake frown a little bit, an expression that quickly fled. "What is it you want from us, exactly?"

Will shook his head. "I know you can insert an ID into the Concord mainframe for him, give him the papers he might one day need. Right now PETS can show up and take him away. With those papers we can kill the pet and let the man walk away."

The programmers exchanged a look. Ryan half shrugged and Jess raised an eyebrow before Jake spoke again. "We can do it, no sweat."

"One more thing." Rye spoke for the first time since he'd become the topic of conversation. "Will says you and your team are the best. Can you get into Lerman? Get their files and maybe find out who I am?" He locked eyes with Jake and held them but gave no ground.

"We can," Jake began carefully. "But I'm sorry, we won't."

"Why not?" Will instantly asked.

"Because this station is hot right now and Lerman is too secure to risk it. If so much as one part of the data packet gets forgotten they'll trace it to us--and Lerman isn't a warm, fuzzy, forgive-and-forget kind of group. I won't risk it, this station is under enough of a threat from the Flossin Guard as it is." Jake sighed. "I am sorry, truly I am. In a couple of years when things have cooled off, we'll give it a crack."

Rye closed his eyes. "The threat is greater to your station in a couple of years then it is right now."

"How so?" Ryan questioned, toying with a stray piece of grass he'd plucked.

"Flossin Guard aren't stupid, they won't make a move against any of you right now. They'll wait a year, two, maybe five, until you've forgotten and they can come at you unaware. They aren't the sort to walk away from anyone that's dealt them such a blow." Rye spoke in a monotone from knowledge he didn't know he carried.

"Maybe." Jake nodded. "I'm not worried about myself. They can slit my throat any time they want, just so long as they don't go after the station again."

"So you can do what I ask, you're just not willing to?" Rye challenged once more.

"I'm sorry."

Something sad flickered across Rye's face. "So be it."

❧

They finished dinner as the garden slid from late afternoon into early evening. Crickets and frogs began to sing in the growing dimness and small blue lights along the walkways flicked on one by one. The conversation flowed easily, but there was an undertone of tension that was happily avoided.

"Seriously," Jess nodded, looping one arm with Amanda's like long friends and leaving Ryan to carry the picnic basket and blanket. "You and the others have to come to the Dive tonight. It'll be fun."

Amanda glanced to Ichi and Rye before shrugging. "We'll see. We did sleep on the shuttle."

"There you go, just for a little bit. I know everyone is dying to get a look at you. We don't get a lot of visitors here normally."

Will stopped at a slight touch to his elbow; the only other person not already on the walkway back was Jake. He glanced to the group but the only one who noticed that they'd paused and stayed behind was Narin. The tall, pale man glanced across the pair of humans for a moment before turning and following the rest of the group.

"Will?"

"Yes, sir?"

"Stop that." Jake sighed. "You're mad at me."

Will lifted a shoulder but dug the toes of one shoe into the grass, suddenly feeling seventeen again. "Maybe a little."

"Is there going to be a problem between you and Narin?"

"No, sir."

Jake sighed.

"It's just, do you have any idea what kind of risk you took? I could be spoon feeding you right now!"

"Of course I know, but it was a modest risk at best. Wouldn't you take a small risk to save a friend's life?"

Will scrubbed a hand over his eyes. "Of course I would."

"Then don't blame Narin, he carries enough guilt. This isn't really about Narin though, is it? It's about me."

Will opened his mouth but the words dried up. He shook his head and tried the truth. "I feel like a stupid child, jealous because daddy has a new wife. Isn't that absurd!"

That made Jake smile, the small, cynical smile Will remembered so well from this man. "Not at all, there are only three of us left. And Benton won't talk to either of us, not that I blame her. Will, Narin can't replace what we've been through together, nothing can. You just...." Jake shook his head and glanced up to the fading light of the dome where the stars were slowly peeking through. "You've just done better with this whole... life going on thing. Remember what you told me, the morning of your handfasting when I asked you if you were sure?"

Will nodded.

"Well, Narin's like that for me. He makes me feel worthy of a family again. I'm trying here, Will." He laughed a little. "I'm sorry I wasn't up to being a better friend to you, but you're right, we've seen too much together not to try to fix things. I was wrong to push you away for so long. I'm sorry."

"Nothing to be sorry for." Will quirked a half smile at the only man he'd ever obeyed. "We all had shit to deal with, I'm a selfish jerk to assume you'd always play the big brother role. I was just a kid, you know?"

"I know." The truth was, Jake was only a few years older than Will, but while the stress of war and plague had made Will violent and wild, it had matured Jake too early. "I still can't get my mind around you being a doctor."

"Says the super computer fellow. Anyone can learn medicine, coding is half art."

"Maybe, but a doctor?" He shook his head. "I'm proud of you, Will. I know that sounds condescending, but I am."

That made Will's face light up like a child with new candy. "Thanks." The smile dropped. "Jake, about Rye, you won't reconsider? That poor kid has been through so much already."

"It really is too dangerous to try right now."

"Bullshit. You've never blinked at the risk if it was the right thing to do, ever."

"It's also that he's not ready and, frankly, he's a threat. It'd be better if he never remembers who he was before."

Will stepped back. "I've never known you to be cruel before, Jake."

"I'm not being cruel. Lerman did this to him. He killed those attackers on your station as easy as you and I would have sneezed, he wasn't an innocent victim in this. If he can rebuild a life with your family, best to let him try. I've done him a favor by giving him an out from his own past."

"Jake..."

"When he's ready, really ready, we'll know and I'll do everything I can to get those files."

He crossed his arms over his chest. "And if those files get purged in the meanwhile?"

"Nothing is ever lost on a computer system. We'll find it."

"I don't like it."

"I know. But is that because he wants to know or because you want to know?"

"Smarmy bastard."

Jake laughed. "Yeah, that's me." He tossed an arm around Will's shoulders. "Let's catch up, see if Jess has twisted your wife's arm enough for one night."

Chapter Twenty Two

Jess had done her job well and Amanda had smiled and asked nicely and convinced Ichi and Rye to tag along to the Dive as well. That didn't take much, given Rye's love of music. Ichi found himself being dragged along, reluctantly, to the gathering.

"You're an evil woman," Ichi muttered to her, earning himself a smile.

"Be good to get you out more. You're too much the hermit Ich, it's not healthy. Besides, Rye will love it. Half the folks here play or sing, they'll be switching off all night."

"And you knew he wouldn't go without me, and I couldn't say no to him. Evil, evil woman." He tugged his shirt in place, feeling oddly self conscious even though no one else had changed.

"Hush, you'll have a good time. I promise!"

The Dive had started out as a large open area set to be made into a lab, but while the station was still new someone had put in the first still. It had quickly become a meeting place, a pub of sorts, and a small kitchen was quickly installed. It wasn't the formal kitchen that served the meals, but it was the place where most people gathered. Over the years tables, chairs and lounges were added, as well as a small stage, but the walls were kept rough rock and it gave the space an intimate feel.

The doors opened to let warm light and driving music spill out. Mingled with it was a tumble of voices and laughter, the heavy smell of beer and food, and the comforting sense of people, happy people, which sucked others in to join. Ichi stopped protesting when all three of his companions grinned, stood a little straighter and happily disappeared inside.

Hours later, Ichi was drunk enough not to feel the headache he should have had. The music was louder, the people were everywhere, and he hadn't really understood how used to the smaller station he had grown. He'd fended off a half dozen women all trying to get him to dance--or more--and he was tired of blushing and refusing.

Rye didn't seem to have any difficulties; he'd accepted the offers and had spent as much time dancing as anyone else. He was drinking, too. Ichi had never seen Rye drink before. It made Rye look like he belonged with the wild, vibrant, alive people around him. He was beautiful, and Ichi found himself content to sit off in one of the darker corners sipping his beer and watching the redhead.

Just before the beer was gone and Ichi was thinking about finding another, a man with hair as red-orange as Amanda's sat down next to him and slid a new mug toward him.

"You looked thirsty, mate." He grinned.

"Thank you."

"Bents." The man offered his name and his hand.

Ichi accepted it, a custom he'd adapted to but still was unnerved by. People touching so casually just to introduce themselves would always feel odd to him. "Ichi."

"I know, everyone does." He drew a sip from his beer and nodded to where Rye was standing to the side talking to a man with black hair and bright blue eyes. "That's Arnie, he's sort of my off-and-on boyfriend. He's got a thing for redheads."

"And you don't mind?"

"What? That he's talking to your partner?" He grinned. "Naw, there's only seven of us on the station, we tend to be pretty loose with pairing up. So, is the cutie there just your assistant or...?"

Ichi nearly choked on his swallow of beer. Under the small table Bents' hand slid up his thigh, fingers tickling dangerously close to his groin. "Stop that!"

Bents laughed warmly, the hand left Ichi's leg to rise up and brush a stray lock of black hair back, cool fingers gliding over the hot blush on Ichi's face. "Shy, huh? I heard you might be. That blushing thing is killer hot. Don't pine over the pretty fellow there, Arnie will have him tonight. Have some fun with me instead."

Ichi pulled back from the touch and he glanced to Rye. "He's not... he wouldn't..." But the handsome, dark haired man was leaning over now to whisper something close to Rye's ear and the look on the man's face was decidedly predatory.

"Trust me, Arnie always gets what he wants. Damn sexy fool that he is, which is why I can never say no to him. What do you say we go someplace quieter?"

Quieter did sound nice, but Ichi knew enough to understand what the man was implying. He glanced to Rye again and found the dark haired Arnie was now lightly touching his lover and Rye didn't seem to be protesting the hand on the side of his arm.

"Excuse me," Ichi forced out and stood up so quickly he nearly tipped the table over. Part of him wanted to run over and push the hand off of his Rye, yell at the both of them and be hurt, but that would make a horrible display. It would cause a scene, most likely over nothing. Avalon folk were touchy people, they all seemed to need physical contact. The hand on Rye's shoulder could be nothing.

Ichi hurried away to find the men's room, ignoring the concerned questions Bents tossed after him. He slipped around the crowd unnoticed and found the bathroom built onto the back of the room. It was smaller than most public toilets, four stalled in toilets, four urinals, and a pair of sinks under a mirror. Not the most modern of set ups, but Ichi was grateful for the escape.

The music was quiet in here and the lighting better. He hurried, nearly blinded by emotion and too much beer, into the first stall and shut the door. It sealed behind him and he stood there, calmed by the cool plastic walls and the privacy. He wasn't sure what upset him more, having Bents so openly hit on him, which no one ever did, or seeing Arnie so openly hitting on Rye. His Rye, his mind added, twisting his stomach up in unexpressed jealousy. He didn't have a right to be jealous, Rye needed to make choices for himself and if Ichi was any kind of man he'd stand back and let him. Logic didn't stop him from nearly hyperventilating in an effort to get his control back.

Time slipped away and people came and went around him and slowly Ichi felt more in control. He drew a breath and moved to leave the small, private space, certain now that he could make his way back to their rooms without throwing a fit. It would still be a good idea to avoid people, so he peered out of the small crack in the door to make sure the coast was clear and his breath stopped.

Rye was at the sinks, running water over his hands and splashing it up over his face. As Ichi watched unnoticed, he saw Rye stare himself in the eye in the mirror, looking for something as he always did and not finding it. Ichi had his hand on the lock and nearly threw the door open, nearly tumbled out and to ask Rye to go home with him.

Before he could, Arnie followed Rye into the men's room. "I turned around for a second and you were gone. Are you running from me or did you want to be found?" His voice was smooth and controlled, confident and sexy.

Rye glanced sideways at the other man and splashed one more handful of water across his face. "I've had too much to drink. I should go."

"Perhaps I've been too subtle, let me be blunt. Come home with me."

"I can't." Rye stuck his hands in the dryer but his eyes never left the dark haired man.

"Of course you can, that boss of yours won't even notice. Bents is hunting him, he likes the shy ones, but me? I like redheads and men stronger than me, and you, baby, are both. Been a long time since I found both in one person, I can find ways to convince you." Arnie moved to stand almost pressed against Rye, one hand trailed down the side of Rye's ribs and made him shiver.

"Don't touch me."

Arnie chuckled, low and sexy like dark blue velvet. "Just because your boss has a stick up his ass doesn't mean you need to as well. Unless you'd enjoy that, I can oblige that too."

"Don't speak like that about him." Rye stepped back a little, putting a bit of space between their bodies.

"Who? That ice princess? I can understand if he's your only outlet, but here you've got options. You both do, you should exercise them. How long has it been since you've had a real man in your bed?" Arnie stepped forward again and Ichi couldn't swear to it but he thought the man's hand was again on Rye, and not a place as innocent as the side of his ribs. "I can do things to you that that cold, stuck up prig wouldn't ever even dream of."

The words were whispered, but they twisted Ichi's heart. There was truth in them and the mocking of his own fears and he wanted to break from the stall and run. He stayed put because he was more embarrassed to be discovered than to be humiliated behind his back.

Rye didn't answer, not at first. The touch was teasing, promising, and his body reacted. It felt good and that initial rush of pleasure forced his eyes to flutter shut. It was biological and took a moment to adapt to, to gain some control over. When the shock of that bold contact faded a bit, he caught the other man's wrist.

It took no thought or effort to spin the arm in his grip, twisting Arnie's too bold hand away. Rye kicked lightly and caught the back of the man's leg, dropping him to his knees, arm twisted away at a painful angle. Rye leaned forward, anger burning away unwanted desire.

"Don't touch me, and never speak of Ichi like that again! In or out of bed, that man makes you look like an ugly, unschooled worm. After him, no one else can ever compare, do I make myself clear?"

Arnie didn't answer right away, he was breathing a little harder and Rye wasn't sure it wasn't partly from desire.

Rye twisted the arm further, taking it from merely restrained to actually painful. "Do you understand?"

"Yes," Arnie hissed.

"Do you understand that you're nothing next to him?" He twisted a bit more.

"Gods, yes, just don't break it!" Arnie begged.

Rye considered it, figured Ichi would be mad at him and dropped the man's arm. "I've had too much to drink, I'm leaving. This Bents fellow would be lucky to have Ichi, lucky." He shook his head and wandered from the bathroom, leaving Arnie on the bathroom floor rubbing his sore wrist.

Ichi stood frozen, his heart pounding in his chest and oddly turned on. He was afraid to breath for fear of discovery. When he heard footsteps and whistling in the bathroom he peeked out again.

It was Bents. "Shot down too, huh?" He folded his arms over his chest and leaned against the wall.

"I slipped."

"Yeah, right." He grinned a little and moved to help his friend up. "Saw him leaving, warned you he couldn't be pushed."

"I slipped!"

"Of course you did, dear. Let me buy you a drink." Bents draped an arm around the other man and led him away.

Ichi waited, counting to fifty before he slipped from the stall and carefully from the bathroom. He was pretty sure no one had seen him in there and he slid around the edge of the crowd quickly. All he wanted was to get away from the music and laughter and people, to return to the quiet of his room and maybe find Rye there.

"Hey," Rye called from almost directly behind Ichi, making the Asian man start a little in fright. "Sorry."

"Sneak, didn't hear you there."

"I'm leaving, going back to the rooms. Enjoy yourself, okay?" Rye tossed out and turned to leave.

Ichi reached out and caught the redhead's arm. "That sounds perfect, let's go home."

Rye paused and studied Ichi's face. "You sure you don't want to stay?"

"If you go, there's nothing I want here. I'm sure."

That broke a shy, heartbreakingly warm smile across Rye's lips. He leaned in and whispered right into Ichi's ear. "If I knew it wouldn't make you angry, I'd kiss you right here in front of everyone."

The heat and desire and love in that whisper washed across Ichi and made him feel as if Rye had dragged him up onto the stage and kissed him silly. He was blushing as he followed Rye the rest of the way through the crowd to escape back to their rooms.

Chapter Twenty Three

Rye leaned back from the highly illegal retinal scanner that Jake and his group had produced and blinked to clear his vision. Will and Amanda had gone to the med lab to start setting up for the required physicals, but Ichi was with him, sitting quietly to the side as always. They'd been invited to get Rye's new identity that afternoon and Ichi hadn't wanted to wait.

"Have you thought about what name you wanted to use?" Ryan leaned back in his seat and asked. Any one of them could have done the identity insert alone, but it had turned into a group project.

"No, I haven't."

"We can just use Rye Sullivan if you want?"

They were using his real retinal scans which meant anyone at Lerman looking for him would have little difficulty tracking him down. The name used made little difference. "I'd like that."

"Rye Sullivan it is then."

Coding visors and gloves were pulled on and the group tossed half-sentences back and forth as the identity was slipped into the official databases with frightful ease. Less then a half hour passed before all but Jake logged out, and it was just another moment before he pulled his own visor off as well.

"All finished." He slid a data card across the desk. "We took some liberties making up a loose history for you, but it'll hold up."

"Thanks." Rye slid the card into his palm.

"Frightful how easy you made that look. To think you can delete an identity as easily, that someone can do that." Ichi shook his head.

"Not easy." Jess grinned. "We're just good, and it's way easier to put something into the banks than to remove it. If you slip it into the central listing files, it'll propagate outward from there, but to delete someone you have to hunt them down in like a thousand systems. Not saying it can't be done, just a total pain."

"Still frightful. Thanks again, we'll get out of your hair." Ichi stood up and Rye followed, but he stopped when Rye froze.

Rye smiled softly. "I'm sorry, Ichi." He spoke just as gently.

"Sorry?"

There was no further warning. Rye reached under the loose hem of his shirt and, from his waistband, removed a small, nearly palm sized weapon. He thumbed a switch and it hummed up to full charge and waited. Ichi didn't know the small weapon--made with mismatched bits of metal and hard plastics--but he'd recently learned firsthand what a mag gun sounded like.

Rye aimed the gun steadily at Jake. "I'll have those files from Lerman now."

"What're you doing?" Ichi snapped out.

Jess and Ryan exchanged a look and Ichi saw the subtle way the Ryan glanced to Narin. That's when Ichi noticed it too--Narin, who was nearly telepathic with Jake, wasn't the slightest bit upset. Admittedly, the pale man was rather sedate and steady, but there was nothing in his face or posture to suggest concern.

"Sit down, Ichi." Rye spoke calmly, his eyes or aim never leaving Jake. "The files, please."

"Not going to happen, son," Jake answered smoothly.

Rye shook his head slightly. "It's not my wish to hurt you or your people but I must have those files."

"I'm not afraid to die and killing me won't encourage them to help you. They won't do a thing without my order."

It wasn't an idle threat and Rye didn't doubt his people's loyalty. "It's easy to be bold with your own life." The gun swung now and pointed easily at Narin's head. "Will you sit and watch me kill your friends?"

That made Ryan shift a bit in his seat. Narin raised an eyebrow. "Indeed." The alien's split lip made the word softer, almost mocking in tone.

"I have no doubt you're capable of killing all of us, including Ichi. I've known a lot of folks like you, people without remorse or guilt. Go ahead, kill us, but if you do, you'll be throwing away everything you've found. Avalon's protection, your friends, your lover. Are you prepared to toss so much away?"

Rye didn't even blink. "I'm prepared to face the results of my actions, don't think for a moment I'm not. The files, my tolerance for waiting is ending."

The tension in the room rose, Ichi heard his blood pounding in his ears. He was feeling faint but was afraid to breathe or think. Rye looked like cold, clear death and Jake looked ready to laugh in his face.

"You're not going to shoot anyone today, Rye."

"Don't be so certain."

"Oh, I am, because while I'm certain you can kill us, I don't believe you want to, or will, for one. For another, the man you're so willing to kill is the best programmer we have and the only one of us able to promise that stealing those files will go undetected. You're too smart to kill your best chance at success. More importantly," Jake carefully stood up. "You're smart enough to know all of this already, so put the gun down before you give your boyfriend a heart attack. You've made your point, we have the nice happy excuse now." A half smirk danced across Jake's face but his eyes were bright with amusement. "I'm sufficiently convinced you need these files."

Rye stood for a moment more, frozen, before a smile darted across his face. "What gave it away? Or am I really so transparent?" He flicked a switch and the gun hummed down, losing its charge before Rye spun it around and handed it off to Jake.

Jake let the breath he'd been holding out--he hadn't even known he wasn't breathing. "No, you're too convincing. The gun, it's good but the side latch always scuffs up. Yours is clean, not a scratch."

"What?" Jess asked, breathing again.

"It's a fake." Jake found a seam and pulled, the barely held together forgery broke and fell into a half dozen parts, showing the only thing inside was a small device to mimic the sound of a weapon charging.

"You risked Narin's life, all our lives, on a guess?" Ryan stood up.

Jake shrugged.

"Fuck me, I need a drink!" Ryan exploded and went to rummage into a drawer to find a bottle.

"A fake?" Ichi asked, slow to understand. "What?"

Rye held back. "You'll help me?"

Jake sighed and glanced to his crew, Narin as placid as always, Jess looking wide eyed and in shock and Ryan pouring out drinks for everyone. "We'll get those files, don't you worry. I think we all could use that drink, Ryan." Jake knew he could, his hands were still trembling and none of them would be up to tackling Lerman anytime in the short term.

"A fake?" Ichi asked again from where he still sat, lightheaded and sick.

Rye knelt down and pressed a glass into the shocked man's hand. "Yes, I'm sorry."

"I don't understand."

"Rye was doing us a favor." Jake downed his drink in a quick swallow and didn't even flinch at the sharp burn it caused.

"What?" Ichi was starting to wonder if he'd had a bump to the head, because no one was making any sense.

"Now, if we get caught, we can claim he held a gun to our heads and made us."

Rye soothed a hand over Ichi's knee. "It allows me to take full responsibility if the worst happens. They're innocent because I made them, it will be done from force not favor."

It was a bit more to it then that, a secondary understanding between Jake and Rye neither man needed to speak of. Rye had just proven that he was willing to risk anything, give up anything, to find out what he had been, who he had been, no matter how horrible the truth was. That was what Jake had needed to agree because ignorance was often the last shelter to a horrible past.

Ichi slammed back his drink. "You're all crazy, Avalon folk are all insane."

That made Ryan chuckle. "Can't debate that." But the words were tense and uneasy still.

"I still don't know how you talked Jake into this." Will pried again. It had been the running nag since he'd been told that Jake and his programmers were hunting down Lerman's files. No one was talking about what had happened and days had gone by with Will still left to wonder. He knew Jake was virtually as stubborn as any soul alive and unmovable if he didn't wish it.

"It doesn't matter." Amanda accepted the mugs Will had carried over, setting one in front of where Rye sat. Four days had passed with Rye growing more and more uneasy and Ichi retreating further into silence, the least of their concerns should have been how Jake had been convinced. "It's done now."

Jake had called them an hour ago and spoken privately to Rye. It had been Rye that had requested that only his family be there when he found out just what and who he was. As soon as Will and Amanda had canceled the rest of the day's exams and returned home, Rye had stopped pacing. He'd sat down, rubbed idly at the soft fabric covering his knee and fixed his eyes to a spot a couple of feet in front of him. Even Ichi sitting to one side of him and Amanda the other did nothing to stir him.

Jake finally arrived, Narin following, but not the other two. He looked stubborn, but his face was unreadable. Greetings were exchanged quickly, offers of tea were made and refused before Narin settled in to a chair near the one Will had taken and Jake had pulled a seat over to sit closer to where Rye still hadn't looked up.

"It's okay to have changed your mind," Jake said gently, eyes not leaving the redhead.

Rye swallowed hard and glanced up. "I need to know."

"And you're certain you want everyone here?"

Which was a nice way of warning that not everything was going to be pleasant. Rye nodded. "I'm certain." He slid a hand over and felt Ichi's fold over his own. He'd been surprised when Ichi hadn't been angry over the whole fake gun, fake threat gambit. Surprised, he'd been more than a little surprised and upset that he'd been kept in the dark and so frightened, but not angry. It was a blind, total acceptance that he was unable to refuse and desperate to return the same.

"Ready?" Jake checked one more time, a deep part of him wanting Rye to refuse.

"Jake, you're killing us here!" Will moaned, swayed by the tension growing in the room.

"I'm ready." Rye nodded.

Jake sighed but nodded. He tapped a few keys on his notebook and vid screen in the room picked up the interface and displayed a photo. "Rye, you were Unidentified Child Number 834826 on Haflyn Downs."

The vid screen displayed an obviously official identification photo. The child had been cleaned up and his pale skin was flushed red from the scrubbing. The dark red hair, several shades less black cherry red than Rye's current hair color, had been cut into an uneven line. The boy was too skinny and had a sullen frown plastered on his face. The eyes were the same, the distant, cold gray hadn't been altered in the least.

Rye sat up and tried to find some scrap of memory connected to that face. "That was me?"

Jake nodded. "That was you when they picked you up out of the slums of a neighborhood called Molotov's Mixer. Official report says you were found wandering unattended, eating from the gutter, and that you about castrated the arresting officer." Jake tapped a few more keys and the written report came up. "In fact, the first notes in your file are warnings toward your short temper and violent tendencies. Apparently, you gave the social workers a hell of a time."

"How old was I?" It felt odd, asking personal questions about himself.

"Unknown, they guessed you were about six from medical exams, but it's also noted that you were severally malnourished and quite ill when picked up. Refused or didn't know your name, where you were from or any family. It's written in here that you told one of the case workers that an older boy called you 'the little shit', but you didn't think that was your name." Jake scrolled across reports and more pictures, all showing a scrawny child with too old eyes and a mean look.

"So I was nothing."

Amanda shook her head. "No, it means you were dumped into a bad situation too young."

Rye glanced down but he kept his hand tightly wrapped around Ichi's. "What else?"

"You were deemed too antisocial to be adoptable and placed at Hearts of Eternal Mercy's Home for Unwanteds, a private company that ran and still runs orphanages, group homes, mental wards, soup kitchens and homeless shelters on seven worlds. Two guesses who owns and funds Hearts of Eternal Mercy." Jake had brought up pictures of the home Rye had been sent to but the redhead was watching the still images and promotional footage with not even a flicker of recognition.

Will leaned forward. "Lerman."

"Give the man a cookie." Jake grinned bitterly. "Rye you were one of eighty-three children between the ages of ten and five gleaned from the Lerman controlled orphanages over an eight year period. During those eight years tests were done on new arrivals. They rated intelligence, aggression, adaptability, creativity, as well as rating the likelihood of the child being missed. If the score was high enough, the child interesting enough, Lerman took them."

"To what end?" Amanda asked, as gently as she could.

"This is where things get tricky. Lerman uses coded internal memos, keywords and such, we've been trying to break it apart. I've Jess and Ryan working on it even as we speak."

"Jake," Rye asked softly. "Please, best guess and just say it."

"Very well. Best guess from what we're seeing? The ID numbers on you changed and the pattern matches Lerman employee codes. We believe that these children were raised as Lerman property, isolated and trained for assignments. What we've figured out shows very focused educational training, physical training."

"That's nothing new for Lerman though." Will shook his head. "It's been a quiet secret for years that they'll train agents from little up to be ideal employees. All the big security companies do that with their elite. Don't they?"

"So it's been said, but those children are the offspring of other employees. They live with their parents. These orphans? They went further. The training was stricter, the isolation more intense. Add in the genetic modifications made and only half survived to what Lerman calls 'an applicable age'." Jake sighed and glanced to where Rye sat, staring at the screen with unblinking, empty eyes. "Any of this ring bells, Rye?"

He just shook his head.

"How about any of these pictures?" Jake keyed in the pictures and images of other boys, all about ten years of age, began to flick across the screen. "After this applicable age passed, the survivors were grouped into units. These were the nine other boys in your unit."

Rye watched the faces of the other boys flick across the screen and none of them looked like anything but random strangers. Jake talked in the background about knowing that Rye's first assignment was at this applicable age, which was nine, ten or maybe eleven. The words meant little to him, the facts were there, but none of them belonged to him. Until one face paused on the screen and did more than just casually pass away.

"Wait!" Rye nearly stood up but the face flickered away. "Go back."

The conversation around Rye stopped and the images on the screen froze. "This one?" Jake asked, flipping back to the last photo displayed.

Rye shook his head. "One more."

The boy's picture returned and Rye stood up. The boy was Asian, with black hair, dark golden skin and even as a child his face was squared off. There was none of the almost elegant beauty that Ichi's mixed bloodlines gave him to this boy. His eyes were as black as his hair and he looked as stern and unhappy as all the other faces that had flicked across the screen.

"Who is that?" Rye's heart pounded in fear or memory as he reacted as he hadn't with seeing his own face.

"All we have is an ID number. Here, I've other images, do you know him?"

Rye shook his head. "I don't know."

The pictures on the screen gradually aged. The childish roundness faded from the face and sharp cheekbones emerged. The already squared face grew stronger and Rye watched the changes as his stomach clamped up.

"He's listed as killed in the line of duty at applicable age plus seven. Here, this is the last file image."

"Rye?" Will spoke slowly. "I think we should stop for now." He was starting to feel like a horrible weight was crushing him and that was never a good sign.

"No, I..." Rye shook his head as if trying to clear it. "I know him, I..." He looked to Ichi as if the other man might be able to explain and, in a way, he did. Rye glanced back to the screen and down to where Ichi sat, silent and waiting.

He saw it so clearly, the fear and nightmare that had chased him for so long, Ichi, laying with open eyes in his own blood. Only, when Rye glanced between the picture and the flesh and blood man, the eyes staring at him weren't hazel. They were black and the face was square and there was blood on his hands.

"Oh god, no." He stumbled away, flinching from hands that touched him until he hit something solid. That felt better, something real and tangible and he tucked himself down against it. It didn't matter that voices were trying to be comforting were asking for his attention. It didn't matter that hands stroked and soothed. All that mattered was that he remembered.

It started out with seeing the stern Asian boy laying in the pool of blood, his own blood, on the smooth marble floor. It was Conti's office, Rye knew it was. He remembered the boy had no name, just like he had no name, but the others called him Jude and the dead boy was Mica. They'd been called into Papa Conti's office, which was never a good thing because missions were delivered in a conference room. Rye had even more reason to detest Conti's office, but his mind shied away from that, unwilling and unable to remember yet.

He did remember Mica; proud, strong, beautiful. The other boy smiled a lot, which none of them did often. That's what Rye had first noticed about him, how easily a smile would brighten his eyes even when there was little to smile about. It was when Mica started smiling at him, turning that bright, cheerful grin on just for him, that Rye remembered his heart stopping.

It wasn't like they were ignorant virgins. Rye remembered his first mission had been a blackmail set up with a man that liked pale, young boys. He was pretty sure the others in his unit had worked similar jobs over the years even though work was never discussed. They weren't supposed to be friendly with each other, just training. Nothing more than staying sharp and ready; Papa Conti's daggers waiting to be used. Conversation was discouraged, friendliness outright frowned upon, and only the loosest of bonds allowed. It was useful to know another's skills and limitations when paired for a job, that was all. Rye didn't even feel a twinge when one of the other's failed to return.

He remembered training with Mica, besting the other boy as always but, unlike the others, there was no anger. Mica had just smiled, bright and dazzling. "You're really great, you know that?" he said softly, fearful of being observed conversing.

Rye hadn't answered.

It had taken weeks, months for him to understand what the uncomfortable unease he felt around Mica really was. It was that smile, it made him feel things. And now when they trained the touch of body to body stirred things. They'd jerked each other off in the locker room, quickly and roughly but Mica had smiled again. It was a dangerous, addicting smile.

Things had lost control from there. Quick hand jobs had become quick blow jobs and then to rough kisses which eventually lead to conversations. Rye had been surprised that Mica had never been taken by a man before and oddly sick to his stomach to be the handsome boy's first. He'd worried so much that he barely enjoyed their first union, until Mica had tucked himself into Rye's arms and sighed.

"I love you." he'd whispered, softly, shyly, into Rye's ear.

The words had made him shiver, but he clung to them and believed. It had made life seem easier. The normal sense of freedom being turned loose on a mission gave him was gone, his thoughts stayed home, a place that had always felt like a cage before. For a while things were good and, except having to deal with Conti, Rye had few complaints.

Until they were both summoned to Conti's private office, a place that made Rye ill to even think of. Only a handful had ever gone there, the very best or the very special or the ones soon to be very dead. Rye had been sent there when he'd returned from his first mission, still injured in more than just his body. He'd been sent in to find one of the older boys, one of the best of all the units, with his pants around his ankles. Conti was fucking him, right there over his desk.

Rye had frozen in place and stood at attention, waiting to be acknowledged, trying to pretend he wasn't there. It wasn't enough, the older boy hung his head and his face went red. Rye remembered the wicked, horrible way Conti had smiled and he'd known that this was a punishment for the other boy, knowing someone else saw why Conti considered him special.

He'd be summoned back to the office again, years later. Conti informed him that of all the remaining of his children, Rye was the best. It had made Rye feel so proud, like he'd mattered. Papa Conti had then told Rye that the older boy that had been his special boy wouldn't be returning from his mission and Rye was now his special child. After that, Rye had gone to the office far, far too often and never spoke a word of it to anyone, not even Mica.

So he knew it was bad, but Mica still admired their savior, their father. His faith was as bright as his smile, and Rye followed crisply but with sick dread. There was soon no doubt it was bad. There was yelling and taped evidence of the two boys' affair. Conti beat them both, but Rye more than Mica. Both of them took the cursing and the blows without a word, there was no excuse to be offered. They'd both known their contact was forbidden--and Rye had known doubly so.

"I will not tolerate this!" Conti has screamed. "This ingratitude under my own roof! After all I've done for you boys! You were trash, filth, tossed aside to die and I took you and made you gods among men and this is how you repay me? With betrayal?"

Conti had kicked them a couple of times more. "This ends." He pulled a drawer open and retrieved a blade. "283," the last three digit's of Rye's number, he remembered them, it was the only way Conti ever addressed them. "Your scores and success is higher, you live. Dispose of 918."

The two boys froze and their eyes met. There were no smiles now. This was the cold reality they'd lied to themselves about. They'd both known that discovery would mean death, and some small part of Rye's mind had whispered that maybe that was why they'd grown careless. Never had they dreamed that Conti would order only one death.

Mica nodded. Steady and prepared, not a glimpse of fear in his eyes. He'd often talk to Rye, in stolen moments after their lovemaking, about wanting out, an idea that Rye couldn't even begin to conceive. He'd known there was nothing more, nothing beyond the blood and death and pain of their lives, but Mica had dreamed of an escape, any escape. His eyes said it now: if Rye loved him, he'd give him that escape.

When Rye took up the blade, Mica knelt and raised his chin. They'd been given an order and there was no choice but to obey. Every moment of their lives had burned obedience into them and even though Rye felt himself breaking apart, dying more fully than a physical death could ever be, he obeyed.

The blood had been hot and the knife was sharp. Mica slipped into death quickly and far more painlessly than either of them had ever hoped for. Mica had held his eyes until he was gone, neither one looking away even as the blood dripped from Rye's hands and the knife clattered to the floor.

Conti was there, now alone in the room together. The older man beat Rye some more, cursed him. Screamed at Rye for responding to a piece of filth boy, when even the smallest of response had to be wrestled from him at Conti's hands. Rye hadn't fought, he never did. Conti had made him, created him, was his father. Even when Conti had stripped him half naked and fucked him over his desk, Rye still didn't fight. There seemed no point to it, no point to anything anymore. As Conti took him with more anger and rage than real lust, Mica lay in his blood, watching. Rye wished it was him on the ground but not if that meant Mica would have swapped places with him. He cared for the other boy too much to wish Conti on him.

It was all there, in Rye's head, a lifetime of memories that unlocked and opened one by one. Every horrible thing he'd done or survived, the look on every face of every person he'd killed. Men, women, children. He'd been a dog that if Conti said attack, he'd attacked. How many people had he killed? Rye wasn't sure he could count them, after a time it was just easier to say a whole bunch. He'd ruined people's lives, stolen their money, crushed their dreams and not once had he felt a thing about it. The only thing he felt remorse or pain over was killing Mica, and that was a bittersweet pain.

Rye felt smothered, crushed under the weight of so much. It seemed impossible to balance what he had been with anything remotely worthy of the life he'd found. He curled into a small ball, his side pressed to whatever solid surface he'd stumbled against and sobbed. It was shock, some part of his still functioning mind knew it was just shock, but he was hysterical and couldn't stop. When a stinging sharp feel of something being injected into his blood stream came, Rye welcomed the darkness the drugs brought with it.

Chapter Twenty Four

The darkness cleared slowly, like veils being pulled back from his eyes one thin drape at a time. Rye found his throat hurt, and his eyes, but he was curled up on something soft and felt generally warm and safe. It was a feeling he'd recently taken for granted but suddenly found it to be almost startlingly new. Even before he could get his eyes open, a soothing hand stroked across his hair.

"Hey you, welcome back." Ichi spoke softly. "Amanda said you should burn off the sedative pretty quickly but she gave you way too much."

Rye frowned to find Ichi sitting in a chair pulled close to the bed. It didn't seem right, but he was selfish enough to be almost desperate to have the man near. "I'm glad you're here." The words slipped out and Rye sighed, apparently remembering his past didn't end his stupid habit of blurting truths out.

"Where else would I be?" Ichi smiled and slid a hand across the rumbled hair. "How're you feeling? I've some water here, thirsty?"

"Please." He pulled himself halfway to sitting to accept the bottle. The water was mostly warm but still soothing. Ichi didn't push, didn't ask, didn't crowd him and he could have kissed the man for his quiet patience. "I remember," Rye said softly, licking a drop of water from his lips and lowering the bottle.

"Who that boy was?"

"That and more. All of it. His name was Mica. That was his real name, he told me. We didn't have names, just numbers. When we'd go on our first assignment, we took the first fake name we used so we'd have something other than a number to call each other. Mica, he told me, he had them use his real name. No one else knew it was the name his parents gave him."

"He was your friend?" Ichi asked carefully, unwilling to trigger another fit of hysterics but equally unwilling to not show concern.

"No, he was my lover." Rye forced a small smile. "Must have a thing for Asian men."

That made Ichi blush a little. "Must have."

"How long was I out?" He wasn't ready to tell Ichi he'd killed Mica, not sure he could yet.

Ichi had to glance at a clock. "Nearly three hours. We didn't want to sedate you, but it had been over an hour and you were only getting worse. Amanda was afraid you'd hurt yourself."

"I was hysterical, it's okay." It was so odd to piece together what he had been with who he was. "Is Will okay?"

"He is now, Jake and Narin took him. They said something about communing would settle him better than drugs. Apparently it worked, but he's staying over in their rooms for now. He wanted to give you the space to rant as much as you liked without worry." Amanda had stayed, she was out in the living room in case she was needed.

"I'm not a good man, Ichi, and I know I should disappear, get as far from you as I can but I'm too selfish. I can't stand the thought of leaving you. I love you too much to leave, even if you tell me to." That sounded a touch intense, but he knew himself now and Rye knew he was, by nature, not a man to give up. He drew a breath and braced himself. "So, think of the worst thing you can imagine, the very worst, and double it."

"Rye..."

"Just do it."

"Okay."

"Now, I've done that, and more. I'm a killer, Ichi, I'm good at it."

"Doesn't matter now, you're a different person."

Rye thought about what it had felt like to kill those pirates. "Not too different. Ichi, I'm good at it and I enjoy it. I killed Mica, I took a knife and slit his throat."

Ichi saw no lie in Rye's voice or face, just open guilt. "But you said he was your lover?"

"He was and he loved me and I cared for him."

Ichi glanced down to study his own hands. "You would never hurt me." He believed that as sure as he believed anything.

"I would die before I allowed harm to come to you."

It wasn't a morality question he'd ever been presented with. "I've said it before, I don't care what you've been, or done, so long as you're here with me."

"I will kill again, Ichi. Can you love me knowing that?"

Logic said in a society murder was wrong. In Ichi's black and white world before he'd left his home he would have refused to speak to Rye, shunned him, no matter how deeply he may have held emotions. Life wasn't so black and white any longer, there was no clear and easy answers.

Will had taken human life as well, and Ichi knew his friend and brother was equally ready to kill again should he have to. Should Ichi cut all emotional ties with Will, or brush it off as circumstances? Was Rye's past and his threat of violence in the future such an insurmountable hurdle? Was Rye not just as much a creature of his past as Will?

Ichi leaned forward and brushed his lips across Rye's. The kiss was soft, quick and chaste. "Don't be silly, I'm selfish too."

The look that darted across Rye's face was such broken desperation that Ichi had to look away. That meant he missed seeing the hand that snaked out and caught his arm, pulling him easily onto the bed and into Rye's arms. One of Rye's hands came up to cradle the back of his head and the other wrapped around his body. The hug was tight and nearly crushing, but Ichi tucked his face against Rye's neck and didn't complain.

"I know I never did anything to deserve you."

Ichi held still and Rye's unsteady breath tickled the side of his neck. The hug loosened enough to let him breathe but he was unwilling to pull away. The hand ruffling across his hair was skilled enough and strong enough to just as easily snap his neck; the body he was resting against was tense, graceful and deadly. The idea that so much chaos, so much of everything he'd been told was wrong and antisocial was bound in the man against him should have repulsed him. Instead, it drew him like a moth to an open fire and Ichi happily risked the flames.

"Conti used to fuck me, before he made me into a pet," Rye whispered against Ichi's dark hair. "He found out what Mica and I were doing, beat us, ordered me to kill him and I did. He died in a pool of his own blood, eyes open, watching while Conti took me over his desk. Afterwards, he made me dispose of his body and clean up his blood."

Ichi pulled against the arms holding him and leaned away enough to look at Rye. "I'm sorry. That's why you've been so worried about letting me care for you."

He nodded. "I didn't know, didn't remember, but it wasn't totally lost. I kept seeing you in his place. He died because he loved me, I killed him." Rye closed his eyes and drew a long slow breath. "He wanted out, used to talk about being free. Mica never cared about how, he just wanted out. The only way out was to die and he just knelt and let me do it."

Ichi didn't try to say anything comforting, there weren't words for that. He just sat and listened.

"After I killed Mica I started to understand what he meant. I started putting money aside, identities aside, in secure accounts on a dozen different worlds. Things Conti didn't know about, that no one knew about. I didn't plan on getting out, it just…it kept me from going crazy. I kept saying I was doing it to get Mica out, he used to say he had an uncle, a family. I thought, maybe I could find them, tell them about him. I don't know, it just made things easier." The words felt stale and flat but he needed Ichi to know.

"Is that why Conti did this to you?"

He shook his head. "As far as I know he never found out about the accounts, or Mica's uncle. I was sent on an assignment to kill a target and anyone else that might witness his death. The target was a seven year old boy, the location was a public transport. I sat next to that child for two hours, he talked to me, to other people. He was so full of life and hope, he was so innocent. I couldn't do it. I just, I couldn't do it."

"Understandably so."

"No! I've killed more children then I can remember, this boy was no different. I just couldn't do it."

"You were what was different."

Rye nodded. "I just, I really saw what a monster I was. I got off at the next stop and let the boy go. I should have run, taken the hidden accounts and ID's and disappeared, but I couldn't. I, Ichi, Conti was all I had. I couldn't go, I…"

"Shhh, I think I understand."

"I went back thinking he would kill me. Told him I didn't want to be a monster anymore. He beat me and, well, eventually had me turned into this." He glanced to his hands. "He should have killed me but he didn't. Ichi, he made me into a toy because of Mica. He never forgave me for enjoying Mica's touch but not his."

"So he made it so you'd have to enjoy his." The horror of the truth settled like lead at the bottom of Ichi's stomach.

"He let clients use me, people I'd worked jobs for, who knew what I had been. Yet he didn't kill me. Ichi, he should have killed me when he disposed of me yet he didn't." That was the most important problem, the largest mystery he needed to solve.

"Maybe he had feelings for you?"

That was a cold thought and it made Rye shiver. "No, I was never anything more than an object. We all were, just tools to be used. He was angry that I had given something to someone else that I wouldn't give to him, but that was from spite." It clicked into place and Ichi nearly got dumped onto the bed Rye stood up so quickly. "He's going to come back for me. There can't be too many of us left and I was the top of all the units, he couldn't afford to kill me outright. This was just to humble me. He's going to come for me." That set his heart to thudding in near panic and Rye could almost feel Conti's breath on his neck already.

"You don't know that." Ichi spoke carefully and didn't move from where he sat on the bed. Rye looked startled and ready to bolt.

"That's the only reason I'm still breathing, Ichi. Conti doesn't make mistakes and he has no mercy. He couldn't have known I'd find someone kind, someone that would help me heal."

Ichi moved now, he slid off the bed with none of the grace Rye showed. Remembering his past only seemed to make the man more graceful, more fluid, and Ichi knew he could watch him for days and be happy. His own clumsiness didn't seem important, he moved to stand in front of Rye and caught his eyes.

"Stop, just stop," he ordered in a firm voice. It was the same voice he'd used to give Rye orders when he'd first arrived. It worked, Rye shut his mouth and swallowed the words he'd been ready to pour out. "You've only known this for four hours, three of which you were unconscious for. Take a couple of breaths, calm down, and then we'll sit down with the others and figure out what to do from here. We have Lerman's files, you have your memories, and you aren't alone anymore."

Rye blinked at the total command in Ichi's voice and manner. Instantly, the unfocused panic faded and the cold fear stepped down. He was trained to obey, it was all he knew, to follow a stronger man--he just hadn't thought Ichi was going to understand that and fulfill that role. The difference was this time he had a man worthy of following.

"That's better." Ichi saw the clarity return to those gray eyes. "Now, Amanda's out there and she's pretty worried about you. She said you should try to eat something when you wake up. So, how about we get dinner, check on Will, give it a bit and then worry?"

It was sensible idea and one Rye nodded and agreed to, but there was no point or need for discussion. Conti knew he was alive and would eventually come for him. Most likely, Ichi and other innocents would be hurt along the way because he doubted anyone would simply hand him back to Conti. That left only one course of action--kill Conti or die in the process of trying.

It took a while to get ready for dinner. Amanda wanted to check Rye over and Rye wanted a shower. He wasn't sure how he could stand being at the public kitchen and spent most of the time in the shower just letting the hot water soothe him. It was odd to have his memories in place, to be able to page through them like a book. He wanted time to sort it out, time away from watching eyes. Time alone. He'd spent most of his life basically alone and contact with other people had only ever brought pain.

But he wasn't owned by Conti anymore, he wasn't housed in a unit of drones anymore. Rye shut the water off and tried to catch his breath. Every instinct screamed at him to run before people got hurt, but he didn't want to leave. Will and Amanda and even Jake and Narin were friends, family even, or as close as he was ever likely to find. They weren't competition for survival within his unit. Ichi, well, Ichi went beyond family, he was vital.

It left him feeling torn in two. Unable to leave and near panicked just from the thought of harm touching any of them. He knew how to fake a relationship, a friendship, in fact he used to be quite good at it, but inside he'd always known it was a fake. Nothing had prepared him for having those ties become real. But he'd learned one thing: hiding alone in his thoughts wasn't going to keep them away.

That thought made him smile a little. He could keep his distance all he wanted, bite his tongue and refuse to speak to them, but they wouldn't abandon him. They'd go on and make horrible, futile plans anyway and do everything in their power to protect him. Since he knew he could cut off his own legs easier than he could leave them behind, he resigned himself to accepting their company and perceived help, even if Rye knew it was going to be up to him to protect them.

Dinner turned out to be in Jake and Narin's room, a two bedroom suite similar to the one the four of them shared, which settled some of Rye's nerves. He was grateful to be away from unwelcome and unknown eyes. Will was already there, looking a little pale but otherwise normal and he greeted the three of them with a wide, warm smile.

"Hey."

Amanda moved over to press a kiss to her husband's forehead. "I see communing didn't scramble your brains."

"Not that we'd be able to tell with Will," Jake teased.

"Hey!"

"Seriously, how was it? I wish I was a stronger psi." She sat down as Narin slid platters of food onto the table.

Will drew a slow breath and studied the plates of food, all simple fare meant to be picked at, light too as if Narin knew that the conversation would settle heavily on human stomachs. "It was different, better than I expected, less vulnerable then I'd thought. It helped a lot."

"Will's not that much stronger of a psi than me but he's twice as empathic. Seems communion works to settle a lot of the backlash of that down." Jake nodded to Rye and Ichi but settled down across from them. "So, is it a safe guess to assume you've remembered, Rye?"

Rye nodded. "Pretty much everything."

"How much protection can Avalon really offer?" Ichi wanted to cling to Rye, but unless the man reached for him he found it almost impossible to cross the gulf to him.

Amanda glanced to Jake and shrugged before answering. "A fair amount through legal channels. By all rights, Rye is still considered property, Avalon property. He can't be removed without a legal fight and it's one I doubt Lerman or PETS would risk becoming a public fight."

"No, they won't come at me openly. Avalon can't protect me from that. The moment Conti thinks I might remember, he'll send for me."

"Send for you?" Will leaned forward.

"A recall order that I'll have to follow, if I don't, he'll send someone and they'll kill anyone that gets in their way."

"You're sure about this?"

"Will, I'm sure." He'd been sent to retrieve one or two of them over the years. One of the other boys he'd found living with a woman, all he wanted was to be left alone. Rye had killed the girl and dragged the boy back. The other, one of the female children Lerman owned, had missed her recall order because she was dead. He'd dispatched those around her body and brought that back.

"So we just have to make sure he never finds out you're better," Amanda said, as if that was simple and easy.

"I don't think that's possible, not for the long term." Jake caught Narin's eye but the pale man was silent, respectful of a situation that didn't directly affect him. The pale blue eyes were hardly disinterested, they absorbed every word with the hunger for knowledge of the Lorekeeper he'd once been.

Rye drew a breath. "The safest course of action is for me to disappear."

Anything else he might have said was cut off by all three Avalon folks talking at once. Oddly, the loudest sound was Ichi's silence, and Rye found himself acutely aware of the Asian man's harsher, shorter breathes.

"I agree, it won't do any good." Rye finally cut into them. "They'll still come here looking for me and I can't swear my absence will protect you. This isn't going to end until I'm dead, or until Conti's dead."

That shut everyone up.

"I can't sit here on my hands waiting for him to come for me. I have to take this to him." The thought made him feel sick.

"Just like that? You get your memories back and suddenly you're some super hero?" Will snapped, feeling an edge of panic from Ichi seep into his brain and cold dread from Rye.

"If you can think of another way, I'll listen," Rye challenged, knowing there wasn't another way.

"Conti is a paranoid fucker, it's not going to be so simple to just walk in there and kill him!"

"Will, don't think for a single heartbeat that killing Conti will be anything close to easy. For better or not, that man is my father and short of the last year, the only person in my entire life to give a thought about whether I breathed or not. Reaching him will be the easy part." Even Rye was surprised at the vein of loyalty he'd found, but that horrible knack to speak from emotion still popped up and out the words spilled.

"How can you defend him? He stole any chance you may have had for a normal childhood, turned you into some weapon, and when that was no longer useful turned you into a sex toy! Wake up Rye, this man is filth and deserves death, not your protection!"

"Will," Amanda warned.

Rye stood up, his hands balled into fists. "I know better than you'll ever be able to dream what a monster Conti is, but he is my father, he is all that ever mattered to me. I lived or died on that man's whim, I was his and no matter what...." Rye flinched a little from the quick flashes of memory but he drew a breath. "No matter what he's done, he's all I've ever had." That sounded weak, empty and more than a touch broken.

The two men locked eyes. Rye couldn't help remember all the reasons he should agree with Will, they scratched at his sense of self and drew blood. Worse, he remembered vividly why he of all people had reason to hate his father. It had little to do with being a pet.

Will went three shades paler just before he turned green. "Oh, fuck me," he hissed and ran off to a bathroom.

Rye's anger disappeared. "What just happened?"

"Will's gifts bond him to his family," Jake explained carefully. "He's been getting flashes of your memories. He must have seen something new. Amanda, want to settle him down, or should I?"

"No." Rye shook his head and started to follow Will. "I'll go." He glanced over to where he'd been sitting, and how pale Ichi looked as well, he hadn't touched a bite of food. Soothing Will's nerves wasn't the only nerves he'd be settling down.

Rye found Will washing his mouth out and splashing cold water across his face inside of Jake's bathroom. He glanced up and saw Rye reflected in the mirror, not Jake or Amanda.

"You'd think with how much I puked this afternoon I wouldn't have anything left."

"I'm sorry."

He waved it off. "Isn't your fault. Poor Narin, Olesckians don't vomit like we do, it scares him." Will grinned and sat on the toilet lid. "He thought I was dying." The grin disappeared. "Does Ichi know? Have you told anyone?"

Rye leaned against the doorframe. "Told anyone, what?"

"That Conti abused you, beyond the obvious, I mean." Rye's only reaction to his words was to drop his head and hide his eyes. "I saw it, Rye."

"Conti made it clear there was only room for the best in his children, I was one of the best but I wasn't special. He had favorites. After my first mission, he made sure I knew what made the other boy special, made me watch to shame him. When that boy was killed a couple of years later, Conti told me I was special now. I fought him, Will, I refused him. He beat me for it, screamed at me that the big secret was that he owned me and I had no right to say no to him. When he was finished, I spent a week in the infirmary. I never refused him again." He spoke in a flat, dead voice, reporting facts that felt disconnected from his actual person.

"But you never gave in to him either. I saw that, Rye. You may not have been able to stop him but you never, ever gave in." Things clicked in Will's head and he paled again. "Oh, that's what you tried to tell me. That night after your nightmare. That's why you thought it was from before you'd been made into a pet. It was Conti using you and your body didn't respond. Graces, it wasn't Ichi in the blood but that boy and you killed him, they made you, oh…" Will moved quickly and retched into the sink. There wasn't even bile left to vomit out, but over and over his stomach dry heaved.

Rye moved to help support the man, holding his head for him and letting him purge physically what couldn't be purged. When Will calmed, he helped him rinse his mouth and settle, shakily, back on the toilet lid.

"I'm supposed to be settling you down, not making you worse."

Will waved it off. "It's okay, better to get it out now. That's why he did this to you? Because you denied him, he made it so you physically couldn't. Rye, that's evil, that's beyond evil. He needs to be killed, if for nothing more than his sins, he needs to pay."

That set a cold knot in Rye's stomach. "I know that but can you see why I say it's not so simple? He's my father, as horrible as he is, he's all I've had. I owe the man my life."

"Rye..." Will shook his head and locked onto those broken, torn gray eyes. "You owe him nothing, he used you and made a huge profit on you, I'm sure. You've paid him back enough. No matter what he's said to you, taught you, or beat you into believing, you didn't deserve this, any of this, and he isn't your savior."

"You can't understand."

"Like hell I can. I was luckier than you, Jake's a good man. If he'd been a sick fucker like Conti, I would be standing where you are."

That left Rye silent for a long moment. Will was right, there was little difference between them. They'd both been wild, violent men, both had been harnessed by stronger men. Will had simply been luckier, but they both were lucky to have been found at all. "I'll kill Conti, to ensure you and Ichi and the others stay safe. But you're wrong Will, I still owe him."

Chapter Twenty Five

Rye sat, mostly silent, as the small group debate and talked. He let them figure out plans and methods, but for the most part he ignored them. They didn't know Conti, they didn't know his facility and Rye did. Their plans made them feel better, less out of control, and he was smart enough to shut up and leave them that.

Only Ichi seemed to sense the truth and stayed distant. He barely ate and hardly commented, sitting with just a touch too much distance between him and Rye. Subtle things, but things Rye had long learned to read from the quiet man. It was a series of little things that added up to the other man thinking too much and being worried.

That set Rye's teeth near to grinding, knowing there was nothing he could do until he got Ichi alone. Minutes passed in painful slowness until the group started to repeat themselves, having exhausted all their current ideas.

"Perhaps we should finish this another time?" Narin broke in gently, giving Jake a warning look and reminding them all how exhausted Rye had to be.

Rye made a mental note to thank the pale man because he had little doubt that the alien knew his real reasons for wanting to escape. The wide blue eyes seemed to miss little.

So, thanks to Narin, Rye was soon following Ichi back to their room. Will and Amanda had elected to stay behind with Jake and Narin and catch up on old times, or maybe simply to give the other couple some space. Rye didn't know, he was just grateful for the privacy. Ichi would be much easier to get talking if they were alone.

Only, as the door shut behind them there was no need to pry the words from Ichi. "I don't want you doing this."

"Doing what?" Rye asked but he knew already.

"Going after Conti, you don't know what his intentions are. You could be walking into a trap, or worse, you could get killed for nothing." He kept his back to Rye, unable to look at the other man and speak.

Rye moved and wrapped his arms around Ichi and tucked his face against the back of the slender neck, holding the other man's back to his chest. "I won't risk him sending for me and you or the others being caught in the middle. You're right, I could sit and wait--but it's just false security, he will send someone for me eventually. I won't be able to keep you all safe, which person would you have sacrificed? Will? Mark? Rosie?"

"Not you!" The words nearly choked him. "I won't sacrifice you!"

"Ichi, if I don't do this, you'll lose me anyway. This is the only chance." He could feel the tight, fearful anger in Ichi's body.

"All it takes is a lucky shot, one mistake."

"I'm tough, I've survived worse." And he had, his nightmares of worms suddenly were memories and he pushed it aside. "You know that, you've known for weeks that those nightmares were real." The Gorpahn worms were about as close to dying as he'd come, for a day or so he'd nearly killed himself to stop the pain. "You didn't tell me..." Even Rye could hear the hurt in the words.

"No." Ichi pulled and broke from Rye's arms. "I didn't. What good would it have done? I had Will look and there was nothing but dead ends, it gave no clues to your past other than that you'd nearly died."

"You didn't think it would have done any good to tell me?" The words came out in a startled gasp.

"You were more fragile weeks ago. What good could have come from you knowing that at some point, some time in your past you'd gone through something like that? It upset you enough to think it was just a dream."

"Because I thought I was losing my mind."

Ichi didn't know if they were fighting or not, he just felt cornered. "I did what I thought was best. It's okay because now that you remember Mica it's clear I was just a poor replacement for him. I'll never be as strong as he was or as good at doing what's right, so I'm not even going to try."

Rye actually took a step back, he was caught so off guard by the sudden turn in the conversation, and land mine of pride he'd just blindly stepped on. "What the hell? Just because he was

Korean and you're, what? Part Japanese? Aren't you the same guy all worried that I'd suddenly remember that I don't like men? I'd think you'd be happy I do and, better, that you're my type!"

"It's supposed to make me happy to find out that you're only attracted to me because you vaguely remembered him?" Ichi heard the harshness in his voice, knew he was getting as close to yelling as he ever got. He wasn't even sure why he was angry but he knew he was scared.

"Oh yeah, my being attracted to you has nothing to do with the fact that you're kind and smart and unbelievably sexy and everything to do with the fact that my first lover was a cold blooded killer that I happened to live with and who just happened to be Asian!" Rye shouted back. "God, for such a smart man you can be a real moron!"

"I'm not a moron!"

"And you're the only one here even thinking that my loving you has anything to do with Mica!"

Ichi was nearly shaking in rage. "Look me in the eye and deny it." He snarled back and tried to think logically how all of this mess had started. Like most things having to do with emotion, he found himself clueless.

Rye locked his eyes with Ichi. "Moron."

"Don't call me that!" He stalked nearer to Rye.

"How about idiot, moron?" It was getting childish, but Rye found himself pushing.

"Stop it!"

"You aren't cold, you're clueless!"

"You don't know what you're talking about!"

"Coward, clueless! What do you want, Ichi? What has to be done to get it through that thick skull of yours that I love you! No one else, not even Mica, you! Do I need to make you hate me to make it okay to love you?"

Normally, shouting made Ichi walk away. He'd never screamed in his life, but the fear and emotional ups and downs had pushed him too far. "You can't love me!" he heard himself screaming. "People like you don't love people like me!" The truth was raw and mean and horrible.

Rye wasn't sure if he was more hurt or angry. "I'm not good enough for you?" He suddenly felt filthy. Ichi was so clean, so innocent and sheltered, he must seem the monster in his eyes.

It wasn't what Ichi had meant and the odd turn to the fight stopped his hurt anger in its tracks. "What?" he questioned, unsure, trying not to be the clueless coward he'd been accused of.

"Well, now I know why you have no desire to take me... I've never tried to hide how many men have used me." He glanced down, hurt surging over anger. "You're right, people like you aren't loved by the likes of me."

"What?" He shook his head. "People like me? Cold, empty, bookish, robots? God, Rye, you're beautiful and dangerous and alive and so fearless, if I could be half as brave as you! You should have loved Mica, not someone boring and dull and clueless and... and cowardly like me."

The hurt was dripping in Ichi's words like blood drawn from a deep wound and Rye suddenly understood he'd confused the situation again. His admiration for Ichi was so high that he often forgot the other man thought so little of himself. For Rye, knowing what he was, the bad and the worst of his past, it was all just facts, but Ichi built his sense of self around his perceived failings.

Rye stalked back to where Ichi stood, angry, hurt and tense in the center of the room. He was close enough to smell the other man, and it made him want to nuzzle his face into the dark hair. Those mocking, closed off, hazel eyes were lowered and Rye dropped hard onto his knees.

"I'd give anything for you to be able to see yourself as other people see you, even for a moment," he whispered. "Take me."

"What?"

Gray eyes glanced up and Rye found he had difficulty breathing when hazel met his own. Ichi wanted him, he could see it there under the hurt and anger and fear, but the man held himself in tight check. Rye begged with his eyes, wondering if this was too much, too soon for Ichi. He knew he couldn't ask, there was no way he could tell Ichi how badly he needed to be fucked into the ground. He wasn't sure he could explain how deeply he needed to let go and give himself into Ichi's hands. He wasn't sure Ichi would ever be able to understand.

Rye underestimated the effect his eyes, lustful and begging, combined with being on his knees and Ichi's already unstable emotions would have. Their eye's meeting was like lightening striking them. Ichi felt his chest tighten, his heart beat painfully, and there was no anger left. It was like that first morning, seeing Rye naked and waiting and Ichi wanted him.

He let one hand cross the gulf of space and angry words between them to ruffle across Rye's hair. Those gray eyes fluttered but stayed locked to his own, begging, asking, needing, and Ichi found his hand gripping into the handful of red he held. He tugged slightly and Rye followed, rising up on his knees as Ichi bent lower to meet him halfway for a kiss.

When Rye normally kissed him he was aggressive, chasing after Ichi and claiming what he wanted. This kiss was different, passive, hungry, asking instead of taking and it made Ichi feel bold and so hot he thought his skin might catch on fire. He wanted to open his pants and feel himself grow hard inside of Rye's mouth. He wanted to be as much a creature of wild, brave life as Rye ever was.

Wanting and doing were two different things and Ichi broke the kiss and found himself at a loss. Rye's eyes, when they slid slowly open, were clouded with need and longing and, more, there was trust there. Ichi let go of the tight fist of hair and soothed the black cherry locks again.

"It never crossed my mind that you'd want to bottom," he whispered, unable to lie or hide with those honest eyes on him. He felt his face blushing hotly red but Ichi didn't look away. "No one's ever wanted me to, I've never... I don't know how."

"Anything you want," Rye whispered, his voice harsh with need, trembling on the edge of knowing Ichi might be able to give him all he wanted.

Ichi understood and it made him shiver. Being dominant wasn't one his stronger skills, but logically he understood. Rye responded to strength, he'd been raised from childhood on up to follow and Ichi had just naturally been filling the role outside of the bedroom. What Andrew had scolded him for-- calling it Ichi's stubborn, bossy, perfectionist streak--made Rye feel safe. They fit, the two of them, they made a good pair, filling in each other's needs and strengths and Ichi saw it for the first time.

With Rye on his knees, trembling with want, all of his normal bedroom dominance, all of Rye's normal confidence in control and being the aggressor between them, had taken a back seat. For right now, Rye needed to surrender. He needed to obey and follow and Ichi knew it was more. It was something they'd been dancing around and flirting with since their relationship had turned sexual. Rye needed to know he could give in and not always be in control and that it would be okay. He needed physical, solid proof that these sides of him were okay and accepted and safe to explore.

It finally clicked. Ichi's logical and emotional minds met each other and shook hands in agreement. He understood and it was okay and nothing else mattered. He loved Rye, more amazingly Rye loved him, and the differences in their personalities, their pasts and their ways fit together like two broken parts to make a better whole. Everything else--the fear of Rye going after Conti, the twisted sense of morality over the blood on his lover's hands, his own insecurities and fears--none of it mattered.

Ichi's love, his beautiful Rye, needed him. Ichi's love, his beautiful Rye, trusted him. It made him feel both strong and small at the same time. He felt light-headed and almost drunk as understanding dawned and it left no room for anything but the moment they stood in.

The fantasy returned, the shivering, delicious vision of growing hard in Rye's mouth. It was something from a dark, buried, naughty dream, something sexy and not normally in his day to day life. For all the sudden faith and knowledge, Ichi teetered, unsure about sliding over that last edge.

Rye saw it, saw the startled wonder. He saw the slow understanding and he saw the moment of doubt. He checked himself, ran across everything he'd ever known or done and found nothing that he wouldn't enjoy at Ichi's hands. He licked his lips and widened his eyes. "Anything," he repeated, voice husky and dark with need.

Ichi was already harder than in his fantasy, but trying to verbalize what he wanted made him blush more and knocked some of his desire back down. Half hard and more than half scared, Ichi tugged a little at the closure of his pants. His hands seemed to have forgotten how to do the simple task.

Rye's hadn't. With only that little bit to guide him, he batted the hands away and expertly got the fabric to cooperate. He didn't wait, the first glimpse of the small v of golden skin the fabric showed was one of Rye's favorite spots on Ichi. Below his waist, and above more sensitive parts, that first exposed v was always a siren song to him. He pressed his face to the warm flesh, suckling gently and delighting at the hitch in the already rapid breath.

He pushed the fabric lower and was surprised to find that Ichi was only half hard. Rye glanced up and saw the brilliant blush painted across the man's face, how red his ears were, and knew it was more than the idea of a simple blow job that had Ichi so embarrassed. That made him grin, surprised again by such a kinky, lusty streak hidden under the cool, distant exterior.

Rye ran the side of his face along that half hard, half soft, velvety length and felt Ichi shiver in response. That was all the welcome he needed and all the warning he offered. He moaned softly as he brought Ichi into his mouth and earned an answering, echoing moan from the still standing man. It was something that Rye had considered doing late at night. He'd wake up and on those delicious, rare occasions when Ichi had let himself fall asleep nude, Rye would wonder what it would be like to take the soft, sleeping length into his hand or mouth and wake it. He hadn't been bold enough yet to risk it, unwilling to disturb Ichi who slept as soundly and as innocently as an angel.

A dirty, wicked, lusty, horny angel. Rye grinned as he lightly teased. Ichi was gasping, short, lost breaths like a fish pulled from water. Rye wondered if he kept teasing, would the length in his mouth keep growing? It was a silly idea, but it made him feel playful and he worked even more to draw sighs and moans from his lover. He nearly came when Ichi dug a hand back into his hair, it felt that good.

Only the tight grip didn't encourage him on, instead it pulled his head away. Rye surrendered his prize, thinking of the now aroused hardness in terms of possession. It was in his mouth, he'd made it so hard and twitchy, so it should be his to toy with. The idea made him grin wickedly. Inch by inch he reluctantly pulled away until they both moaned in disappointment when the very tip slid from Rye's lips.

Gray eyes peered upwards. Slightly puffy lips stood parted, waiting, hungry. Ichi nearly fell to his own knees at such a sight. He swallowed hard and got his brain working, at least half way.

"Go to the bedroom, strip naked, get the lube and wait for me," he heard himself whisper.

Rye's only answer was a small, wolfish grin before he stood up with all of the grace he could show when he wanted. Ichi watched as the other man moved silently to the bedroom, stunned again just by looking and still startled that the beautiful creature wanted to bind their lives together.

He needed the moment alone. Ichi tugged at his clothes and, while there was no way he could close his pants without cutting something vital off, with his shirt loose he wasn't so lewd. The idea that Amanda and Will could return at any moment was what had saved him, otherwise he would have happily given in and let Rye suck him to climax.

That wasn't what Rye wanted, and in truth it wasn't what Ichi wanted either. He was nervous, yes, but excited too at the idea of topping. It wasn't something he'd ever given serious thought to, it seemed too bold for him, too much for him, and Ichi had simply been grateful that there were men occasionally in his life that had wanted to top him. It was just the sight of Rye that first morning, presenting himself, that Ichi couldn't shake. He'd almost given in that day, almost done what he'd never done before and after, well, he just assumed that Rye wouldn't ever want to bottom again. It wasn't like he was going to complain, having Rye top him, well, those weren't thoughts that were helping Ichi gain better control over himself.

When Ichi was fairly sure he could stand the sight of a naked Rye and not melt to a pile of adolescent goo, he followed the redhead to the bedroom. There, he found out he should have put ice into his pants because the sight of Rye nearly knocked him backwards. His hand fumbled behind him to flick the lock on their bedroom door.

"Oh, my, god," Ichi heard himself whisper.

Rye had stripped. He was all bare, creamy pale skin over long, lean muscles. Of all the poses Rye could have picked, of all the places he could have waited for Ichi, he'd picked the center of the bed. There he knelt, raised up slightly, clutching the lube in his hands, the way he had that first morning. Only this time, there was no fear, no dread in the redhead and he clutched the lube in hungry need not worry.

Ichi stumbled back to lean against the locked doors as those gray eyes devoured him. "I'm wearing too many clothes," he heard himself mumbling.

That made Rye laugh, a warm, dark chuckling sound that filled the room with lust and life. It crinkled his eyes a little and made the hard length that jutted from a nest of dark black cherry curls bounce. "I think you're always wearing too many clothes."

Another desire floated up in Ichi's mind and he was glad for the support of the door at his back. "Rye?"

The merriment dissolved instantly in the fires of the intensity that burned from that single word. "Anything," he confirmed again.

Ichi drew a slow breath and let his gaze sweep over the stunning sight again. "Prep yourself, touch yourself… I want to watch, and I want to see you come." The words dripped like honey wine, thick and heavy, from Ichi's lips.

The lube slid from Rye's hands, gone numb at the bold words. Ichi's voice washed over him, bathed him in desire, and Rye struggled not to obey just from the mere suggestion of release from his lover. His knees slid further apart, his spine arched backwards as a full shiver raced across his body. So insensible was he from the delight of those whispered words that he was unaware he'd arched so far back that his shoulders brushed the bed beneath him.

"Oh god," Ichi whispered at the sight. He watched, mind too shut down to even remember how to undress, as Rye slowly regained some control. Ichi watched as Rye rose up from the bed, a light sheen of sweat making his skin glisten in the dim light and as he fumbled after the lube. There was something needy and desperate in the gray eyes and Ichi knew what it was they wanted.

Rye knew he had to be quick because if Ichi wasn't fucking him senseless soon he knew he'd go crazy. He struggled to catch his breath and arched back up to kneeling instead of half lying backwards on the bed. The lube had simply dropped beside him instead of rolling away where he'd have to hunt it. It slicked up his fingers and Rye didn't wait, there was no time left in him to be gentle or slow. He plunged two fingers into his body, moaning in that voice that was so desperate, so needy that it sounded close to pain.

It was a struggle now to keep his eyes open, but he needed to see that look of shocked, surprised lust on Ichi's face. With his free hand, Rye slid lube across his own cock and began to lightly stroke himself. It was a torment, one he'd endure forever if he could, and the moment that his body eased to two fingers he moved to three.

There was a choice and Rye made the choice to deny himself. "Only you," he gasped, not sure he'd even spoken as his free hand slid down to lightly tease his balls before gliding up to stroke himself more.

Ichi wasn't sure he was going to make it long enough. Those eyes, the moans, how stunningly beautiful Rye was all worked together to unravel his control. Even his inexperienced eye could see that Rye was prepping himself a little too quickly, a little too roughly and he wondered if it was from a desire to move quickly or if Rye liked things a little rougher. His train of thought derailed at the hoarse words that made little sense to Ichi.

"What?" he gasped out as he caught his hands moving toward his own groin. Ichi shook his head, he wasn't going to jerk off, he wasn't like Rye, he couldn't come five times in twenty minutes.

Rye moaned. "Only you, Ichi, that spot, only for you, I won't touch it." He wanted to, god he could feel the fireworks that it would set off. Ichi's eyes on him, watching the show, his pants split open and his own hard cock peeking out of the sheltering fabric, that made him want to show off, made Rye want to be as sexy as he could so the other man would enjoy the show as much as possible. It was something he held back from. "I want you… you to do that for me."

It was a lot to ask of someone that was basically a virgin top, but hearing Rye ask for something so intimate with no shame and total confidence, Ichi felt his pride swelling. He'd do it, he'd do it well and proper and be worthy of that faith. "I'm going to make you scream," Ichi heard himself promise, half meaning it for his ears only and mildly embarrassed at saying something so bold.

Rye did hear him and it was the matching look in those hazel eyes that pushed him over the edge. Ichi looked like some shy bedroom god and Rye knew he was going to be target of whatever thoughts were swirling behind those eyes. His climax gathered him up and shorted out his brain. Distantly, he heard himself whimpering, felt his own come splash across his chest, felt a fourth finger join the other three but even this wasn't enough. He'd arched backwards too far and fell on his back on the bed, his fingers sliding unwillingly from his body. His legs fell apart, spread wide, begging and slutty and needing to draw Ichi over to join him, but his mind was too fried to form the words.

He didn't need words, when Rye's vision cleared enough that he could see again, Ichi was standing over him. The sight made him moan and arch a little off the bed, his cock still hard, trembling and unsatisfied. For the moment he was too boneless, too spent to even think about touching himself and he lay there, waiting, wanting, trusting.

Ichi bent down, caught a handful of hair again and fisted it tight in his grip. It had to be painful, but Rye moaned. When his lips found the pair below his, they were parted and ready. He kissed the redhead with hunger and need, hovering over the shivering body and inhaling the scent of sex and Rye.

When he opened his eyes and broke the kiss, Ichi saw a fleck of come against the gold of the nipple ring. He grinned, and it must have looked as wicked as he felt because Rye's eyes widened in reply. Slowly, Ichi leaned down and with the flat of his tongue swiped the speck from Rye's pierced nipple.

Pleasure exploded, better than coming, better than fucking himself with even four fingers. Nothing he did alone could compare to anything Ichi did to or with him, nothing. The wicked, teasing look in those normally serious eyes made him shiver and he moaned, begging without words for anything Ichi wanted to give him.

He didn't expect to feel that hot, wet, tongue against his chest a second time. Rye arched and glanced down to watch as Ichi very slowly bent over him and lapped the come from his chest and stomach as daintily as a kitten licking up milk. Small, pointed-tongue licks that barely flicked wet across his skin were counter balanced with wide, flat, swipes, and each contact made Rye sob.

Ichi was making little sounds in the back of his throat that sounded so much like contented purrs that Rye had to fist his hands into the sheets to keep from grabbing the other man, throwing him on his back and impaling himself on Ichi's cock. That wicked tongue, those happy, sighing purrs, the very fact that Ichi was licking him clean had Rye moaning, begging to come again and Ichi was still dressed.

Ichi glanced over and the head of Rye's cock was close by. Beaded at the tip were small drops, as pearly and bright as the stains across Rye's pale flesh. It was natural to swipe them away when the last of the come was licked clean from the stomach below. Rye arched from the bed, gasping on a moan that half strangled on its way out.

The sound made Ichi feel amazing. He was doing this, he was, nothing else, he was driving Rye crazy. There were advantages to taking the more dominate role in the bedroom and he was finding he liked being able to do anything he wanted. He swiped at the head of Rye's cock again and the whimper was needier this time.

That put a wicked thought in Ichi's mind. He parted his lips, just enough to slide only the head into his mouth. Trapped there, he sucked on his treat, swirled his tongue, tormented just the sensitive end of the aching cock, and below him Rye writhed and moaned. Ichi reached out and trailed his hands across Rye's legs, mapping the strength there, brushing them aside if they closed too much, ghosting touch across hypersensitive skin. He didn't stop or pause or retreat until Rye arched up, his hips leaving the bed in their effort to bury his length into the warm mouth tormenting him. Ichi was waiting for that and kept just the tip inside of his lips, but he swallowed the release quickly, easily.

Rye fell, exhausted and still writhing on the bed, nearly blinded by a blow job that only covered a bare few inches of his flesh. "Oh," he moaned. "Oh, please, fuck me, please, Ichi please, fuck me, please," he begged, eyes shut because he couldn't stand to watch, he needed so deeply.

"Too many clothes," Ichi moaned as he struggled to undress. His shirt twisted and held him prisoner for a moment, but he tugged and turned and got himself free. Cloth was removed and tossed across the room, baring flesh and dragging more moans from Rye. Even his shoes seemed to fight him and Ichi nearly lost his balance and fell as he tried to yank them off.

Finally nude, Ichi crawled onto the bed, drawn by the pale skin and warmth of the panting redhead. Rye arched upwards, seeking and receiving another kiss, and Ichi let his hands wander over the offered body. A little thought at the back of his mind wanted to stop and get detailed instructions before continuing, maybe read up on the subject of being top instead of bottom. He wanted everything to be right, with no mistakes or flaws, but when he looked into Rye's eyes that small logical voice faded away.

Ichi slid across the other man, skin catching and dragging along skin in delicious friction. He reached one arm out, stretching above them to pull pillows free and Rye didn't even have to be asked to raise his hips and let them be placed gently at the small of his back. Without really knowing how he got there, Ichi found himself hovering over Rye, slender legs around his own.

A lube-slick hand found his cock and Ichi shivered and groaned. He hadn't heard Rye getting the tube back open, but he saw it drop from his free hand. There was no doubt now, he was really going to do this, and a wave of uncertainty and almost-fear crested over him. What if he wasn't any good? What if he hurt Rye? What if he was a disappointment?

"I love you," Rye whispered, his eyes fluttering shut as his hips arched up to meet Ichi's.

He paused, no longer feeling so frightened but still just as uncertain, hovering over Rye and certain time had frozen just for them. Ichi felt his heart might break if he went on and was equally sure it would shatter if he stopped. "Rye? I've never…"

"Shhh…" Rye hissed out between panting breaths and considered just raping the man. "You won't hurt me, do it, please, Ichi, please." Ichi moved against him, every touch of skin to skin making Rye more crazed. He sobbed when he felt the tip of the other man pressing very gently against his entrance. "Please, please, Ichi, please," he begged and found he really liked begging for Ichi.

The moaning, begging, desperate voice shattered past the last of Ichi's worries. He leaned forward and was surprised at the level of force it took to breach that tight muscle. It was so slow, swallowed by fractions as he eased forward. When Rye's body eased and Ichi slipped inside it was like light exploded around him. His vision sparkled with it, his nerves crackled and Ichi wasn't even sure he was breathing. Rye sounded like a wounded animal, moaning, gasping, and clawing at Ichi's back as bit by bit, Ichi slid into his body.

Legs wrapped around Ichi's waist and pulled him, hard. He lost his control and balance and plunged all the way, deep into Rye. The pleasure was too much, Ichi was trembling, he heard his own gasped breath rumbling out harshly. He understood now, the pained-pleasure look on Rye's face when their roles were reversed, he understood the sense that if he didn't move, if he didn't thrust wildly, he might die.

Rye looked like he might have died already. His head was tossed back, the longer layers of his hair splayed out like dark red ribbons around him on the pale sheets. Those haunting gray eyes were squinted shut, his mouth parted in silent cries. The long, graceful neck was arched and Rye's hands grasped Ichi's shoulders, his back, his arms, anything they could find in an effort to pull the man closer.

Something about how lost, how passionate Rye looked shorted out a part of Ichi's brain. He knew, logically, he should wait until Rye was adjusted and ready to move at all, he knew he needed that time too because the pleasure flooding his body was beyond any words, but seeing Rye broke all thoughts into dust. Before he knew what he was doing, Ichi had slid from that tight body and, with a groan, back deep inside.

Rye's entire body arched, bowed up like a too tightly wound rope. His eyes popped open in startled surprise and he moaned a muffled scream. "Oh!" Rye shuddered, his eyes dilated, his toes curled up and he lost what shreds of control he had when his eyes locked onto Ichi's.

Come splattered up against Ichi's stomach, making him moan, but it was the feel of Rye's body gripping him, clinging to him in a way that nearly broke Ichi. His arms were trembling already but with the sudden, unexpected pleasure they gave out entirely. His weight fell against Rye's chest but those arms held him close, those legs enfolded him further.

"Oh, god, oh I think I'm going to die." Ichi moaned, barely able to breathe, with no hope of thinking when he felt this good.

"So good... so good..." Rye whispered into the damp tendrils of dark hair as he came back down a little from the startling climax.

He tried to hold his weight back up off of Rye, but Ichi found his arms were more like limp noodles than muscles. "I can't, I..."

Rye wiggled, moaning a little as their bodies slid together and the cock, so hard inside him, slid as well. "Here... Ichi... here...easier..."

Slowly it sunk in what Rye was trying to do and Ichi managed to lift himself up enough that the redhead could squirm free. Only, as he moved, it created a new torment and it took all the fragments of Ichi's broken control to allow Rye to slowly slide away from him. When they finally parted, both men groaned and Ichi heard himself sobbing. That sudden feeling of abandonment was worse when topping.

"Easier..." Rye sighed again and managed to get himself turned over. Frankly he loved this position, as top or bottom, and when he got his knees under him and his ass in the air the sight earned an approving moan from Ichi as well. Rye glanced over his shoulder and slid his legs further apart.

"Oh, god." The sight of Rye on his hands and knees, ass in the air waiting to be fucked, burned itself like a white hot brand into Ichi's mind. He sat where he'd tumbled, dumbfounded for a moment, lost in the inviting lust in the gray eyes.

"Fuck me, Ichi, please, hard, as hard as you want, please," Rye begged again.

That was all the invitation Ichi needed. He hurried to kneel behind the redhead, his knees unthinkingly spreading Rye's legs wider. Everything lined up perfectly and as he leaned forward Ichi was shocked to realize he could now watch as his cock slid inside of Rye's body. His hands slid across the pale flesh, up over Rye's hips, across his back, stroking, touching, and Ichi found his body moving on its own.

"Harder!" Rye moaned. "Oh, Ichi, please."

Rye had been right, this way was easier. Ichi settled his hands on those wonderful hips and didn't have to worry about anything else but giving in and letting himself take Rye as hard as he wanted to. Only the harder, the deeper, the more he moved, the more Rye moaned and begged. It was like tossing fuel onto a fire and Ichi wasn't sure he was capable of giving Rye what he was so obviously needing.

Until, on a whim, Ichi moved slightly and the angle of his thrusts changed fractionally. The difference was minor to him, barely noticeable, but Rye literally screamed. His arms collapsed and he half curled up, his body shivered, trembled and came again leaving Ichi breathless and half-mad from the second intense wave of tight grasping muscles.

Ichi wrapped his arms around Rye's waist and held the man close as he fell apart into a panting, moaning heap. He should have stopped and given Rye a breather as they normally did, but he couldn't. There was no way Ichi could stop thrusting into the tight, willing body, at best he was able to slow down a little. Ichi felt breathlessly male, primal, strong, to know that Rye--so strong and vital and completely masculine himself--was reduced to near tears from the pleasure Ichi was giving him.

Rye was gasping for breath and wasn't sure he could stand to get hard again. Unfortunately, Ichi's slow, deep thrusts took the choice from him. His body responded and with each stroke his cock started to harden again. "Oh, you found it," he managed to gasp out, feeling Ichi trembling with the need to finish, the twitching against the other man's legs pressed so closely to his own. "Ichi's spot, you found it." Rye muttered again, exhausted and limp everywhere but in one, admittedly important, spot.

The meaning of those words sunk in slowly, past the fogging layers of lust and pleasure and Ichi heard himself half growl. "Mine!" He gripped those hips and pulled Rye higher up, moving a bit harder, deeper, needing blindly now.

"Make me yours..." Rye gasped in challenge.

Ichi couldn't stand to watch any longer. He closed his eyes and turned his world into blackness filled with unbelievable sensation. His hips were snapping with a mind of their own and each time he found that bright spot--his spot--deep inside of Rye's body, the redhead below him would twitch and whimper, too exhausted and spent to scream anymore. Each strike left him limp and weakened, needing more and unable to do anything but take all that he was being given.

"Iku.... Iku...." Ichi moaned in warning, reaching blindly along Rye's legs. His fingers tickled along bare flesh, stroking up over tight balls which earned him a new pitch to Rye's moans, and forward to grasp his weeping, demanding length.

Rye didn't need to speak Japanese to know what Ichi was saying. The stuttering rate of his thrusts mixed with the near anguished pain of his voice was all he needed to know that Ichi was about to come. Rye wasn't sure he would be able to follow so easily, exhausted, wound too tightly and unable to find that level of satisfaction that would put his cock to rest for good, he didn't know how Ichi could notch up the already mind numbing pleasure he was providing to carry Rye over the edge for the big fall, the last one he needed.

Fingers tickled across his legs, ghosted between them and found their mark. Ichi's hand was barely wrapped around him and his vision went black. "Oh, oh fuck yes, oh, Ichi!" He nearly screamed and came so hard he lost feeling of everything but his own release.

His mind cleared just enough, just soon enough to feel the last stuttering deep thrusts into his body and the burning hot fire of Ichi's release. The man was silent, gasping in breaths as his mind was too overloaded for words. Rye moaned, absorbing the moment deep into his soul. If nothing more, if never again, he had this moment and nothing could take it from him, not even Conti had been able to steal his memories.

Rye collapsed forward, Ichi falling with him to land on his back. He could feel Ichi's breath, hot and panting, against his skin, feel the kisses the other man pressed to his sweat-glossed flesh as he came down from his own release. Rye would have been happy to lay with Ichi's weight against him until time ended, but all too soon Ichi squirmed.

When Ichi managed to remember that he was pillowed on and most likely crushing Rye, he struggled to get his body to work and his weight lifted. His now spent and limp cock slid unhappily from the home it was nested in and Rye moaned long and low at the loss. Before Ichi could think of anything to do or even where he should try to lay down, strong, pale arms found him and pulled him down.

Rye wrapped himself around Ichi, pressed his sweaty and sticky body to every bare inch of Ichi he could find. "Love you... so much," he sighed out, every muscle fiber in his body trembling in twitchy exhaustion.

"Did I..." Ichi sighed as Rye pulled him impossibly closer. "Was it okay?" That was the first thought to drift up when thoughts returned.

The chuckle was low and warm and rocked them both. "No, no, okay doesn't cover it--amazing, wonderful, perfect, that's closer. What did you think, of topping?" Rye found himself kissing the side of Ichi's neck in lazy, sated exhaustion.

"Amazing, wonderful, perfect... but..."

"Hmmm?"

The kisses against his skin, the body snuggled so close to his own was lulling Ichi down into well earned sleep. He hated sleeping all sticky and sweaty but maybe, this once, he could make an exception. "I like the other way better." He sighed and hoped Rye wouldn't be too disappointed.

That warm chuckle welled up again and Rye tossed a leg across Ichi's. "Me too, baby, me too but is nice to sometimes play Pet and owner, hmmm? God," he sighed, drifting quickly to sleep. "That was so... so... amazing."

Pet and owner. Ichi hadn't thought about it, but how Rye had been waiting for him on the bed was just as he'd waited while a pet. He wasn't entirely sure those sort of games were totally healthy but if some part of Rye would occasionally need to let go and fall into that role again, Ichi wasn't going to blame him for it. Not when the results were so mind blowing and delightful for them both.

As he drifted into sleep inside the circle of Rye's arms, a second thought floated up and his sex-addled and sleep seeking brain blurted it out. "I'm going with you... for Conti..."

Rye didn't protest, he was already asleep. Ichi glanced over and saw the man hadn't really heard his declaration and shrugged it off. He'd made his stance clear, Rye hadn't protested, the matter was now officially settled. Content, warm, and not caring how sticky and sweaty they both were, Ichi let himself drop into exhausted and happy sleep.

Chapter Twenty Six

The hotel was far nicer than Ichi was comfortable spending money on. He was frugal by nature and raised to detest the trappings of excess, which made the suit he was wearing even more uncomfortable; it cost a disgusting sum of money all to earn it a designer label. The absolute worst part was that Rye had paid for it all.

Ichi had dug his heels in about going with Rye when he left, expecting to have to fight Rye tooth and nail, but the redhead had merely gone silent and nodded. When pushed, Rye simply admitted he'd feel better knowing Ichi was safe, personally knowing, and the only way to do that was to keep him close at hand. But Ichi had refused to be baggage, knowing his role as pet owner could get them at least into the same secure office complex that Lerman rented. He'd stood his ground until Rye accepted him as an equal.

It had made Will sick with worry. He'd protested more than Rye had and in the end had been upset enough to be angry. Only, when the day came for them to leave, he'd hugged them both and seen them off. They'd traveled via Avalon transport back to Concord space, and from there to a colony in the middle of nowhere. Officially, they were going there for Ichi to evaluate the logistics of adding a new species to his collection. In reality, it was one of the locations Rye had used as a drop.

In the span of a few hours, they'd picked up Rye's stored information and he'd taken another name. A visit to a local bank and a short wait made them wealthy men--not that Ichi didn't have plenty of money of his own, his family was quite comfortable and his own personal money was well invested, but this was ready, on-hand, accessible cash.

He had stopped protesting when he saw how easily Rye moved in this world. When Rye took him to buy new clothing, he hadn't protested. When Rye had made reservations, Ichi had agreed. He'd let Rye make the plans, so long as those plans included him.

It had led them to Lerman's doorstep, with Ichi in a suit that cost an indecent amount of money, checking into a hotel that was far more than he needed. Rye stood behind him, naked but for one of his longer, custom made kilts. Around his neck was an ornate collar they'd bought new and a new leash was attached. Ichi held the other end uneasily, knowing it had to be done and still not liking it.

"Ah, here it is, sorry for the delay Mr. Vitorui, everything is arranged. If you require anything, please, contact the front desk. Will you be requiring a caretaker for your pet while planetside?"

"No, that won't be necessary." Ichi tried to sound cold, aloof, superior as Rye had suggested but he felt frightened and worried. Lucky for them both, when he felt scared he tended to sound just as Rye wanted.

He waved off the help of one of the hotel bellhops and shouldered his own traveling bag. They'd made the choice to move light and, still holding the end of the leash, Ichi led them down hallways to the room they'd rented. Once inside, he dropped the leash and locked the door.

Rye still didn't move, not until Ichi opened their bag and pulled out a small handheld electronic scanner. He turned it on and it hummed slightly before beeping and glowing green. Rye sighed and clawed at the collar, desperate to get it off. When the latch gave way he tossed it onto the nearby bed.

"Did you really think they'd have the room bugged?"

"Better safe." Rye nodded to Ichi and moved to set the small device to continue scanning and to automatically block anything it might find. He glanced up to where Ichi was half frowning. "I have to do this."

"I know."

"Getting in will be easy, finding Conti will be easy, the rest?" Rye shook his head. There was no way to smuggle a weapon in without drawing notice to them, he'd either have to find one or kill Conti with his bare hands. The thought alone turned his stomach.

"And this can't wait until the morning?"

Rye dug out the small satchel they'd put together before the ship landed and tossed it toward Ichi. "Can't risk it, I can't swear that Lerman doesn't monitor the docks. If they do, they'll have captured my face and if I'm still in the files it'll pop up in the daily reports on Conti's desk in the morning."

He caught the satchel and draped it over a shoulder, suddenly sick with nerves. "And they're going to just let us in?"

"They're going to just let us in. You're a pet owner, you've an open invitation to visit the plant anytime you wish. Once there, I'll get us diverted, easy as can be." There had been a distance between them since the morning Ichi had declared he was going with Rye. During the entire trip, Rye would catch

Ichi staring at him with a lost, hurt look in his eyes, but no amount of asking got the man to speak. "Remember, this is my home. I know that compound better than anyone alive."

"I know." Ichi nodded and smoothed out a wrinkle from his suit. "What do you think our odds are of living to see the morning?" His voice just above a whisper, he asked the question that had gnawed at him for days.

That stopped Rye's fussing and brought his head up so quickly it almost made him dizzy. "What?"

"You heard me."

"Ichi." He moved to where his lover stood, eyes worried and dark. "Nothing is going to happen to you."

"I'm not afraid to die."

Rye's hands came up to cup either side of Ichi's face, his thumbs traced the line of his cheekbones. "Nothing is going to happen to you, nothing."

"And if something happens to you?"

"You do just like we talked about, Lerman won't hurt you if they think you've got proof of all of this. Turn around, walk out and don't stop until you get back to Avalon." Rye had gathered an extensive collection of evidence against Lerman over the years and he'd tucked that away just as securely as he'd put aside fake names and cash.

"If something happens to you there is no turning around for me." Ichi met those cold gray eyes and didn't flinch.

"You promised me."

Ichi just shook his head as much as he could while Rye held it. "What are the odds?"

For as much as he wanted to tell Ichi everything was going to be fine, Rye knew better than to lie to the smart man. "Less than half, but if I... we, don't do this, we've no chance. They will come for me eventually."

"I know."

"Even if I left you and never saw you again."

"Don't even think that."

That quiet stubbornness made Rye smile softly before he leaned forward and kissed Ichi. Their lips barely brushed against each other and it was more for comfort than passion. "Let's go."

There was nothing that could be said from that point on. Rye put the collar back on and fell easily into the role of pet. Ichi took up the end of the leash and guided them to a cab and from there to the very industrial complex that housed Lerman and PETS Living Companions. It took every ounce of his will and every fragment of his faith in Rye to not simply turn them around.

Rye had the skills, training and expertise to simply disappear. If he'd never met Ichi it would be a simple matter of making a choice between revenge and hiding. Ichi had no illusions about his own skills at such covert things--he couldn't disappear, he had his work, his family, his life. The very thought of being forced to give up everything that defined him, to run and hide for the rest of his life without ever making a mistake seemed like an impossible task.

There were no choices and the cab dropped them off at the main entrance. Ichi slid out, trying to hide his fears, and Rye followed where he was led. The secure complex had only three entrances, one was private, one was secured for deliveries and shipping, and one was the public main entrance. Before, Rye had used the smaller, private entrance, but he knew the level of surveillance there and knew he'd be noticed.

The delivery and shipping entrance was exploitable. Yes, it was secure but Rye had grown up running scenarios for infiltrating buildings his entire life. He could think of four ways they'd most likely gain entrance that way, none of them were a sure thing, and all of them could easily lead to detection.

The main entrance was a different story. Less monitored, more heavily trafficked, just as secure but easier to slip by in. There were local deliveries made here, office workers came and went, visitors to PETS as well, sometimes even groups of school children were invited to the tour. There was a gift shop for PETS of all things, and even Lerman didn't bother to scan every face that came through the door.

It was busier than Ichi had expected, and made him less nervous. He'd been most worried about being the only two people there, standing out, looking odd, gaining attention Rye had warned was a bad thing. Instead of being empty, the place was modestly busy. There was even another man standing to the side holding a gold chain leash, only his pet was a female wearing the simple kilt and a single band of fabric over her breasts. Her blonde hair fell to below her waist, her eyes downcast, but even Ichi, who didn't think twice about women, had to admit the female was stunningly beautiful.

He glanced to Rye and felt the fear dissolve. A smirk tugged at his mouth, for as beautiful as the blonde was, she looked like she'd been hit by an ugly stick compared to Rye. It made him feel a sense of pride that straightened his spine and gave him the perfect amount of confidence to approach the help desk.

He scanned his thumb print and a holograph of the same recorded woman that had announced his surprise upgrade appeared. "Greetings--" A half-beat too long pause. "Mr. Kenichi Vitorui of--" Another half beat too long pause. "Avalon Station S14592." The holograph smiled blindly. "Welcome to the home of your Pet, the Living Companions division. I see you've brought your Pet along for this visit. Would you like to arrange a training session?"

"No," he answered coldly.

The holograph paused and the response processed. "Very well. We have many wonderful training sessions available, should you reconsider. In as little as a week, your Pet could learn many useful new things all for very affordable rates. Is there a current difficulty or problem with your Pet that you would like addressed?"

"No."

"Good! It's nice to see a satisfied customer. Would you like to tour our facility?"

"Yes."

"Excellent. Please follow the gold light on the floor, it'll guide you to the lifts. Please continue to follow the gold light during the tour, it will show you all the best that Living Companions has to offer. And don't forget to visit our gift shop before going home, you'll find many wonderful items for you and your Pet." She smiled again and blinked off, but now gold light glowed on the floor just below Ichi's feet.

He followed it and wasn't surprised that it led near the other man and his waiting pet. The man was in his late middle age and wearing a suit that made Ichi's look cheap. He had a slick, wealthy look that reminded Ichi of the patrons that funded research because it was expected, not because they had any love of science.

"Well," the man greeted as Ichi came toward him. "Didn't expect another of us to be here."

"Small world." Ichi nodded back, refusing to back down to the other man.

"Quite a looker you got yourself. Well trained, is he?"

"Well enough."

The man smiled. "He's new to you."

"Less than a year." Ichi felt no need to lie.

"Ah, Ju-Ju here, I've had here for almost six. Thinking about having her upgraded a bit while we're here. Darken the skin maybe, getting tired of a blonde."

The man spoke so casually and it made Ichi ill. Until he really looked at her and saw that no one was there, there wasn't even a glimmer of intelligence. From day one, Ichi had seen life in Rye and just assumed it was normal for a pet. The difference between how Rye was when he arrived and the blonde woman was as dramatic as the difference between night and day.

"Well, now would be the time to do it," he heard himself agreeing absently.

"Ju-Ju started out as a redhead, like my first wife, but, well, red isn't much fun without the personality to match."

Ichi was saved from answering by the gold lights blinking and a lift door opening. The older man and the blonde moved right away but Ichi held back.

"Coming on the tour? They say it has all the newest modifications for spring."

"Bit crowded with four, I'll catch the next one."

The man shrugged. "Suit yourself."

The doors shut and on the glossy black surface the recorded woman appeared. "Another lift will be along momentarily, Mr. Vitorui."

The wait was only a few moments but Ichi had to bite the inside of his lip to keep from bouncing his weight from foot to foot. They hadn't planned on running into anyone else taking the tour and he hadn't really been prepared to deal with having to share a lift with anyone. It would look odd to refuse to share a second time. When he thought he might scream, the lift doors opened and he lead them inside, but he held his breath until the doors slid gently shut.

Just as Rye had said, the third panel from the door popped open to reveal a keypad and the six digit number Ichi quickly typed in shut the lift down. The instant the lift stopped moving, Rye was pulling the collar off.

"How much time do we have?"

"Two minutes before the override clicks off and the sensors come back on." Rye pulled open the satchel and pulled out the clothing. The kilt stripped off quickly and he was pulling on the smuggled clothing.

Black, which hadn't surprised Ichi, but it was made of a light-weight, synthetic fabric stronger than leather and more supple. Rye pulled the pants on and they clung to his body in all the right ways and made Ichi forget the danger they were about to be in. All that pale skin framed around the black pants just made him want to do inappropriate things. Fortunately, Rye pulled on the long sleeved shirt of the same material and that helped him look more dangerous and remind him of where they were.

"Shoes?"

Ichi already had them out of the satchel. Again, they were made of the same material but with a detachable, reinforced sole. The pair sealed tightly and reached nearly to the knee, they offered the same flexibility and protection as the rest of the outfit with the added strength of the sole, but with the sole removed, the pair folded flat and was easy to smuggle in.

As Rye got his feet secured, Ichi gathered up the collar, leash and kilt, and in less than two minutes Rye went from Pet to person. "Ready?"

He didn't trust his voice, Ichi just nodded.

"If we're lucky, Vince hasn't been killed since Jake stole those files," Rye warned again, typing in a string of numbers. Just how Rye had the other children's access numbers Ichi hadn't asked, but it made sense to use one of them.

Rye keyed in the last number and they waited. Seconds crawled by with nothing changing and Ichi was starting to think this was a very bad idea. The lifts were small little prisons, they were basically cornered here.

The panel flicked to blue and the lift moved again. Rye let out the breath he hadn't known he was holding and nodded to Ichi. "This will let out inside of Lerman."

"This seems too easy."

That made Rye grin a little bitterly. "We're the only ones other than Conti to have full access. Trust me, for anyone else, this wouldn't be easy. If we come across anyone on the way to the internal lift, act like you belong. Dressed like that, with me, you'll look like a high-paying client and no one will risk asking. One weakness of a secure system: once inside, everyone assumes that if you're there, you should be there."

Ichi had to admit that in his elegant, expensive suit looking cold and aloof, and Rye in a black outfit that literally moved as he breathed, they did look like they belonged. A high-price client and a high-cost killer. No one would be foolish enough to question them, Rye looked like death on two legs, even unarmed.

The lift doors opened and Ichi shouldered the satchel again. They moved and he tried to remind himself to look confident and important. Rye hovered nearby, scanning hallways as they went and, sure enough, within moments they passed a few people. They glanced their way but their eyes quickly darted away at the hard look Rye gave them. None seemed surprised to see him, or showed any signs of knowing him, they just knew his type and knew he was higher on the food chain than they were.

It took all of five minutes to cross the hallways and corridors to reach the internal lift. This one wouldn't even let the doors open without the proper identity code, which Rye quickly entered. The doors slid open instantly, no delays or processing this time, just as they'd always done. From here he could reach the private dorms he'd been raised in or the back entrance to Conti's private office.

"Remember what I said. If anything happens, you get out."

"Rye..."

That drew stubborn, cold gray eyes to Ichi. For a heartbeat more they stayed cold and then with a sighed breath they melted. "Love you."

"Rye..." But before he could say anything more, the lift doors opened and Rye strode out into the plain, elegantly and simply decorated waiting room. A few chairs lined the warm wood paneled walls and soft carpet lined the floors. A door stood at the far end, sealed with a keypad waiting next to it.

Only, the room wasn't empty. Standing between them and the door was a slender blonde man. His hair was cut short, not quite military short but too short to get a grip on. He had the generic, ordinary look of someone used to blending in and being overlooked. There was nothing menacing about him, or overly worrisome. Ichi saw it, how the man stood, how his eyes watched them, the steady way he waited. The blonde reminded Ichi very much of Rye.

"Vince," Rye said carefully as he stepped closer to the blonde and motioned for Ichi to move off to the side.

"Should have known it was you, Jude. None of the other's would have the balls to use my code."

Rye just shrugged. "Was sort of hoping you weren't home."

"Papa said you'd been killed."

"Papa says a lot of things."

Vince sniffed a little. "You look like a whore, but then that was always your specialty."

"Jealous?" Rye grinned and it was dark. "How long have you been Papa's favorite?"

"Long enough, and coming back from the dead isn't going to change that."

"Do you like it? Being bent over his desk, him grunting like an animal?"

There was just the slightest of narrowing to Vince's blue eyes. "It's his right."

"Bullshit. He's a pig."

"You owe him better than that," Vince spat back but there was just a touch of doubt to the voice.

"No, I don't. He made me into a Pet, Vince, instead of killing me, where's the honor in that? And when he cast me aside he took you in my place. I don't want to kill you Vince, just step aside." Rye shifted his balance just a little but Vince saw it.

"You know I can't do that."

"You could. You're human, you know. He doesn't own us, we aren't property."

"He's our father! Have you forgotten that?"

"A father that fucks his own children and throws them away to be killed is no father! Haven't you ever wanted more?" Rye asked--but it was Mica's voice, begging and distant that he heard pleading with him as he was pleading with Vince.

"Since when does it matter what we want? Our place is to obey, not question." But there was longing there under the proper, programmed answer.

"Last chance, Vince, step down."

"Can't."

Rye nodded and made sure Ichi was off to the side. "One favor?"

"If I can."

"If you take me down, walk him out. He's innocent here, I've blackmailed him into helping me."

"You're a horrible liar." Vince grinned but he shrugged. "So long as he goes quietly, he's no threat."

"Thank you."

"Welcome." The kindness in Vince's tone was betrayed by him pulling a knife from a sheath that was attached to his waistband.

"I'm unarmed." Rye tried to guilt the man into evening the odds.

"Mores the pity for you."

Vince scuttled forward, his feet shuffling along the soft flooring without lifting and his eyes never left Rye. Vince was good, they all were good. Training and the years had weeded out all but the best. This would be no simple fight between barely trained pirates, this would be a real fight, one that Rye hadn't had to face in over a year, not since before his latest modifications. And while double terminated nerve endings made Ichi's touch extraordinary, they made pain horrible.

The knife slashed out in a tight, controlled arc, one Rye easily avoided. "Please, don't insult me."

That made Vince smile broadly. "Just thought you might have gone soft."

"You wish."

There was no need for further bantering. The two men were confident to the point of arrogance for good reason. When Vince attacked again, the blade slashed with blinding speed and followed with fluid, quick movements. Rye dodged but it wasn't with the same ease as the first attack. He ducked one slash and the blade came close enough that a few strands of dark red hair fluttered to the floor.

Rye kicked out and Vince blocked and brought the blade around faster than Rye remembered him being able to move. The edge drew sharply toward Rye and he was able to brush it aside with his arm. It cut his arm open and he hissed at pain that he'd never have felt before. Vince was careful and gave Rye virtually no mistakes to exploit. The blonde's reaction time was as good as Rye remembered and the two moved around the room like a pair of dancers.

With a quick grab, Rye caught Vince's wrist and spun them so the man's back was to his chest. He held the arm and blade out aware from them both, struggling to overpower the other man. Vince's free hand lashed back and Rye managed to catch it in time, locking the elbow into a joint lock that would have had another person begging for mercy. Rye knew better, he knew Vince wouldn't even flinch until the joint was broken.

Blood slid down to Rye's arm to the hand that was holding the blade away. As they struggled, locked together by will and temper, Rye felt his grip slipping. Vince groaned and yanked, nearly breaking his elbow, but the hand holding the blade popped free from Rye's grip. Without pause, he brought his freed arm back, smashing an elbow into Rye's face.

The pain was blinding. It was just a black eye at most, but Rye saw stars. He was going to have to adjust to the new sensations, and adjust quickly, or he knew he stood no chance at all. With a startled cry Rye let go of Vince and stumbled backwards, shaking his head to clear it.

A heartbeat was all he had, Vince pressed his advantage. The blade drew blood again and a third time, slashing along Rye's back and across a leg. Each line Rye offered to the knife earned him a blow to Vince and he was pleased to see that the blonde wasn't unaffected. One quick punch had bloodied and most likely broken the other's nose, and if the last kick Rye managed to land hadn't broken a couple of ribs, he was in trouble.

At least Ichi had the sense to be elsewhere. Whenever Rye glanced for the man out of the corner of his eye Ichi was safely out of reach. He'd made the man promise to not do anything stupid, and since Ichi didn't even know how to throw a punch let alone fight or keep himself alive that meant avoidance. That was good because Vince was taking all his concentration. At least it was Vince, the man wasn't likely to attack Ichi so long as Ichi stayed out of his way.

A kick lashed out and Rye missed seeing the warning because half of his attention was on Ichi. Vince's boot caught Rye's knee and the joint lit up in pain. Rye dropped like a rock, falling hard onto the carpet. He rolled as he hit and it carried him away, staining the carpet in smears of blood. Only now when he came back up his knee hurt too much to hold his weight.

Vince smiled a little as Rye tried to balance his weight on his good leg. The man he'd known and grown up around wouldn't have flinched at such a minor blow. That was one of the reasons Rye had always been in the top, even half-dead he'd been too stubborn to give in. To see him limping was encouraging and made Vince double his attack.

The damaged leg slowed Rye down, making him almost clumsy. Vince landed another kick but Rye managed to deflect the follow up punch tossed his way. To dodge it, Rye twisted his knee and something popped. He felt it, heard it, and the pain blinded his vision and turned his stomach. All Rye wanted to do was fall down and not get back up, but Vince was still advancing and the knife thrust out sharp and deadly toward Rye.

The knife was going to gut him. Rye saw the angle, knew he didn't have the focus or strength to get away before that sharp point ended up in his stomach. He did the only thing he could do, he tossed up his arm and let the blade find a home there. It took a second but it felt like forever for the blade to slide between the bones of his arms. Rye screamed and had enough presence of mind to hit Vince's wrist with his free hand. The blonde's grip spasmed and he released his hold on the hilt of the knife.

Rye let his body fall. His knee refused to work, his body glowing in pain. He cradled his impaled arm close to his chest but still could feel when the impact of his body hitting the carpet made the blade vibrate. The pain stole his breath and there wasn't anyway Rye could get back up and keep fighting. He was down and was going to stay down and he lay where he'd fallen, trying to catch his breath and clear his vision. Rye had barely enough thought left to hope that Vince would be honorable and not harm Ichi.

"You have gotten soft," Vince said as he came closer. With one booted foot he kicked the arm with the knife in it away from Rye's body, nearly making the man black out. "Time I remember, this would be barely a scratch for you."

Vince brought his booted foot down on Rye's wrist, pinning it in place as he leaned down. One hand wrapped around the hilt of the blade and tugged the blade from Rye's arm. Rye gritted his teeth but still he screamed, vision fading this time but not going black. Every fraction of metal that left his flesh he could feel and there seemed no way to adjust to the higher sensitivity Conti had forced on him.

The blade finally slid free and Vince frowned. "I'll make it quick, you deserve that much."

Rye wasn't sure that was something he could thank the other man for. Before Ichi, he would have, a quick clean death was all any of them had wanted. But now he had something worth holding on for. All he wanted was just another moment, another breath, to love Ichi, but he knew emotion and sentiment would mean little to Vince. Emotion wouldn't have moved Rye before and it wouldn't move Vince now.

Movement behind Vince caught Rye's eye but it was too sudden for him to register. That was good because it meant it was too sudden for Vince to register, the blonde had a half-second to notice Rye glance behind him, but that was all the warning he got. One of the heavy wood chairs that lined the wall came crashing down, splintering over Vince's neck and back. It knocked the blonde down, the blade falling from startled fingers as he tried to brace himself on his hands and not fall flat on his face on top of Rye.

"What the hell?" Vince swore as he pushed himself up, more startled than hurt.

Rye shivered. "Ichi!"

Vince was moving as soon as he was on his feet, angry that the bookish looking man he'd pegged as no threat at all had managed to land any blows on him. Worse, he'd be picking splinters out of his neck and head for the rest of the day, and all because he'd assumed the man was merely an ally and nothing more to Rye.

Ichi scurried backwards, hands clutching the satchel and trying to look helpless. Rye had spent days telling them that only a handful of the people he'd worked with at Lerman actually killed for pleasure, it was just a job to the rest, and if they thought Ichi wasn't a threat they'd leave him alone. He'd schooled Ichi to look as non-threatening as possible, to stay out of the way, but Rye had screamed. Killer or not, Vince had made Rye scream and Ichi simply couldn't stand by and watch his love be murdered without doing something. Even if all it accomplished was his own death, he had to try.

Vince caught Ichi easily, one hand going around the slender neck. He pushed hard and slammed the slender man back into the wall. The impact made Ichi's head crack loudly against the wood paneling.

"Who is he?" Vince asked, glancing to where Rye was struggling to move on the floor. "Did you make friends, Jude? What did Papa teach us?" Vince accented each word by pulling Ichi just far enough from the wall to crack him back against it. "Friends are vulnerability!"

The grip on his throat was just tight enough to hurt and block some of his air without killing him. Ichi wasn't sure if Vince meant to kill him or not. His attack had a sense of bitter anger, a tinge of jealous want more than any real desire for violence. But that didn't mean Vince wasn't going to take his head off.

Ichi saw that Rye was still struggling to move. Blood soaked the dark fabric around the slashes and pooled under his left arm, his injured leg was splayed out at an odd angle, but it was his eyes that told Ichi that Rye really was down. They were almost black, the pupils were so wide and unfocused and they didn't appear to be seeing anything going on around them.

That meant if he didn't want to be killed like a lamb to slaughter, Ichi had to do something. There was no way he could pry Vince's hand from this throat, that wasn't going to happen, and he knew he couldn't hurt Vince enough to let him go. One of Ichi's hands fumbled and tangled into the satchel, but he encouraged that and shoved his hand inside the bag. His fingers found the collar and than easily found the sharp prong on the latch. It wasn't a knife, but it was metal and pointy and beggars couldn't be choosers.

The collar came out of the bag, leash and all, and Ichi brought the prong down onto the back of Vince's hand with all the force he could muster. The blonde screeched more in shock than pain but his hand came away from Ichi's neck, dropping the dark haired man to slump down the wall. The collar hung from the impaled prong, leash dangling below, and Vince's eyes went wide.

"What the fuck?" Vince stared in disbelief as blood welled from the back of his hand from the ornate metal of the collar. He pulled back his foot and kicked at the fallen man, hard. "It's not nice to piss me off!" He kicked again, and again.

The prong on his hand was yanked because the collar it was attached to was still attached to the leash which was quickly pulled to the side. Vince growled a little but knew to let his hand follow the pull, it just took a half-second for him to understand why his hand was being pulled. When he glanced from the fallen Ichi to see why, his eyes locked on Rye and from there to the blade now in Rye's hands.

That was all the warning Vince was given before the blade plunged into his side. The blonde gasped and stumbled backwards, eyes going wide with surprise at the hilt that had appeared in his side. He'd been distracted, angry that any of them had found a friend and maybe a real life outside of Lerman. He'd viewed Rye's collapse as a sign that Papa Conti was right, friends and connections made them weak and had to be avoided. Vince had spent his life fighting, he knew defeat when he saw it, knew when a person was hurt too badly to go on and Rye had been there.

Only now the redhead was standing again, blood flowing and gingerly putting weight on his knee. One hand, slick with red, still gripped the hilt of the dagger as their eyes met. The confusion in Vince disappeared, behind the pain in the gray eyes, behind the dazed uncertainty, he saw protective love. He shook his head. "How?"

That was all Vince was able to ask. A wood chair leg smashed down across the back of his skull and the man fell unconscious to the ground leaving Ichi standing behind him, the chair leg in one hand and the other wrapped around his ribs. He half smiled and dropped the heavy wood stick.

Chapter Twenty Seven

"You look awful," Ichi forced out.

Rye only nodded. "You promised to stay out of the fighting."

Ichi shrugged. "I lied." He glanced down to the unconscious blonde. "What now? Kill him?"

"That would be the most logical choice." It was the choice Rye would have made before. He knelt down and ran a hand across Vince's side before he pulled the blade from his body. "The wound's not fatal, he'll be out long enough. Do you want me to kill him?"

"Yes, he hurt you but no, not really." He took the bloodied collar and leash from Rye and tucked it back into the satchel. "There's no way we can walk back out of here, you can barely stand and we both look like we've been in a knife fight."

Rye nodded and accepted Ichi's help to stand. "Let's finish this and then worry about that."

Finish it. Ichi had almost forgotten about Conti, waiting on the other side of the sealed door. All he wanted was to get Rye safely away, but that couldn't be done, not yet. He was angry at himself for allowing this, for not thinking about bringing even a basic med kit even if it had looked suspicious, for a thousand things, but all Ichi did was slide under Rye's arm and help support him. Together they half-hobbled to the far end, blood dripping down Rye's left arm to fall in fat drops to the carpet below in a trail that led from where Vince lay.

There was no way Rye could punch the code in with his left hand, the entire arm was throbbing badly, sending sharp spikes of pain from the tips of his fingers up to his shoulder. He hissed a little as he made the hand curl around the hilt, freeing up his more functional right hand.

"It's good that it hurts, right? I mean, if the nerves were severed it wouldn't hurt as badly. Guess maybe it doesn't matter though, given what Will and Amanda said about your immune system." Ichi knew he was babbling, but he was scared.

Rye typed in Vince's pass code again and paused before pushing the final button. "I'll be okay, Ichi, promise." Rye waited until Ichi nodded before he hit the last button.

The door clicked and unlocked, sliding easily aside to let them into a small side room. Rye remembered it well. The secure waiting area was posh, decadent even, with gold trim on rich red wood and soft, plush furnishings. It was were Conti met with guests that he didn't want in his private office or one of the other more formal meeting rooms. He found an odd, perverse pleasure in letting blood drip on the costly room.

"You're sure he'll be in?"

"He's a creature of habit and he never leaves the center of his web during work hours." Rye knew better than anyone Conti's habits, he'd had years to study the man. "Stay behind me."

Ichi just nodded and let Rye go first into the next room. Whatever he'd been expecting from the external shows of wealth, the plain, efficient office wasn't it. The walls were cream, tan and soft greens, soothing colors. The floor was bare wood, sanded and polished in matching warm tones with a geometric rug tossed in front of the desk with colors that matched the office perfectly.

There was no overt signs of power, no obvious signs of fortune. Neither was there the menace that Ichi had expected. From this office a million murders had been ordered, countless lives ruined or raised, entire political systems stopped or started--and it reflected nothing of that. On a smaller scale, this place, this office was where Rye had endured so much that it almost seemed a mockery to have nothing stand as testament to that.

If the office was a let down in it's simplicity, Conti was even more so. An aged man, he sat behind his desk wearing goggles similar to the ones programmers used. Office goggles that allowed fast and quick interface to information, the man's hands were covered in the input gloves and they twitched as he keyed in whatever new scheme he was hatching. Heavy set, he may have been a powerful man once but now he was wrapped in his own weight and of little physical threat. Even his shoulders appeared slumped and worn down by age and time.

He could have been someone's grandfather, someone once vital in youth but now bidding time until retirement could lead him to card games and travel. There was the look of someone who chronically overworked--his hair was just slightly in need of a trim, his clothes a touch out of style for a man in his position. There was a sense the chair he sat in was nearly molded to his body and his skin was too pale for anyone that lived planetside.

Conti was as ordinary as his office, perhaps a touch more outdated and weaker, but just like the office there was no stain on the man that marked him. It didn't seem right that someone as evil as Conti must look so ordinary. Ichi found himself wondering if they had the right man, wondering if maybe this was a ringer or stand in. It didn't seem right that Conti should be a fat old man that could walk past everyone on the street and go unnoticed.

"You're early, your orders were to arrive a half hour from now." Conti spoke without even stopping his work.

The voice... Rye had braced himself to see this man but not to hear his voice. It made him tremble and want to run. Ichi slid a hand onto his arm and it was there that Rye found his strength. "It's not Vince, Papa," he forced from a throat that felt too tight.

The hands froze a second before Conti reached up and pulled the goggles off. He dropped them onto the desk, eyes going wide a moment before narrowing. "Jude." It was the first time Rye had heard the man speak his name. It had always been a number, or an insult.

"Surprised to see me?"

Conti carefully pulled the sensitive input gloves off and dropped them to his desk. When the second one hit the surface his hand dipped just below the edge. Rye didn't wait, he threw the knife and it lodged into Conti's flesh, deep where the arm joined the body on the chest. It was perfectly aimed. Conti's arm lost control and the small gun slid across the desk to drop to the floor below. The blade was deep enough to make the man cry out but damaged nothing vital.

Rye was across the room before Conti could react, the adrenaline in his system dulling down the hideous pain in his knee and the throbbing in his arm. He scooped up the gun and half leaned on the desk for support. The same desk--the man had never bothered to get a new one--Conti had raped him on, raped countless of his siblings on. Ichi was standing almost on the spot where Mica had died. The rug was new but Rye remembered every crack, every crevice in that floor he'd scrubbed the blood from.

"Fucking ungrateful, idiotic, moronic, worthless twat!" Conti cursed but was cut off when Rye yanked the blade from his shoulder. "Have you forgotten what you are?" he hissed.

Rye leaned there and stared down at the only family he'd known, a man he'd once obeyed blindly.

"You were gutter street trash and I made you glorious! I made you! The most powerful in the universe have cowered at your feet because I made you! How dare you raise a hand to me! You exist because of my whim!"

That voice, it made Rye want to vomit. It was easy to say it was the pain and shock, the blood loss, but it was Conti's voice that made him tremble. It made him wonder just what he was doing, what foolishness had infected him. Mica's plans were silly dreams, there was no place in the world for men like them. They were killers, it was all they were good at and it was their father that offered them everything. Like dogs owned by a kennel, it wasn't their place to think, just attack and leave it up to the master to think.

"Now, 283, place down your weapons and back away. That's an order, boy!"

That voice, it made his head spin. Like a vein being opened, Rye felt his will bleeding away. It would be so much easier to give up and die, to find an escape. He understood completely why Ichi had knelt and let his throat be slit, Rye was ready for that surrender too.

Only, it wasn't Ichi he remembered laying in his own blood. That was Mica. Rye drew a slow breath and steadied his head. He'd killed Mica, it was Mica that had viewed death as the only escape. Ichi was here, yes, but not here looking for death. Ichi was here looking for a future, a promise of more, a life, with him. Ichi--the quiet, reserved, blindingly intelligent man that he'd fallen so madly in love with-- stood behind him. There were no delusions there, Ichi knew him, knew what he had been and was and loved him anyway. That, and only that, gave Rye another purpose.

"Fuck you." Rye whispered.

Conti actually blinked in startled shock. "What did you just say, 283?"

"I said fuck you, Papa." He wanted to hit the man, to pound his face to a bloody mash but his own body was too sore, too battered to manage it. Instead, he reached out and dug a thumb into the bleeding knife wound in Conti's shoulder. It made the man grit his teeth around a scream but Rye used the touch to push Conti's chair back, moving him away from any other hidden weapons or emergency call buttons that might be there.

"You don't own me!" Rye heard himself shouting as he hovered over the man. "I'm not your property!"

Conti started to chuckle, dark and low and with sharp edges of mocking humor. "Is that what this is about? Revenge? Getting even? How quaint."

Rye hauled back and hit Conti, with enough force to break the man's nose even if the impact caused him to see stars as well. "Even! For us to get close to even I'd have to kill everything you love, let you be gang raped and then break every bone in your body and we'd still barely be in the same zone as even!" It didn't matter if it hurt now, Rye was hitting Conti, hard. He hit Conti with enough force to open up gashes on his face and knock the man from his chair. When Conti fell, Rye moved to stand over him. Unable to kick him like he wanted to, he flicked the small gun on and aimed it steadily at the older man's head.

"You're not going to kill me." Conti spoke with confidence. "You don't have the balls for that."

Rye turned the gun up a notch, causing it to whine as it charged.

"With me dead, what will you do? Where will you go? Hmm? Put on a suit? Work in an office? You'll always be someone's thug, someone's sad little boy who bloodies his hands. Without me you're just a second rate loser drawing blood to get off! If you kill me, you might as well kill yourself right after because without me, you're less than nothing!"

Rye frowned. There was truth in what Conti said. "I'll take that chance."

Conti struggled to sit up straighter, his right arm useless, one eye swelling shut, looking sadly like an old man that had been violently mugged for his pension check. He nodded his head and the angry frown turned to a half smile. "Proud of you," he whispered.

Rye's hand tightened on the gun and fired. Conti's head dissolved into broken chunks and vapor. As the small gun whined to itself, recharging for another shot, Rye stumbled a few feet away before he collapsed and his stomach turned over. He lay where he'd fallen and retched, exhausted and broken.

Until a hand soothed across his hair and stroked across his shoulders. "Shhh," Ichi tried to soothe, his own nerves frayed and snapped. "Shhh, it's over now, it's over." He petted the bloodied, sweat-damp hair some more. "We're okay, come on now, come on Rye, let's get out of here? Hmm? How do you get out of here?" How long could Conti be out of touch before someone came to check on him? The man must have had a slew of secretaries at the least that were used to their boss updating reports and files.

Rye ran a hand over his mouth and was trained well enough to know he couldn't fall apart until Ichi was safe. "Back to the lift, down, out the service entrance if we're lucky." They looked bad, anyone that saw them now would notify security and that would be as far as they got. "Take the knife." The gun was a better choice for Ichi, but since he wasn't sure if the other man could use it without shooting himself the knife was better than nothing. Rye tried not to shake his head when Ichi retrieved the knife and tucked it away into the satchel, totally missing the point of the man carrying it.

It took three tries to get Rye off the floor and back on his feet. Ichi staggered under the weight and gasped in short, hidden pain. "Where're you hurt?"

Ichi shook his head. "I'm fine."

"Where're you hurt?" Rye demanded again.

"Just, banged up from being kicked." He wasn't going to say that he thought a rib might be broken because he knew Rye would rather drag himself along the floor rather than accept help that might be hurting him. "I'm okay, let's go home."

There was no doubt Ichi was lying but Rye could respect the dark haired man's reasons. He spared one last glance around the office he knew so well, one final glance to where Conti lay behind the desk before he nodded.

"Yeah, let's go home." Which was so much easier to say than do. He really had no idea how they'd get back out. It all depended on how much time they had until Conti was discovered, how far they could go unnoticed, how many people would risk stopping them. He wasn't up to much more fighting, that was the bottom line, and Ichi--well, Ichi wasn't a fighter.

Those were worries he kept to himself as he leaned on Ichi and let himself be lead back to the door they'd come in at. There was some worry about going out past Vince, they had thick skulls and it was even odds the other man would be coming around. He couldn't fight him again, he'd have to shoot him.

Codes were entered and doors opened and they staggered back out into the waiting room, but it was when the door opened to the outer room where they'd left Vince that the pair froze.

"Aw, shit," Ichi sighed.

The room still looked like a knife fight had happened there, but instead of Vince laying where they'd left him he was sitting stiffly on one of the chairs. Kneeling beside him, working on getting a pressure bandage across the stab wound, was a blonde man. His hair had no brown tones and was a soft, butter yellow blonde. It fell in all one length, slicked back from his face, to below his shoulders. He was dressed in dark, classy pants with a very stylish shirt that screamed money.

When the door opened pale, ice blue eyes slid over to study the pair in the doorway. The blonde was handsome, with a long nose and strong features. In another place, Ichi would have found him attractive, sensual. Only, the blonde man wasn't the only one in the room with Vince. Standing to the side, careful of keeping expensive shoes from the splatters of blood, were two more blondes.

"Rye? I'm seeing the same man in three places," Ichi said softly. It was the same man, same face, same hair, even the same clothes. There were three sets of ice blue eyes staring at them.

"The triplets," Rye whispered, as if that explained everything.

"Of course." Ichi sighed. "What now?"

"Please," one of the blondes standing spoke. "Join us."

Rye pushed away from Ichi and got the gun aimed at the nearest blonde. "Get away from the lift."

The triplets passed a look between them and the other one standing spoke this time, in the same voice. "283, we intend you no harm, just a word. Or would you rather Jude?"

There was no point to stand in the doorway, the easiest way out of Conti's suite of rooms was this way. They had virtually no chance of escape if they didn't make it into the lift right here. Rye limped forward, trying to hide how badly he was hurt.

"Please, sit, you must be badly hurt to limp so much." Standing blonde-one said and moved to bring a chair closer to Rye.

The raised gun stopped the man and he smiled gently without the smile touching his eyes and carefully set the chair down, facing them.

"As you wish. Do you know us?" Standing blonde-two spoke.

"Papa's nephews."

The blonde near Vince stood and moved to his brothers. "Yes," he said easily. "And the new CEO's of Lerman..."

"Unless..." The middle blonde spoke.

"You didn't kill him." The third finished.

It was enough to give Rye a headache. He nodded. "I killed him." He braced himself for their revenge and wondered if he could barter to get Ichi out alive. "I don't care what you do to me, let him go. He's no part in this." Rye nodded a little to the side and where Ichi was hovering.

"You don't understand...."

"We have no intentions..."

"Of even thinking about revenge."

Rye wasn't sure if he was speaking to one person or three. "You expect me to believe that?"

There was a shrug and an exchanged look and the center blonde stepped forward. "I am Harper Dubois. My brothers Julian and Oliver." He waved slightly to the brother on his right first, then to the one on his left. "We hold you no ill will, Jude. In fact, you've done us a great service."

"Just as we had hoped..." Julian spoke.

"Actually." Oliver finished and the three smiled softly, that same empty, sly smile that didn't warm their icy eyes.

"Oh, stop looking so suspicious." Harper gently teased. "Do you imagine you and your siblings were the only young boys Uncle Howard couldn't keep his hands off of? The man was a pig."

"We would have killed him years ago..." Oliver nodded.

"If it wasn't for his will." Harper finished.

"Harp, he's bleeding still." Julian nodded to Rye and the blood that still dripped from his arm.

Harper nodded and Julian gathered up the med kit that had been opened to treat Vince, but as he got closer Rye raised his gun and was more than happy to kill any of them. "Perhaps your friend would care to help you instead?" He set the kit down and pushed it with a foot closer to where Ichi hovered.

Ichi didn't move until Rye nodded slightly, and only then did he crouch down to snag the med kit. It was well stocked and had pressure bandages in sizes far larger than most kits came with. He hurried to get one open and Rye's sleeve torn away. The red head didn't flinch as he worked and the gun never wavered.

"We're Uncle Howard's only family…" Oliver explained.

"We get everything." Julian finished.

"But, Uncle was paranoid. If we killed him, we get nothing." Harper added.

"Our hands were tied."

"So to speak."

Harper glanced to his brothers. "When Uncle Howard ordered you be disposed of, we knew what he meant but we talked about it."

"It would have been like smashing a stained glass window." Oliver shook his head.

"We may not approve of Uncle Howard's treatment and creation of you and your siblings but you're amazing agents." Julian glanced from his brothers to where Vince sat with eyes downcast.

"So, we had you tossed out into Pets' random upgrades."

"Hoping I'd remember and kill him." Rye was shocked, chilled, and it wasn't just the shock of his injuries.

The triplets shrugged. "It's a chance we were willing to take to be merciful to you."

"It's such a shame about Uncle Howard," Oliver sighed.

Julian grinned wickedly. "By dying at your hand, he's been killed in an industrial accident."

It didn't confuse Rye, he'd had assignments before where deaths had to appear a certain way to circumvent revenge or a solid will. This was just the first time he'd been used unknowingly. It mocked him, he'd killed his father for profit, not for the protection of those he loved. It was almost too much and if the triplets hadn't just confessed to being the ones to send him to meet Ichi, he may have killed them right then and there.

He had to get Ichi away, that was all that mattered. "So, what do we do now?" Rye asked, feeling exhaustion settling in and needing to get them out of there before shock dropped him.

The triplets exchanged a look but it was Harper that spoke again. "Uncle Howard's projects, while innovative, are no longer viable."

"Lerman is moving in a new direction, more streamlined, more flexible," Oliver added.

"Sadly, this new streamlined system leaves no room for you and your siblings." Julian finished.

That snapped Vince's head up, proving he was paying greater attention then he'd shown. Rye didn't spare him a look, he didn't trust the triplets and kept his attention and gun on them.

"I don't care what Lerman does, I'm out."

"Indeed." Harper nodded and let one of his brother's brush his hair back from his shoulders. "It would be prudent of us to see to it that Uncle Howard's hobbies died with him. Some would look at us and wonder if he practiced those hobbies with us and view that as weakness."

"The only two still alive that know what a pig Uncle Howard was are both here."

"It would make logical sense to not allow either you or your brother here to walk away," one of the triplets finished.

Rye tightened his grip on the gun.

"However," Harper continued quickly. "The problem still stands, we respect you and your siblings, you're well trained. We would hate to destroy you needlessly. If you were willing to walk away and remain silent, knowing the value of silence, we're certain a man of your skills would do nicely running his own freelance security firm. Avalon has quite a fascination with security right now and we're certain Lerman would be delighted to offer a company run by such a trained agent right of refusal on projects contracted to them."

It was an idea he had half considered, late at night during their travels. "I've no plans to continue in this line of work," Rye answered carefully.

"Please." Julian rolled his eyes and waved toward Ichi. "We don't care how pretty he is, being his lapdog will drive you mad."

"You'll miss it. It's in your blood, as it's in ours."

"Within a month, you'll be setting up your own freelance firm anyway. All we're doing is offering you your first contract." Harper finished.

"This isn't the place for that negotiation."

Harper laughed at that and glanced to his brothers. "God, we like you. No wonder Uncle Howard was obsessed with you."

"Do we have an understanding?" Oliver asked, impatient with his brother's amusement.

Rye didn't even need to think about it, it was a concern he didn't have. "I have no plans to ever speak of my past."

"We have an understanding." Julian nodded.

"One that will be kept, because there are innocents that shouldn't be harmed in the crossfire if a word of honor is broken." Oliver pushed.

"I understand." Rye didn't need them to glance to Ichi to know their meaning.

"Good. Your employee number is functioning. The lift is operational. Take it to the docks, berth thirty-two. The ship there isn't the best yacht but it's nice, consider it severance pay."

"We're to just walk away?"

"Of course."

"But…"

"If you do, we'll be forced to destroy Vince and turn out the rest." Oliver finished.

He should have walked away, he owed them nothing. "We both know they can't survive out there alone. Not after this long."

Harper nodded. "Lerman still employs eight of your siblings, seven of which are on assignment, five are expected to return. Only Vince here was kept back."

"Uncle Howard liked his comforts," Oliver spat out.

"Take him with you." Julian added quickly and glanced to his brothers. "There's been enough pain for him, and if anyone can understand and help him, I believe you are the one."

It was the first time one of the triplets had spoken of themselves singularly and Rye had little doubt which of the three Conti had found special. "He's not property to be given away."

"You don't really believe that, do you?" Oliver mocked.

"All of you and your siblings are Lerman property, even if not officially."

"Property we must now dispose of," Julian reminded them all.

"You sick bastards you can't just kill him, he's a human being!" Ichi snapped out for the first time. He was angry, frustrated, and didn't know why they were having this debate.

S. A. Payne

"We have no desire to destroy the others but Vince here was special."

"Stop, I'll take him." Rye forced out and wondered how he was going to keep Vince from killing them in their sleep. "I'll keep his mouth shut."

"And the others?" Harper asked carefully.

"Release them as you'd planned, tell them they can go about their lives but they're welcome in Avalon. They have a home there, work there. That I'll take care of them." And if by work he meant trying to teach them what it meant to be human, well, that was fine. Any of the survivors that showed up Rye would manage, somehow.

Harper didn't look thrilled with Julian's idea but neither did he look willing to contradict him. "Fine. Take this one now, we'll send the others as they return. Go, before we change our mind."

Rye tried to take a step forward but his knee locked up and it turned into a stumble. The last thing he wanted was to fall but as he struggled to get his leg moving, Vince darted across the room. As suddenly as he was moving, he was under Rye's arm, his undamaged side against Rye, supporting most of Rye's weight. It was surprising enough that Rye nearly pulled away.

"It's okay," Vince spoke in a small whisper.

Together they hobbled toward the lift, keeping their backs toward the wall and their eyes on the triplets. At the lift, it was Vince that punched in his code and the doors quickly opened. Ichi scurried inside first to be out of the way.

"We'll be in touch, Rye Sullivan," Harper said as the doors slide shut and the lift waited for directions.

"They know your name," Ichi whispered into the waiting silence.

"I'm sure they know a lot more than just that." Rye staggered back to lean against the wall with a grimace. He turned to where Vince stood, one hand pressed to his side. "Think the ship is a trap?"

He shrugged. "From my dealings with them? They don't bother with elaborate games. They want to use our training but don't want us on the lists. They want us as freelance, no point in killing us now."

Rye nodded. "Agreed."

He let Vince punch in the access code that would take them to the company controlled docks within the compound. The gun was a dead weight in his hand and he was tired, horribly tired.

"You really killed him?"

"Yes." Rye answered simply.

Vince stood silent for a long moment, eyes seeing something that wasn't in the small lift with them. Finally, he nodded. "Good." Vince's eyes fell on the grim, silent man following Rye so blindly. "The two of you…" he didn't quite ask.

Rye felt a small smile tease his face. "It's good, Vince, really good. We can have a life, we're real people, not just weapons."

"For you, maybe," he disagreed.

That made Rye push himself off the wall and stand as straight as he could. "Will we have a problem, Vince? Do I need to worry about my back being to you?"

For a moment the blonde looked willing to fight, willing to threaten, but after a tense breath he shook his head and dropped his eyes. "No, sir."

"Good." It was a gamble. Rye knew firsthand how desperately they all needed a strong leader. If he didn't fill that role, his siblings would be wild and dangerous. Ichi gave him a touch stone, he could manage to be that for them. He leaned back against the wall and for a heartbeat closed his eyes. "Good." It was a start, a small, very tiny, start.

⬥

Lerman's private docks were in three levels. The first were local transports, the second held planetary transport and the third were long-range, true spaceships. Berth thirty-two was on the third level, second slot, and from the access hall there was little to be seen of the ship itself. The other two levels were always busy as employees came and went from company provided transportation but the third level was always nearly deserted. The ships in dock required little to no maintenance and the ground crews only came in for the look over when a ship returned to port. The only people that would be moving about here were other agents coming and going or Lerman executives.

Vince glanced from the lift and down the hallway. "No one in sight."

"Triplets would have cleared it. They wouldn't want us spotted." He had to bite his lip to keep from groaning as Ichi helped balance him.

"I've got him." Vince nodded and moved to take up his place on Rye's other side.

"I'm okay," Ichi said and meant it, even if it wasn't possibly true.

Vince just shook his head. "Even odds I cracked one of your ribs, just let me."

Ichi glanced to Rye and at his slight nod backed off. "Never mind the whole stabbed in the side thing," he heard himself muttering.

"I'm used to it, I'm stronger than you and I did this." Vince explained as he helped Rye hobble out into the hallway.

By the time they made it to the second access tunnel and Vince got the code punched in, Rye was seeing black spots floating in his vision. His body just didn't take shock well anymore, it was a limit he'd have to keep in mind. It didn't seem to matter that he was slowly adjusting to the pain, he was hitting his limit and it was way sooner than it had been before Conti had modified him into a pet.

The inside of the ship was comfortable and almost home like. Vince helped Rye stagger forward, past a small kitchen area to a lounge. "They gave you one of the Pep Cruisers."

"They can afford it." Rye groaned as he happily dropped into one of the plush seats. He glanced up again. "Where are your loyalties, Vince?"

The blonde didn't even pause. "With you."

"Get us out of here, aim us for Avalon." Pep Cruisers were made so one person could pilot from anywhere on the ship, but there was a formal bridge. Really, piloting was a kind word, it was a simple interface with a great deal of automation that could be overridden if the owner desired. Right now, Rye didn't desire; in fact, the only thing he wanted to was to curl up and cry his eyes out.

"We're in atom," Vince announced as he returned to the lounge.

"Shhh, he's asleep." Ichi slipped Rye's head from his shoulder and got him propped on the arm of the lounge. "We need to get you both to a doctor."

"We'll survive. You?"

Ichi grimaced and staggered back toward the kitchen. "Same, I'd imagine."

He paused to look and saw Vince as someone other than an adversary. He knew the uncertain look in the blonde eyes from Rye. He knew it covered a real fear and Ichi felt his heart break a little. How old was Vince when Lerman picked him up? How old was he now? If he was like Rye, he'd never sat and listened to music for enjoyment, or learned to dance or laugh freely or love.

Ichi paused in the kitchen. "I don't want to be your enemy."

That made Vince shake his head quickly. "You aren't."

And Ichi knew the blonde meant it, but they needed to get beyond that. In Vince's world there were three sorts--enemies, competition, and non-threatening useless civilians. "I'm not going to be your competition either."

Vince just snorted in agreement at that. "Not even if you started trying today."

He moved to the table and saw their luggage sitting, waiting on the table and a small note card. "I'd like for us to be friends." Ichi very deliberately turned his back to Vince and trusted the man that had been trying to kill him less than an hour before.

That left Vince floundering. As much as he hated Conti and often hated the life he'd been living, he understood it. He could logically know what to expect. This was new and while he knew what to say, how to fake things, that wasn't what was required.

Finally, he shook his head a little bit. "My loyalty is to Jude."

Ichi turned, holding the card. "That's fine." He smiled gently as seeing the uneasy, almost painfully uncomfortable look on Vince's face. "I'm sorry for what Conti did to you."

That only made the confused unease worse. "It was his right."

"No, it wasn't." But just like Rye, Vince couldn't be convinced so easily or so quickly. He glanced down to the card and if he wasn't so emotionally exhausted he'd have swallowed his own tongue in shock. Living Companions had granted both Ichi and Rye restitution, a shocking, frightfully high sum of money, all legal and proper. He knew they were being bought off but, frankly, he couldn't bring himself to care.

Epilogue

Ichi grinned at the Mercury Fire Ants as they moved in ant-like agreement carving out their new home. They were an odd species, breeding just enough to fill the space and resources open to them, like goldfish in progressively larger bowls. He was guessing that once the queen made herself at home he'd have several hundred ants within a month. The new lab was far better laid out and he was taking advantage of starting over.

A footfall too soft to be someone from Avalon sounded behind him. "Hello, Vince," Ichi spoke to the air, knowing it had to be the blonde. He could move silently but was smart enough to give his new friends fair warning when he was behind them.

"Mr. Ichi." No amount of being told different had been able to convince Vince or the handful of his siblings that had shown up to be less formal than that. Even if the formality, the distance they placed between themselves and everyone else, made the folks from Avalon uncomfortable.

It was something Ichi understood. Vince had been circling closer and closer to him like some timid, kicked dog, more so over the last few weeks with Rye and Gardner off on a job. Vince was both more skittish and--in some ways--less than his siblings, and as the weeks had passed he seemed unable to fit in with his siblings or the folks from Avalon.

It was only those times when he'd show up and just sit in the corner of Ichi's lab that the blonde seemed to relax at all. Even if having the other man sitting, studying everything he did was unnerving, Ichi tried not to mind. It was important to Rye that the few remaining siblings he had were given a chance at connecting on a human level and it was a small enough thing for Ichi to do to help.

Ichi didn't glance from his ants. "Any word from Rye?" He knew there wouldn't be, old habits died hard. Just as Vince was taking Rye's request to 'look after Ichi' as seriously as if it were a to-the-death command.

"About that, sir..."

Those were frightful words. Ichi felt his heart stop beating and his blood go cold. Rye was hurt, or dead, he wasn't going to make it back. It didn't matter that he'd been very strict with what kind of jobs his fledgling security company accepted. He'd so far tracked down a runaway teenager from a wealthy family and stuck to testing of already established security on companies and military bases. Thief work, Vince had called it, but none of the siblings had complained too loudly about not having to kill anyone to survive.

Just because it was low risk didn't mean accidents didn't happen. Rye had insisted he join each sibling on their first job, to make sure they were stable and okay. He'd been gone for the better part of the last two months and Ichi had grit his teeth and accepted it. They were still figuring things out but Rye was smart, he was establishing a system that, once in place, would allow him to stay close to Ichi at all times.

Except Vince had come to him, quietly, with his flat emotionless voice that could announce cold death without a hint. Ichi sat upright but didn't turn around. He couldn't look at Vince, couldn't see nothingness in his blue eyes, or worse, sympathy.

"What about, Rye, Vince?" He asked carefully, prepared to dismiss Vince and fall apart in private.

There was a pause and a soft shift of feet. "Hey, baby," a warm, delicious voice spoke.

Ichi about startled from his seat. "Rye!" He spun around now, ants forgotten, and standing in the doorway was Vince, Gardner and Rye. The blonde was grinning like a madman at his part in the surprise and Gardner, a dark haired man that was so ordinary looking that Ichi had a difficult time remember just what he looked like, stood beside Vince carrying a small box. Rye, however, stood just inside the lab doorway and he was smiling widely.

There was no thought to being shy or being reserved, Ichi literally flung himself against Rye with enough force to stagger the stronger man back a step. Warm arms wrapped around Ichi's waist and lips parted to his own. Ichi heard Rye moan softly, deep in his throat, a moment before one of the hands at his waist slid lower to the top of his ass and pulled their hips together.

"Shit, get a fucking room," Gardner mumbled and earned himself an elbow into his ribs from Vince.

Rye broke the kiss but kept his forehead pressed to Ichi's for a moment. "Missed you."

"Same," Ichi whispered back but Rye didn't seem willing to let him go.

"And watch your language, Gardner." Rye's voice took on a sterner tone.

It made the dark haired man duck his head slightly. "Yes, sir."

"What're you doing back so soon? I thought you had some tracking job…" Ichi tended not to ask for many details, but Gardner was the best tracker of the surviving siblings, the man could find anything if given enough time.

"We did. Got it and came back." He nodded to the box Gardner carried.

It was only then that Ichi remember how frightened he'd been with Vince being so discreet and assuming the worst. He pulled out of Rye's remaining arm and thumped the redhead hard enough to get his attention. "Never scare me like that again! I thought, with Vince, I thought something had happened!"

"Ow, hey, don't." Rye half laughed. "Blame Will and Amanda too, I made them swear to secrecy. Been planning this for too many months and you're too smart of a man to fool easily."

"What are you talking about?"

"If you were anyone else, I'd have bought you chocolates or flowers but, happy birthday." He waved to the box Gardner was holding.

Ichi blinked, surprised and counted up the days. Sure enough, today was his birthday. Normally he only remembered because Will and Amanda teased him for being old but they hadn't. "I'd forgotten."

"I know, I asked everyone to not remind you. Go on, take the box."

"Birthdays aren't that important to me, you know you didn't have to do anything," Ichi started but as soon as he saw what kind of box it was he began to get excited. The weight was right too when he took it from Gardner. The read out on the top confirmed it. "Oh, my god."

Rye grinned wider. "Seven Trillions to start your new swarm. All from different hives, too, so they'll be a good breeding set."

"How… how did you manage this?" Ichi hurried the box over and started pulling up the details from the read out. "I had to get my original swarm one at a time, it took years to get seven."

"We had eight."

"One of the little fuckers bit me and I smashed it without thinking," Gardner protested, showing the spot on his arm that was still black and swollen from the toxin.

"Language," Rye warned softly.

"Sorry."

The idea of Rye stumbling on a hive, waking a hive, being brought down by a hive, made Ichi ill. As much as he wanted his swarm back, he never would have allowed Rye to be the one to replace it. It was easier to risk his own safety, his own life, not Rye's.

Ichi stood so long just staring at the sealed cold storage box that Rye wondered if he'd done something wrong. He'd seen folks from Avalon celebrate birthdays, seen other people as well, but had no real experience with it. When he'd realized Ichi's was fast approaching, he'd spent hours in discussion with Will trying to learn what was proper and right. They'd gone over all the traditional gifts, a few Rye had indulged in as well that were waiting back in their apartment, but none seemed proper.

"Will said, he told me, that a birthday gift should be perfect for the person receiving it. He said, it should make the person happy and surprise them." Rye tried to explain and wondered if he'd done something horribly wrong. Nowhere in all his research had he ever seen anyone giving the person they loved highly dangerous insects for a gift.

Ichi sniffed softly, refusing to sob like a child over the romance of how thoughtfully perfect the swarm was. He glanced over to Rye with a small grin on his face but at the worried, uncertain look on his love's face the smile grew wider. In fact, he was grinning so largely that his face hurt and it felt a little like someone else's smile. He'd been feeling that way a lot since he'd met Rye.

"It's the most thoughtful, most perfect birthday surprise I could imagine," Ichi finally announced. Three faces lit up but all Ichi could see was Rye's.

"We've a party planned too," Vince announced. "Will planned it, but we helped." None of them had been to a party for pleasure before but the rest of the folks on the station from Avalon had helped and it felt, almost, like a real family.

"A party?" Ichi felt overwhelmed, torn between the expectant humanity in the siblings so eager to try a real celebration, his own excitement at meeting his new swarm, and simply dragging Rye away for some private time.

"There's a cake." Vince nodded but while his voice was empty and careful, his blue eyes sparkled.

"A cake?"

"Alright!" Rye stepped in, his eyes having never left Ichi. "Both of you, out. Gardner, go see Will or Amanda, get that bite looked at."

Matching 'yes sirs' preceded the pairs' departure and the door shutting tightly behind them, leaving Rye alone with Ichi. "I'm hoping at least four come out of cold storage okay," He said into the empty silence of the lab.

"They're hardy, they can take a lot." He felt feverish with the way Rye was watching him, those gray eyes so intent. "The, ah, the journal accepted my paper on the nesting habits. They were quite impressed. There's been talk of my actually presenting the paper at several universities."

Rye couldn't wait any longer, he hurried over and gathered Ichi back into his arms, pinning him between the work top and his own chest. "Of course they were, you're brilliant," he whispered just before he licked Ichi's ear. "Happy birthday, god I missed you."

The lick made Ichi whimper and his knees go weak. "I should, the swarm, I should get them settled…"

"Soon, I'll help… need you too much though." He sighed and rubbed his hips across Ichi's, not at all surprised to find the blushing entomologist equally aroused.

"Door… still doesn't… oh god… lock." Ichi sighed out and tilted his neck for Rye to exploit.

Rye chuckled. "Don't care, going to take you right here. And tonight?" He bit Ichi's neck hard enough to earn a surprised yelp. "Don't expect to get any sleep."

The threat was real and one Ichi had been thinking about making to Rye when he returned. He moaned and found his hands working to open Rye's pants for him, eager, needing, and only half caring about the unlocked door. Behind him his new ants were carving out their home and beside him sat the swarm waiting to be released into their new enclosure, but all Ichi's mind could process was the feel of Rye holding him.

"Missed you, missed you so much." Ichi groaned, but it wasn't in response or reference to the strong hand that had managed to worm it's way into his pants.

"I know, I love you too." Rye grinned and answered.

And for that single moment, both clung to each other and spoke of love with flesh and sighs; they saw the future stretched out before them. A time filled with many more birthdays and anniversaries, filled with laughter, family and friends. There would be work and accomplishments, threats and failures, joys and fears. It was a future they'd risked so much to see, lost so much to gain, and so long as they could cling to each other it was one that held no fear for either.

Lightning Source UK Ltd.
Milton Keynes UK
27 September 2010

160419UK00001B/32/A